ROCK CANDY MOUNTAIN

VOLUME ONE

WRITTEN & DRAWN BY

KYLE ✳✳✳✳✳ STARKS

COLORED BY
CHRIS SCHWEIZER

DESIGN BY
DYLAN TODD

PUBLISHED BY IMAGE COMICS INC.

ROCK CANDY MOUNTAIN, VOL 01. FIRST PRINTING. SEPTEMBER 2017.

Published by Image Comics, Inc. Office of publication: 2701 NW Vaughn St., Suite 780, Portland, OR 97210. Copyright © 2017 Kyle Starks. All rights reserved. Contains material originally published in single magazine form as ROCK CANDY MOUNTAIN #1-4. "ROCK CANDY MOUNTAIN," its logos, and the likenesses of all characters herein are trademarks of Kyle Starks, unless otherwise noted. "Image" and the Image Comics logos are registered trademarks of Image Comics, Inc. No part of this publication may be reproduced or transmitted, in any form or by any means (except for short excerpts for journalistic or review purposes), without the express written permission of Kyle Starks, or Image Comics, Inc. All names, characters, events, and locales in this publication are entirely fictional. Any resemblance to actual persons (living or dead), events, or places, without satiric intent, is coincidental. Printed in the USA. For information regarding the CPSIA on this printed material call: 203-595-3636 and provide reference # RICH – 762718. For international rights, contact: foreignlicensing@imagecomics.com. ISBN# 978-1-5343-0317-1

CHAPTER ONE

"One evening as the sun went down."

*"good road
to follow."*

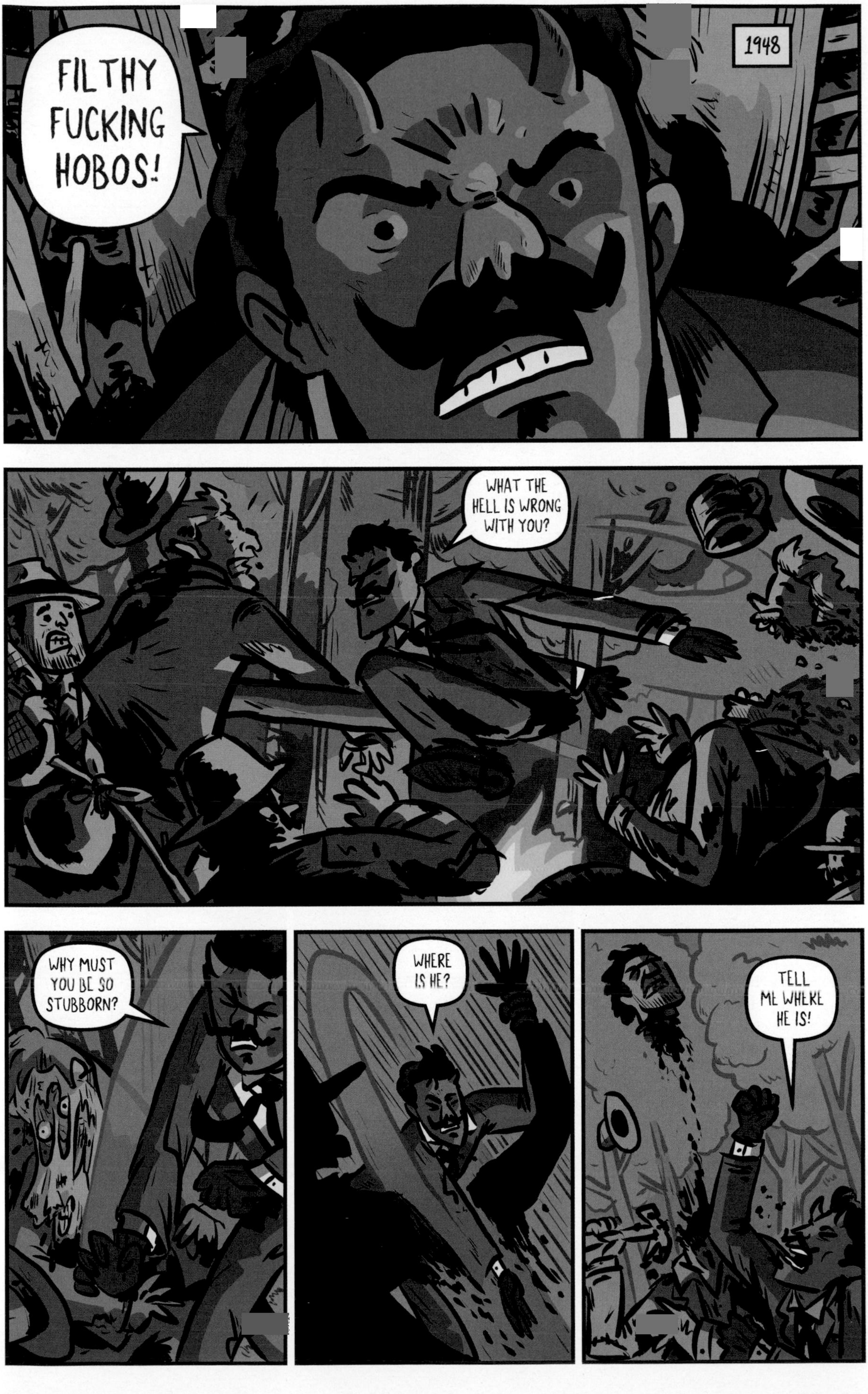
1948
FILTHY FUCKING HOBOS!
WHAT THE HELL IS WRONG WITH YOU?
WHY MUST YOU BE SO STUBBORN?
WHERE IS HE?
TELL ME WHERE HE IS!

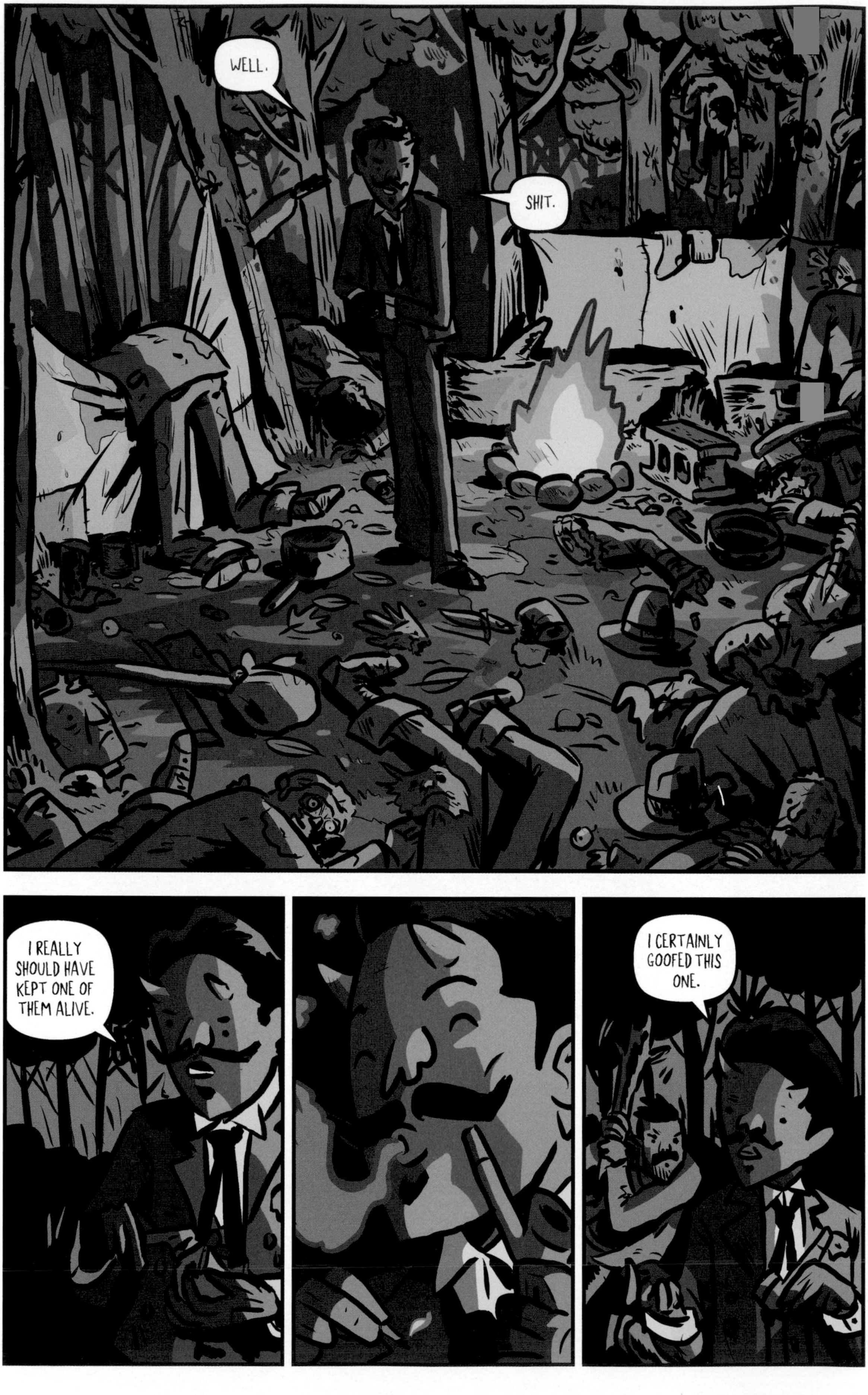
WELL.
SHIT.
I REALLY SHOULD HAVE KEPT ONE OF THEM ALIVE.
I CERTAINLY GOOFED THIS ONE.

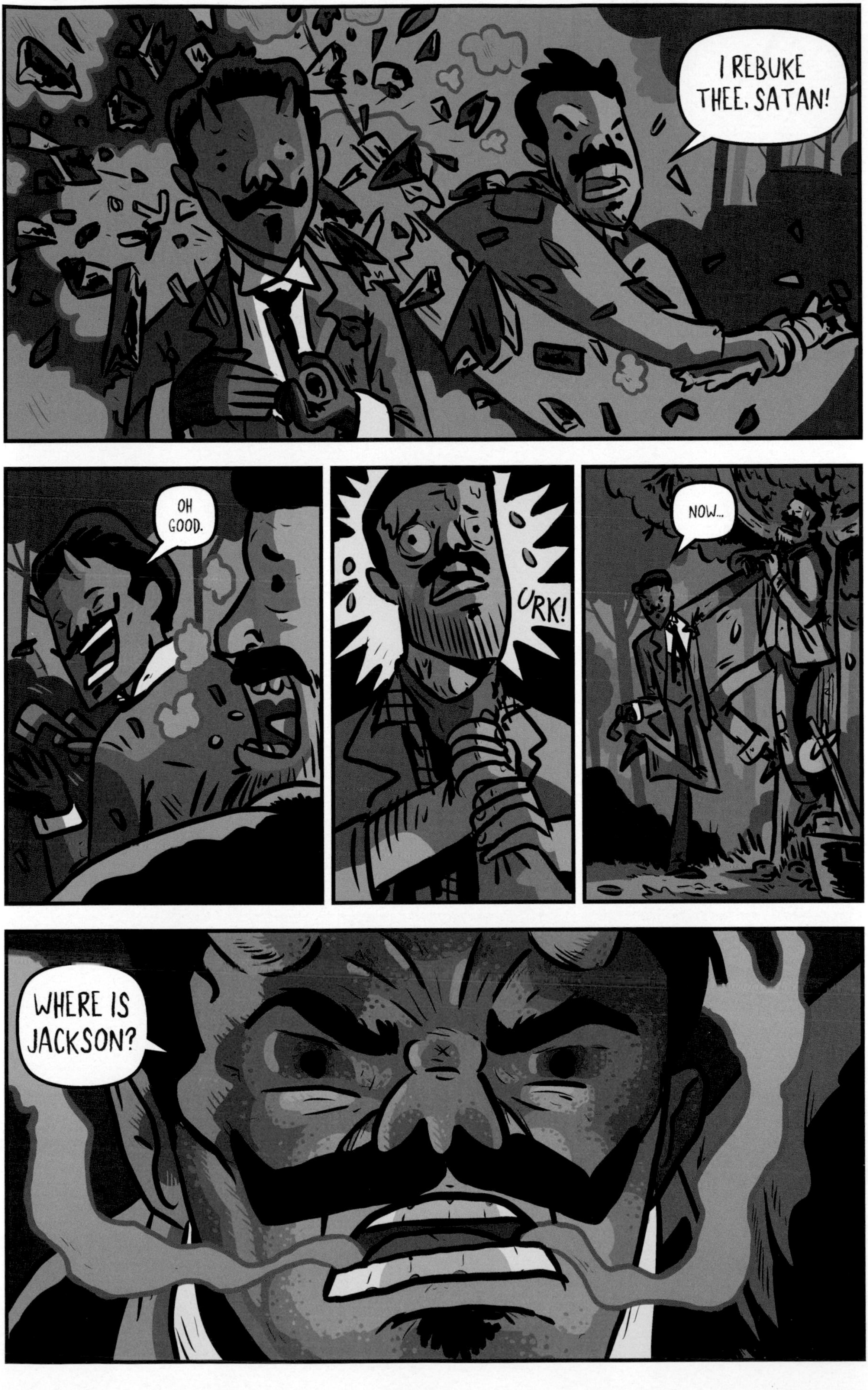
I REBUKE THEE, SATAN!
OH GOOD.
URK!
NOW...
WHERE IS JACKSON?

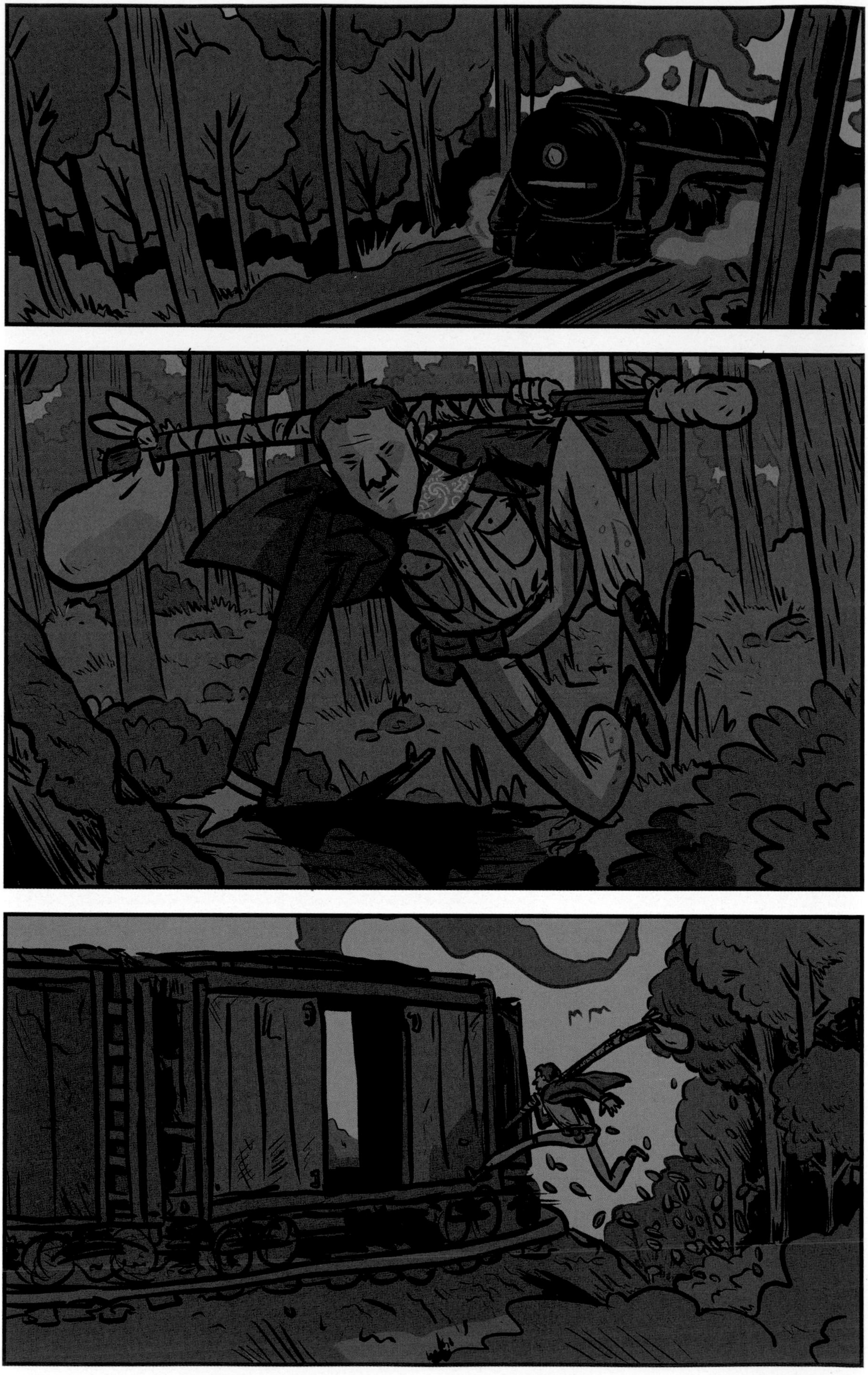

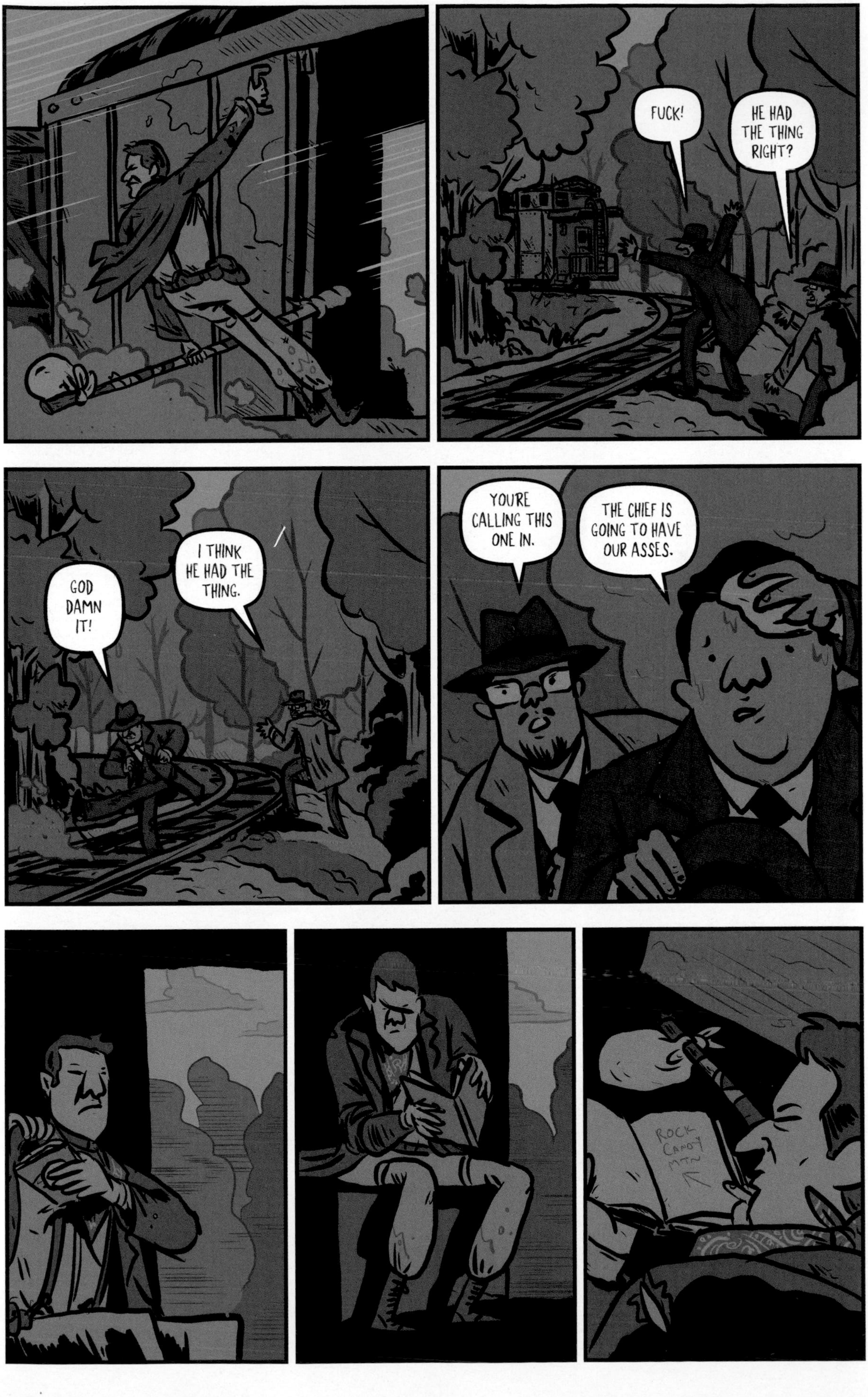
FUCK!
HE HAD THE THING RIGHT?
GOD DAMN IT!
I THINK HE HAD THE THING.
YOU'RE CALLING THIS ONE IN.
THE CHIEF IS GOING TO HAVE OUR ASSES.
ROCK CANDY MTN

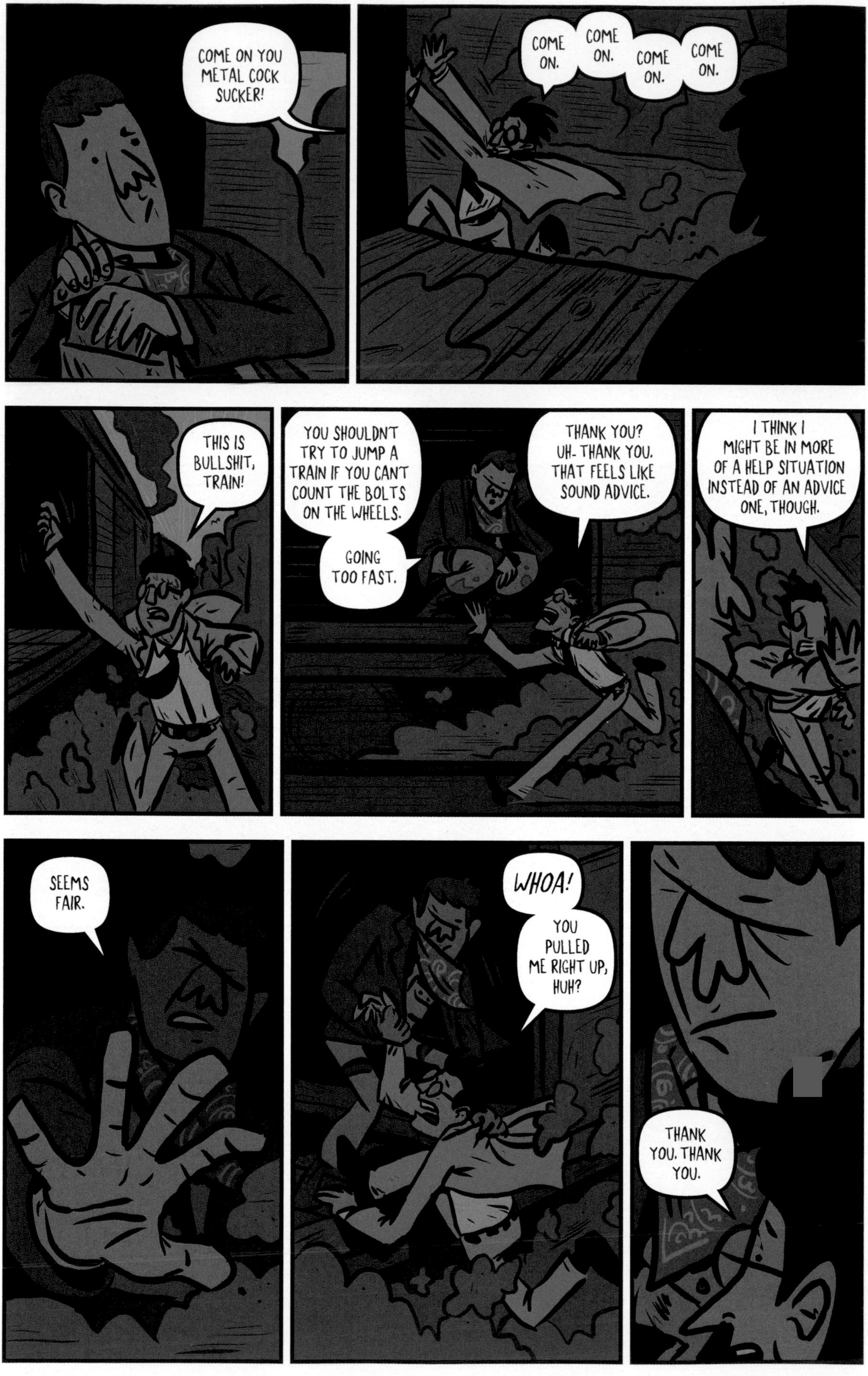
COME ON YOU METAL COCK SUCKER!
COME ON.
COME ON.
COME ON.
COME ON.
THIS IS BULLSHIT, TRAIN!
YOU SHOULDN'T TRY TO JUMP A TRAIN IF YOU CAN'T COUNT THE BOLTS ON THE WHEELS.
GOING TOO FAST.
THANK YOU? UH- THANK YOU. THAT FEELS LIKE SOUND ADVICE.
I THINK I MIGHT BE IN MORE OF A HELP SITUATION INSTEAD OF AN ADVICE ONE, THOUGH.
SEEMS FAIR.
WHOA!
YOU PULLED ME RIGHT UP, HUH?
THANK YOU. THANK YOU.

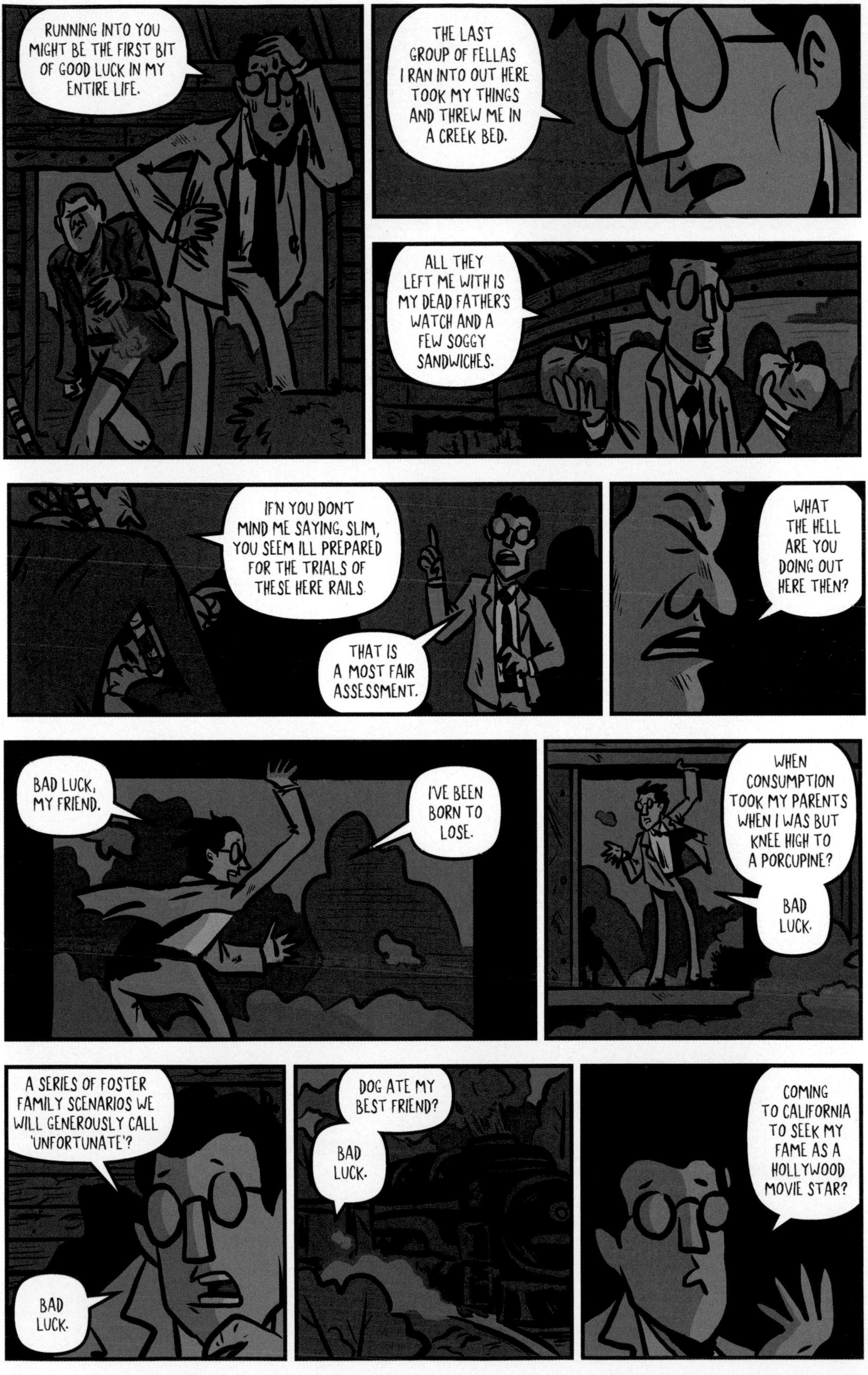
RUNNING INTO YOU MIGHT BE THE FIRST BIT OF GOOD LUCK IN MY ENTIRE LIFE.
THE LAST GROUP OF FELLAS I RAN INTO OUT HERE TOOK MY THINGS AND THREW ME IN A CREEK BED.
ALL THEY LEFT ME WITH IS MY DEAD FATHER'S WATCH AND A FEW SOGGY SANDWICHES.
IF'N YOU DON'T MIND ME SAYING, SLIM, YOU SEEM ILL PREPARED FOR THE TRIALS OF THESE HERE RAILS.
THAT IS A MOST FAIR ASSESSMENT.
WHAT THE HELL ARE YOU DOING OUT HERE THEN?
BAD LUCK, MY FRIEND.
I'VE BEEN BORN TO LOSE.
WHEN CONSUMPTION TOOK MY PARENTS WHEN I WAS BUT KNEE HIGH TO A PORCUPINE?
BAD LUCK.
A SERIES OF FOSTER FAMILY SCENARIOS WE WILL GENEROUSLY CALL 'UNFORTUNATE'?
BAD LUCK.
DOG ATE MY BEST FRIEND?
BAD LUCK.
COMING TO CALIFORNIA TO SEEK MY FAME AS A HOLLYWOOD MOVIE STAR?

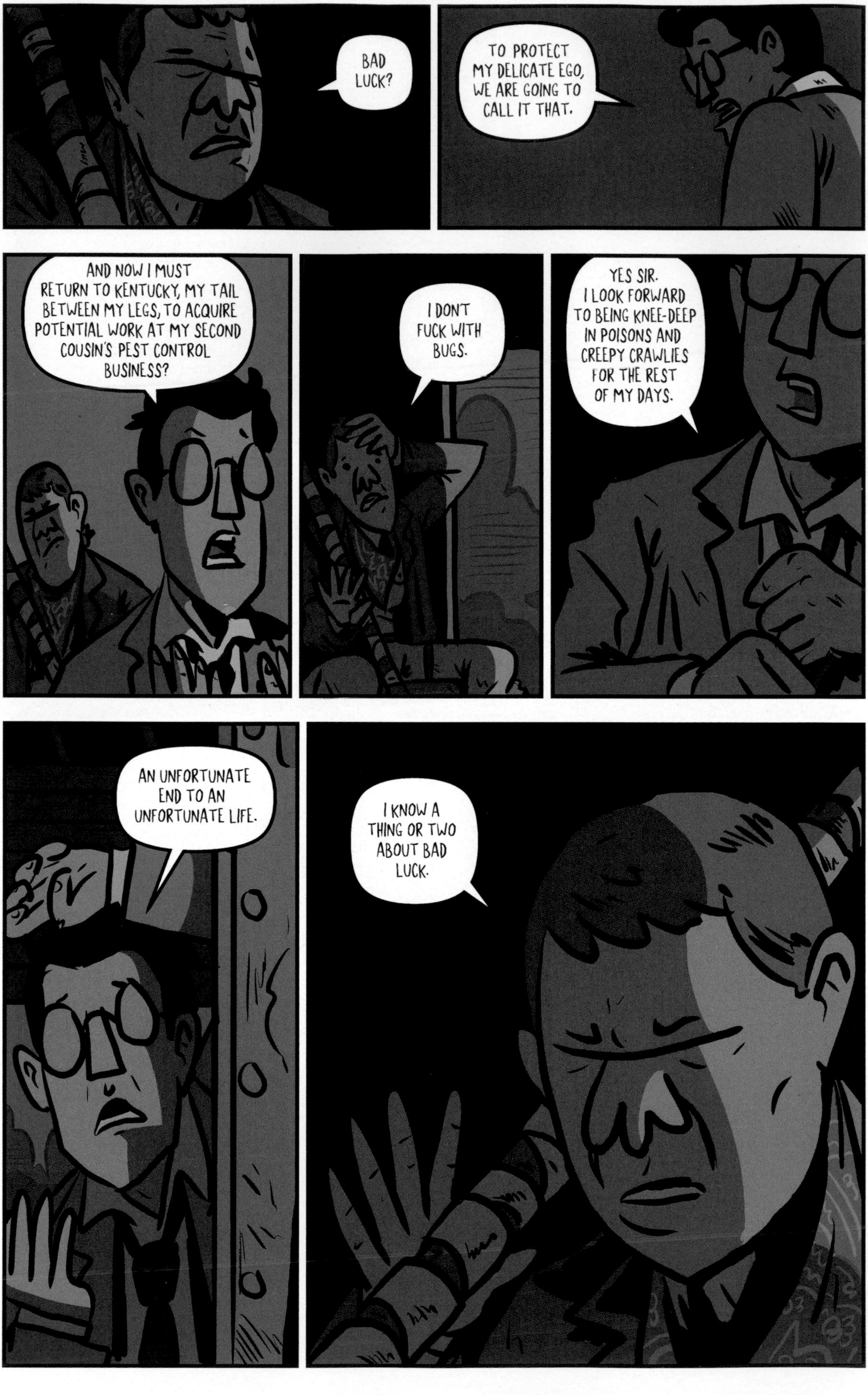
BAD LUCK?
TO PROTECT MY DELICATE EGO, WE ARE GOING TO CALL IT THAT.
AND NOW I MUST RETURN TO KENTUCKY, MY TAIL BETWEEN MY LEGS, TO ACQUIRE POTENTIAL WORK AT MY SECOND COUSIN'S PEST CONTROL BUSINESS?
I DON'T FUCK WITH BUGS.
YES SIR. I LOOK FORWARD TO BEING KNEE-DEEP IN POISONS AND CREEPY CRAWLIES FOR THE REST OF MY DAYS.
AN UNFORTUNATE END TO AN UNFORTUNATE LIFE.
I KNOW A THING OR TWO ABOUT BAD LUCK.

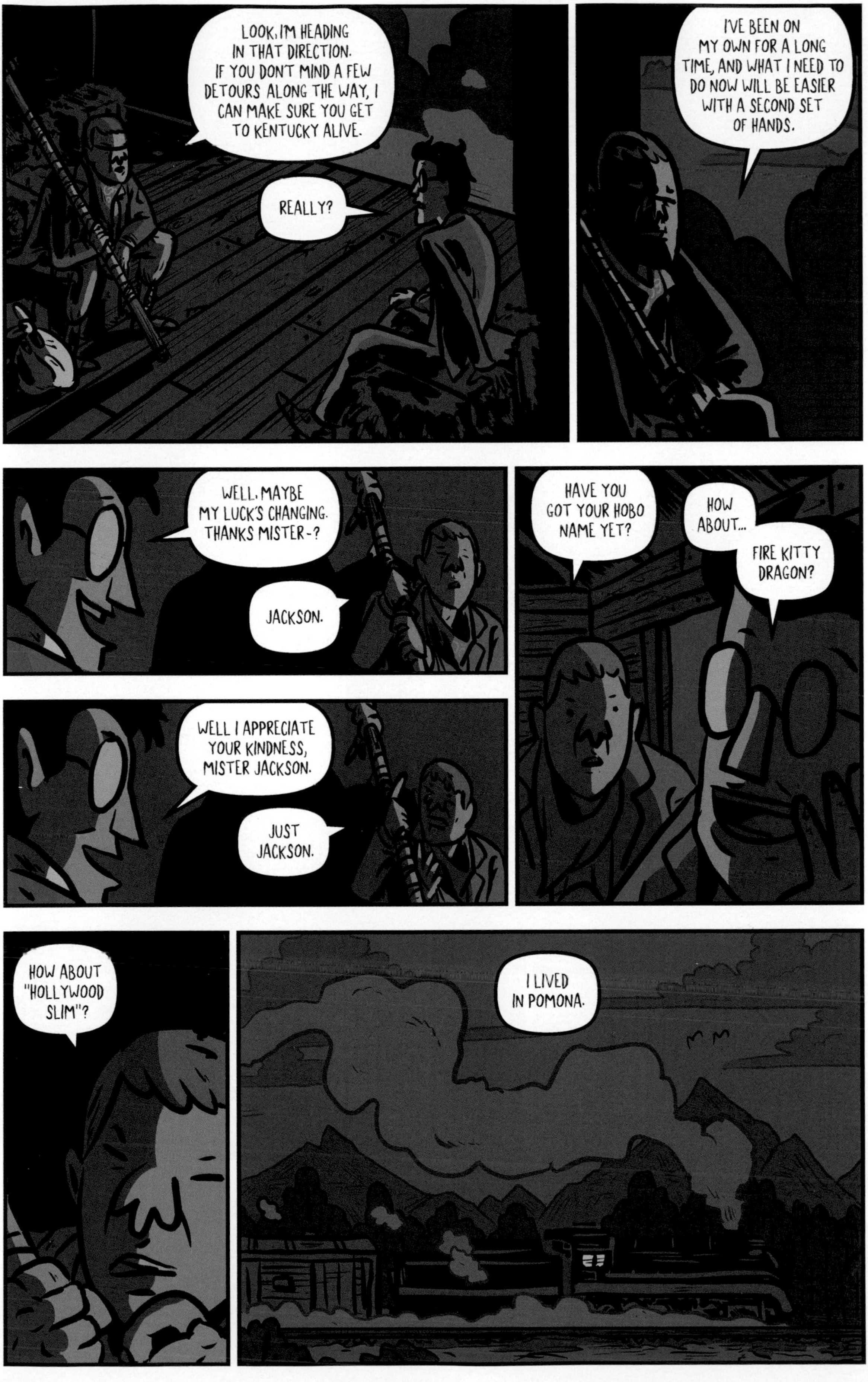

LOOK, I'M HEADING IN THAT DIRECTION. IF YOU DON'T MIND A FEW DETOURS ALONG THE WAY, I CAN MAKE SURE YOU GET TO KENTUCKY ALIVE.
REALLY?
I'VE BEEN ON MY OWN FOR A LONG TIME, AND WHAT I NEED TO DO NOW WILL BE EASIER WITH A SECOND SET OF HANDS.
WELL, MAYBE MY LUCK'S CHANGING. THANKS MISTER-?
JACKSON.
WELL I APPRECIATE YOUR KINDNESS, MISTER JACKSON.
JUST JACKSON.
HAVE YOU GOT YOUR HOBO NAME YET?
HOW ABOUT...
FIRE KITTY DRAGON?
HOW ABOUT "HOLLYWOOD SLIM"?
I LIVED IN POMONA.

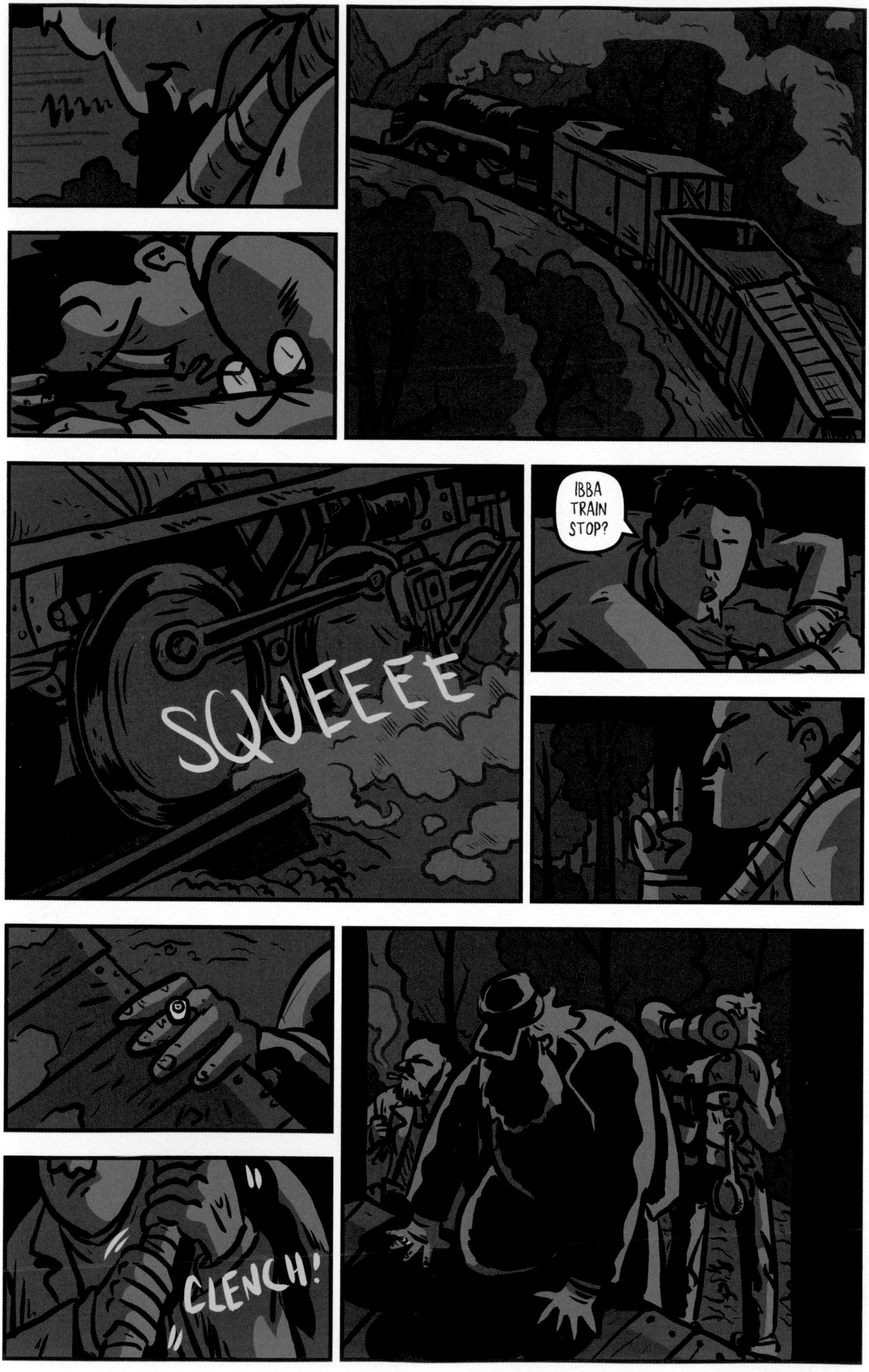
Zzzz
SQUEEEE
IBBA TRAIN STOP?
CLENCH!

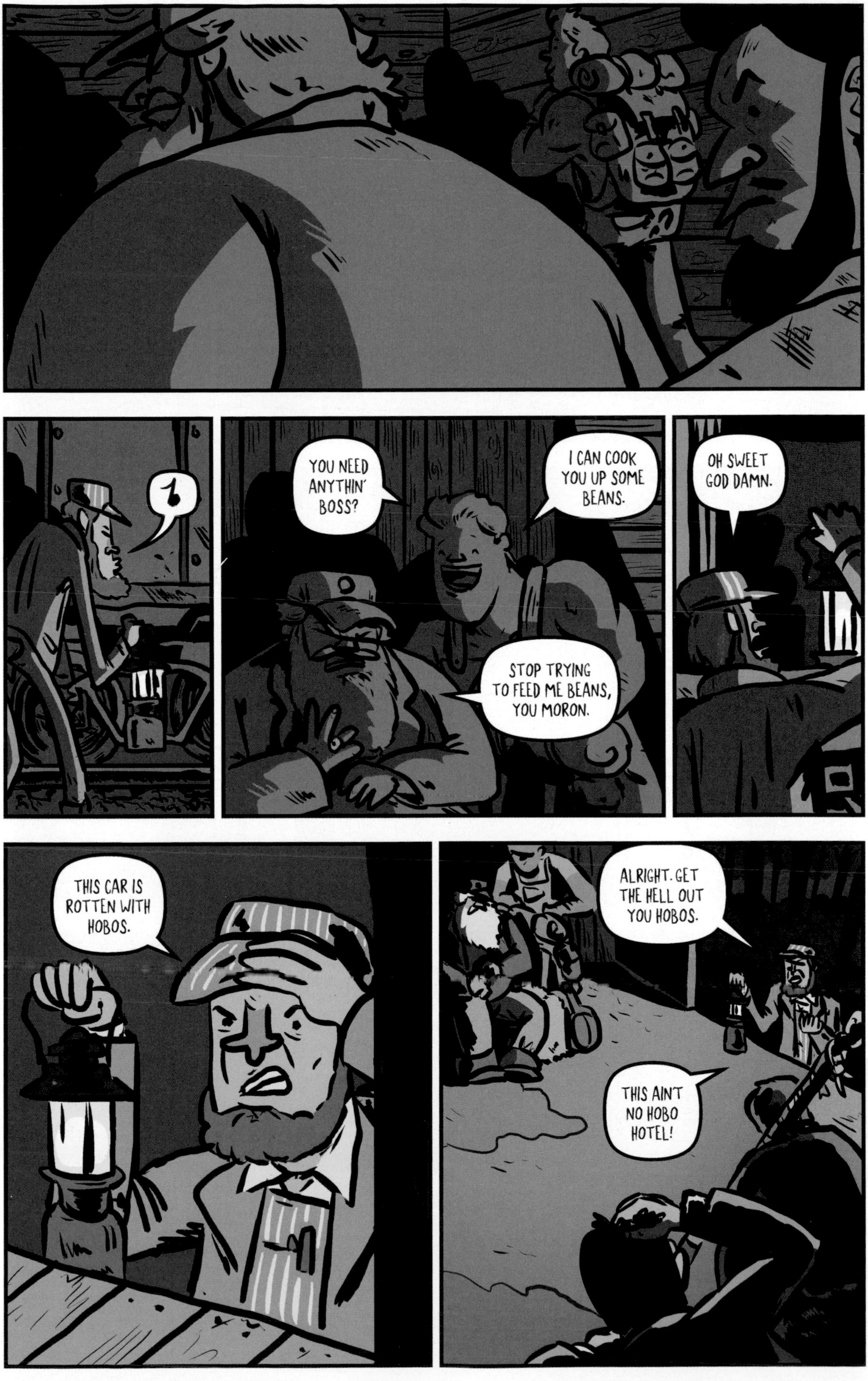

YOU NEED ANYTHIN' BOSS?
I CAN COOK YOU UP SOME BEANS.
STOP TRYING TO FEED ME BEANS, YOU MORON.
OH SWEET GOD DAMN.
THIS CAR IS ROTTEN WITH HOBOS.
ALRIGHT. GET THE HELL OUT YOU HOBOS.
THIS AIN'T NO HOBO HOTEL!

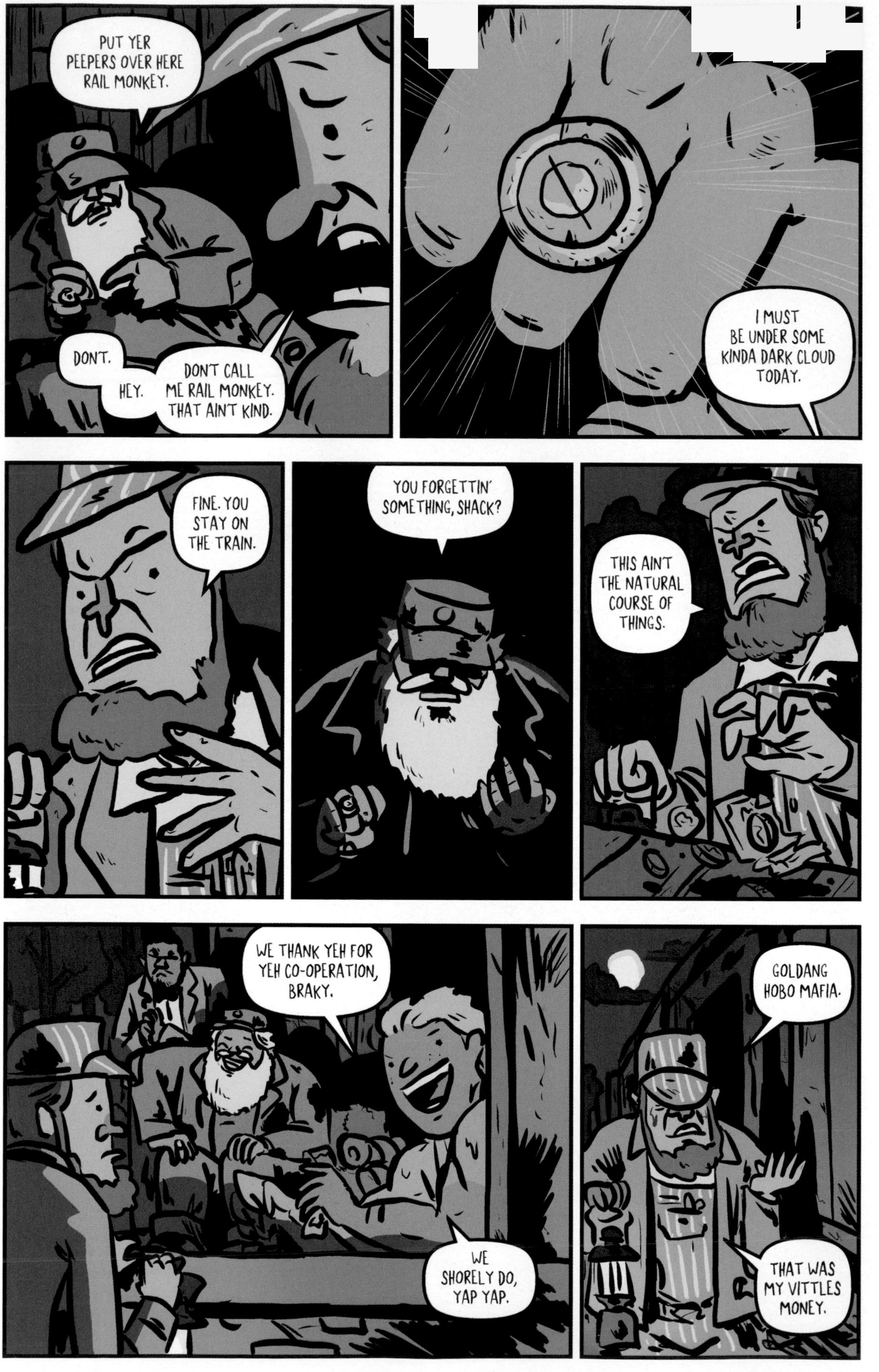
PUT YER PEEPERS OVER HERE RAIL MONKEY.
DONT.
HEY.
DON'T CALL ME RAIL MONKEY. THAT AIN'T KIND.
I MUST BE UNDER SOME KINDA DARK CLOUD TODAY.
FINE. YOU STAY ON THE TRAIN.
YOU FORGETTIN' SOMETHING, SHACK?
THIS AIN'T THE NATURAL COURSE OF THINGS.
WE THANK YEH FOR YEH CO-OPERATION, BRAKY.
WE SHORELY DO, YAP YAP.
GOLDANG HOBO MAFIA.
THAT WAS MY VITTLES MONEY.

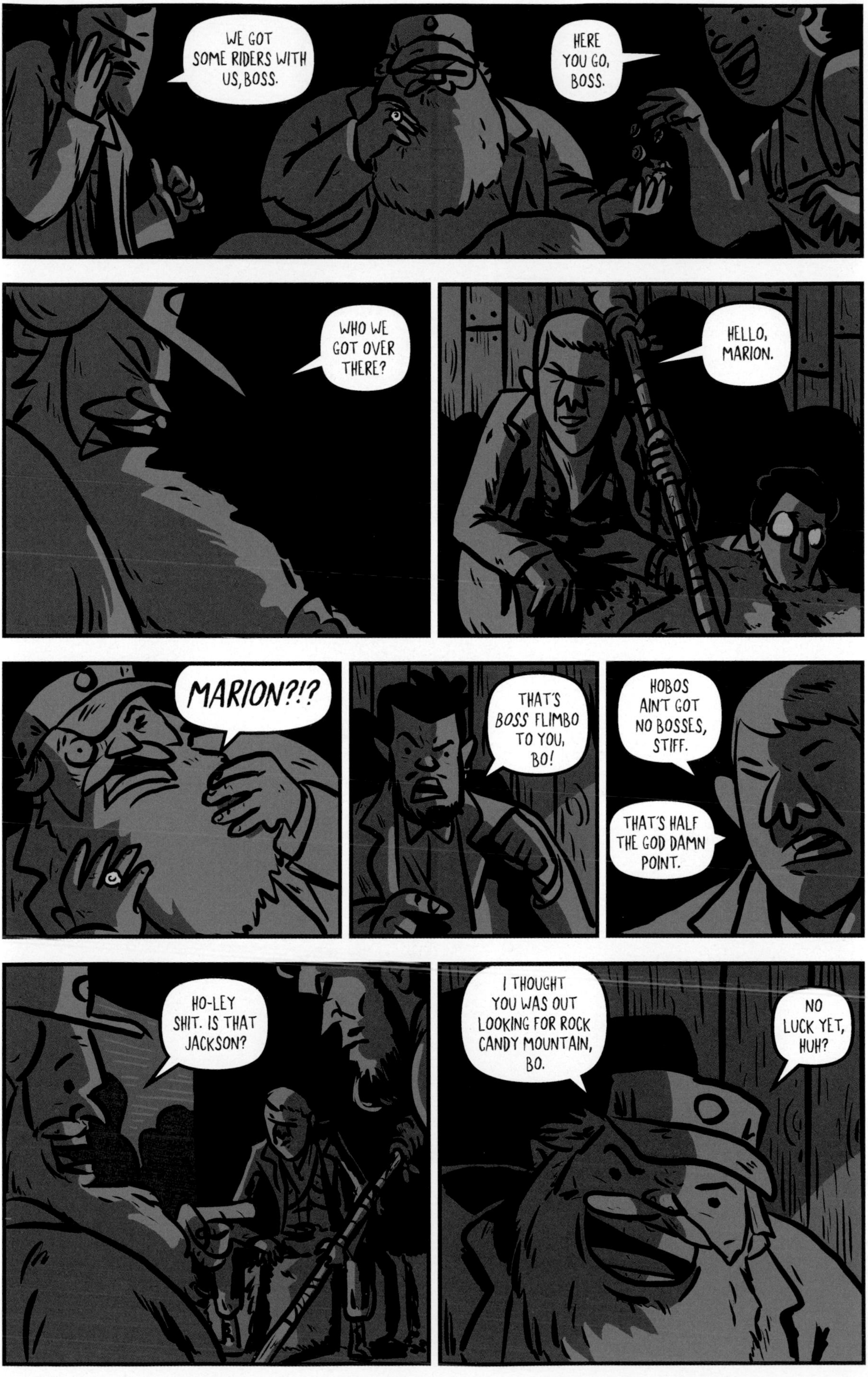
WE GOT SOME RIDERS WITH US, BOSS.
HERE YOU GO, BOSS.
WHO WE GOT OVER THERE?
HELLO, MARION.
MARION?!?
THAT'S *BOSS* FLIMBO TO YOU, BO!
HOBOS AIN'T GOT NO BOSSES, STIFF.
THAT'S HALF THE GOD DAMN POINT.
HO-LEY SHIT. IS THAT JACKSON?
I THOUGHT YOU WAS OUT LOOKING FOR ROCK CANDY MOUNTAIN, BO.
NO LUCK YET, HUH?

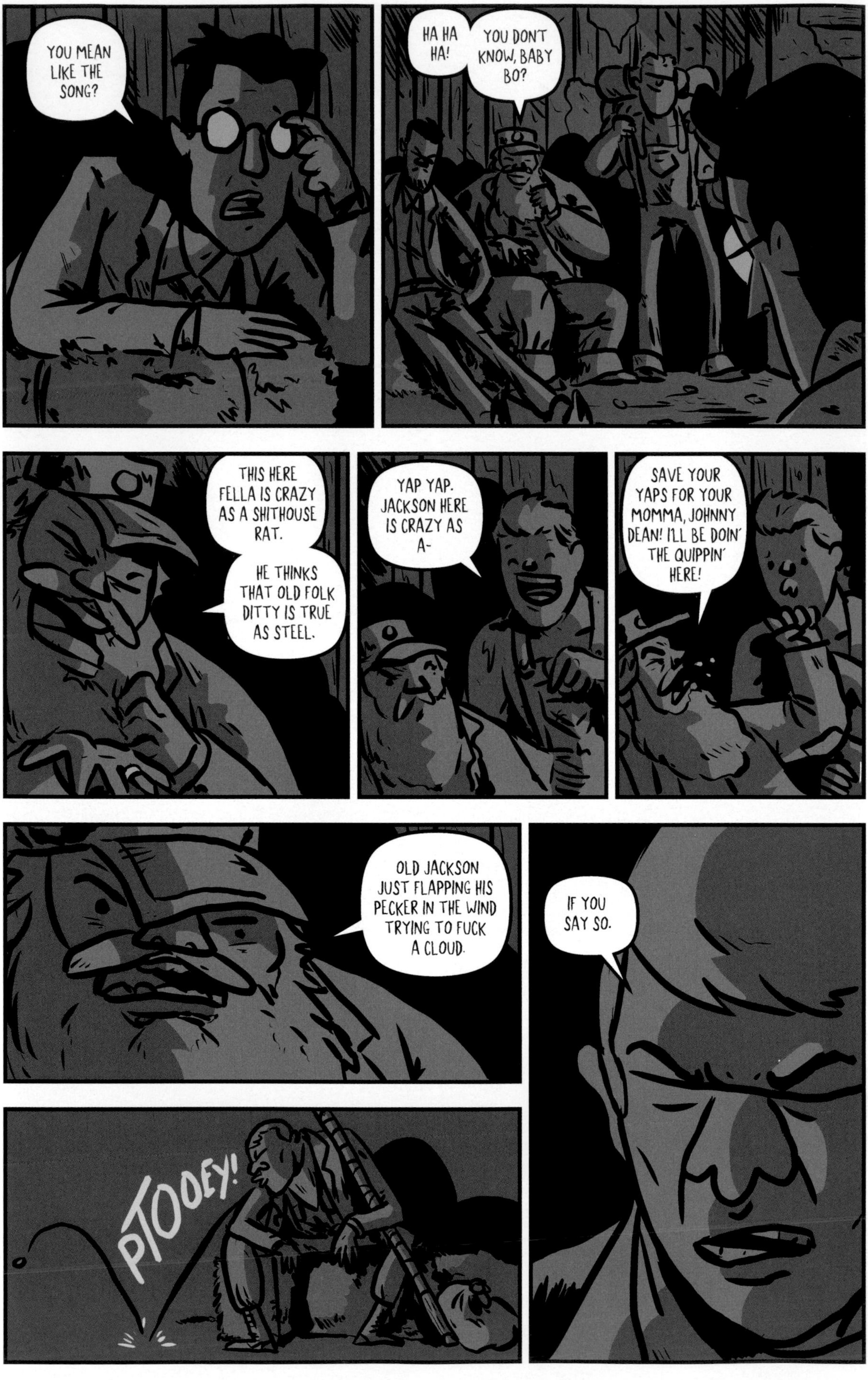
YOU MEAN LIKE THE SONG?
HA HA HA!
YOU DON'T KNOW, BABY BO?
THIS HERE FELLA IS CRAZY AS A SHITHOUSE RAT.
HE THINKS THAT OLD FOLK DITTY IS TRUE AS STEEL.
YAP YAP. JACKSON HERE IS CRAZY AS A-
SAVE YOUR YAPS FOR YOUR MOMMA, JOHNNY DEAN! I'LL BE DOIN' THE QUIPPIN' HERE!
OLD JACKSON JUST FLAPPING HIS PECKER IN THE WIND TRYING TO FUCK A CLOUD.
IF YOU SAY SO.
PTOOEY!

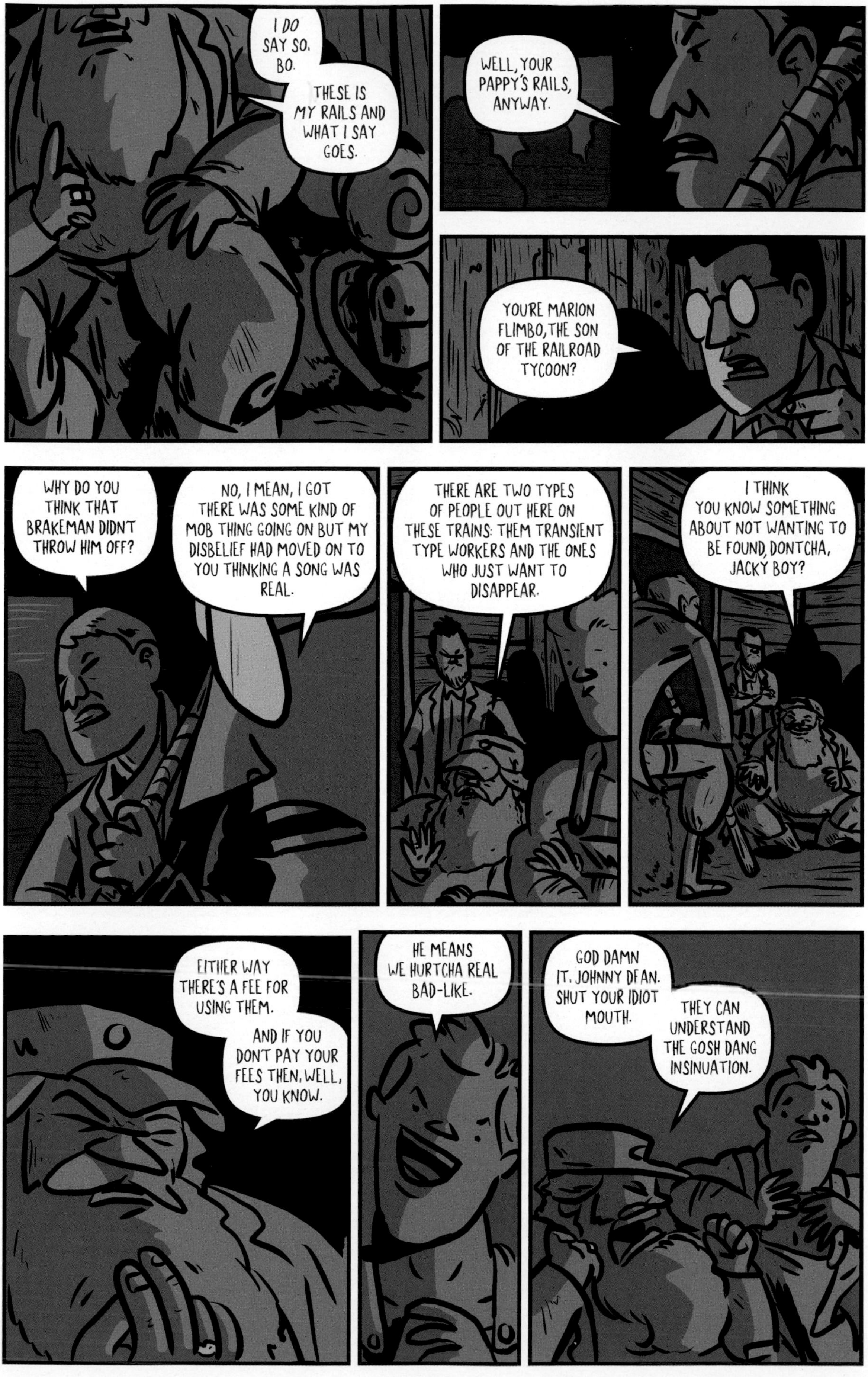
I DO SAY SO, BO.
THESE IS MY RAILS AND WHAT I SAY GOES.
WELL, YOUR PAPPY'S RAILS, ANYWAY.
YOU'RE MARION FLIMBO, THE SON OF THE RAILROAD TYCOON?
WHY DO YOU THINK THAT BRAKEMAN DIDN'T THROW HIM OFF?
NO, I MEAN, I GOT THERE WAS SOME KIND OF MOB THING GOING ON BUT MY DISBELIEF HAD MOVED ON TO YOU THINKING A SONG WAS REAL.
THERE ARE TWO TYPES OF PEOPLE OUT HERE ON THESE TRAINS: THEM TRANSIENT TYPE WORKERS AND THE ONES WHO JUST WANT TO DISAPPEAR.
I THINK YOU KNOW SOMETHING ABOUT NOT WANTING TO BE FOUND, DONTCHA, JACKY BOY?
EITHER WAY THERE'S A FEE FOR USING THEM.
AND IF YOU DON'T PAY YOUR FEES THEN, WELL, YOU KNOW.
HE MEANS WE HURTCHA REAL BAD-LIKE.
GOD DAMN IT, JOHNNY DEAN. SHUT YOUR IDIOT MOUTH.
THEY CAN UNDERSTAND THE GOSH DANG INSINUATION.

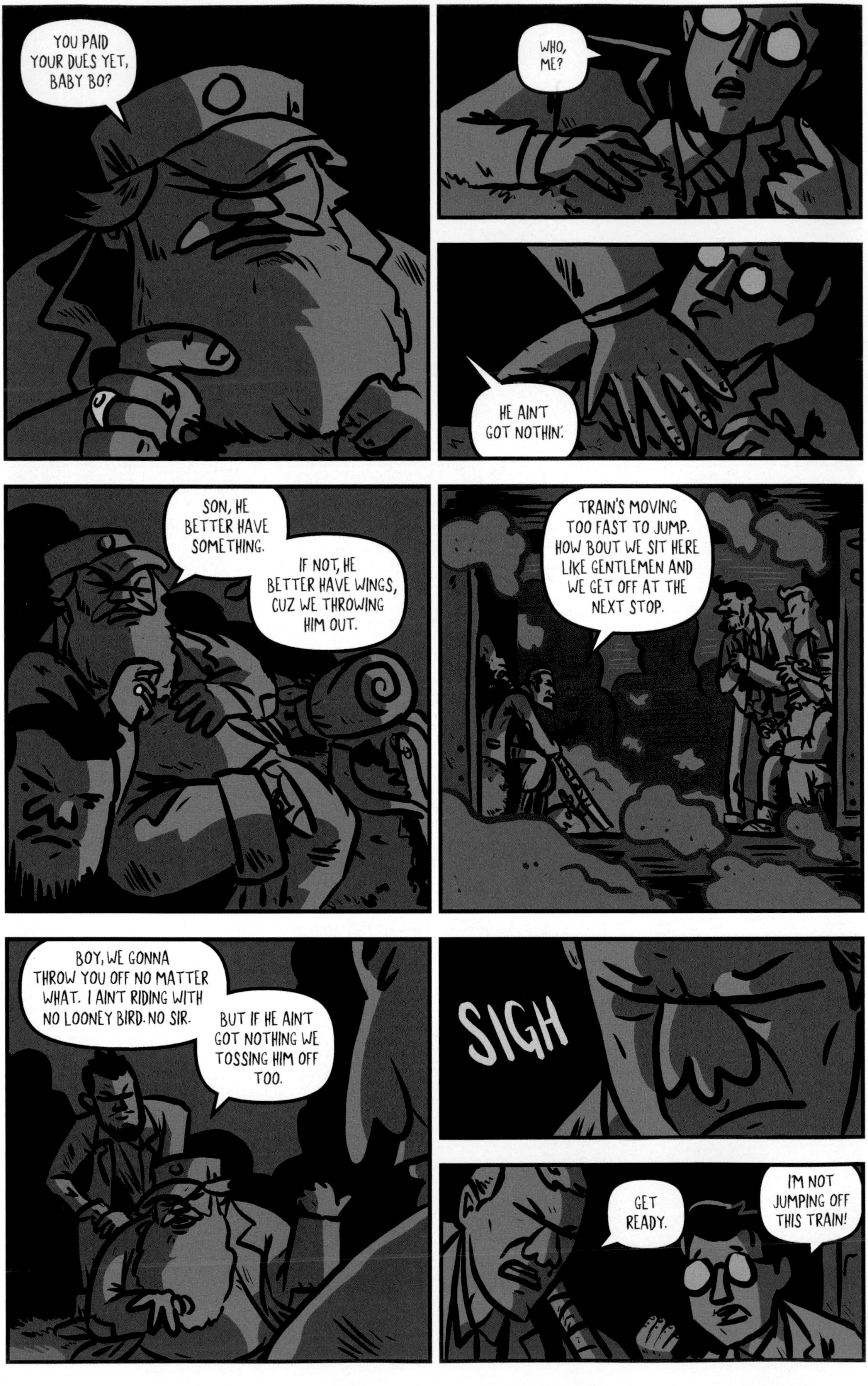
YOU PAID YOUR DUES YET, BABY BO?
WHO, ME?
HE AIN'T GOT NOTHIN'.
SON, HE BETTER HAVE SOMETHING.
IF NOT, HE BETTER HAVE WINGS, CUZ WE THROWING HIM OUT.
TRAIN'S MOVING TOO FAST TO JUMP. HOW BOUT WE SIT HERE LIKE GENTLEMEN AND WE GET OFF AT THE NEXT STOP.
BOY, WE GONNA THROW YOU OFF NO MATTER WHAT. I AIN'T RIDING WITH NO LOONEY BIRD. NO SIR.
BUT IF HE AIN'T GOT NOTHING WE TOSSING HIM OFF TOO.
SIGH
GET READY.
I'M NOT JUMPING OFF THIS TRAIN!

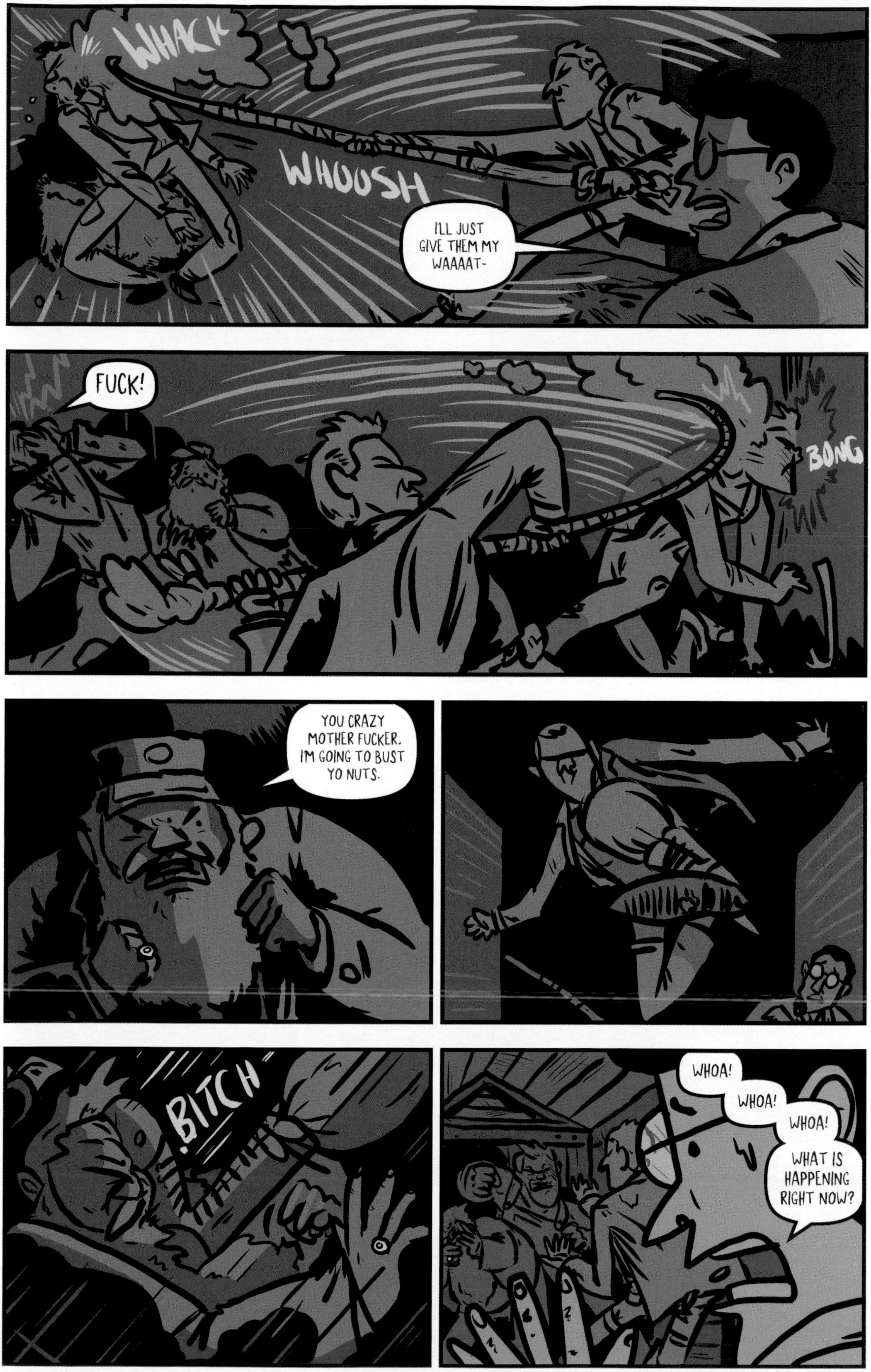
WHACK
WHOOSH
I'LL JUST GIVE THEM MY WAAAAT-
FUCK!
BONG
YOU CRAZY MOTHER FUCKER. I'M GOING TO BUST YO NUTS.
BITCH
WHOA!
WHOA!
WHOA!
WHAT IS HAPPENING RIGHT NOW?

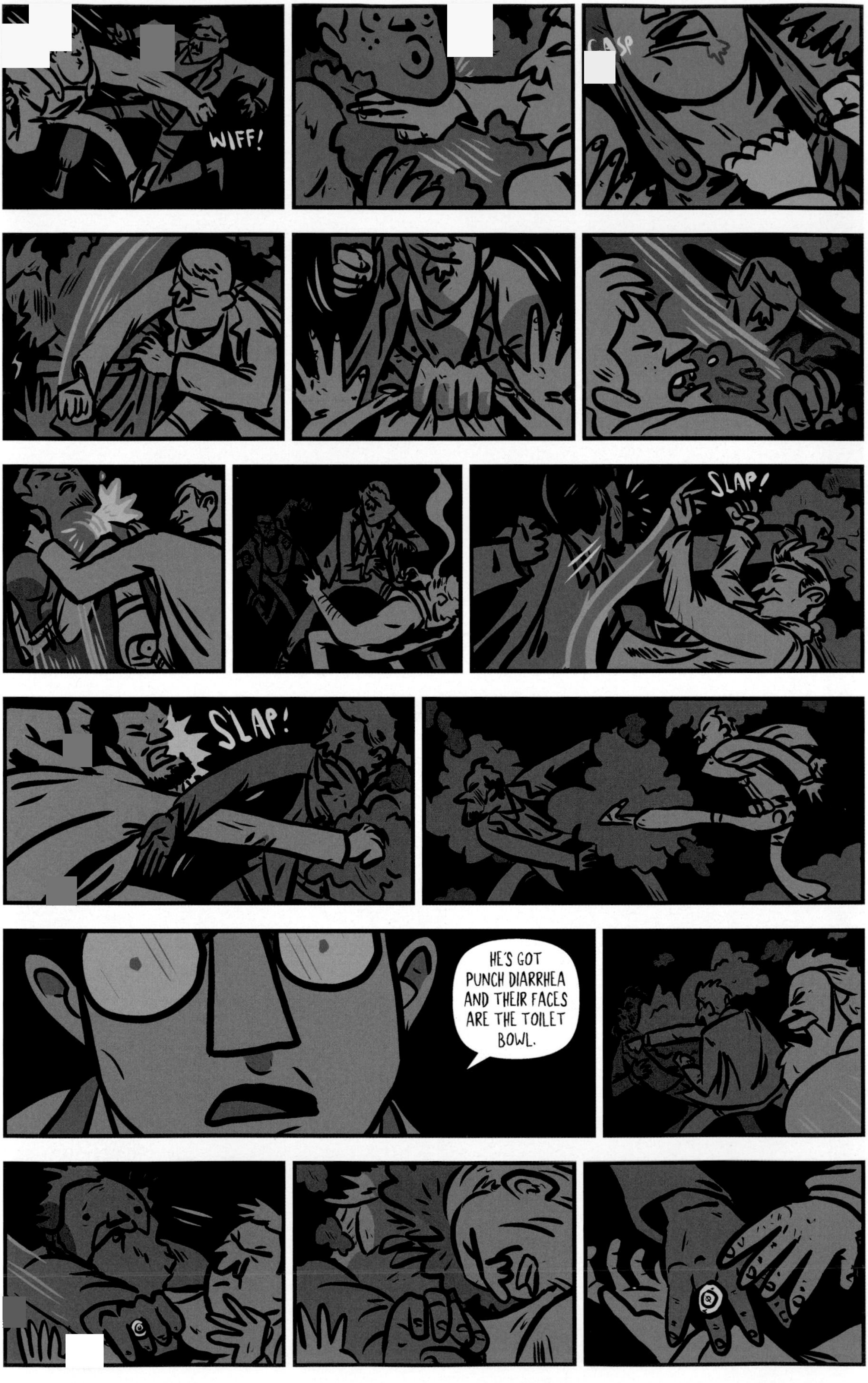
WIFF!
SLAP!
SLAP!
HE'S GOT PUNCH DIARRHEA AND THEIR FACES ARE THE TOILET BOWL.

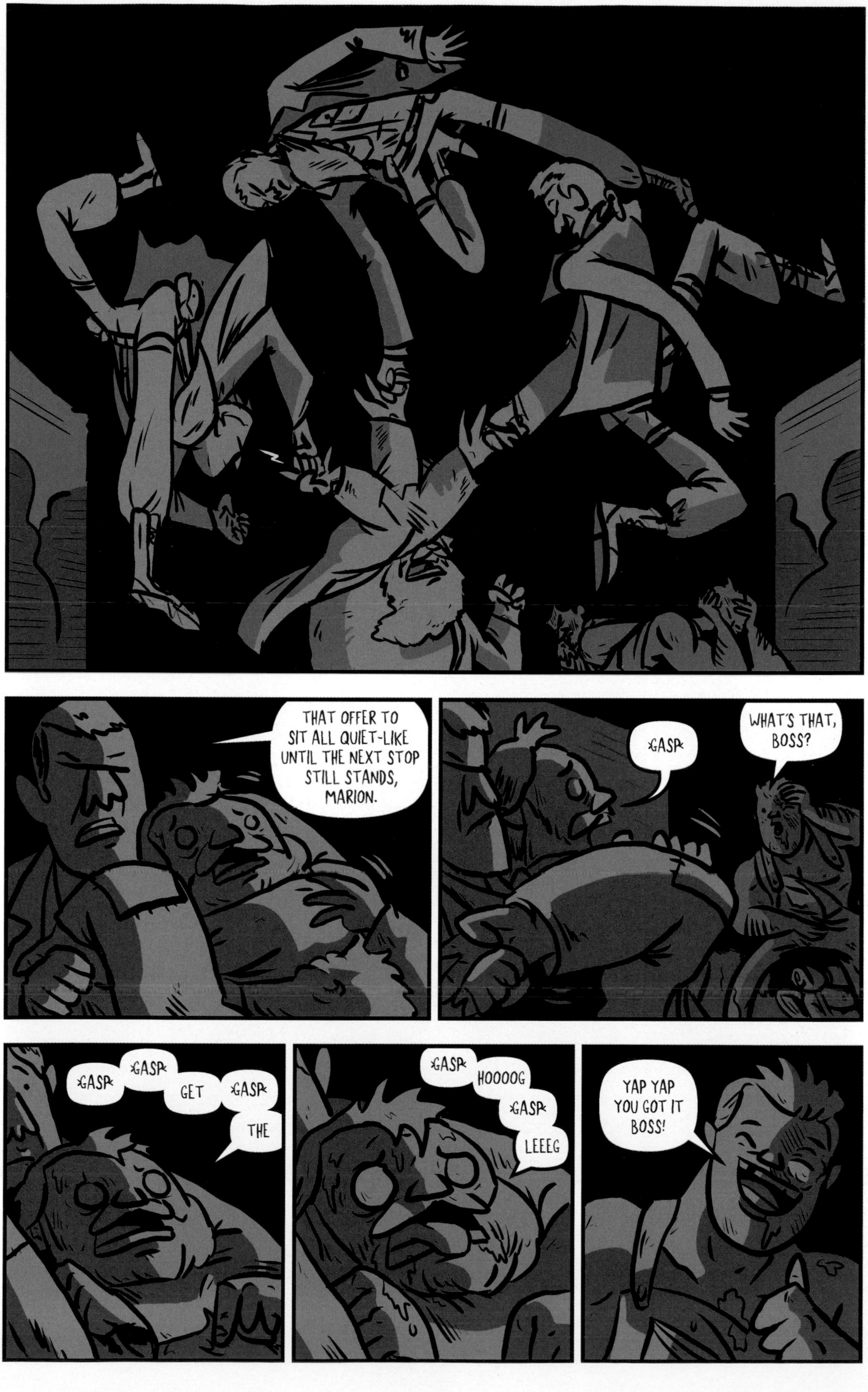
THAT OFFER TO SIT ALL QUIET-LIKE UNTIL THE NEXT STOP STILL STANDS, MARION.
GASP
WHAT'S THAT, BOSS?
GASP
GASP
GET
GASP
THE
GASP
HOOOOG
GASP
LEEEG
YAP YAP YOU GOT IT BOSS!

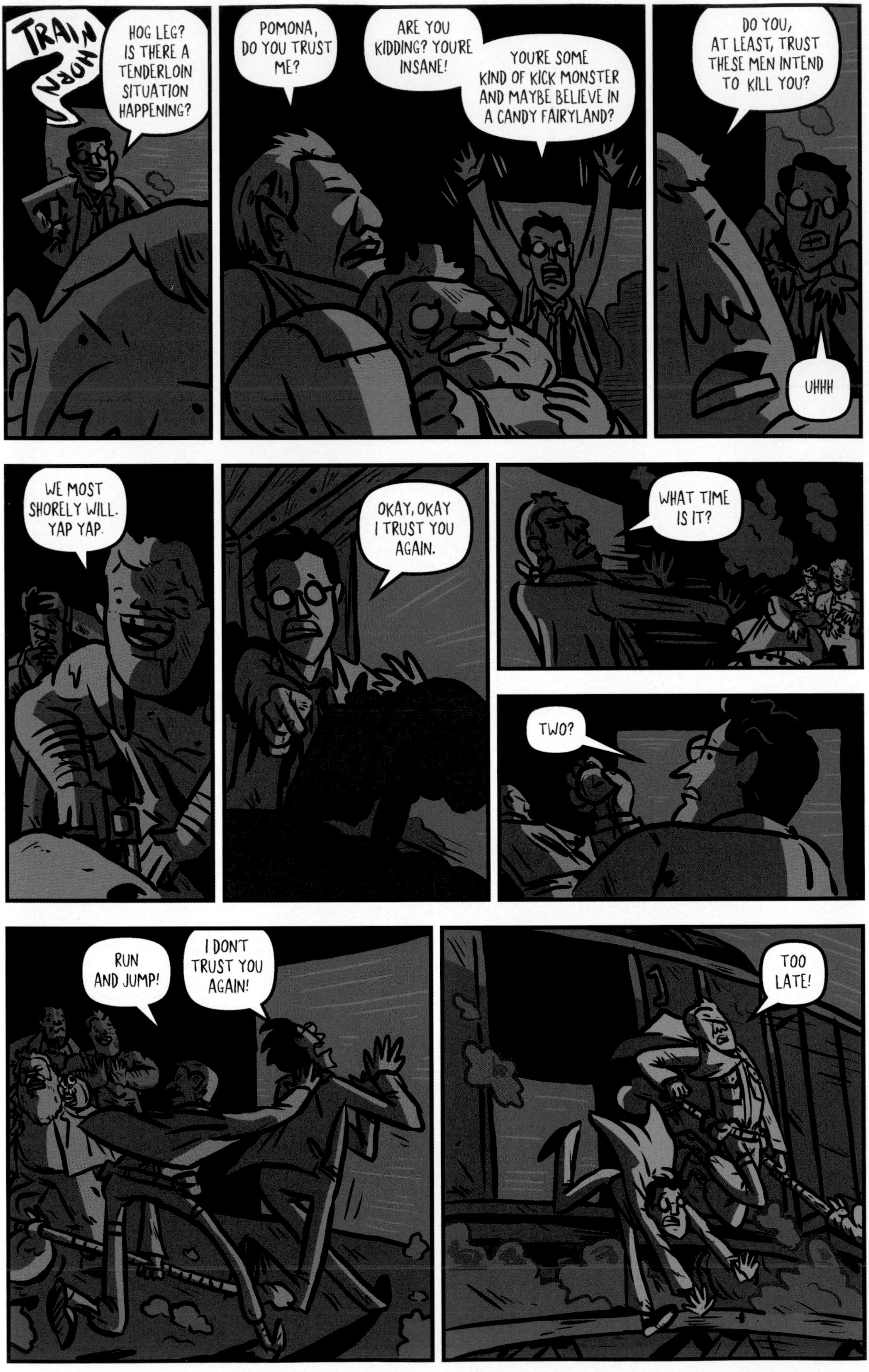
TRAIN HORN
HOG LEG? IS THERE A TENDERLOIN SITUATION HAPPENING?
POMONA, DO YOU TRUST ME?
ARE YOU KIDDING? YOU'RE INSANE!
YOU'RE SOME KIND OF KICK MONSTER AND MAYBE BELIEVE IN A CANDY FAIRYLAND?
DO YOU, AT LEAST, TRUST THESE MEN INTEND TO KILL YOU?
UHHH
WE MOST SHORELY WILL. YAP YAP.
OKAY, OKAY I TRUST YOU AGAIN.
WHAT TIME IS IT?
TWO?
RUN AND JUMP!
I DON'T TRUST YOU AGAIN!
TOO LATE!

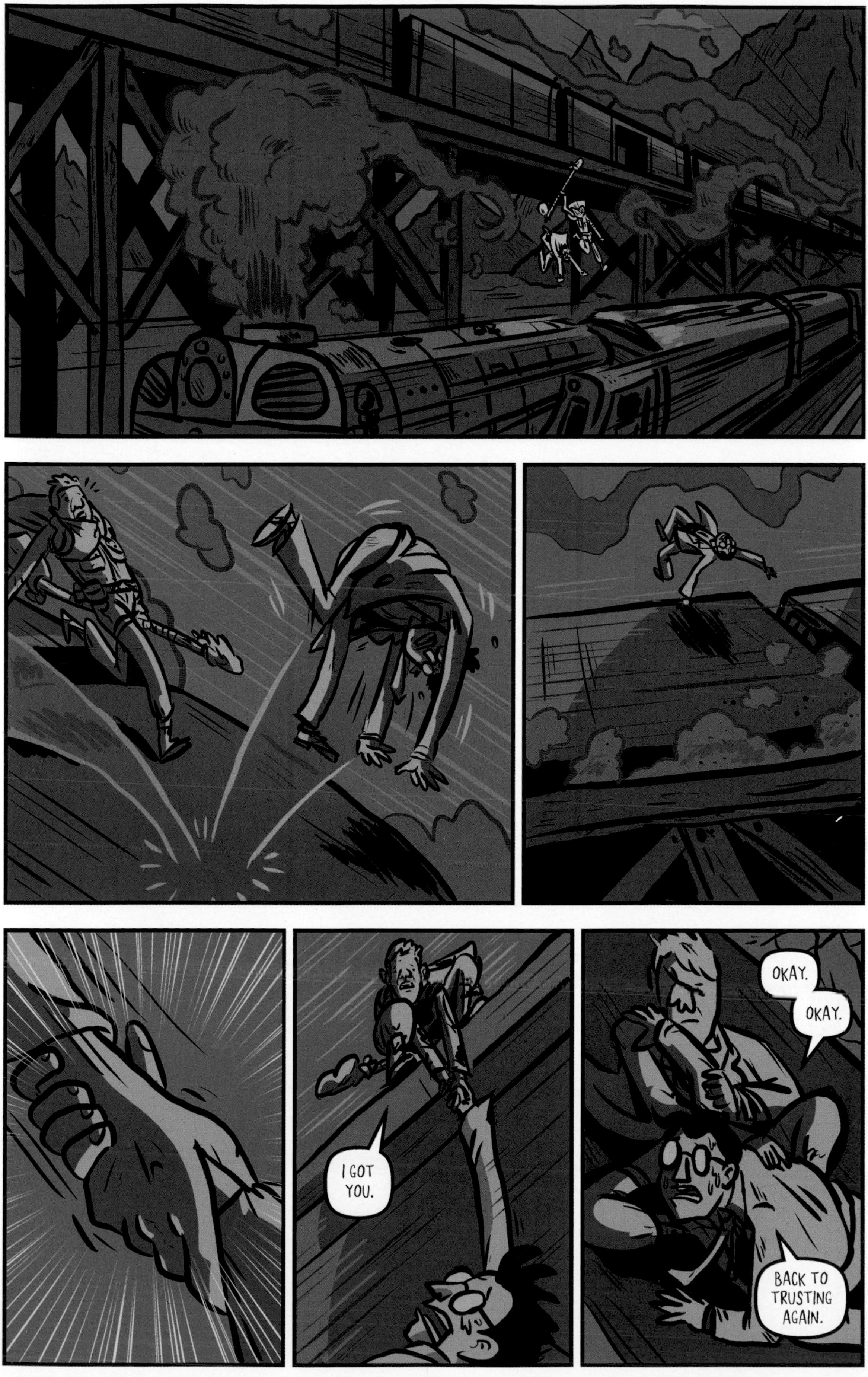
I GOT YOU.
OKAY.
OKAY.
BACK TO TRUSTING AGAIN.

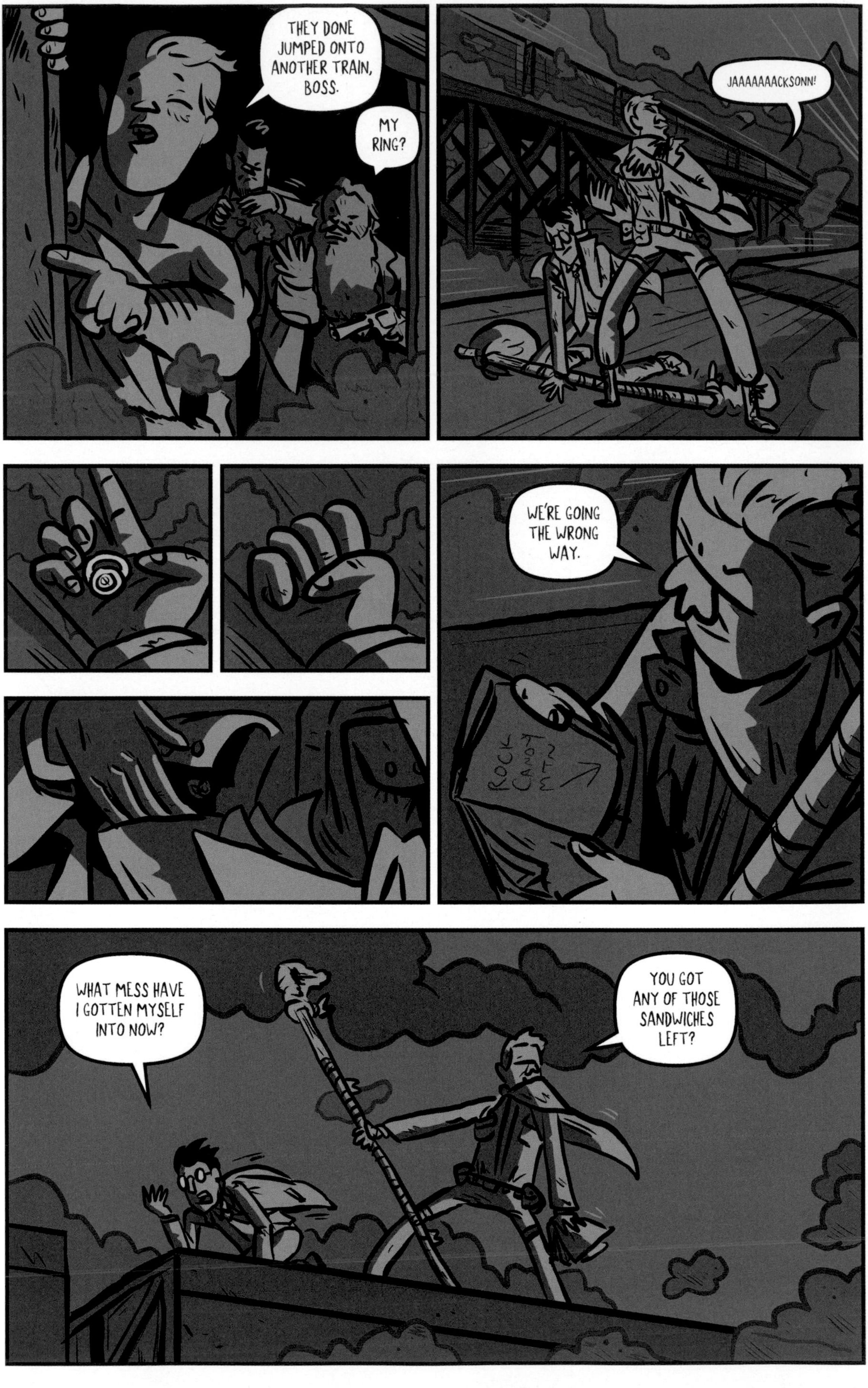
THEY DONE JUMPED ONTO ANOTHER TRAIN, BOSS.
MY RING?
JAAAAAAACKSONN!
WE'RE GOING THE WRONG WAY.
ROCK CANYON CAMP
WHAT MESS HAVE I GOTTEN MYSELF INTO NOW?
YOU GOT ANY OF THOSE SANDWICHES LEFT?

CHAPTER TWO

"The bulldogs all have rubber teeth."

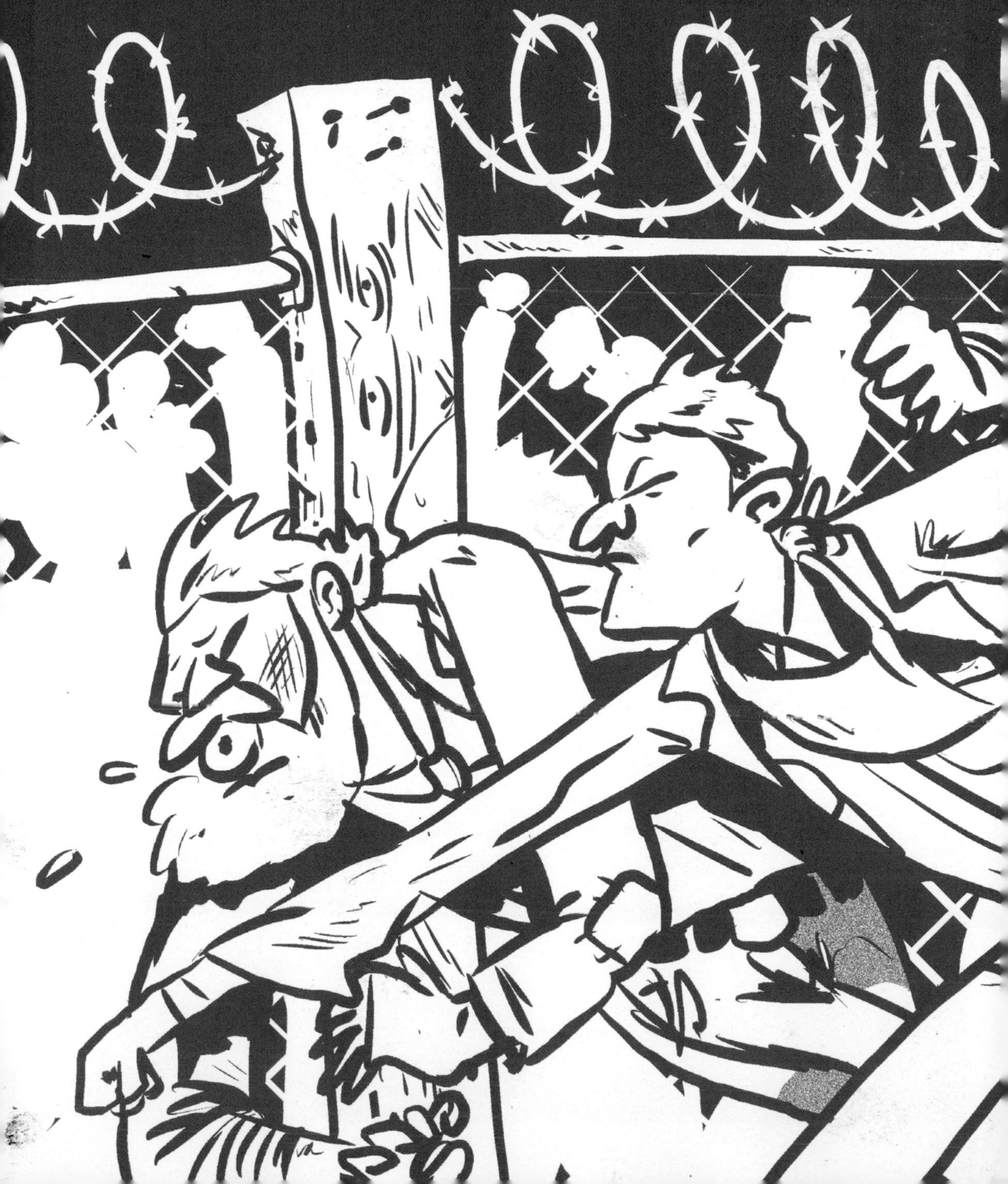

"be prepared to
defend yourself."

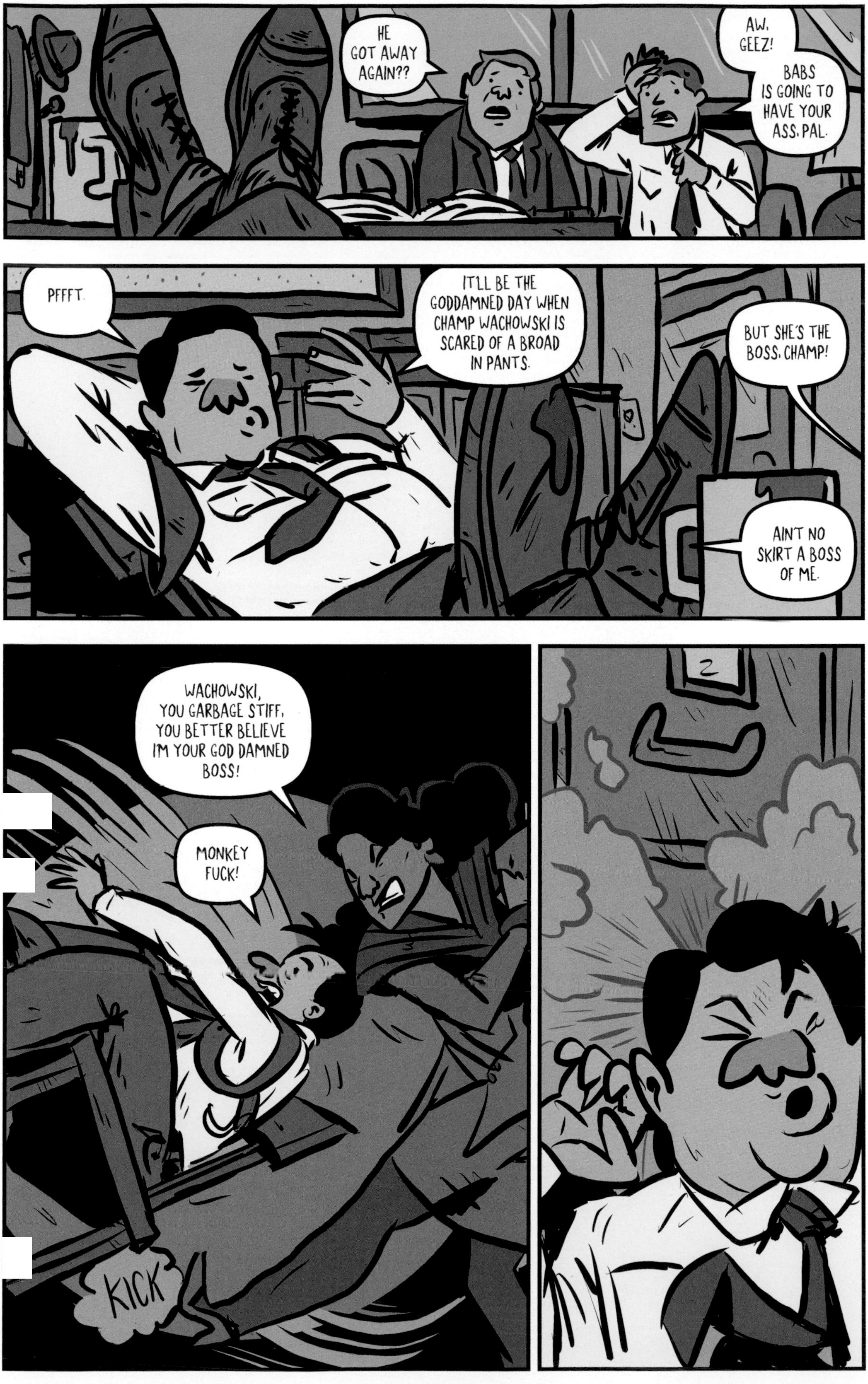
HE GOT AWAY AGAIN??
AW, GEEZ!
BABS IS GOING TO HAVE YOUR ASS, PAL.
PFFFT.
IT'LL BE THE GODDAMNED DAY WHEN CHAMP WACHOWSKI IS SCARED OF A BROAD IN PANTS.
BUT SHE'S THE BOSS, CHAMP!
AIN'T NO SKIRT A BOSS OF ME.
WACHOWSKI, YOU GARBAGE STIFF, YOU BETTER BELIEVE I'M YOUR GOD DAMNED BOSS!
MONKEY FUCK!
KICK

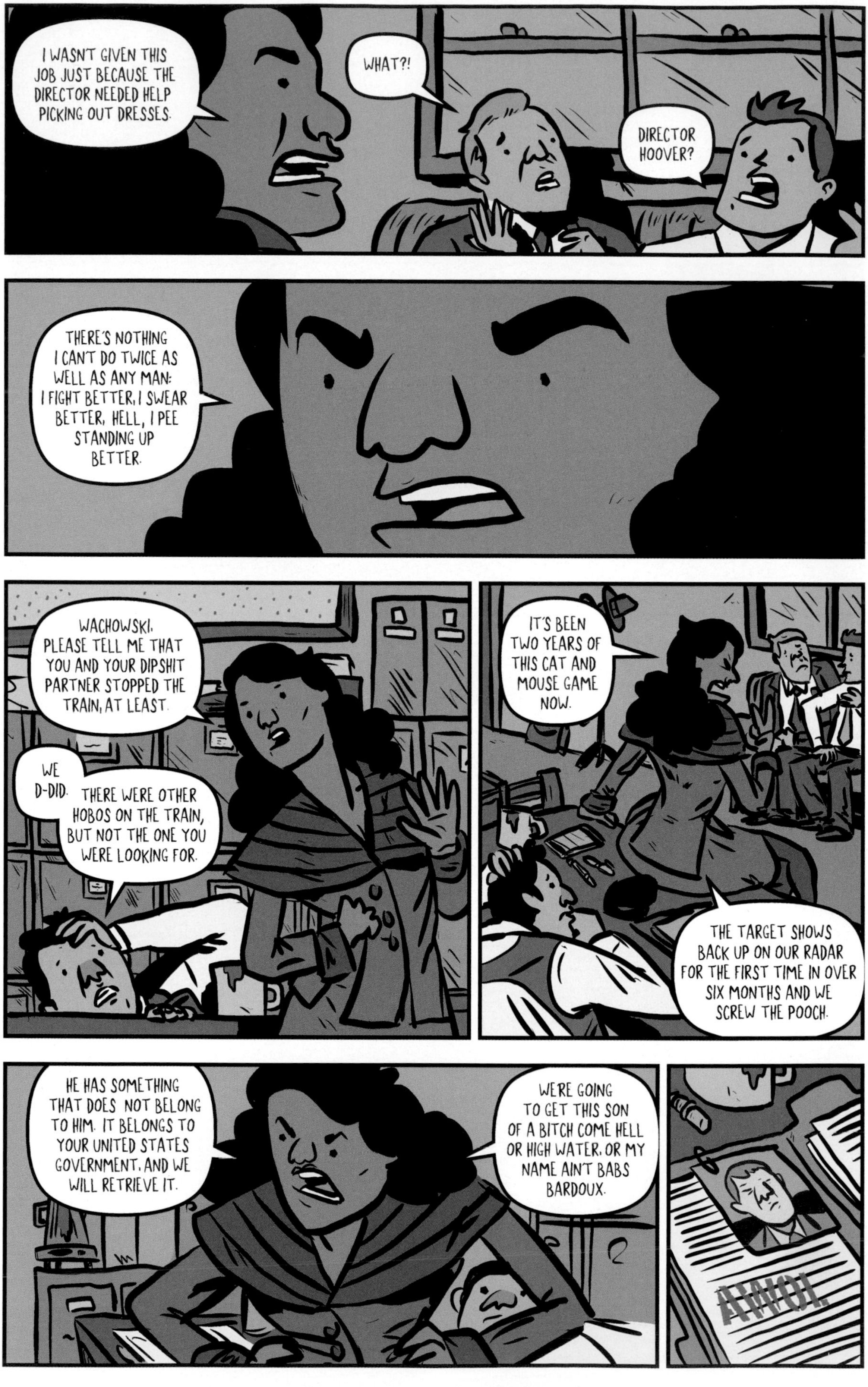
I WASN'T GIVEN THIS JOB JUST BECAUSE THE DIRECTOR NEEDED HELP PICKING OUT DRESSES.
WHAT?!
DIRECTOR HOOVER?
THERE'S NOTHING I CAN'T DO TWICE AS WELL AS ANY MAN: I FIGHT BETTER, I SWEAR BETTER, HELL, I PEE STANDING UP BETTER.
WACHOWSKI. PLEASE TELL ME THAT YOU AND YOUR DIPSHIT PARTNER STOPPED THE TRAIN, AT LEAST.
WE D-DID.
THERE WERE OTHER HOBOS ON THE TRAIN, BUT NOT THE ONE YOU WERE LOOKING FOR.
IT'S BEEN TWO YEARS OF THIS CAT AND MOUSE GAME NOW.
THE TARGET SHOWS BACK UP ON OUR RADAR FOR THE FIRST TIME IN OVER SIX MONTHS AND WE SCREW THE POOCH.
HE HAS SOMETHING THAT DOES NOT BELONG TO HIM. IT BELONGS TO YOUR UNITED STATES GOVERNMENT. AND WE WILL RETRIEVE IT.
WE'RE GOING TO GET THIS SON OF A BITCH COME HELL OR HIGH WATER. OR MY NAME AIN'T BABS BARDOUX.
AWOL

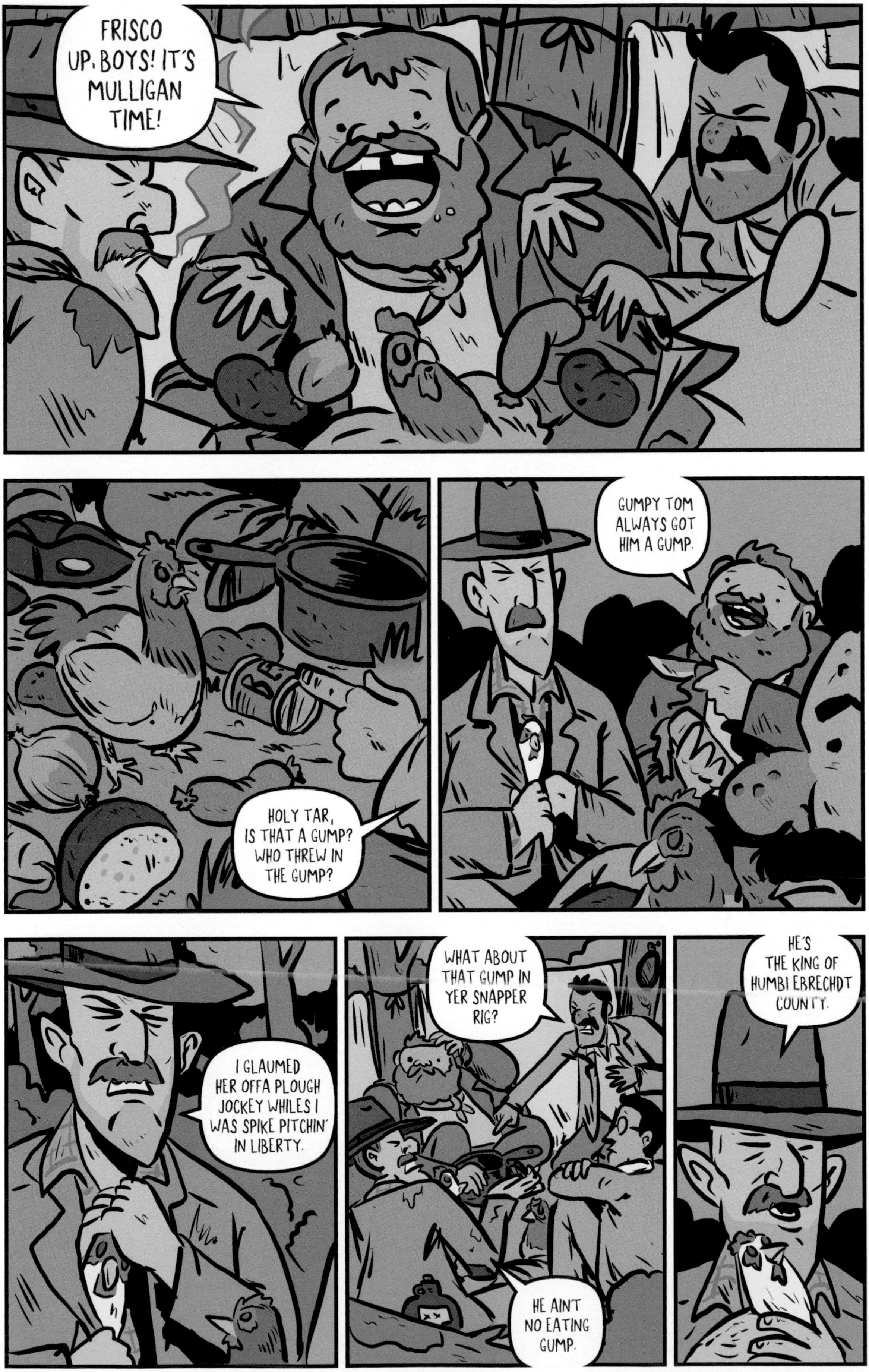
FRISCO UP, BOYS! IT'S MULLIGAN TIME!
HOLY TAR, IS THAT A GUMP? WHO THREW IN THE GUMP?
GUMPY TOM ALWAYS GOT HIM A GUMP.
I GLAUMED HER OFFA PLOUGH JOCKEY WHILES I WAS SPIKE PITCHIN' IN LIBERTY.
WHAT ABOUT THAT GUMP IN YER SNAPPER RIG?
HE AIN'T NO EATING GUMP.
HE'S THE KING OF HUMBLEBRECHDT COUNTY.

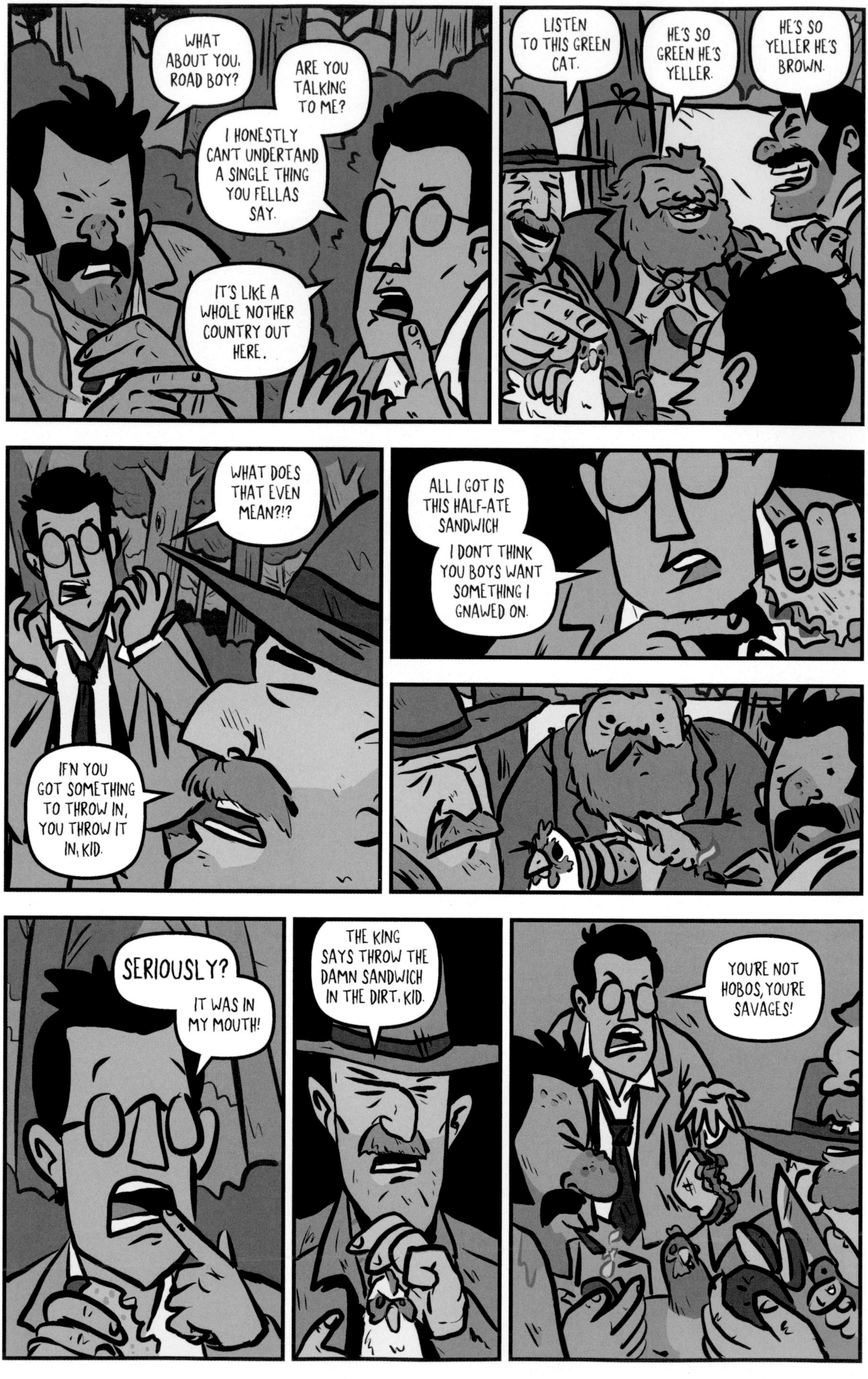
WHAT ABOUT YOU, ROAD BOY?
ARE YOU TALKING TO ME?
I HONESTLY CAN'T UNDERTAND A SINGLE THING YOU FELLAS SAY.
IT'S LIKE A WHOLE 'NOTHER COUNTRY OUT HERE.
LISTEN TO THIS GREEN CAT.
HE'S SO GREEN HE'S YELLER.
HE'S SO YELLER HE'S BROWN.
WHAT DOES THAT EVEN MEAN?!?
IF'N YOU GOT SOMETHING TO THROW IN, YOU THROW IT IN, KID.
ALL I GOT IS THIS HALF-ATE SANDWICH
I DON'T THINK YOU BOYS WANT SOMETHING I GNAWED ON.
SERIOUSLY?
IT WAS IN MY MOUTH!
THE KING SAYS THROW THE DAMN SANDWICH IN THE DIRT, KID.
YOU'RE NOT HOBOS, YOU'RE SAVAGES!

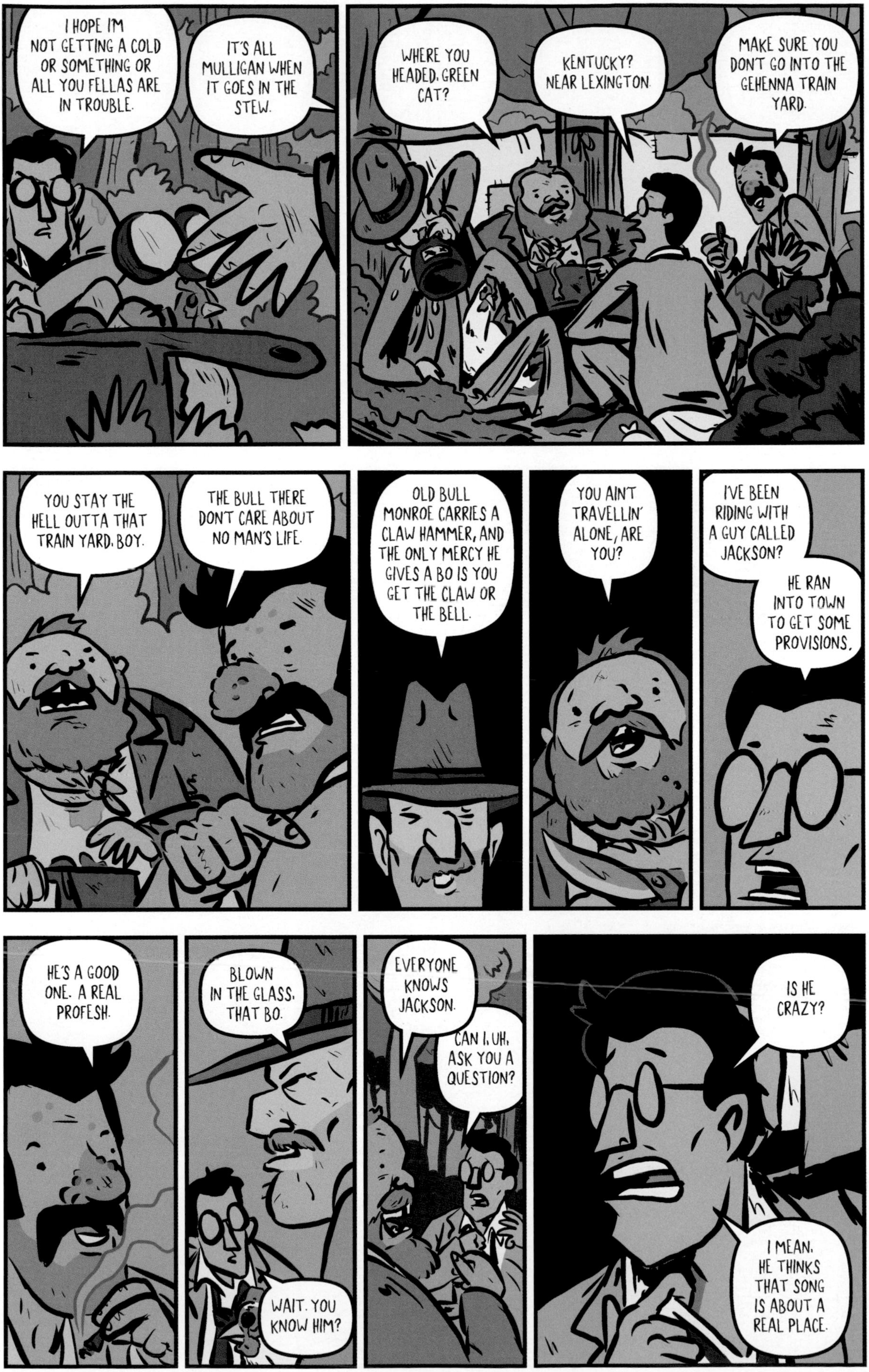
I HOPE I'M NOT GETTING A COLD OR SOMETHING OR ALL YOU FELLAS ARE IN TROUBLE.
IT'S ALL MULLIGAN WHEN IT GOES IN THE STEW.
WHERE YOU HEADED, GREEN CAT?
KENTUCKY? NEAR LEXINGTON.
MAKE SURE YOU DON'T GO INTO THE GEHENNA TRAIN YARD.
YOU STAY THE HELL OUTTA THAT TRAIN YARD, BOY.
THE BULL THERE DON'T CARE ABOUT NO MAN'S LIFE.
OLD BULL MONROE CARRIES A CLAW HAMMER, AND THE ONLY MERCY HE GIVES A BO IS YOU GET THE CLAW OR THE BELL.
YOU AIN'T TRAVELLIN' ALONE, ARE YOU?
I'VE BEEN RIDING WITH A GUY CALLED JACKSON?
HE RAN INTO TOWN TO GET SOME PROVISIONS.
HE'S A GOOD ONE. A REAL PROFESH.
BLOWN IN THE GLASS, THAT BO.
WAIT. YOU KNOW HIM?
EVERYONE KNOWS JACKSON.
CAN I, UH, ASK YOU A QUESTION?
IS HE CRAZY?
I MEAN, HE THINKS THAT SONG IS ABOUT A REAL PLACE.

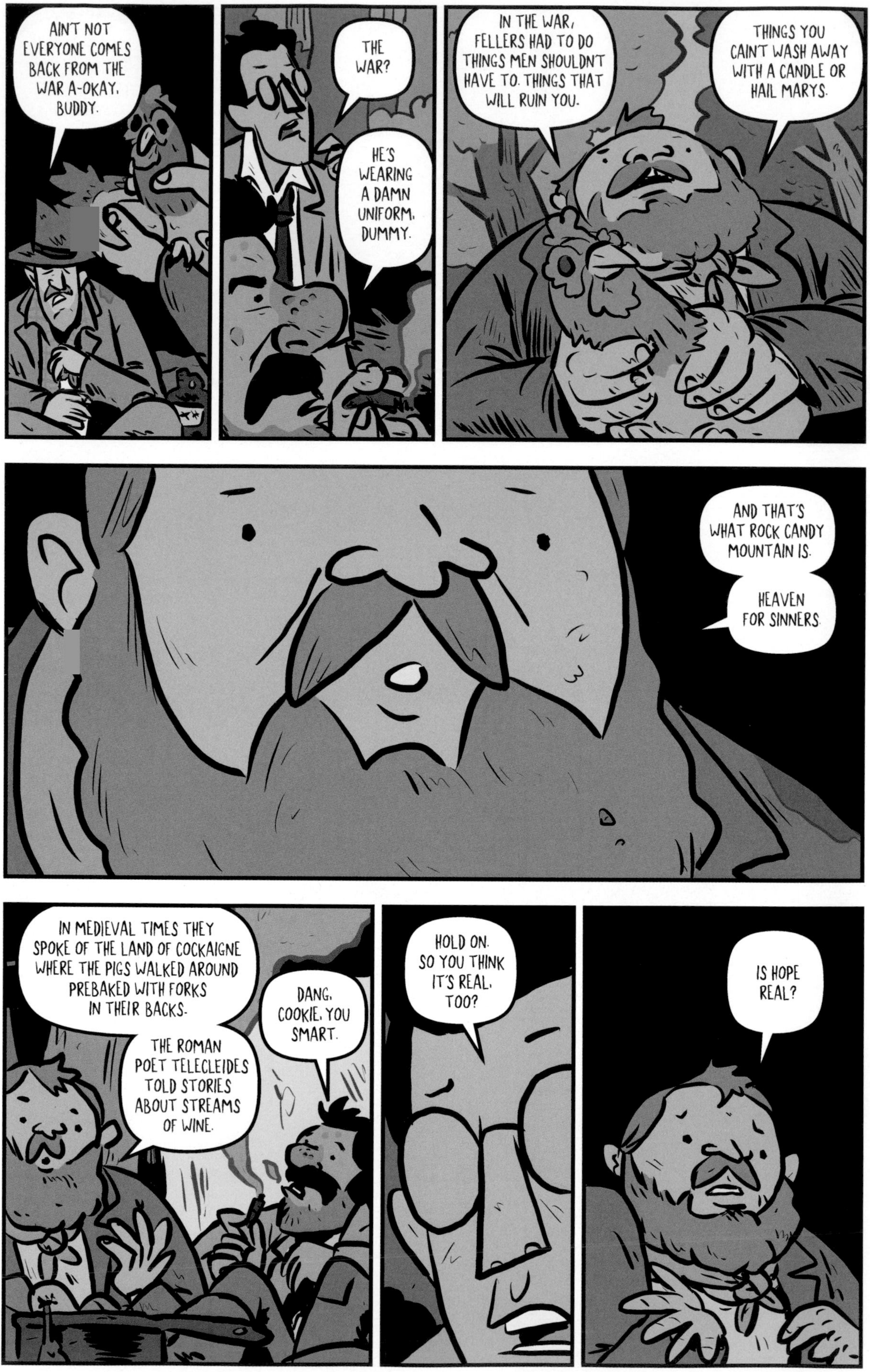
AIN'T NOT EVERYONE COMES BACK FROM THE WAR A-OKAY, BUDDY.
THE WAR?
HE'S WEARING A DAMN UNIFORM, DUMMY.
IN THE WAR, FELLERS HAD TO DO THINGS MEN SHOULDN'T HAVE TO. THINGS THAT WILL RUIN YOU.
THINGS YOU CAIN'T WASH AWAY WITH A CANDLE OR HAIL MARYS.
AND THAT'S WHAT ROCK CANDY MOUNTAIN IS.
HEAVEN FOR SINNERS.
IN MEDIEVAL TIMES THEY SPOKE OF THE LAND OF COCKAIGNE WHERE THE PIGS WALKED AROUND PREBAKED WITH FORKS IN THEIR BACKS.
THE ROMAN POET TELECLEIDES TOLD STORIES ABOUT STREAMS OF WINE.
DANG, COOKIE, YOU SMART.
HOLD ON. SO YOU THINK IT'S REAL, TOO?
IS HOPE REAL?

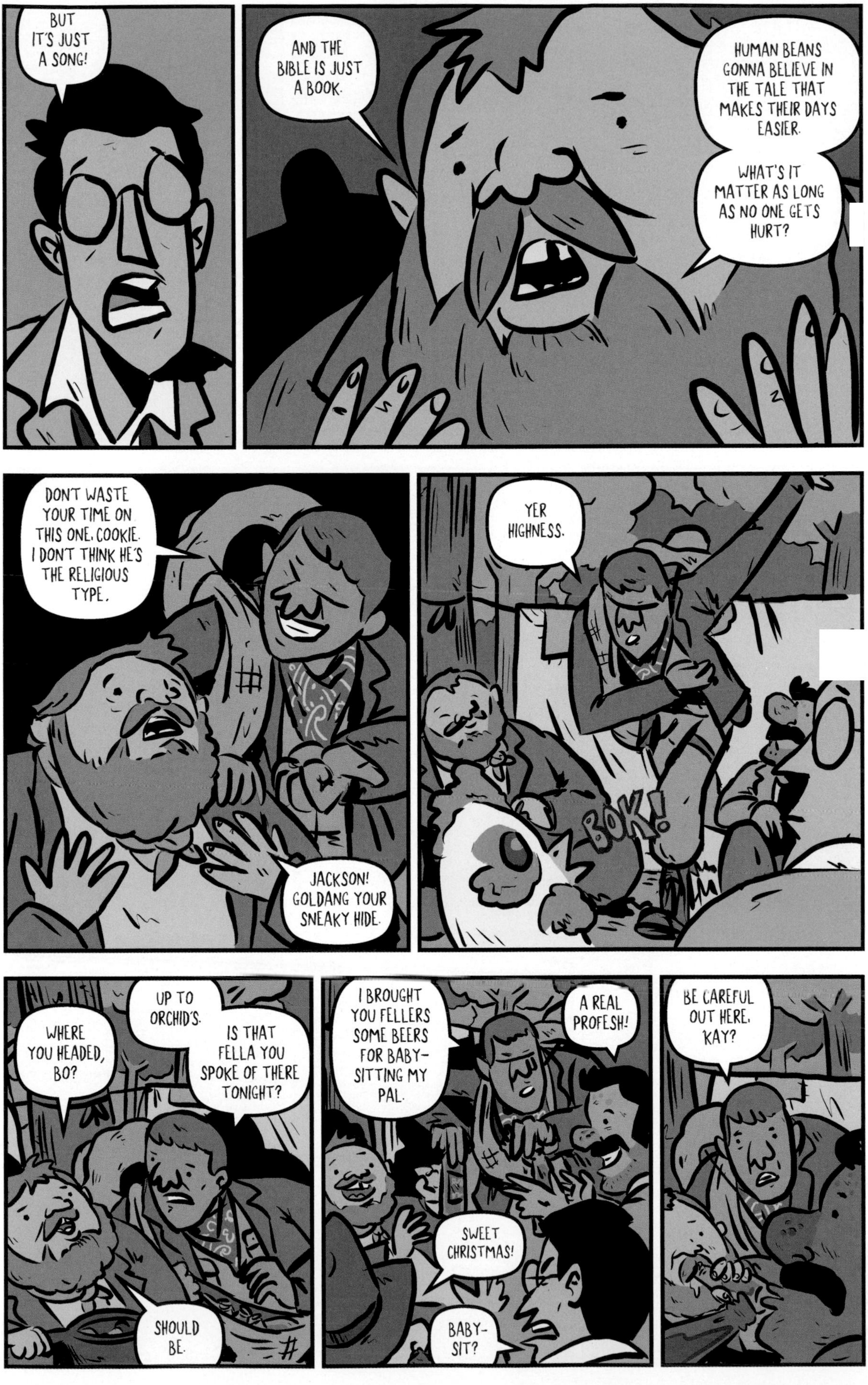
BUT IT'S JUST A SONG!
AND THE BIBLE IS JUST A BOOK.
HUMAN BEANS GONNA BELIEVE IN THE TALE THAT MAKES THEIR DAYS EASIER.
WHAT'S IT MATTER AS LONG AS NO ONE GETS HURT?
DON'T WASTE YOUR TIME ON THIS ONE, COOKIE. I DON'T THINK HE'S THE RELIGIOUS TYPE.
JACKSON! GOLDANG YOUR SNEAKY HIDE.
YER HIGHNESS.
BOK!
WHERE YOU HEADED, BO?
UP TO ORCHID'S.
IS THAT FELLA YOU SPOKE OF THERE TONIGHT?
SHOULD BE.
I BROUGHT YOU FELLERS SOME BEERS FOR BABY-SITTING MY PAL.
A REAL PROFESH!
SWEET CHRISTMAS!
BABY-SIT?
BE CAREFUL OUT HERE, KAY?

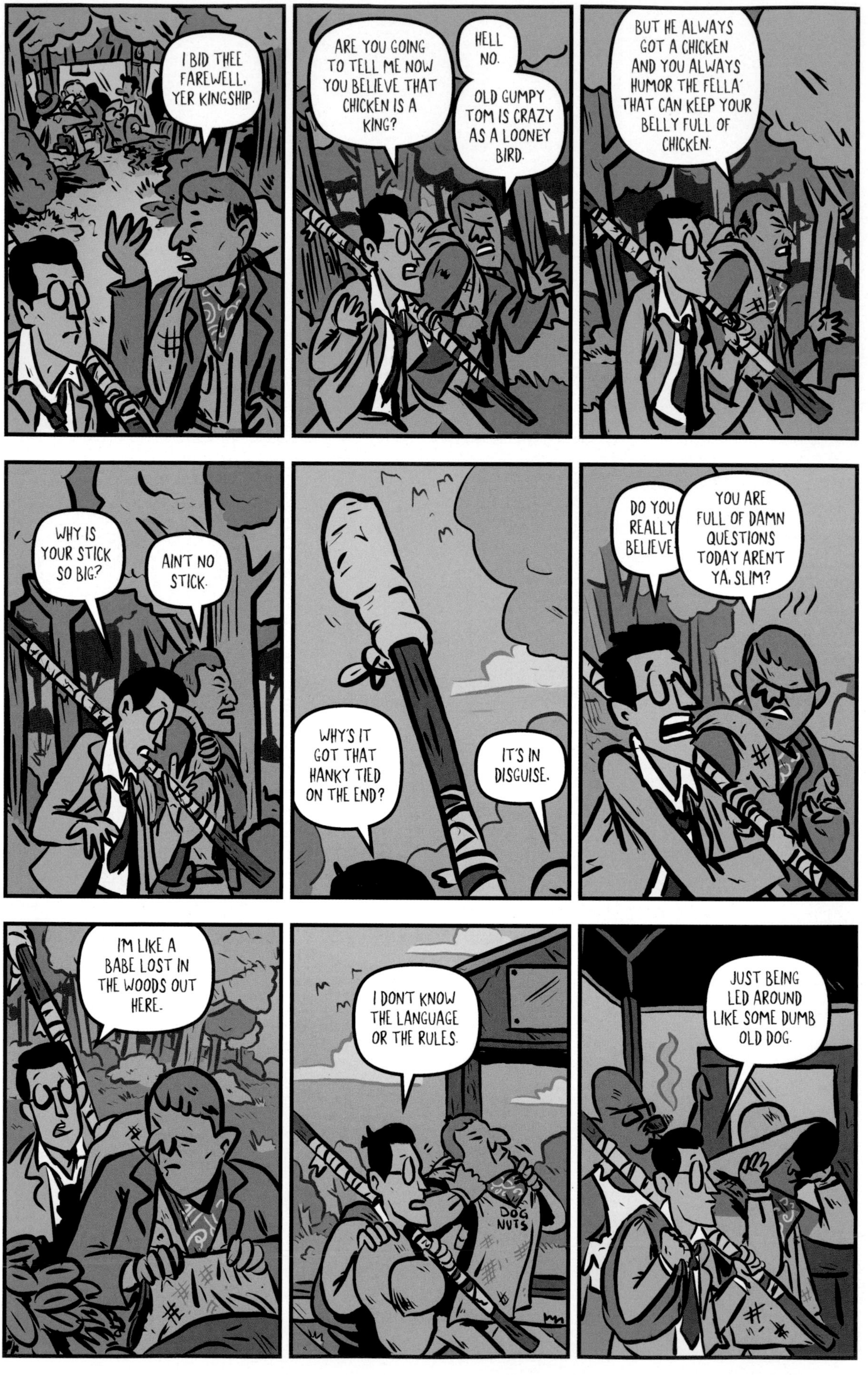
I BID THEE FAREWELL, YER KINGSHIP.
ARE YOU GOING TO TELL ME NOW YOU BELIEVE THAT CHICKEN IS A KING?
HELL NO.
OLD GUMPY TOM IS CRAZY AS A LOONEY BIRD.
BUT HE ALWAYS GOT A CHICKEN AND YOU ALWAYS HUMOR THE FELLA' THAT CAN KEEP YOUR BELLY FULL OF CHICKEN.
WHY IS YOUR STICK SO BIG?
AIN'T NO STICK.
WHY'S IT GOT THAT HANKY TIED ON THE END?
IT'S IN DISGUISE.
DO YOU REALLY BELIEVE-
YOU ARE FULL OF DAMN QUESTIONS TODAY AREN'T YA, SLIM?
I'M LIKE A BABE LOST IN THE WOODS OUT HERE.
I DON'T KNOW THE LANGUAGE OR THE RULES.
DOG NUTS
JUST BEING LED AROUND LIKE SOME DUMB OLD DOG.

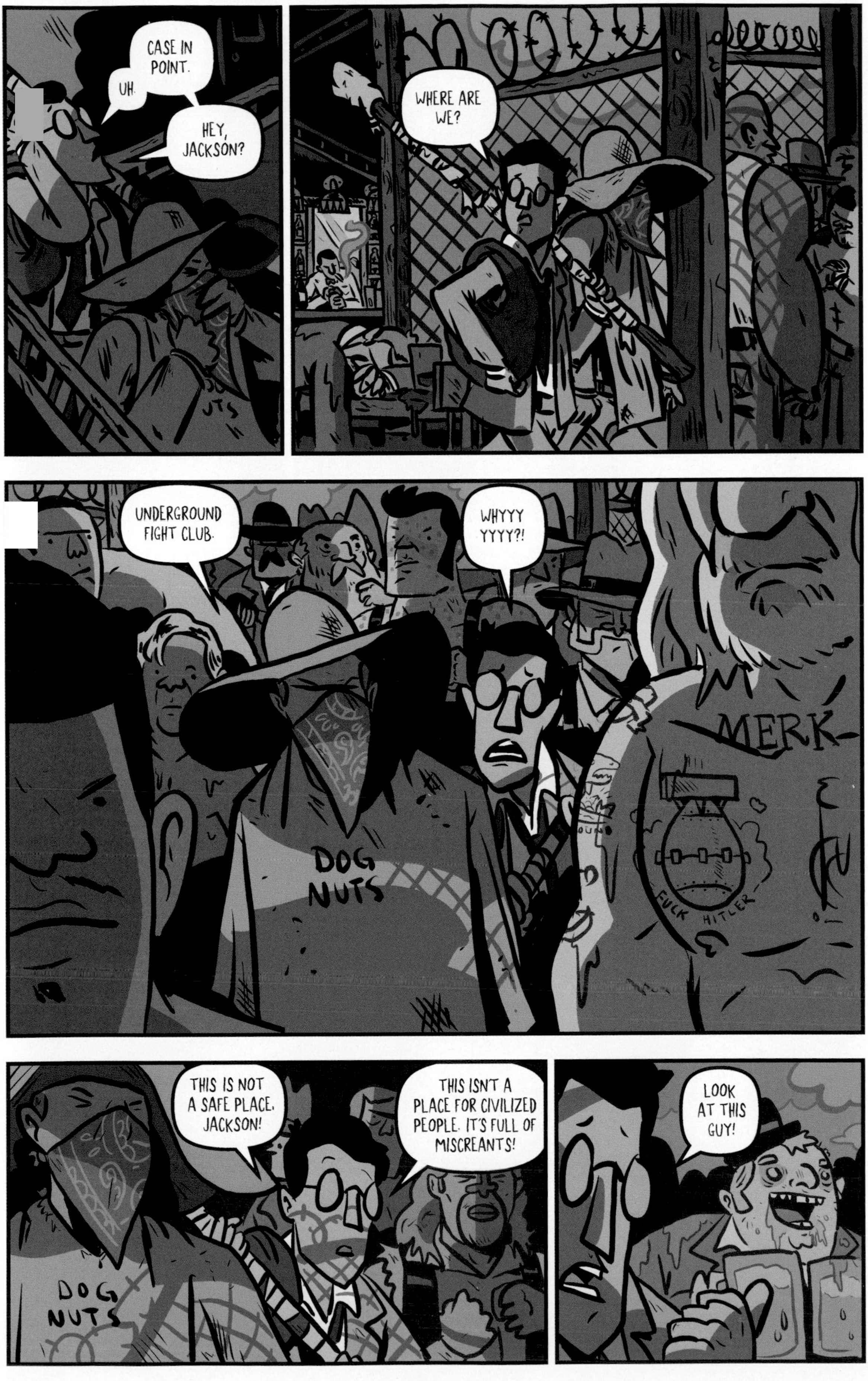
CASE IN POINT.
UH.
HEY, JACKSON?
WHERE ARE WE?
UNDERGROUND FIGHT CLUB.
WHYYY YYYY?!
DOG NUTS
MERK
FUCK HITLER
THIS IS NOT A SAFE PLACE, JACKSON!
THIS ISN'T A PLACE FOR CIVILIZED PEOPLE. IT'S FULL OF MISCREANTS!
DOG NUTS
LOOK AT THIS GUY!

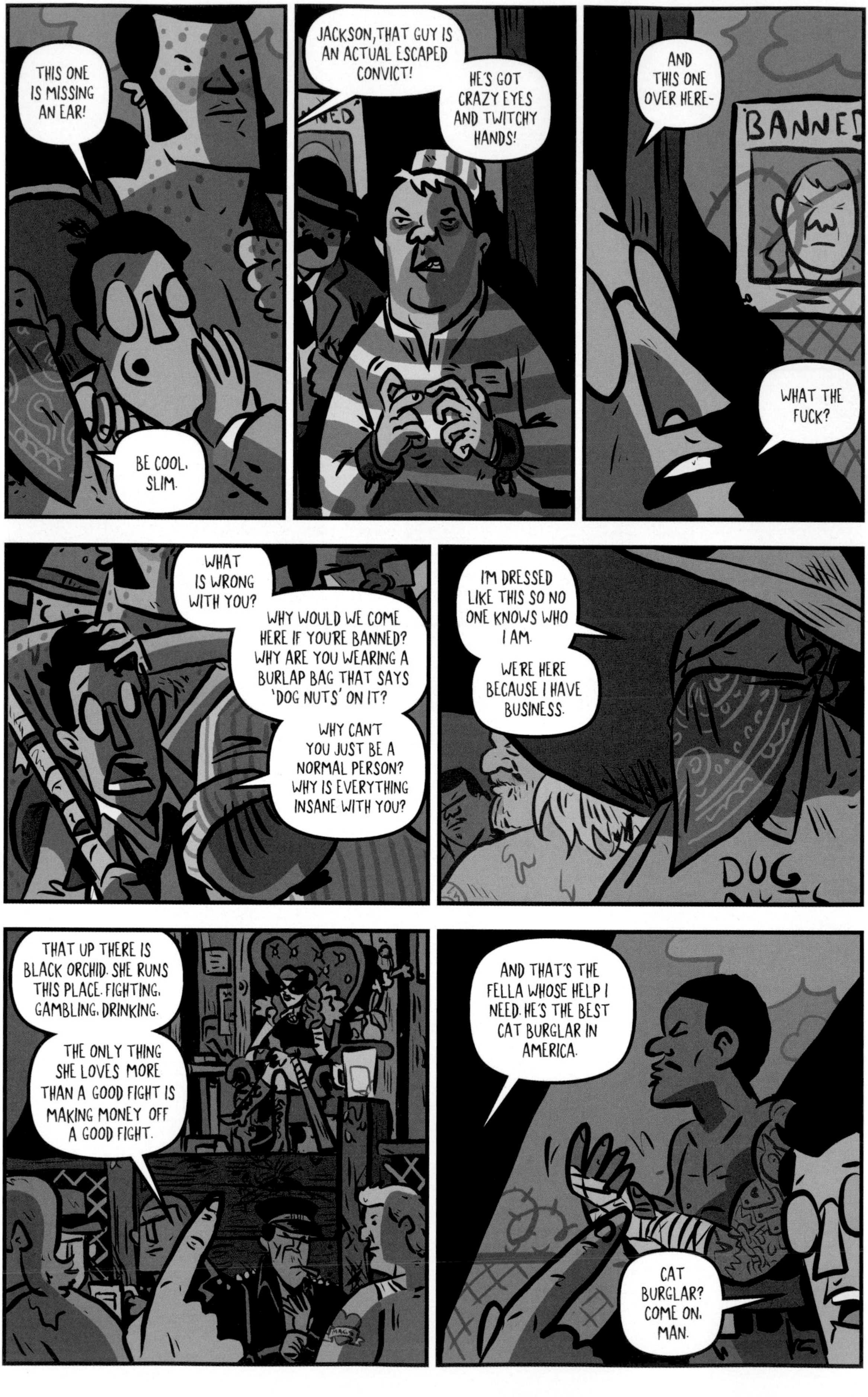
THIS ONE IS MISSING AN EAR!
BE COOL, SLIM.
JACKSON, THAT GUY IS AN ACTUAL ESCAPED CONVICT!
HE'S GOT CRAZY EYES AND TWITCHY HANDS!
BANNED
AND THIS ONE OVER HERE-
BANNED
WHAT THE FUCK?
WHAT IS WRONG WITH YOU?
WHY WOULD WE COME HERE IF YOU'RE BANNED? WHY ARE YOU WEARING A BURLAP BAG THAT SAYS 'DOG NUTS' ON IT?
WHY CAN'T YOU JUST BE A NORMAL PERSON? WHY IS EVERYTHING INSANE WITH YOU?
I'M DRESSED LIKE THIS SO NO ONE KNOWS WHO I AM.
WE'RE HERE BECAUSE I HAVE BUSINESS.
DOG
THAT UP THERE IS BLACK ORCHID. SHE RUNS THIS PLACE. FIGHTING, GAMBLING, DRINKING.
THE ONLY THING SHE LOVES MORE THAN A GOOD FIGHT IS MAKING MONEY OFF A GOOD FIGHT.
AND THAT'S THE FELLA WHOSE HELP I NEED. HE'S THE BEST CAT BURGLAR IN AMERICA.
CAT BURGLAR? COME ON, MAN.

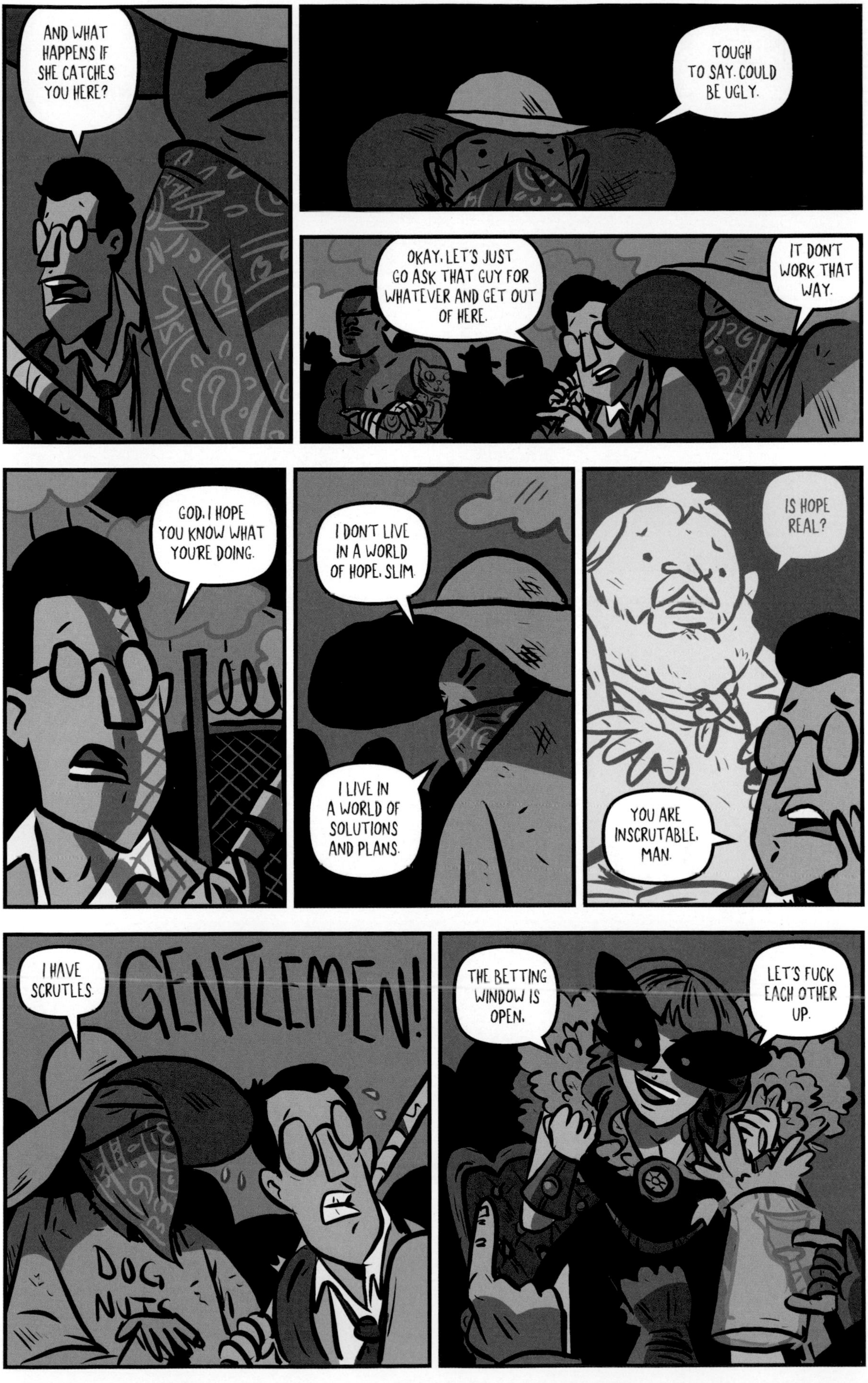
AND WHAT HAPPENS IF SHE CATCHES YOU HERE?
TOUGH TO SAY. COULD BE UGLY.
OKAY. LET'S JUST GO ASK THAT GUY FOR WHATEVER AND GET OUT OF HERE.
IT DON'T WORK THAT WAY.
GOD, I HOPE YOU KNOW WHAT YOU'RE DOING.
I DON'T LIVE IN A WORLD OF HOPE, SLIM.
I LIVE IN A WORLD OF SOLUTIONS AND PLANS.
IS HOPE REAL?
YOU ARE INSCRUTABLE, MAN.
I HAVE SCRUTLES.
GENTLEMEN!
THE BETTING WINDOW IS OPEN.
LET'S FUCK EACH OTHER UP.

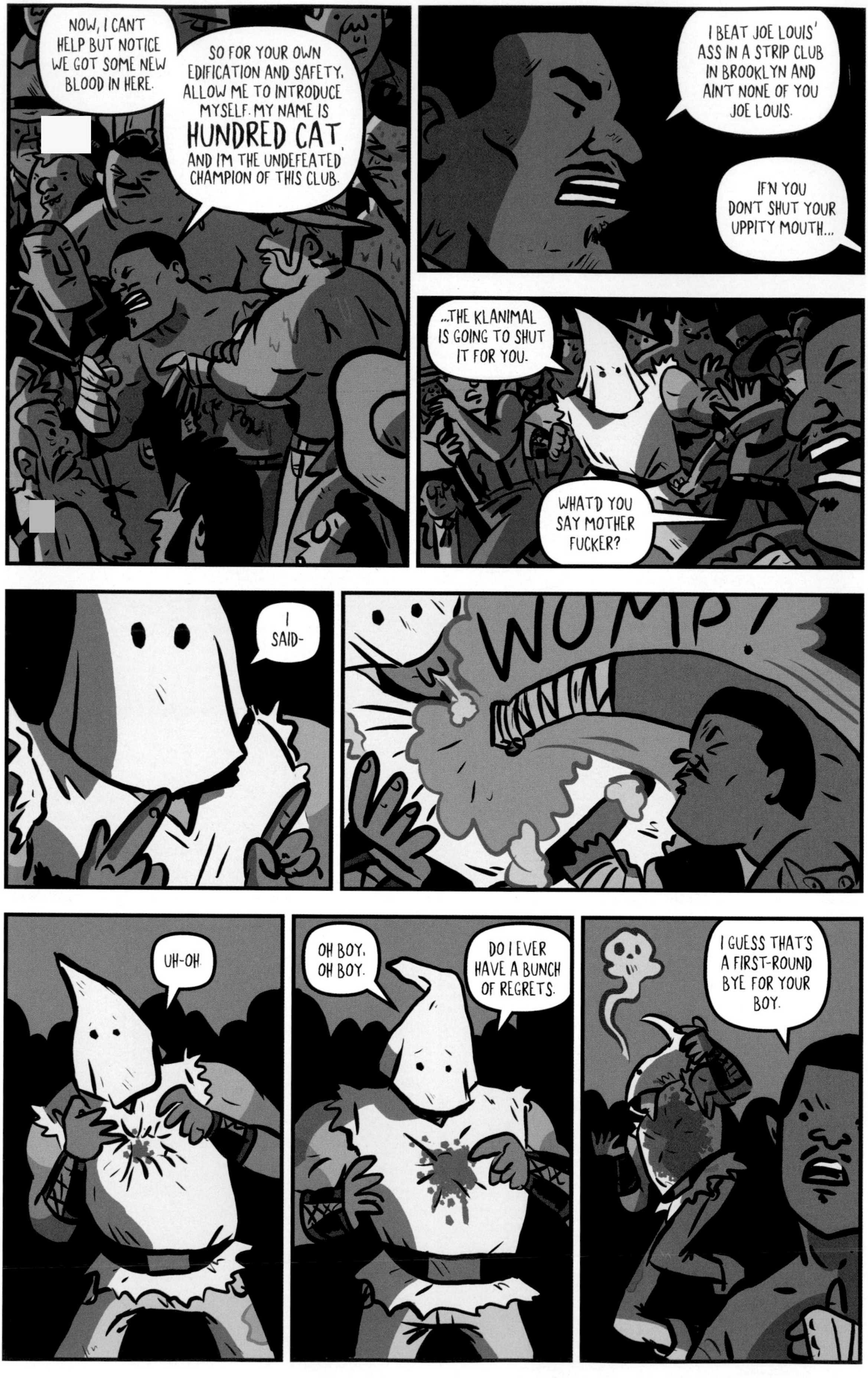
NOW, I CAN'T HELP BUT NOTICE WE GOT SOME NEW BLOOD IN HERE.
SO FOR YOUR OWN EDIFICATION AND SAFETY, ALLOW ME TO INTRODUCE MYSELF. MY NAME IS HUNDRED CAT, AND I'M THE UNDEFEATED CHAMPION OF THIS CLUB.
I BEAT JOE LOUIS' ASS IN A STRIP CLUB IN BROOKLYN AND AIN'T NONE OF YOU JOE LOUIS.
IF'N YOU DON'T SHUT YOUR UPPITY MOUTH...
...THE KLANIMAL IS GOING TO SHUT IT FOR YOU.
WHAT'D YOU SAY MOTHER FUCKER?
I SAID-
WOMP!
UH-OH.
OH BOY, OH BOY.
DO I EVER HAVE A BUNCH OF REGRETS.
I GUESS THAT'S A FIRST-ROUND BYE FOR YOUR BOY.

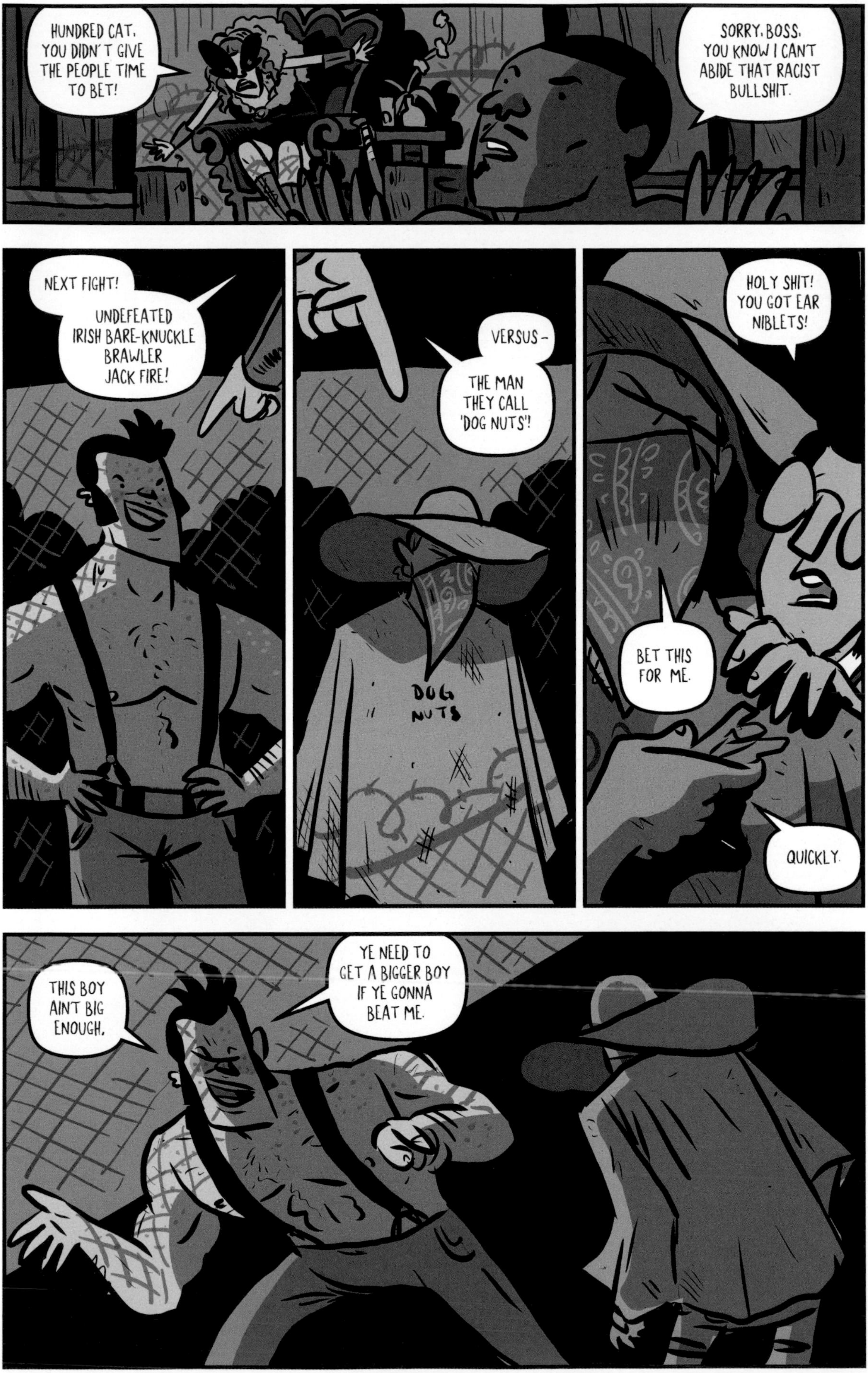
HUNDRED CAT, YOU DIDN'T GIVE THE PEOPLE TIME TO BET!
SORRY, BOSS, YOU KNOW I CAN'T ABIDE THAT RACIST BULLSHIT.
NEXT FIGHT!
UNDEFEATED IRISH BARE-KNUCKLE BRAWLER JACK FIRE!
VERSUS–
THE MAN THEY CALL 'DOG NUTS'!
DOG NUTS
HOLY SHIT! YOU GOT EAR NIBLETS!
BET THIS FOR ME.
QUICKLY.
THIS BOY AIN'T BIG ENOUGH.
YE NEED TO GET A BIGGER BOY IF YE GONNA BEAT ME.

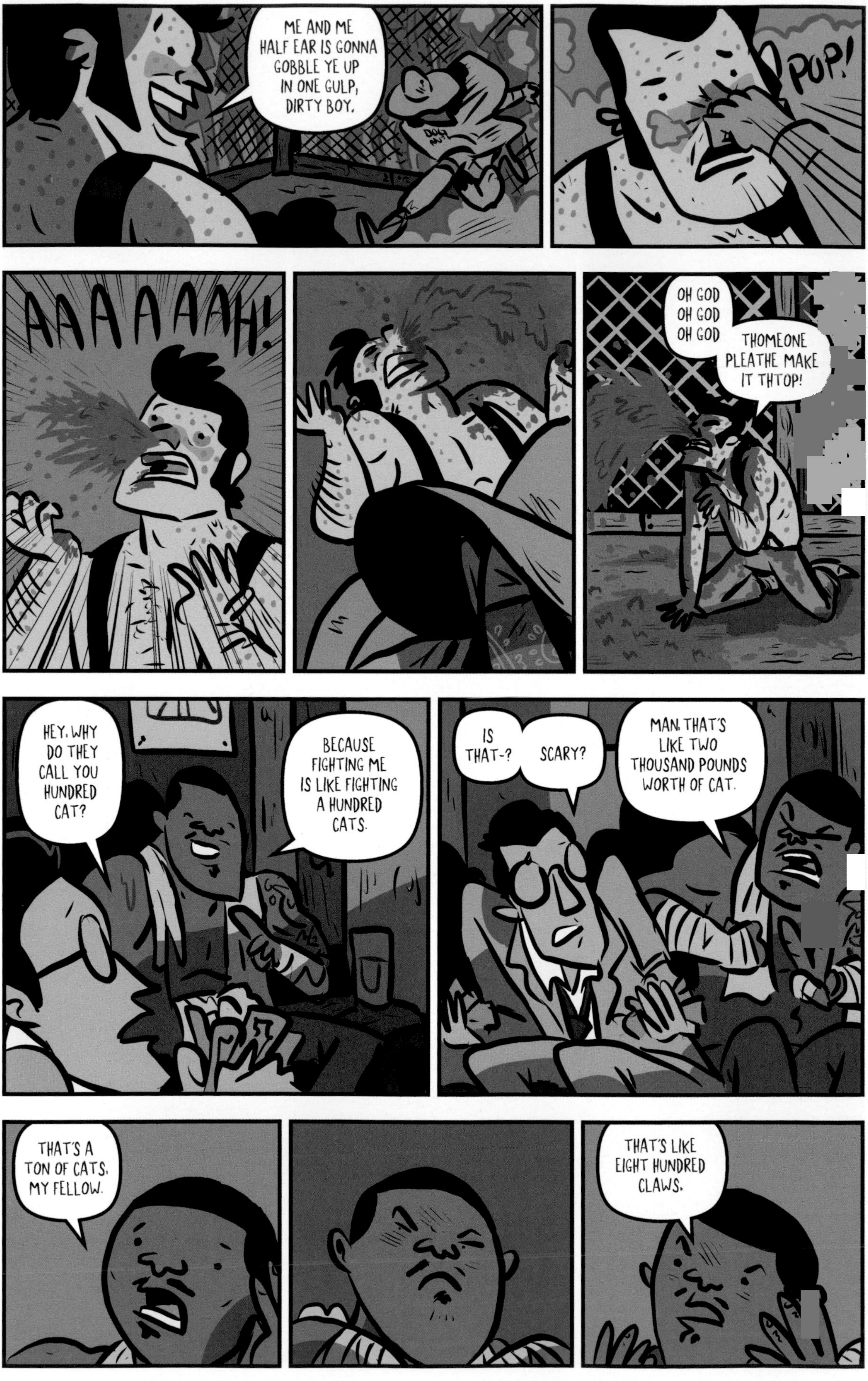
ME AND ME HALF EAR IS GONNA GOBBLE YE UP IN ONE GULP, DIRTY BOY.
POP!
AAAAAAH!
OH GOD OH GOD OH GOD
THOMEONE PLEATHE MAKE IT THTOP!
HEY, WHY DO THEY CALL YOU HUNDRED CAT?
BECAUSE FIGHTING ME IS LIKE FIGHTING A HUNDRED CATS.
IS THAT-?
SCARY?
MAN, THAT'S LIKE TWO THOUSAND POUNDS WORTH OF CAT.
THAT'S A TON OF CATS, MY FELLOW.
THAT'S LIKE EIGHT HUNDRED CLAWS.

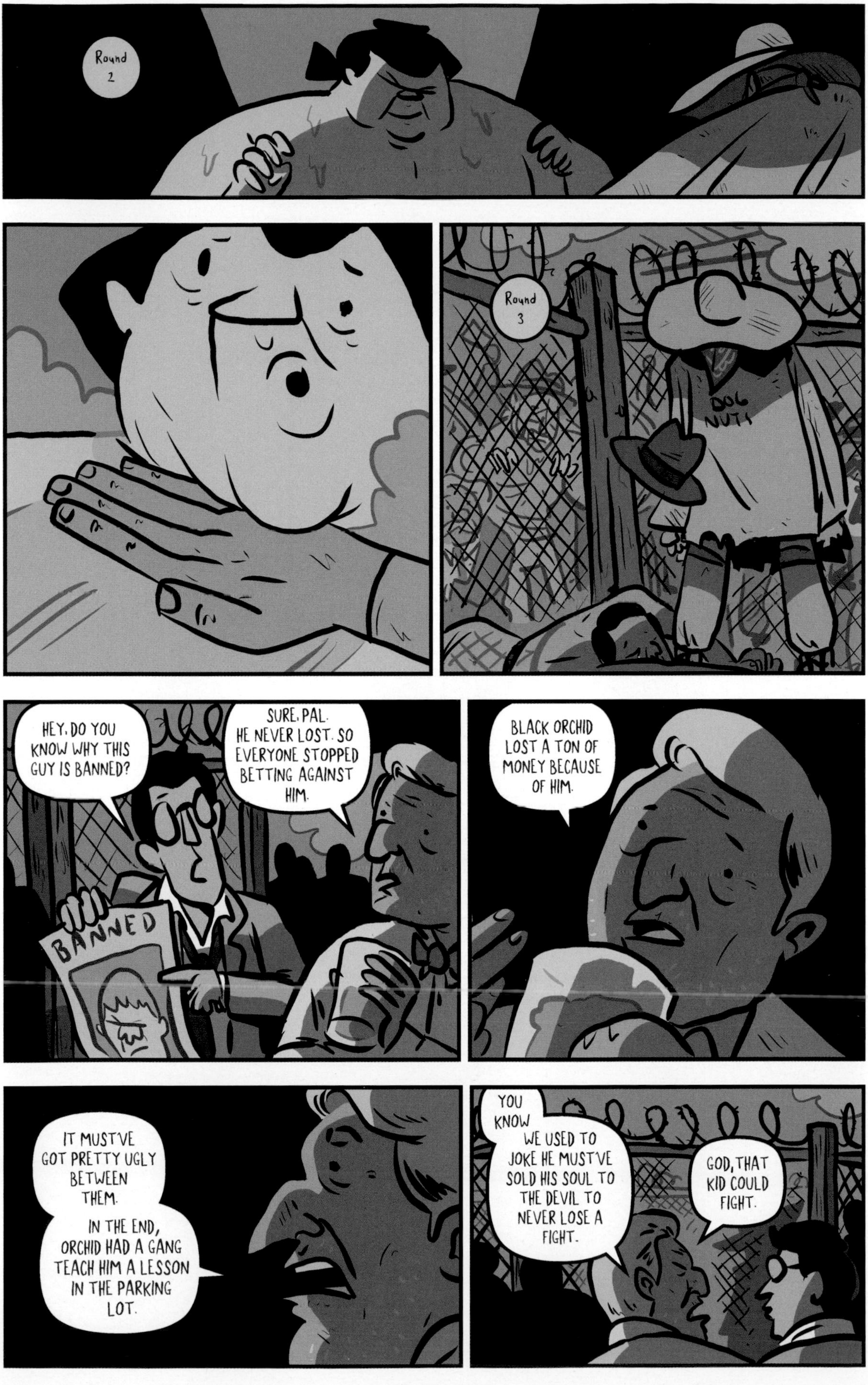
Round 2
Round 3
DOG NUTS
HEY, DO YOU KNOW WHY THIS GUY IS BANNED?
BANNED
SURE, PAL. HE NEVER LOST. SO EVERYONE STOPPED BETTING AGAINST HIM.
BLACK ORCHID LOST A TON OF MONEY BECAUSE OF HIM.
IT MUST'VE GOT PRETTY UGLY BETWEEN THEM.
IN THE END, ORCHID HAD A GANG TEACH HIM A LESSON IN THE PARKING LOT.
YOU KNOW
WE USED TO JOKE HE MUST'VE SOLD HIS SOUL TO THE DEVIL TO NEVER LOSE A FIGHT.
GOD, THAT KID COULD FIGHT.

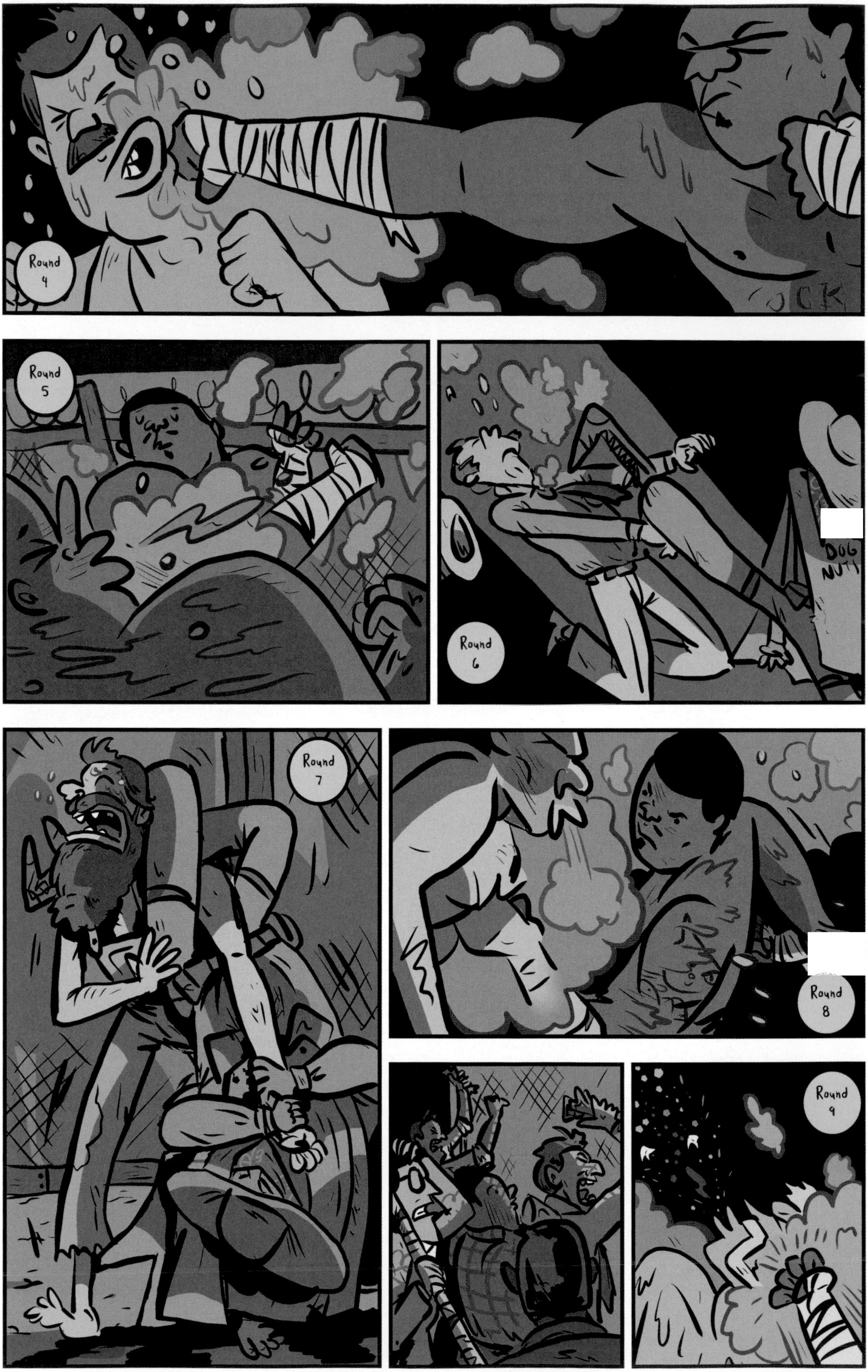
Round 4
Round 5
Round 6
DOG
Round 7
Round 8
Round 9

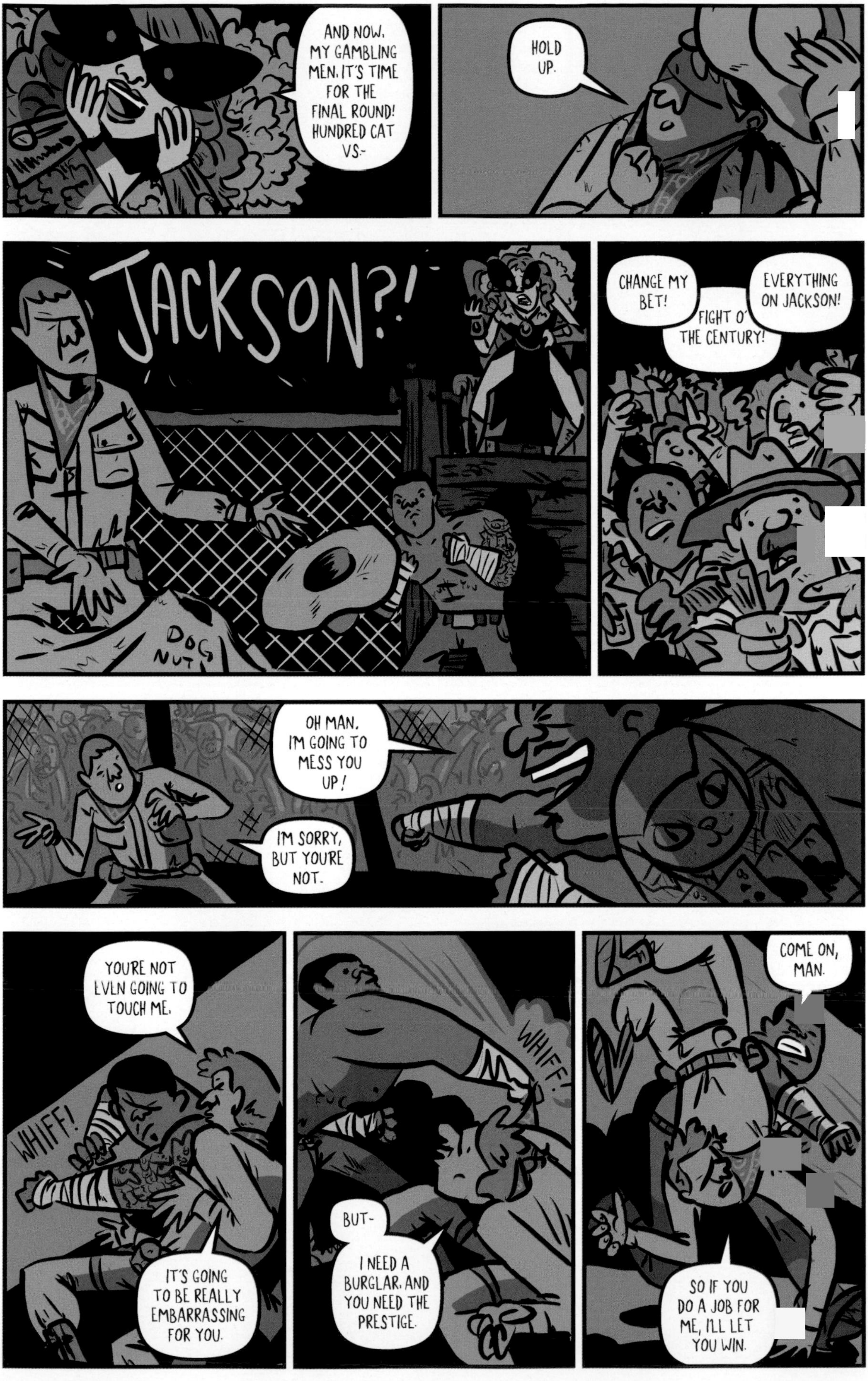
AND NOW, MY GAMBLING MEN, IT'S TIME FOR THE FINAL ROUND! HUNDRED CAT VS.-
HOLD UP.
JACKSON?!
CHANGE MY BET!
FIGHT O' THE CENTURY!
EVERYTHING ON JACKSON!
DOG NUT
OH MAN, I'M GOING TO MESS YOU UP!
I'M SORRY, BUT YOU'RE NOT.
YOU'RE NOT EVEN GOING TO TOUCH ME.
WHIFF!
IT'S GOING TO BE REALLY EMBARRASSING FOR YOU.
WHIFF!
BUT-
I NEED A BURGLAR, AND YOU NEED THE PRESTIGE.
COME ON, MAN.
SO IF YOU DO A JOB FOR ME, I'LL LET YOU WIN.

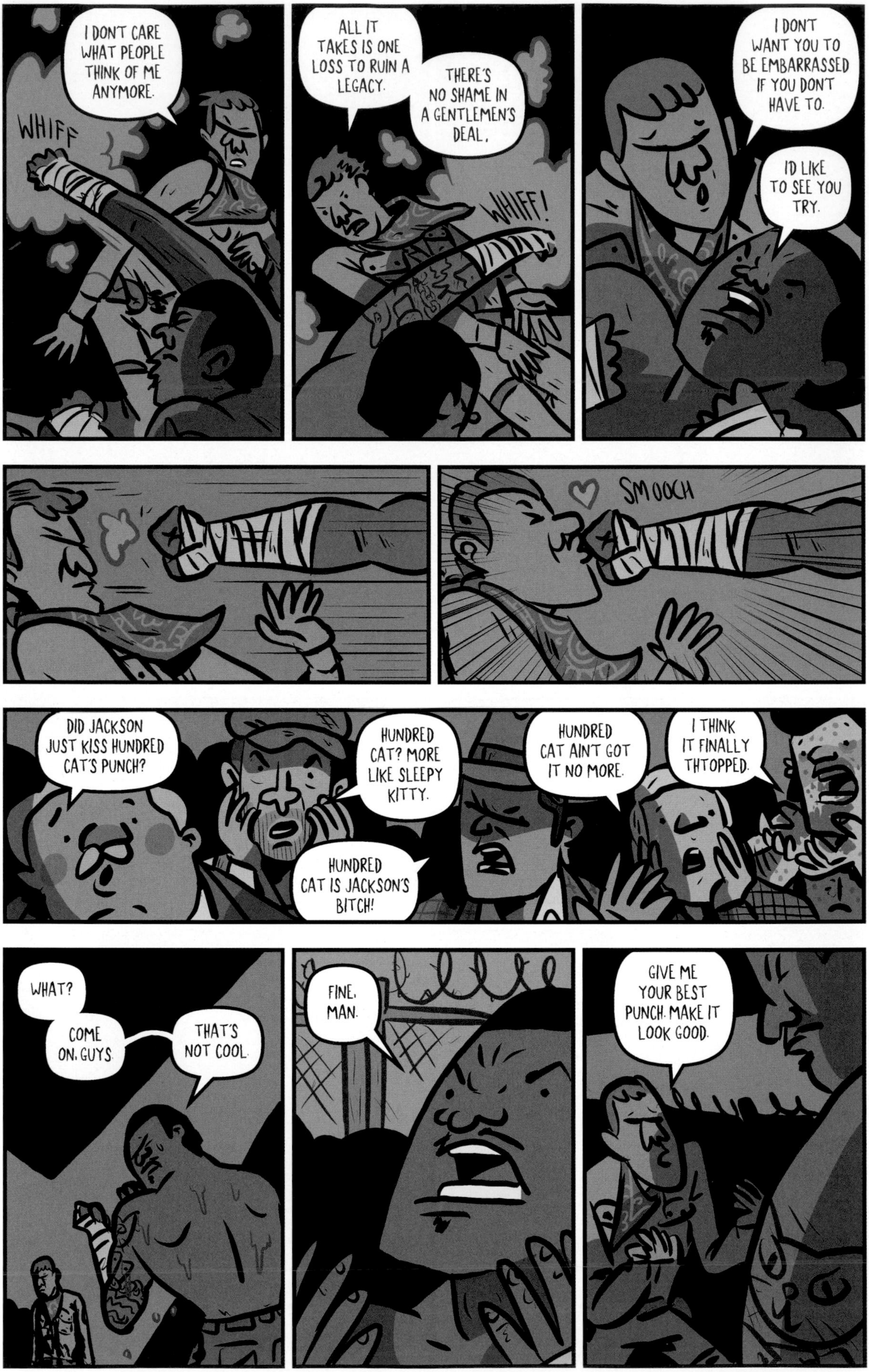
I DON'T CARE WHAT PEOPLE THINK OF ME ANYMORE.
WHIFF
ALL IT TAKES IS ONE LOSS TO RUIN A LEGACY.
THERE'S NO SHAME IN A GENTLEMEN'S DEAL.
WHIFF!
I DON'T WANT YOU TO BE EMBARRASSED IF YOU DON'T HAVE TO.
I'D LIKE TO SEE YOU TRY.
SMOOCH
DID JACKSON JUST KISS HUNDRED CAT'S PUNCH?
HUNDRED CAT? MORE LIKE SLEEPY KITTY.
HUNDRED CAT IS JACKSON'S BITCH!
HUNDRED CAT AIN'T GOT IT NO MORE.
I THINK IT FINALLY THTOPPED.
WHAT?
COME ON, GUYS.
THAT'S NOT COOL.
FINE, MAN.
GIVE ME YOUR BEST PUNCH. MAKE IT LOOK GOOD.

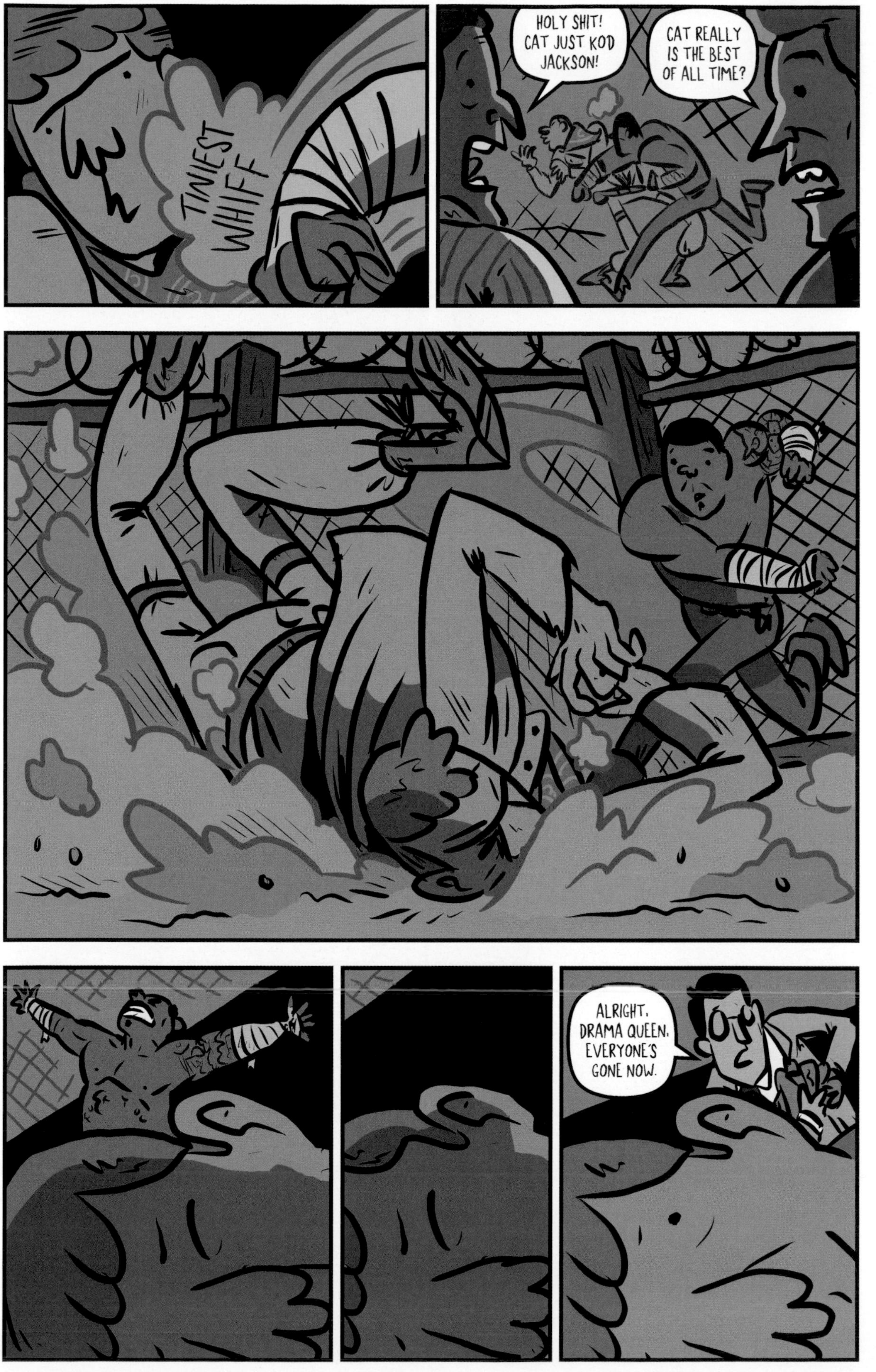
TINIEST WHIFF
HOLY SHIT! CAT JUST KO'D JACKSON!
CAT REALLY IS THE BEST OF ALL TIME?
ALRIGHT, DRAMA QUEEN, EVERYONE'S GONE NOW.

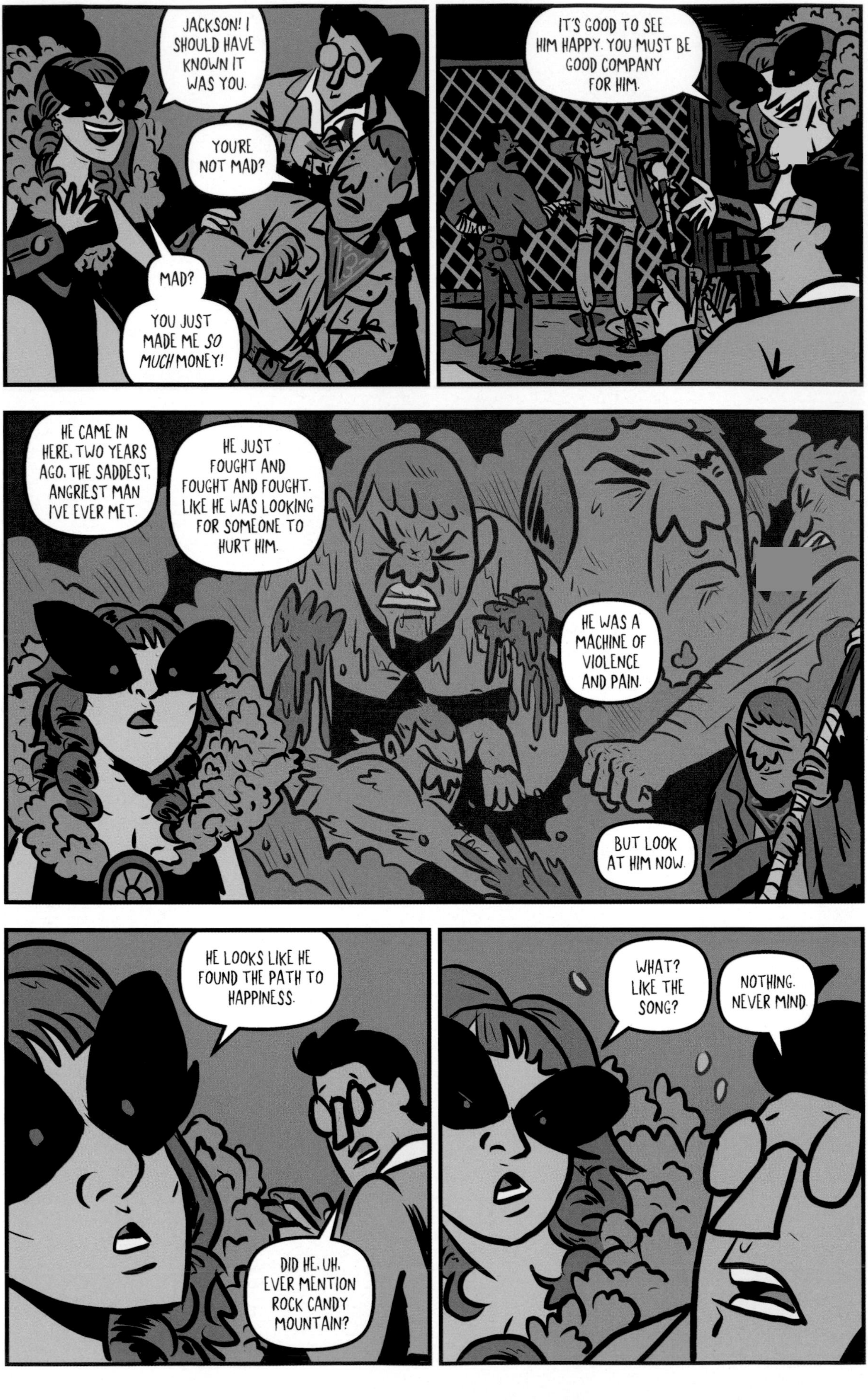
JACKSON! I SHOULD HAVE KNOWN IT WAS YOU.
YOU'RE NOT MAD?
MAD?
YOU JUST MADE ME *SO MUCH* MONEY!
IT'S GOOD TO SEE HIM HAPPY. YOU MUST BE GOOD COMPANY FOR HIM.
HE CAME IN HERE, TWO YEARS AGO, THE SADDEST, ANGRIEST MAN I'VE EVER MET.
HE JUST FOUGHT AND FOUGHT AND FOUGHT. LIKE HE WAS LOOKING FOR SOMEONE TO HURT HIM.
HE WAS A MACHINE OF VIOLENCE AND PAIN.
BUT LOOK AT HIM NOW.
HE LOOKS LIKE HE FOUND THE PATH TO HAPPINESS.
DID HE, UH, EVER MENTION ROCK CANDY MOUNTAIN?
WHAT? LIKE THE SONG?
NOTHING. NEVER MIND.

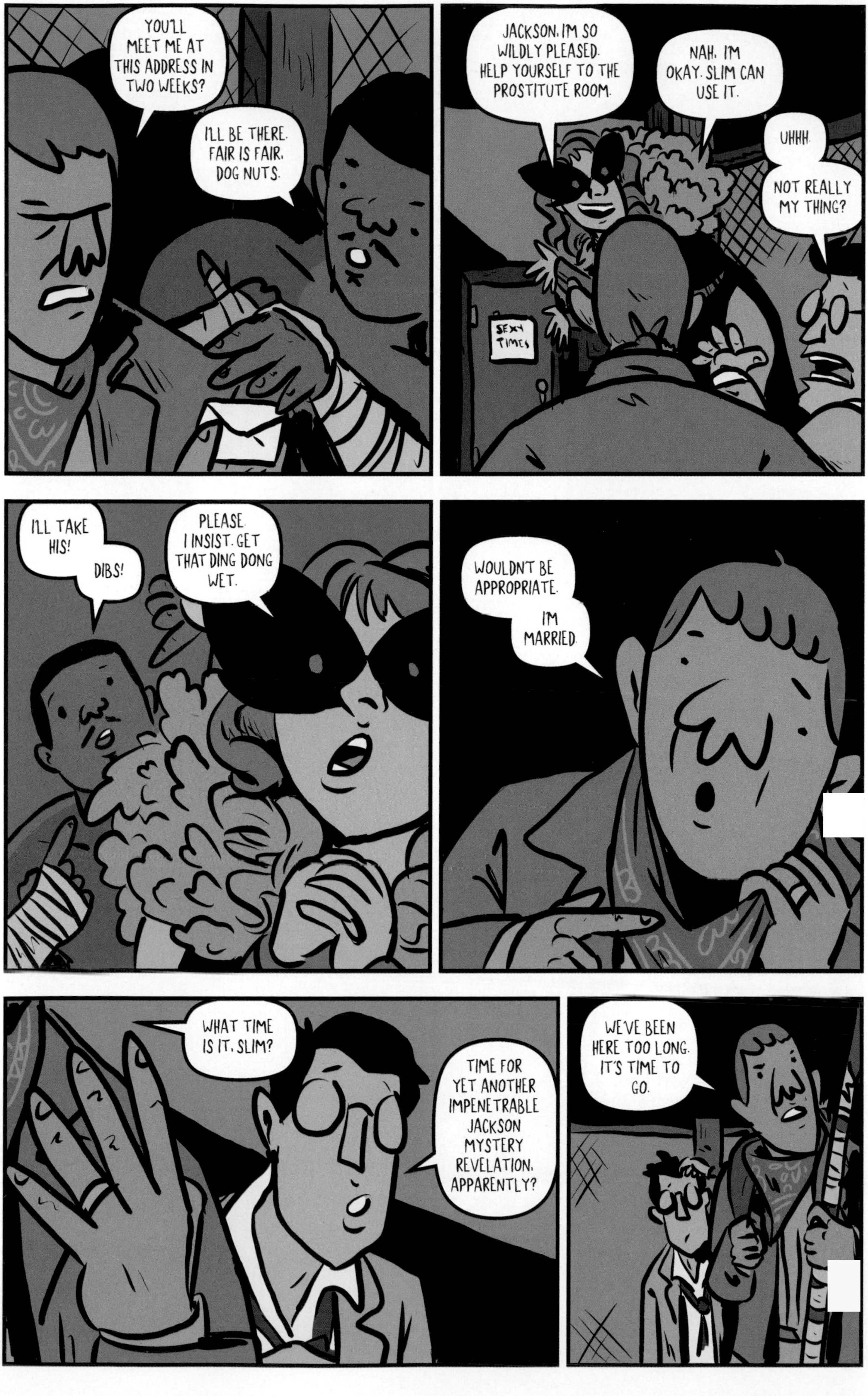
YOU'LL MEET ME AT THIS ADDRESS IN TWO WEEKS?
I'LL BE THERE. FAIR IS FAIR, DOG NUTS.
JACKSON, I'M SO WILDLY PLEASED. HELP YOURSELF TO THE PROSTITUTE ROOM.
NAH, I'M OKAY. SLIM CAN USE IT.
UHHH.
NOT REALLY MY THING?
SEXY TIMES
I'LL TAKE HIS!
DIBS!
PLEASE. I INSIST. GET THAT DING DONG WET.
WOULDN'T BE APPROPRIATE.
I'M MARRIED.
WHAT TIME IS IT, SLIM?
TIME FOR YET ANOTHER IMPENETRABLE JACKSON MYSTERY REVELATION, APPARENTLY?
WE'VE BEEN HERE TOO LONG. IT'S TIME TO GO.

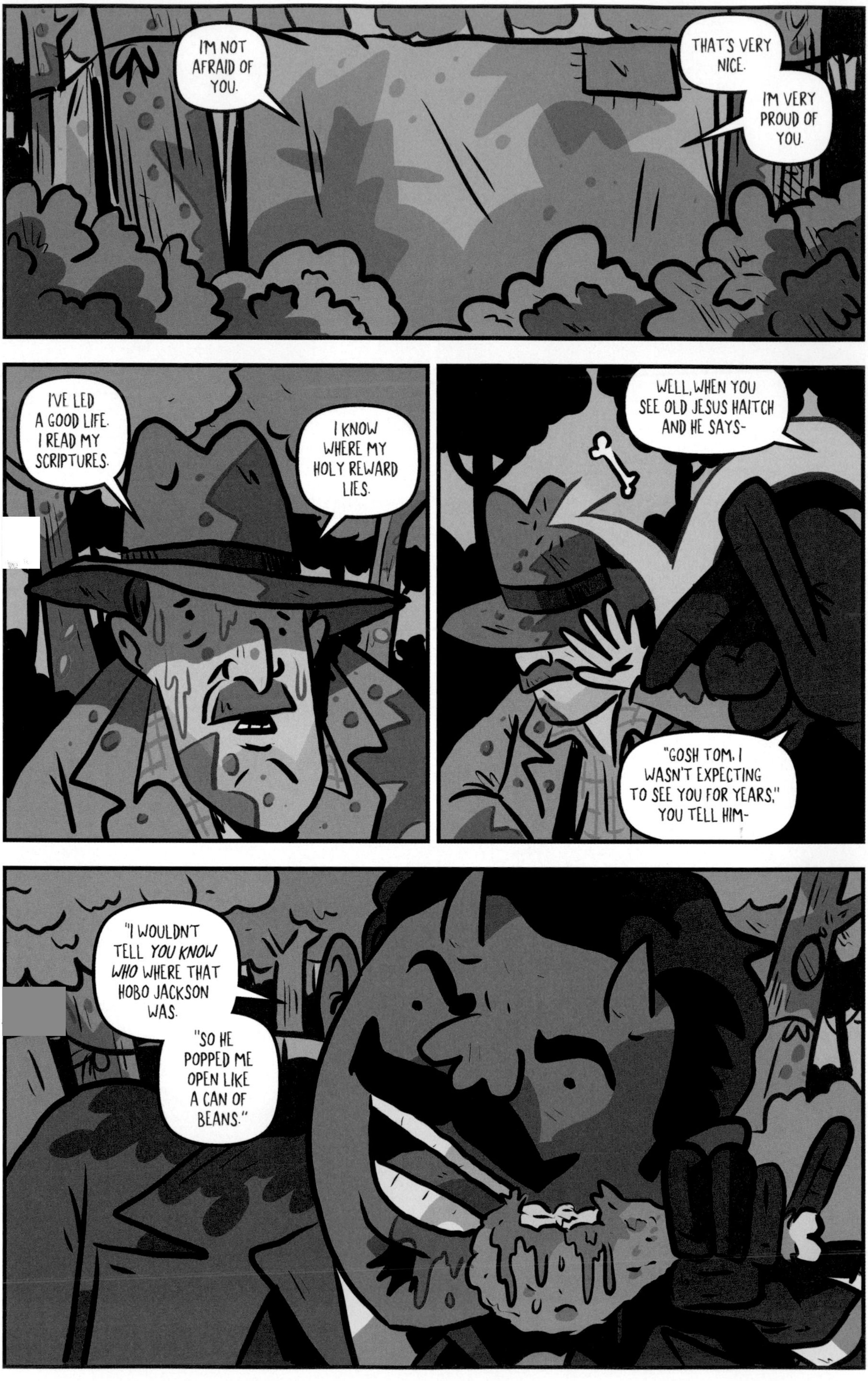
I'M NOT AFRAID OF YOU.
THAT'S VERY NICE.
I'M VERY PROUD OF YOU.
I'VE LED A GOOD LIFE. I READ MY SCRIPTURES.
I KNOW WHERE MY HOLY REWARD LIES.
WELL, WHEN YOU SEE OLD JESUS HAITCH AND HE SAYS-
"GOSH TOM, I WASN'T EXPECTING TO SEE YOU FOR YEARS," YOU TELL HIM-
"I WOULDN'T TELL *YOU KNOW WHO* WHERE THAT HOBO JACKSON WAS.
"SO HE POPPED ME OPEN LIKE A CAN OF BEANS."

CHAPTER THREE

"Beside the crystal fountain."

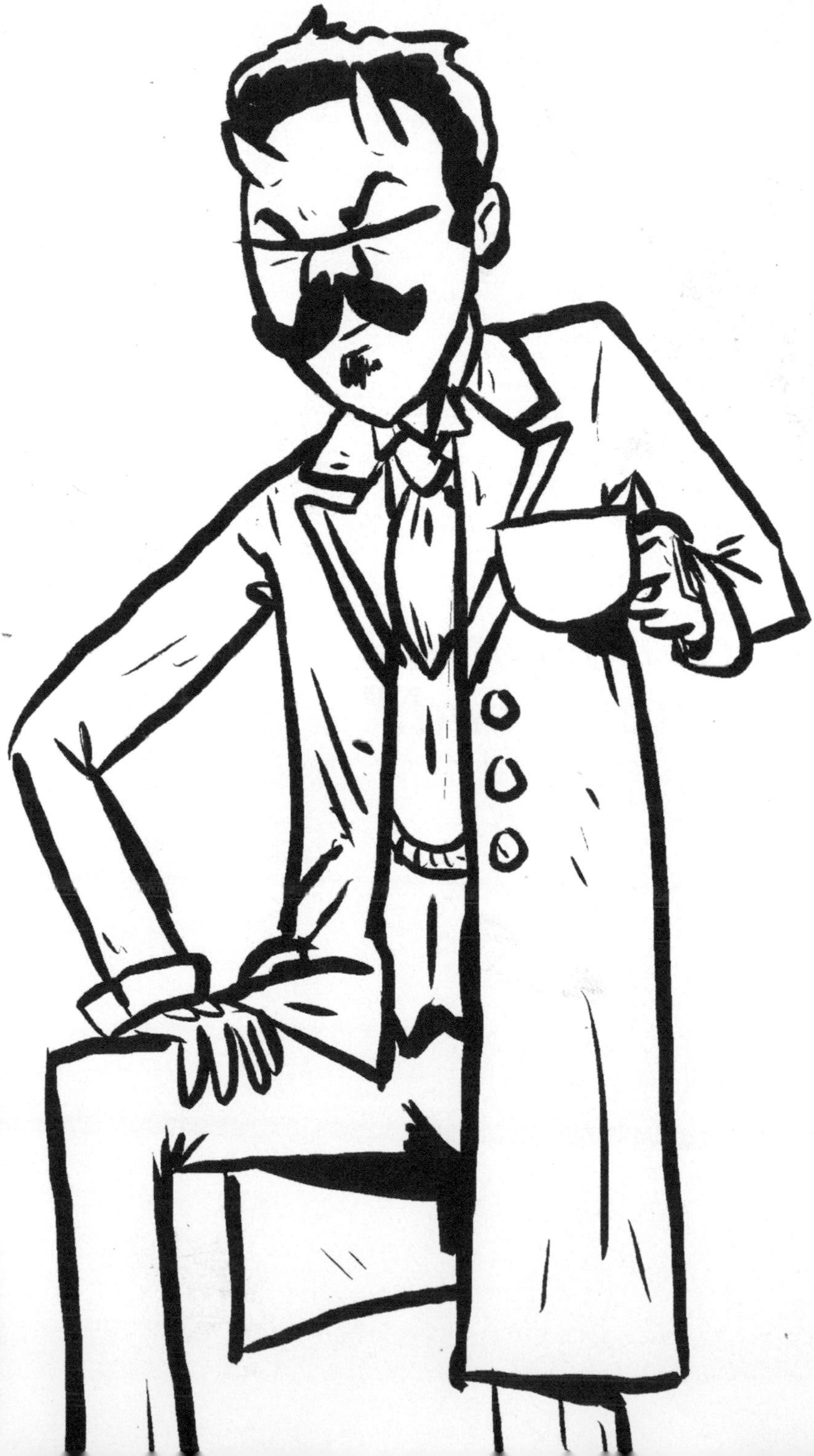

"dangerous neighborhood."

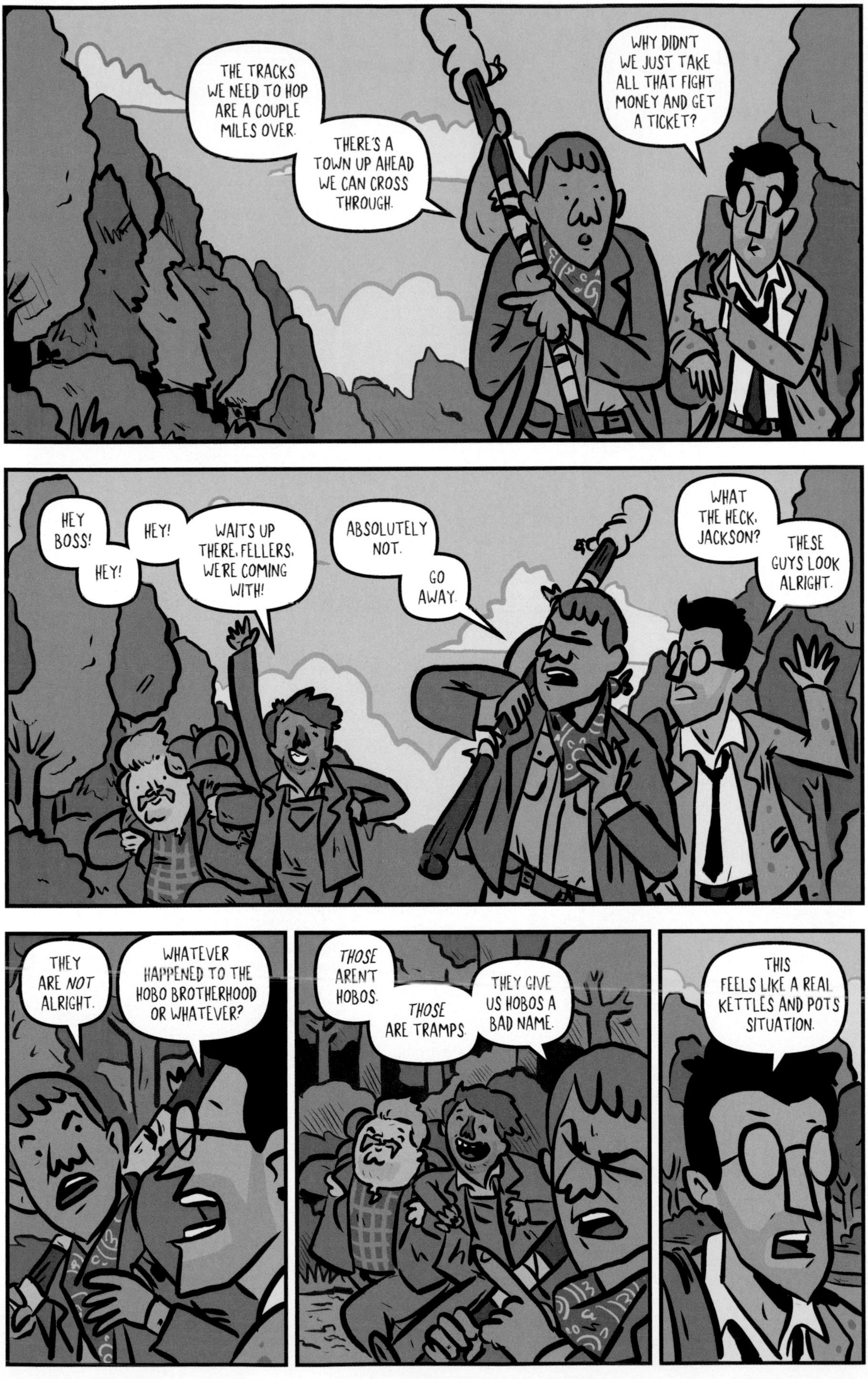
THE TRACKS WE NEED TO HOP ARE A COUPLE MILES OVER.
THERE'S A TOWN UP AHEAD WE CAN CROSS THROUGH.
WHY DIDN'T WE JUST TAKE ALL THAT FIGHT MONEY AND GET A TICKET?
HEY BOSS!
HEY!
HEY!
WAITS UP THERE, FELLERS, WE'RE COMING WITH!
ABSOLUTELY NOT.
GO AWAY.
WHAT THE HECK, JACKSON?
THESE GUYS LOOK ALRIGHT.
THEY ARE *NOT* ALRIGHT.
WHATEVER HAPPENED TO THE HOBO BROTHERHOOD OR WHATEVER?
THOSE AREN'T HOBOS.
THOSE ARE TRAMPS.
THEY GIVE US HOBOS A BAD NAME.
THIS FEELS LIKE A REAL KETTLES AND POTS SITUATION.

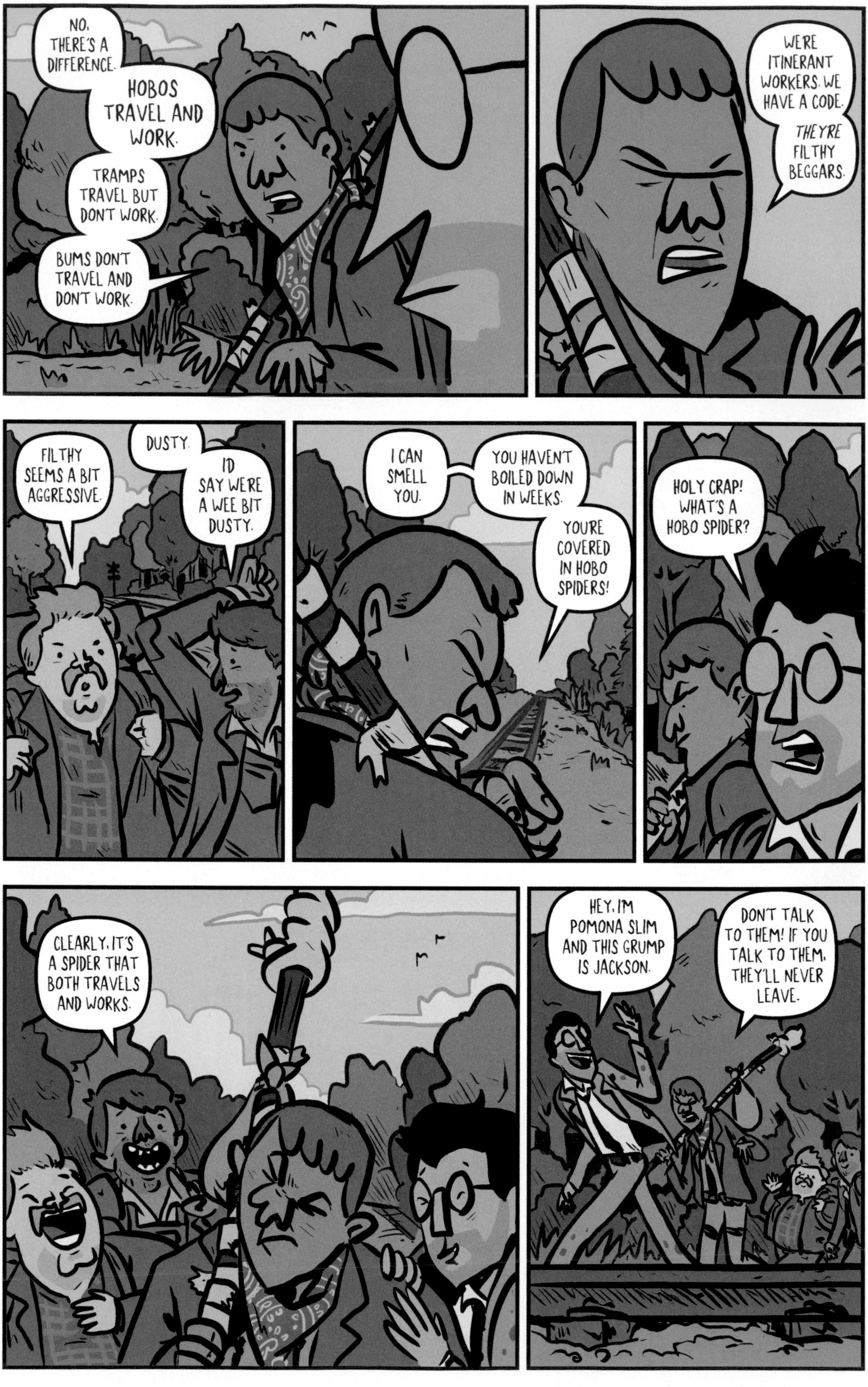

NO, THERE'S A DIFFERENCE.
HOBOS TRAVEL AND WORK.
TRAMPS TRAVEL BUT DON'T WORK.
BUMS DON'T TRAVEL AND DON'T WORK.
WE'RE ITINERANT WORKERS. WE HAVE A CODE.
THEY'RE FILTHY BEGGARS.
FILTHY SEEMS A BIT AGGRESSIVE.
DUSTY.
I'D SAY WE'RE A WEE BIT DUSTY.
I CAN SMELL YOU.
YOU HAVEN'T BOILED DOWN IN WEEKS.
YOU'RE COVERED IN HOBO SPIDERS!
HOLY CRAP! WHAT'S A HOBO SPIDER?
CLEARLY, IT'S A SPIDER THAT BOTH TRAVELS AND WORKS.
HEY, I'M POMONA SLIM AND THIS GRUMP IS JACKSON.
DON'T TALK TO THEM! IF YOU TALK TO THEM, THEY'LL NEVER LEAVE.

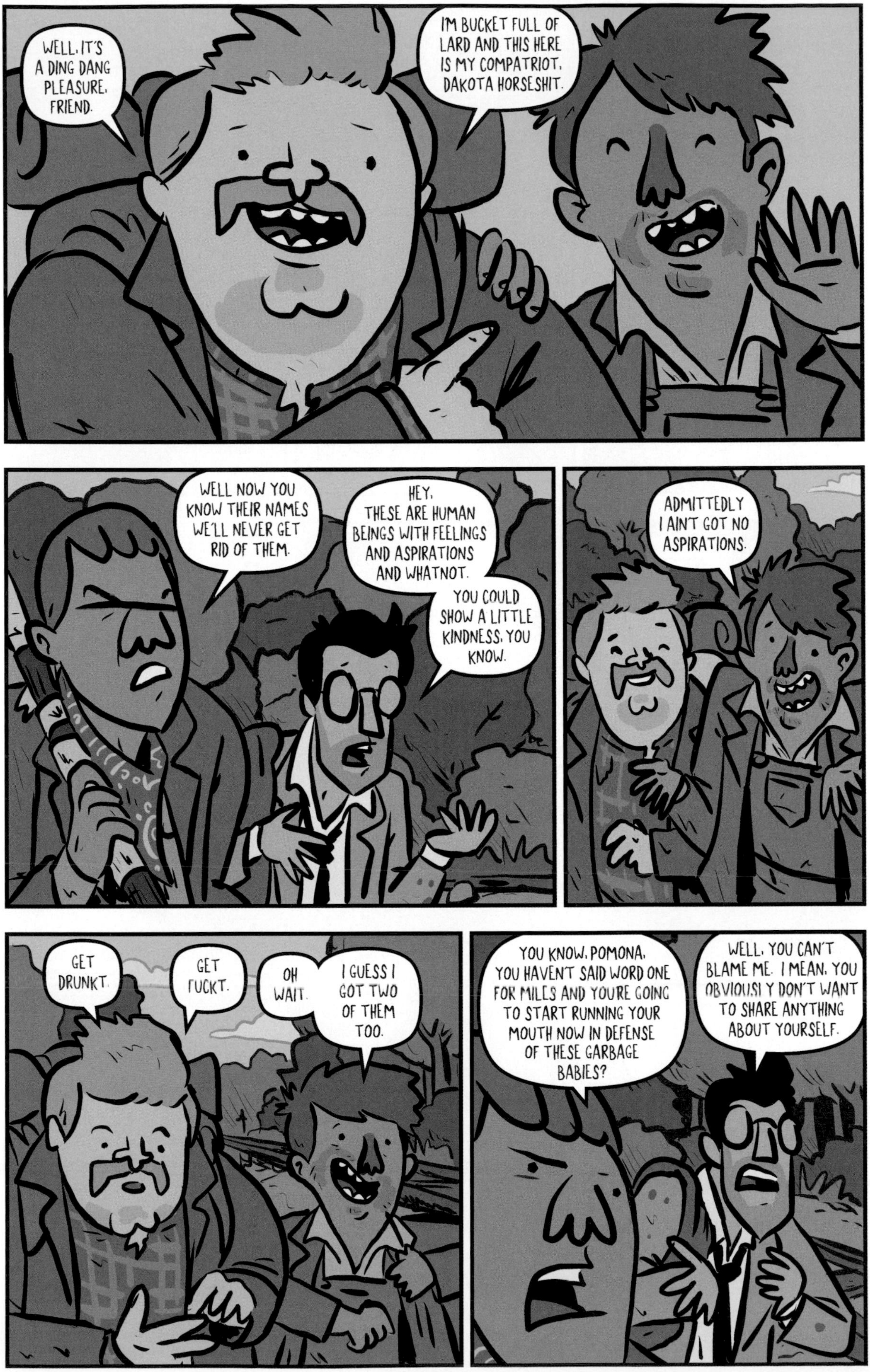
WELL, IT'S A DING DANG PLEASURE, FRIEND.
I'M BUCKET FULL OF LARD AND THIS HERE IS MY COMPATRIOT, DAKOTA HORSESHIT.
WELL NOW YOU KNOW THEIR NAMES WE'LL NEVER GET RID OF THEM.
HEY, THESE ARE HUMAN BEINGS WITH FEELINGS AND ASPIRATIONS AND WHATNOT.
YOU COULD SHOW A LITTLE KINDNESS, YOU KNOW.
ADMITTEDLY I AIN'T GOT NO ASPIRATIONS.
GET DRUNKT.
GET FUCKT.
OH WAIT.
I GUESS I GOT TWO OF THEM TOO.
YOU KNOW, POMONA, YOU HAVEN'T SAID WORD ONE FOR MILES AND YOU'RE GOING TO START RUNNING YOUR MOUTH NOW IN DEFENSE OF THESE GARBAGE BABIES?
WELL, YOU CAN'T BLAME ME. I MEAN, YOU OBVIOUSLY DON'T WANT TO SHARE ANYTHING ABOUT YOURSELF.

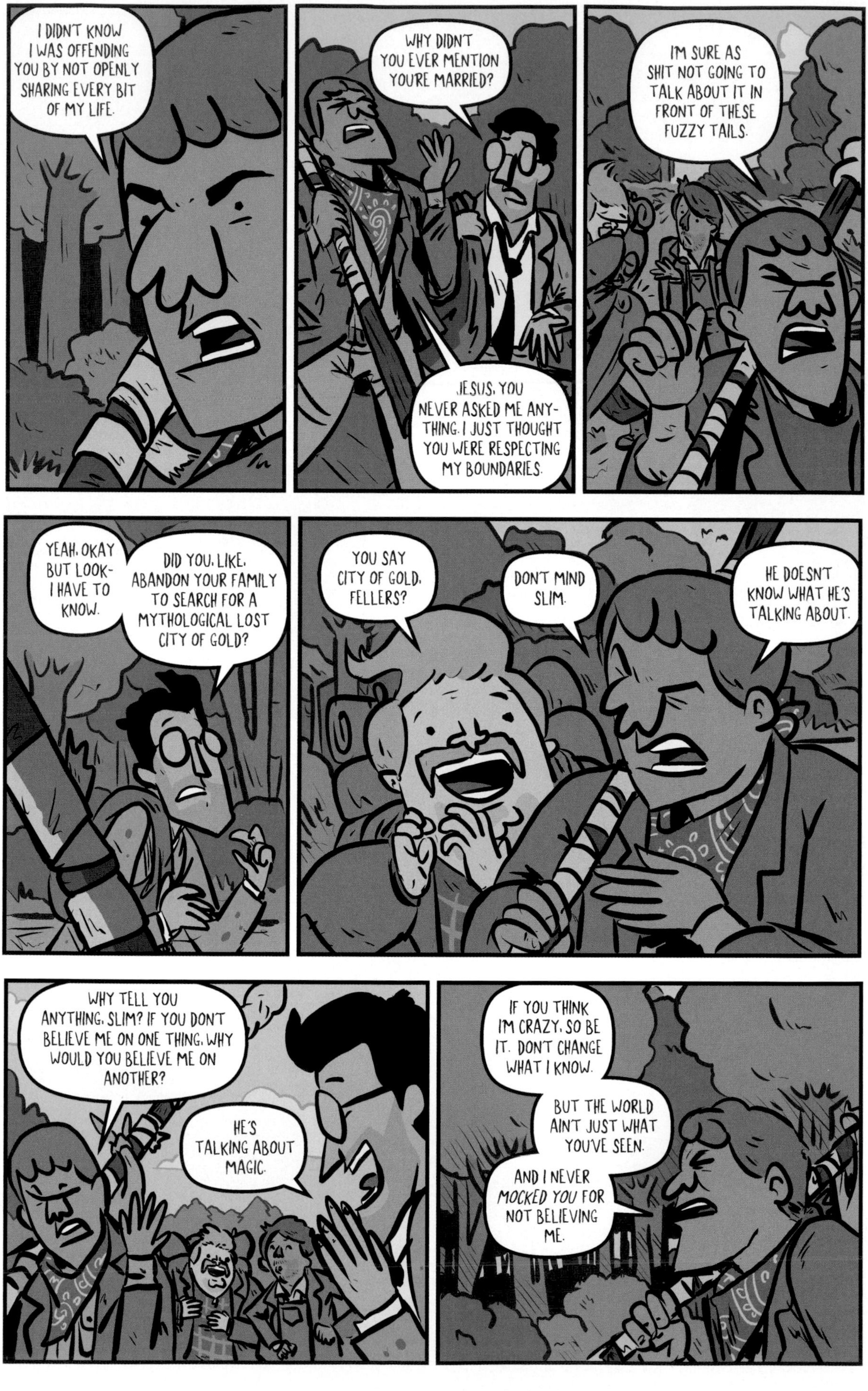
I DIDN'T KNOW I WAS OFFENDING YOU BY NOT OPENLY SHARING EVERY BIT OF MY LIFE.
WHY DIDN'T YOU EVER MENTION YOU'RE MARRIED?
JESUS. YOU NEVER ASKED ME ANY-THING. I JUST THOUGHT YOU WERE RESPECTING MY BOUNDARIES.
I'M SURE AS SHIT NOT GOING TO TALK ABOUT IT IN FRONT OF THESE FUZZY TAILS.
YEAH, OKAY BUT LOOK-I HAVE TO KNOW.
DID YOU, LIKE, ABANDON YOUR FAMILY TO SEARCH FOR A MYTHOLOGICAL LOST CITY OF GOLD?
YOU SAY CITY OF GOLD, FELLERS?
DON'T MIND SLIM.
HE DOESN'T KNOW WHAT HE'S TALKING ABOUT.
WHY TELL YOU ANYTHING, SLIM? IF YOU DON'T BELIEVE ME ON ONE THING, WHY WOULD YOU BELIEVE ME ON ANOTHER?
HE'S TALKING ABOUT MAGIC.
IF YOU THINK I'M CRAZY, SO BE IT. DON'T CHANGE WHAT I KNOW.
BUT THE WORLD AIN'T JUST WHAT YOU'VE SEEN.
AND I NEVER *MOCKED YOU* FOR NOT BELIEVING ME.

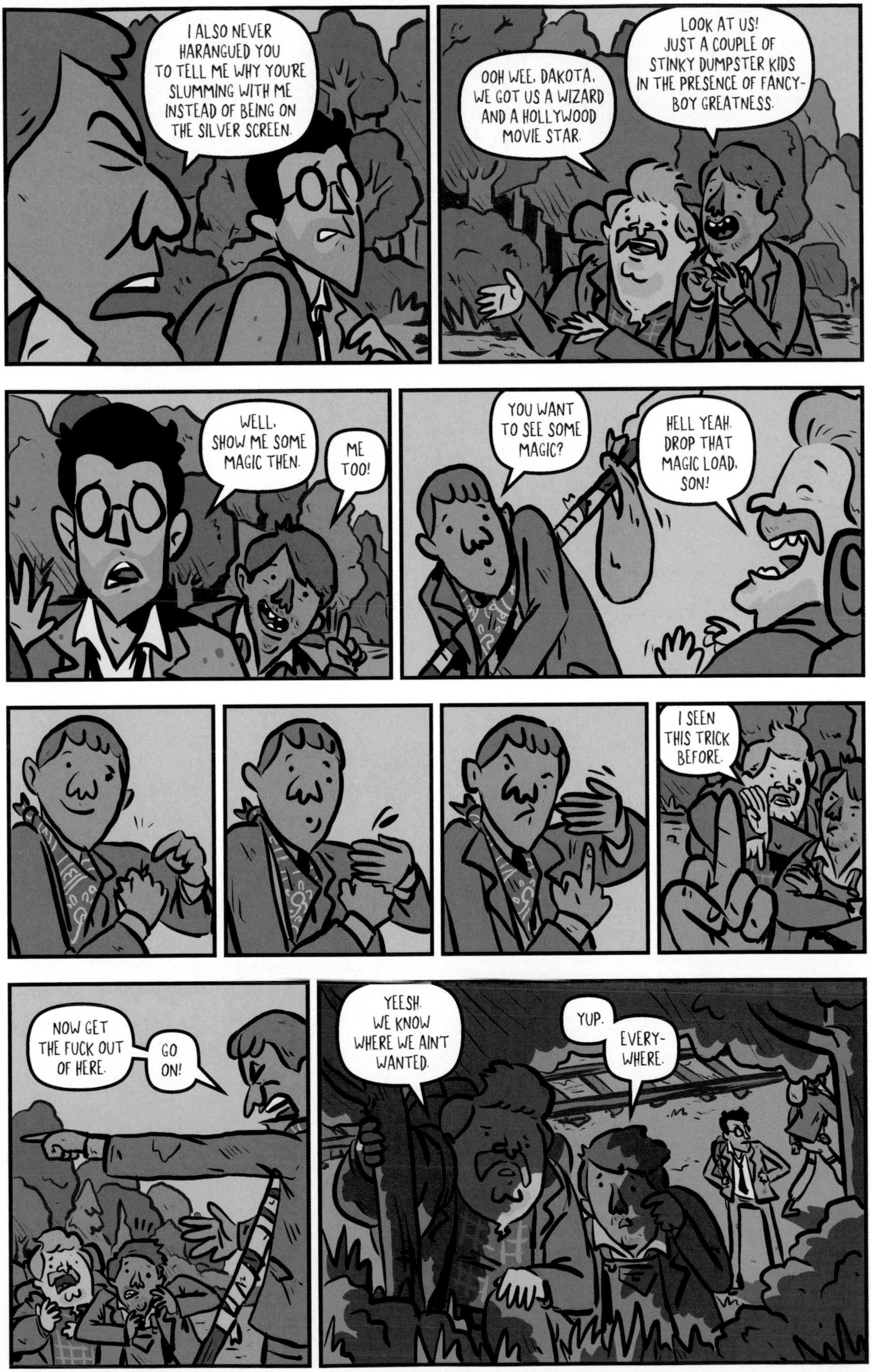
I ALSO NEVER HARANGUED YOU TO TELL ME WHY YOU'RE SLUMMING WITH ME INSTEAD OF BEING ON THE SILVER SCREEN.
OOH WEE, DAKOTA, WE GOT US A WIZARD AND A HOLLYWOOD MOVIE STAR.
LOOK AT US! JUST A COUPLE OF STINKY DUMPSTER KIDS IN THE PRESENCE OF FANCY-BOY GREATNESS.
WELL, SHOW ME SOME MAGIC THEN.
ME TOO!
YOU WANT TO SEE SOME MAGIC?
HELL YEAH. DROP THAT MAGIC LOAD, SON!
I SEEN THIS TRICK BEFORE.
NOW GET THE FUCK OUT OF HERE.
GO ON!
YEESH. WE KNOW WHERE WE AIN'T WANTED.
YUP.
EVERY-WHERE.

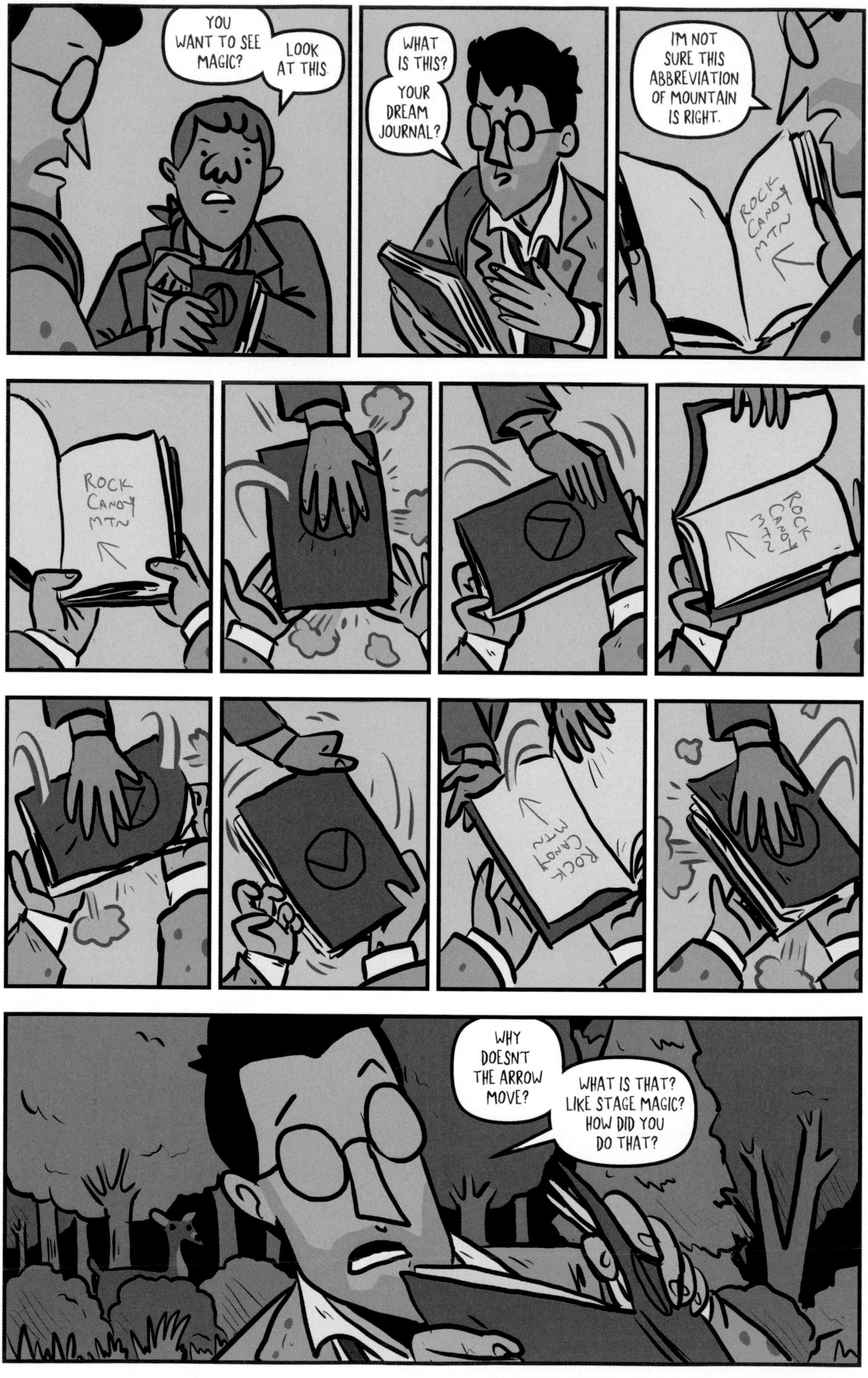
YOU WANT TO SEE MAGIC?
LOOK AT THIS.
WHAT IS THIS?
YOUR DREAM JOURNAL?
I'M NOT SURE THIS ABBREVIATION OF MOUNTAIN IS RIGHT.
ROCK CANDY MTN
ROCK CANDY MTN
ROCK CANDY MTN
ROCK CANDY MTN
WHY DOESN'T THE ARROW MOVE?
WHAT IS THAT? LIKE STAGE MAGIC? HOW DID YOU DO THAT?

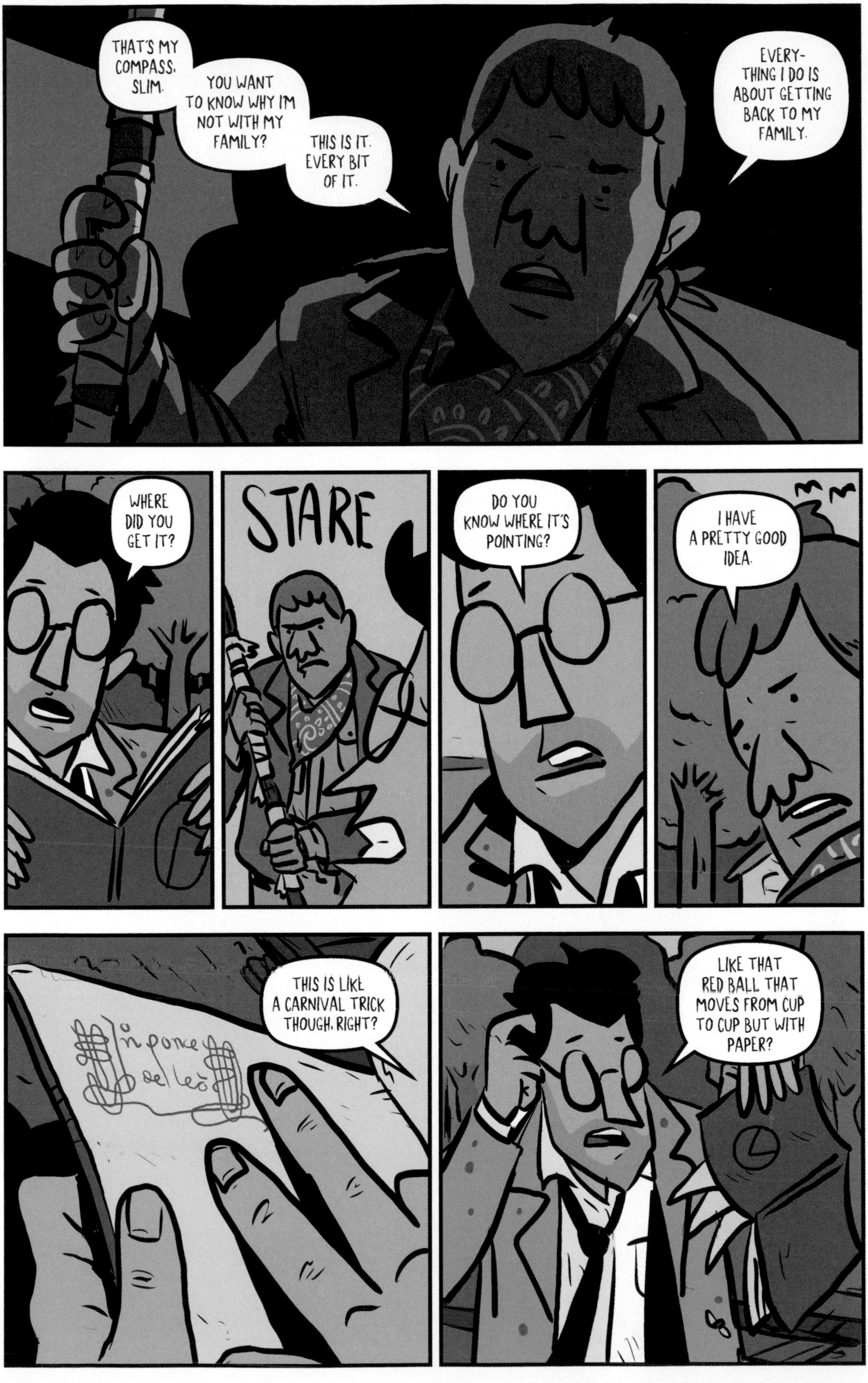
THAT'S MY COMPASS, SLIM.
YOU WANT TO KNOW WHY I'M NOT WITH MY FAMILY?
THIS IS IT. EVERY BIT OF IT.
EVERY-THING I DO IS ABOUT GETTING BACK TO MY FAMILY.
WHERE DID YOU GET IT?
STARE
DO YOU KNOW WHERE IT'S POINTING?
I HAVE A PRETTY GOOD IDEA.
THIS IS LIKE A CARNIVAL TRICK THOUGH, RIGHT?
LIKE THAT RED BALL THAT MOVES FROM CUP TO CUP BUT WITH PAPER?

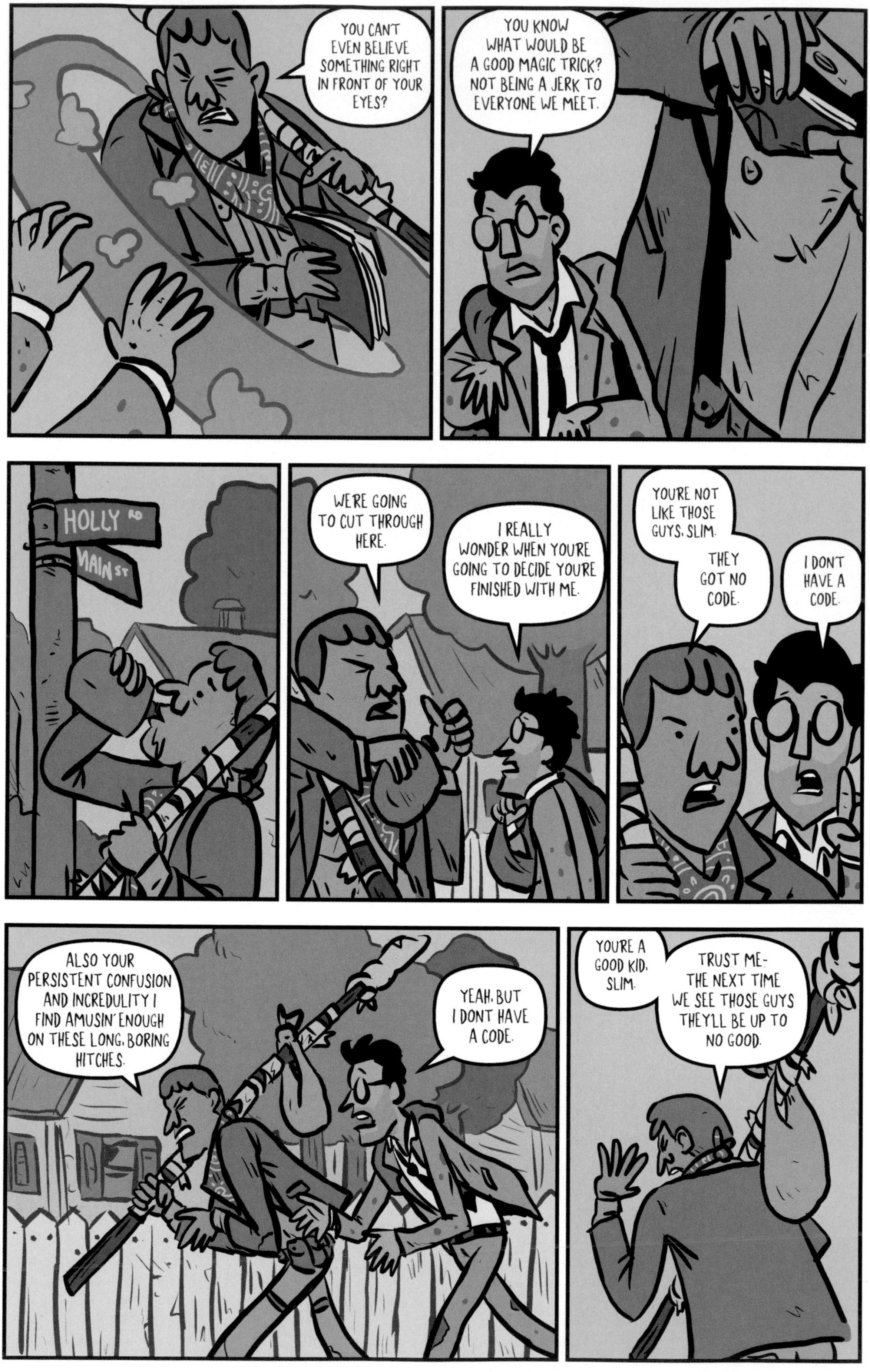
YOU CAN'T EVEN BELIEVE SOMETHING RIGHT IN FRONT OF YOUR EYES?
YOU KNOW WHAT WOULD BE A GOOD MAGIC TRICK? NOT BEING A JERK TO EVERYONE WE MEET.
HOLLY RD
MAIN ST
WE'RE GOING TO CUT THROUGH HERE.
I REALLY WONDER WHEN YOU'RE GOING TO DECIDE YOU'RE FINISHED WITH ME.
YOU'RE NOT LIKE THOSE GUYS, SLIM.
THEY GOT NO CODE.
I DON'T HAVE A CODE.
ALSO YOUR PERSISTENT CONFUSION AND INCREDULITY I FIND AMUSIN' ENOUGH ON THESE LONG, BORING HITCHES.
YEAH, BUT I DONT HAVE A CODE.
YOU'RE A GOOD KID, SLIM.
TRUST ME- THE NEXT TIME WE SEE THOSE GUYS THEY'LL BE UP TO NO GOOD.

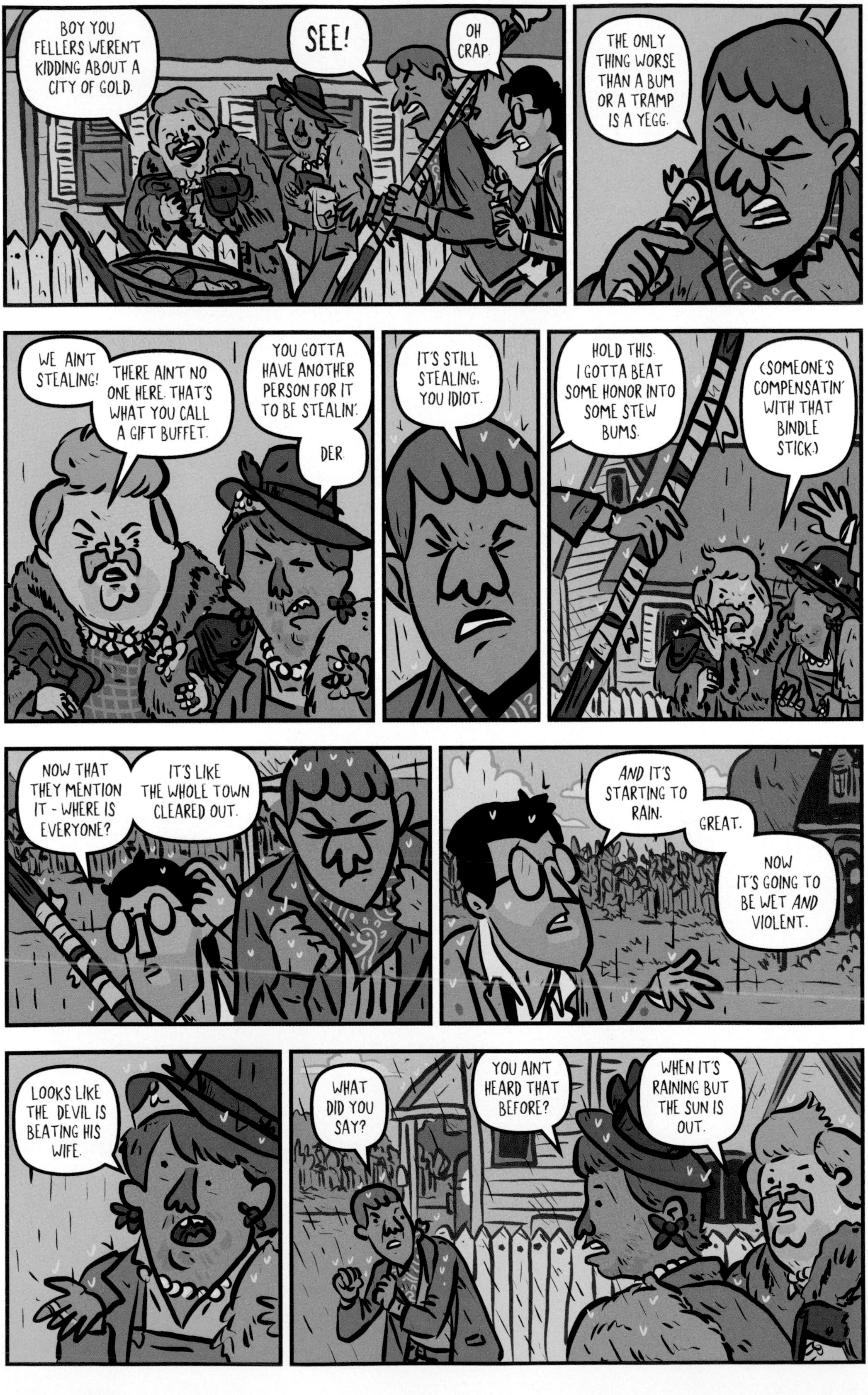
BOY YOU FELLERS WEREN'T KIDDING ABOUT A CITY OF GOLD.
SEE!
OH CRAP.
THE ONLY THING WORSE THAN A BUM OR A TRAMP IS A YEGG.
WE AIN'T STEALING!
THERE AIN'T NO ONE HERE. THAT'S WHAT YOU CALL A GIFT BUFFET.
YOU GOTTA HAVE ANOTHER PERSON FOR IT TO BE STEALIN'.
DER.
IT'S STILL STEALING, YOU IDIOT.
HOLD THIS. I GOTTA BEAT SOME HONOR INTO SOME STEW BUMS.
(SOMEONE'S COMPENSATIN' WITH THAT BINDLE STICK.)
NOW THAT THEY MENTION IT - WHERE IS EVERYONE?
IT'S LIKE THE WHOLE TOWN CLEARED OUT.
AND IT'S STARTING TO RAIN.
GREAT.
NOW IT'S GOING TO BE WET *AND* VIOLENT.
LOOKS LIKE THE DEVIL IS BEATING HIS WIFE.
WHAT DID YOU SAY?
YOU AIN'T HEARD THAT BEFORE?
WHEN IT'S RAINING BUT THE SUN IS OUT.

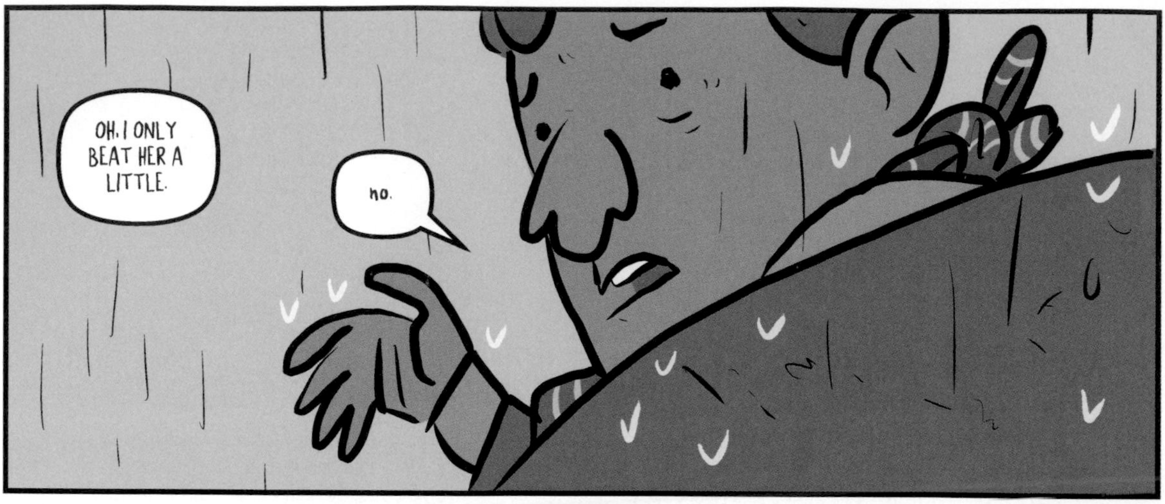
OH, I ONLY BEAT HER A LITTLE.
no.

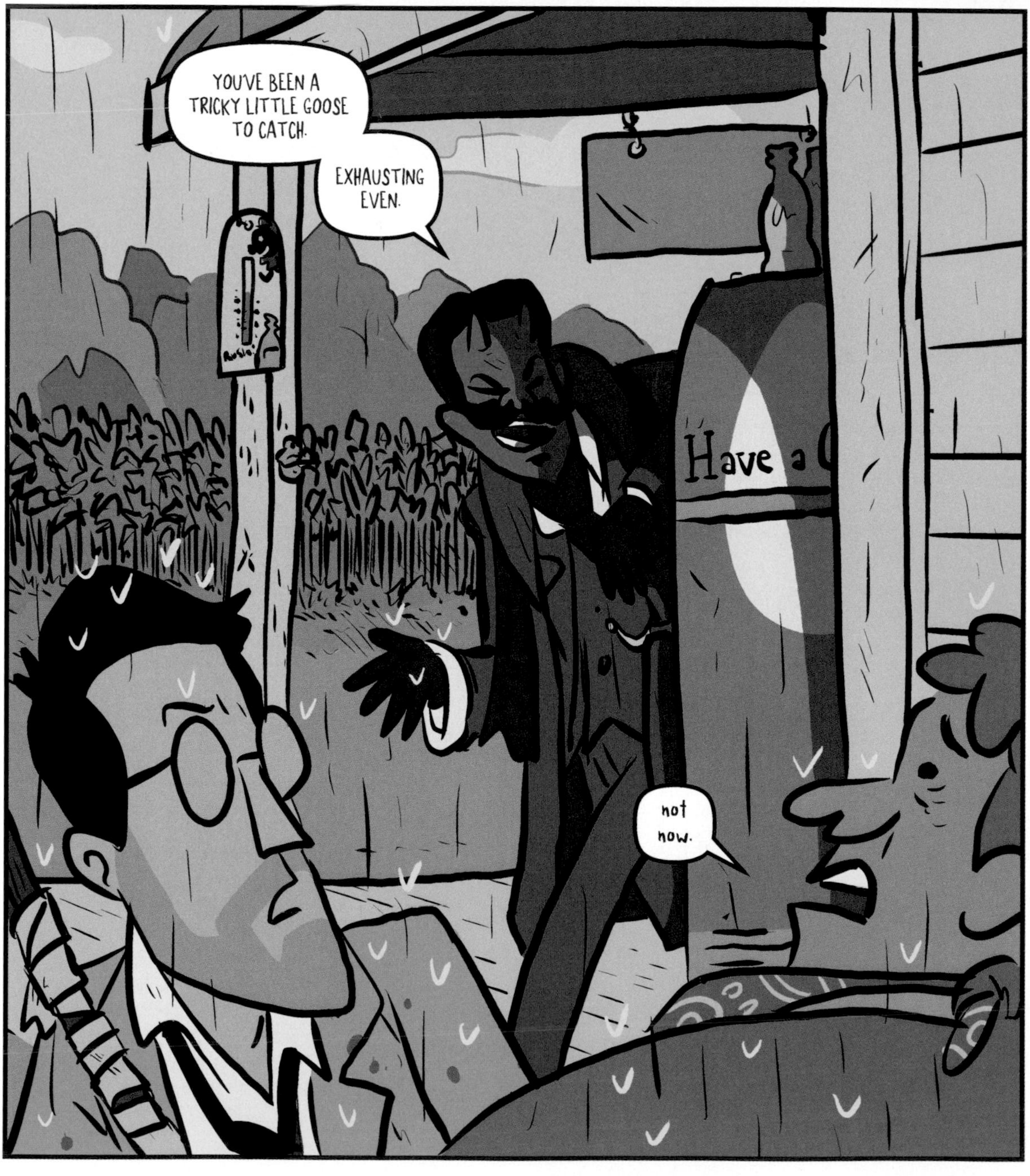
YOU'VE BEEN A TRICKY LITTLE GOOSE TO CATCH.
EXHAUSTING EVEN.
Have a
not now.

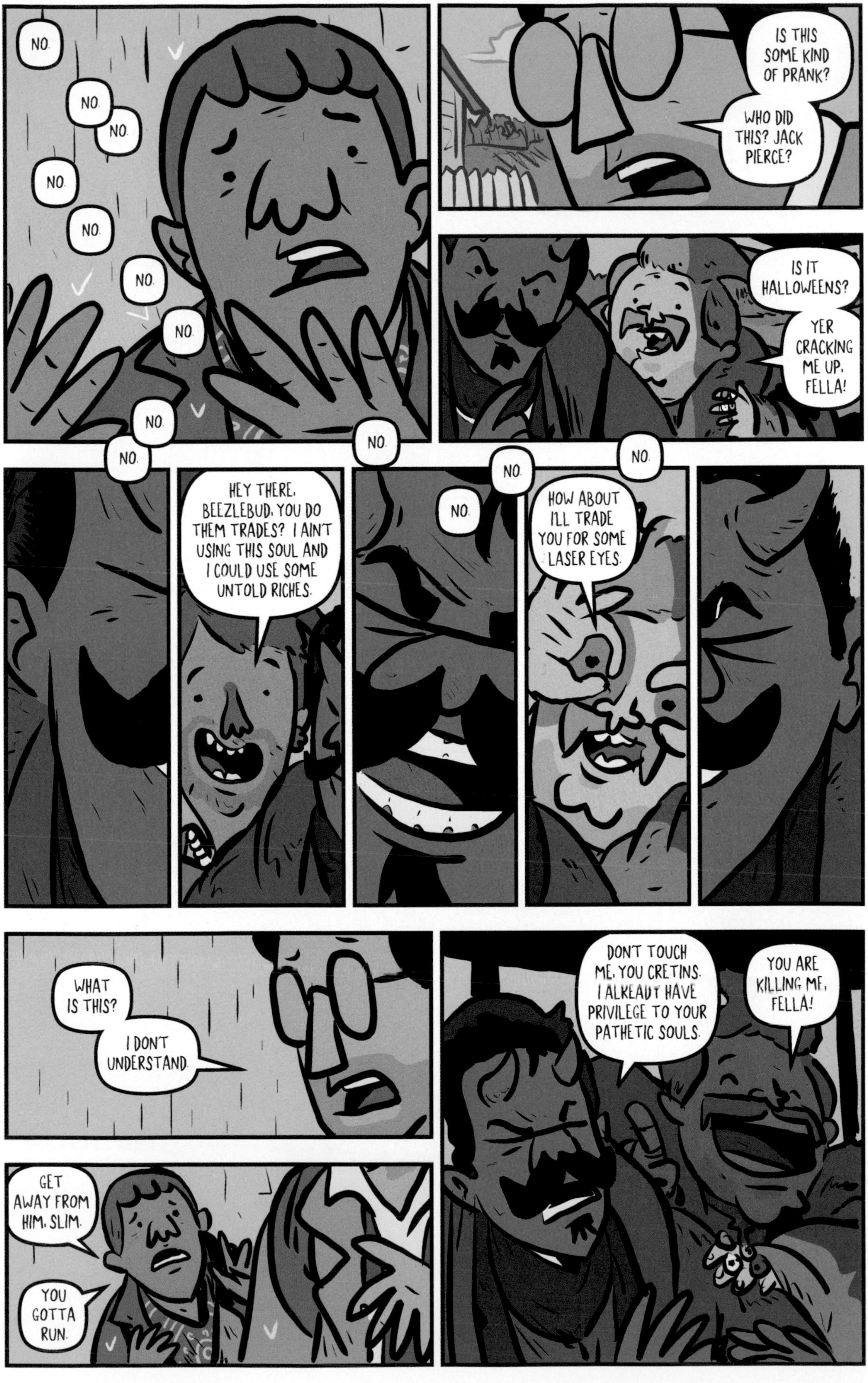
NO.
NO.
NO.
NO.
NO.
NO.
NO.
IS THIS SOME KIND OF PRANK?
WHO DID THIS? JACK PIERCE?
IS IT HALLOWEENS?
YER CRACKING ME UP, FELLA!
NO.
NO.
NO.
HEY THERE, BEEZLEBUD, YOU DO THEM TRADES? I AIN'T USING THIS SOUL AND I COULD USE SOME UNTOLD RICHES.
NO.
NO.
NO.
HOW ABOUT I'LL TRADE YOU FOR SOME LASER EYES.
WHAT IS THIS?
I DON'T UNDERSTAND.
DON'T TOUCH ME, YOU CRETINS. I ALREADY HAVE PRIVILEGE TO YOUR PATHETIC SOULS.
YOU ARE KILLING ME, FELLA!
GET AWAY FROM HIM, SLIM.
YOU GOTTA RUN.

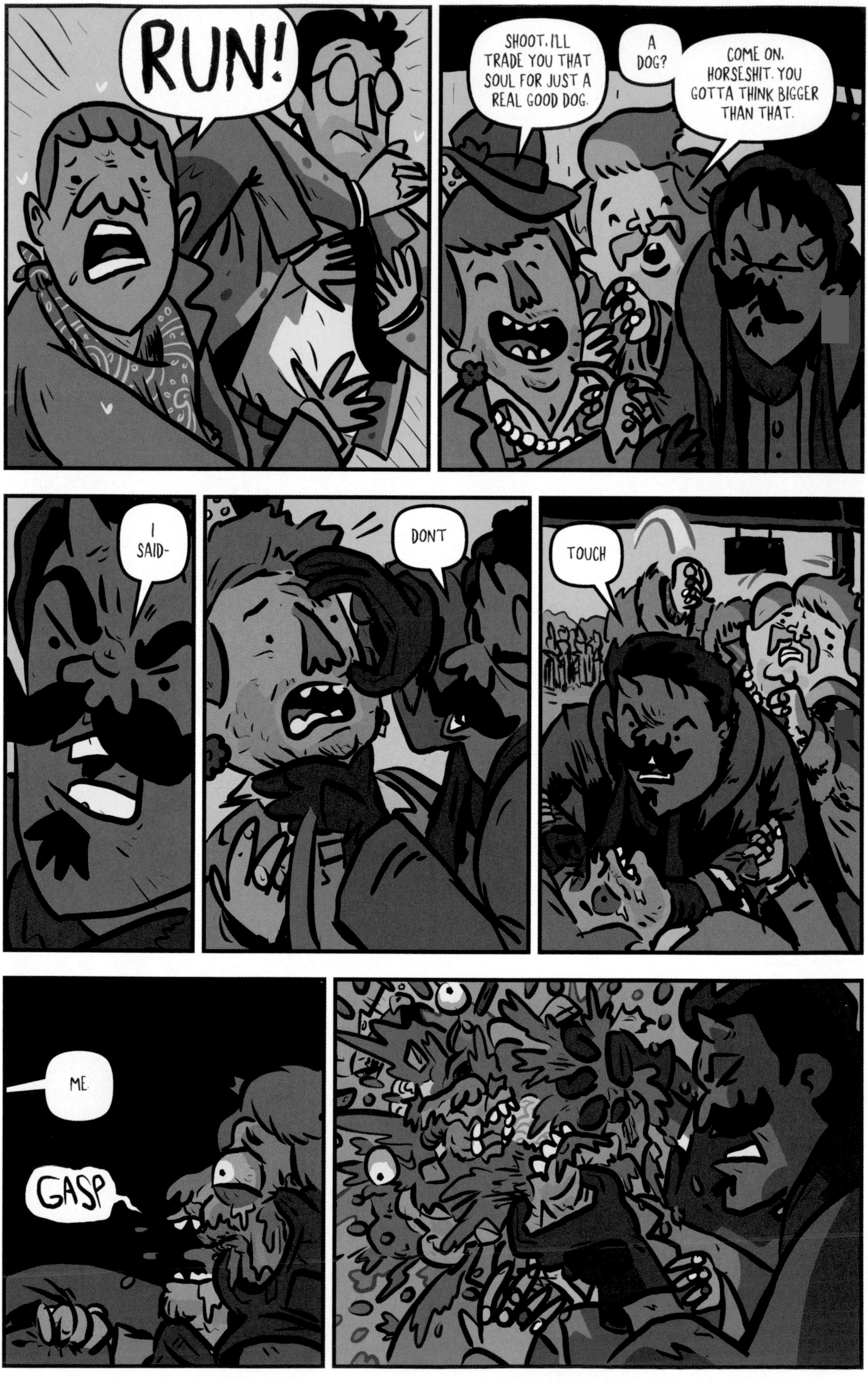
RUN!
SHOOT, I'LL TRADE YOU THAT SOUL FOR JUST A REAL GOOD DOG.
A DOG?
COME ON, HORSESHIT. YOU GOTTA THINK BIGGER THAN THAT.
I SAID-
DON'T
TOUCH
ME.
GASP

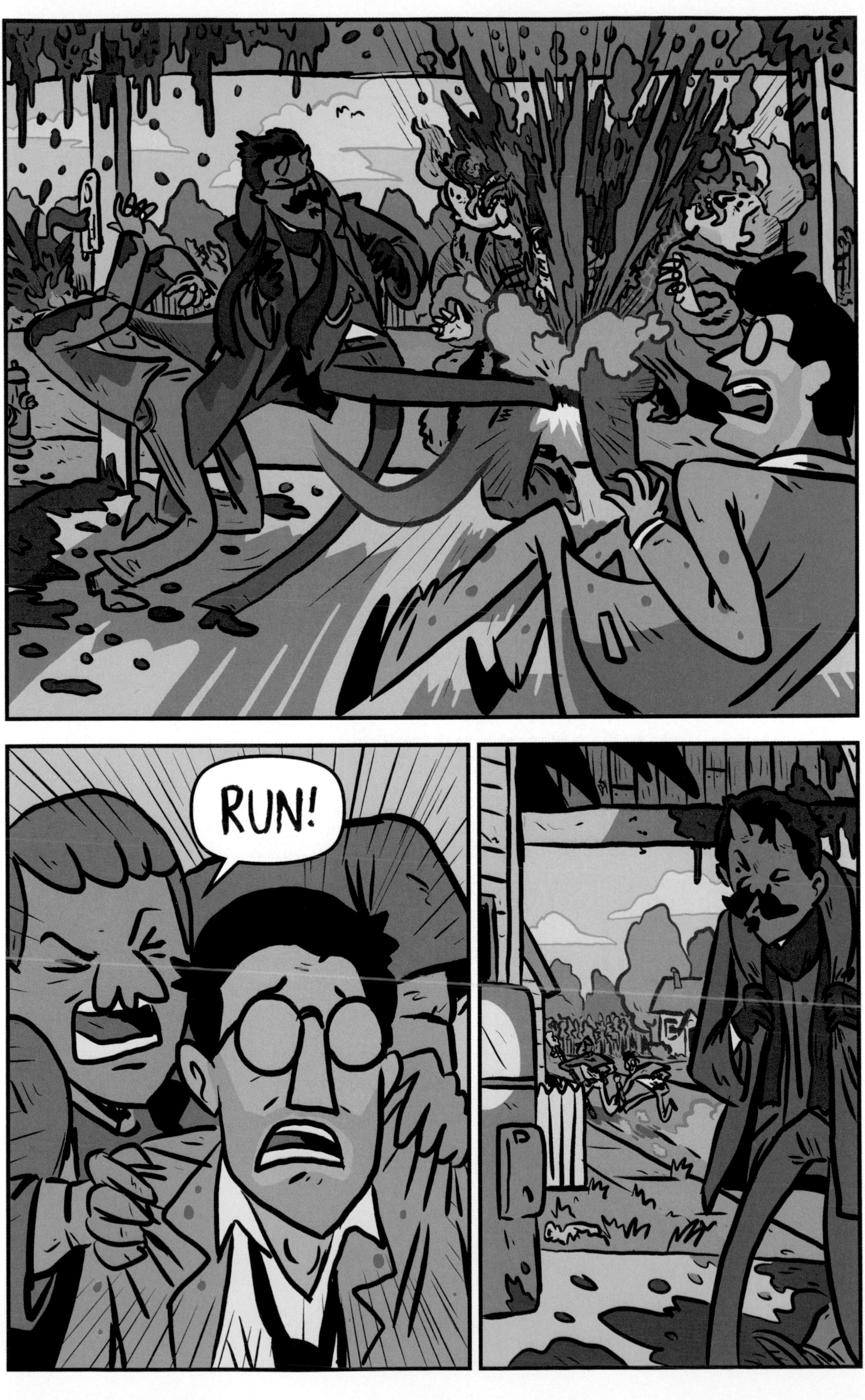
RUN!

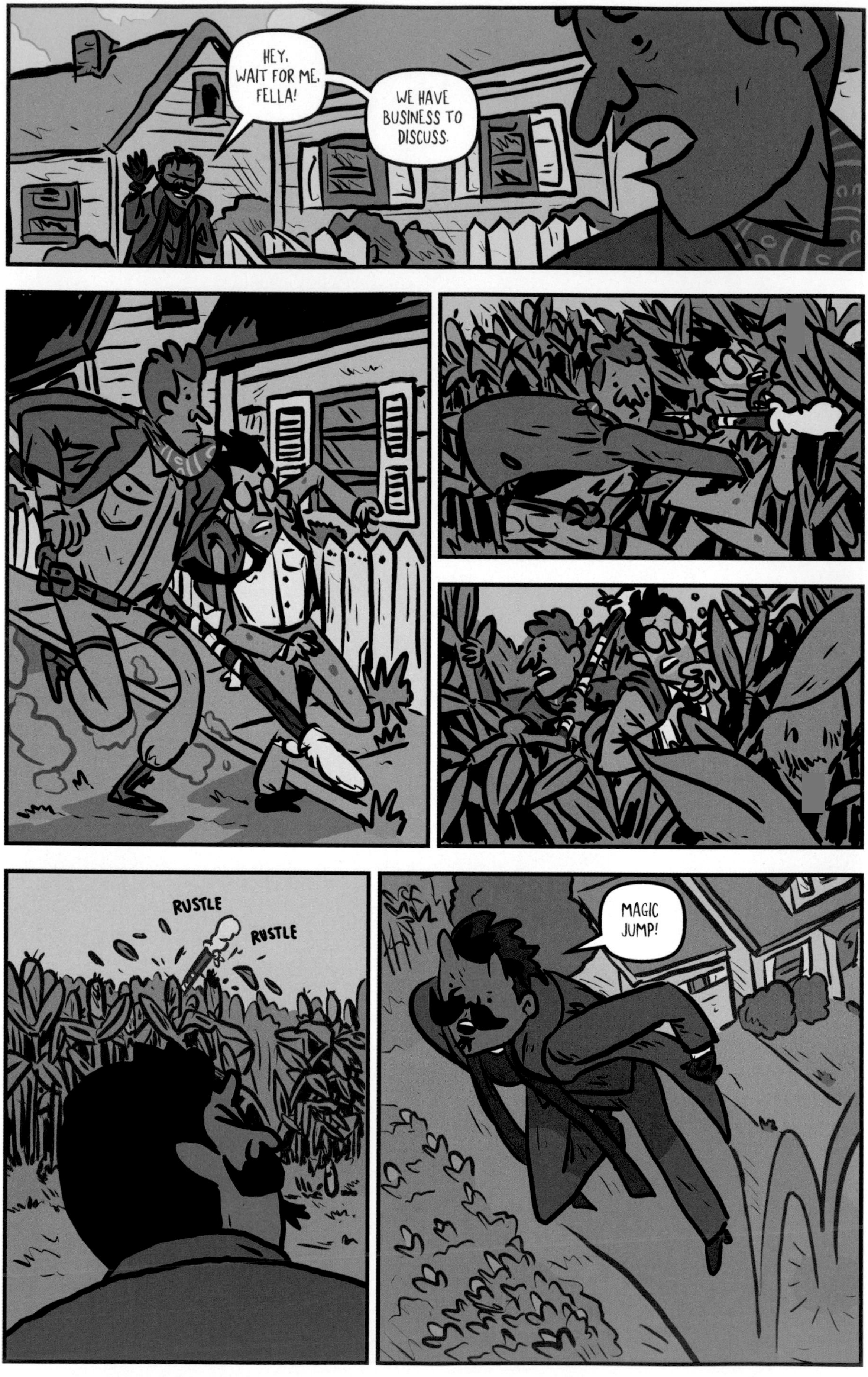
HEY, WAIT FOR ME, FELLA!
WE HAVE BUSINESS TO DISCUSS.
RUSTLE
RUSTLE
MAGIC JUMP!

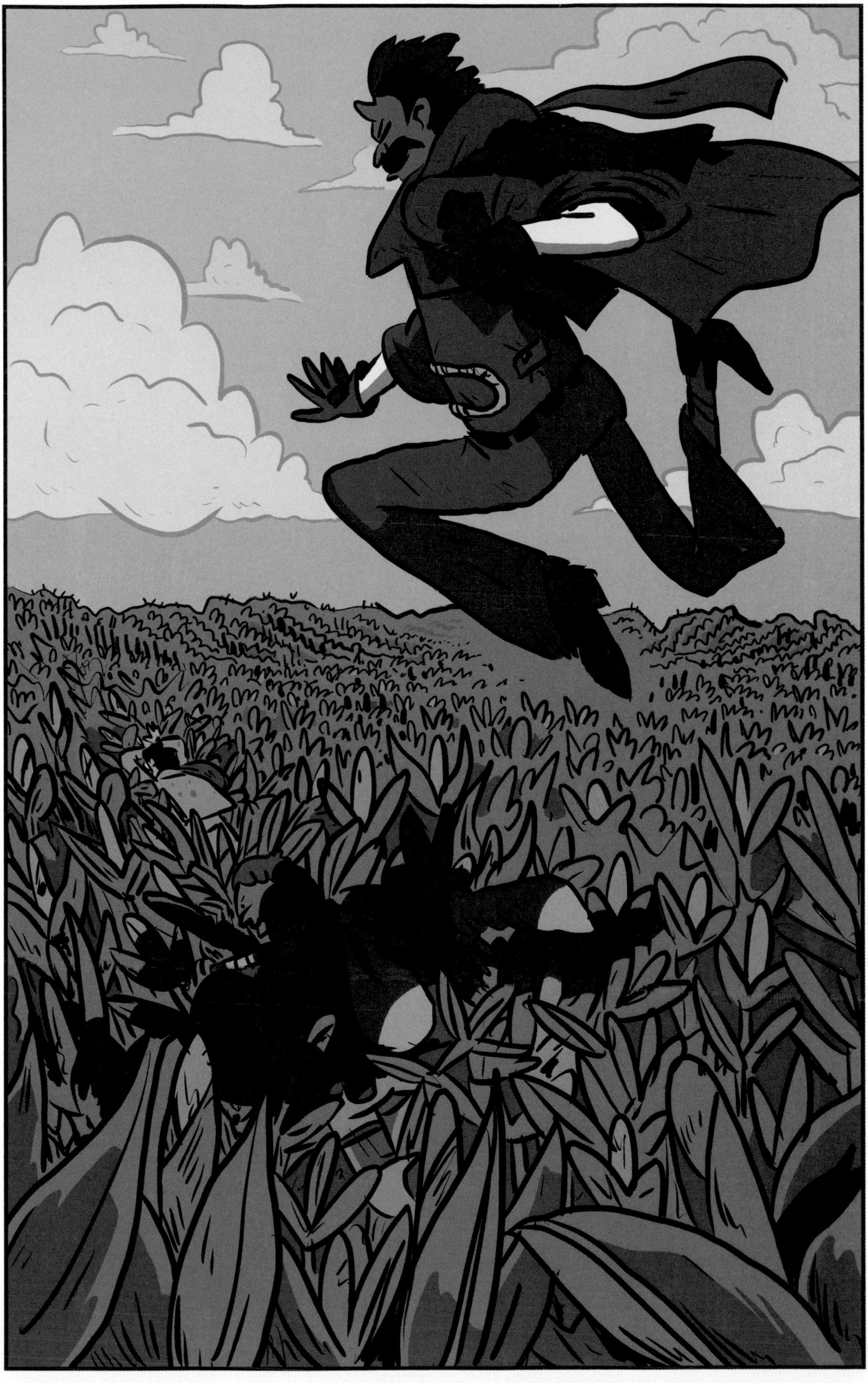

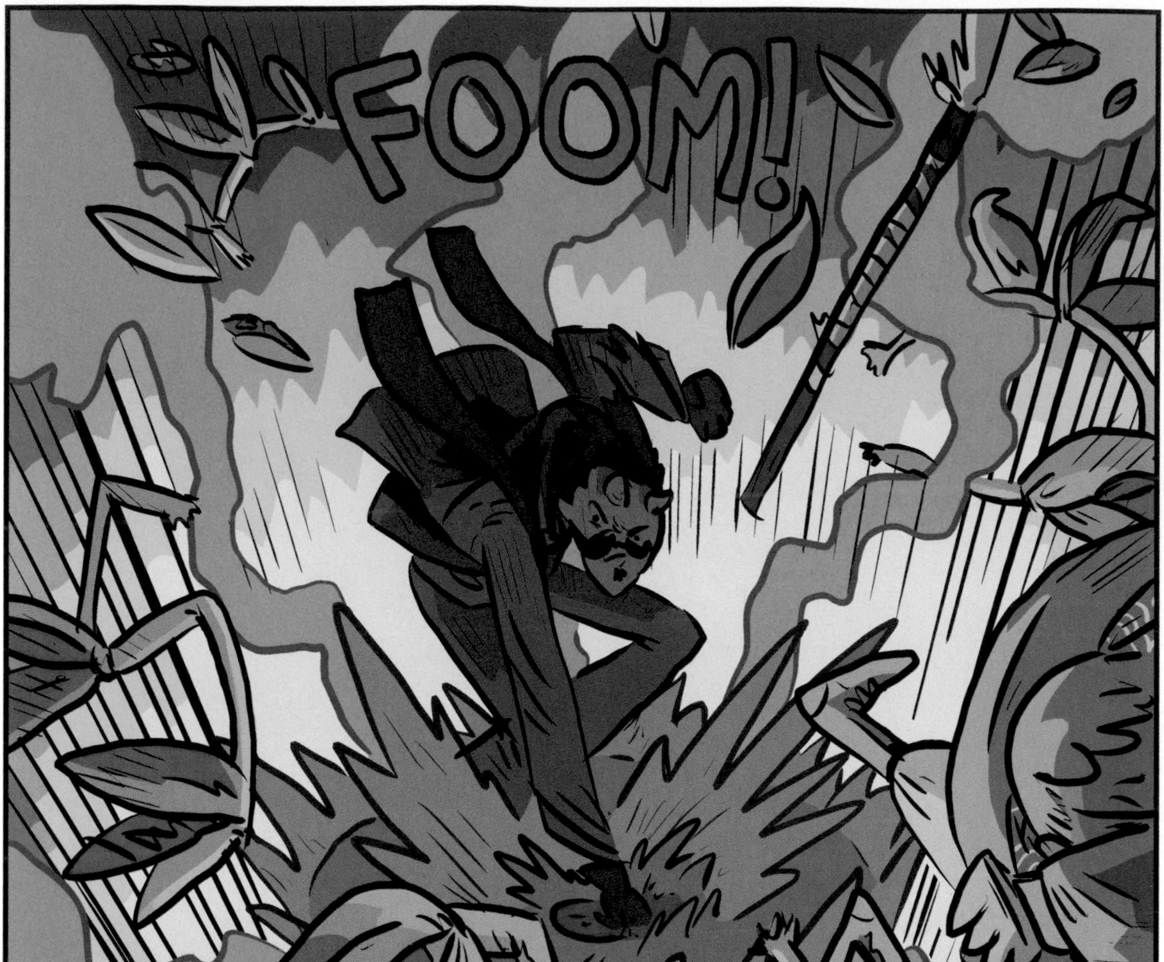
FOOM!

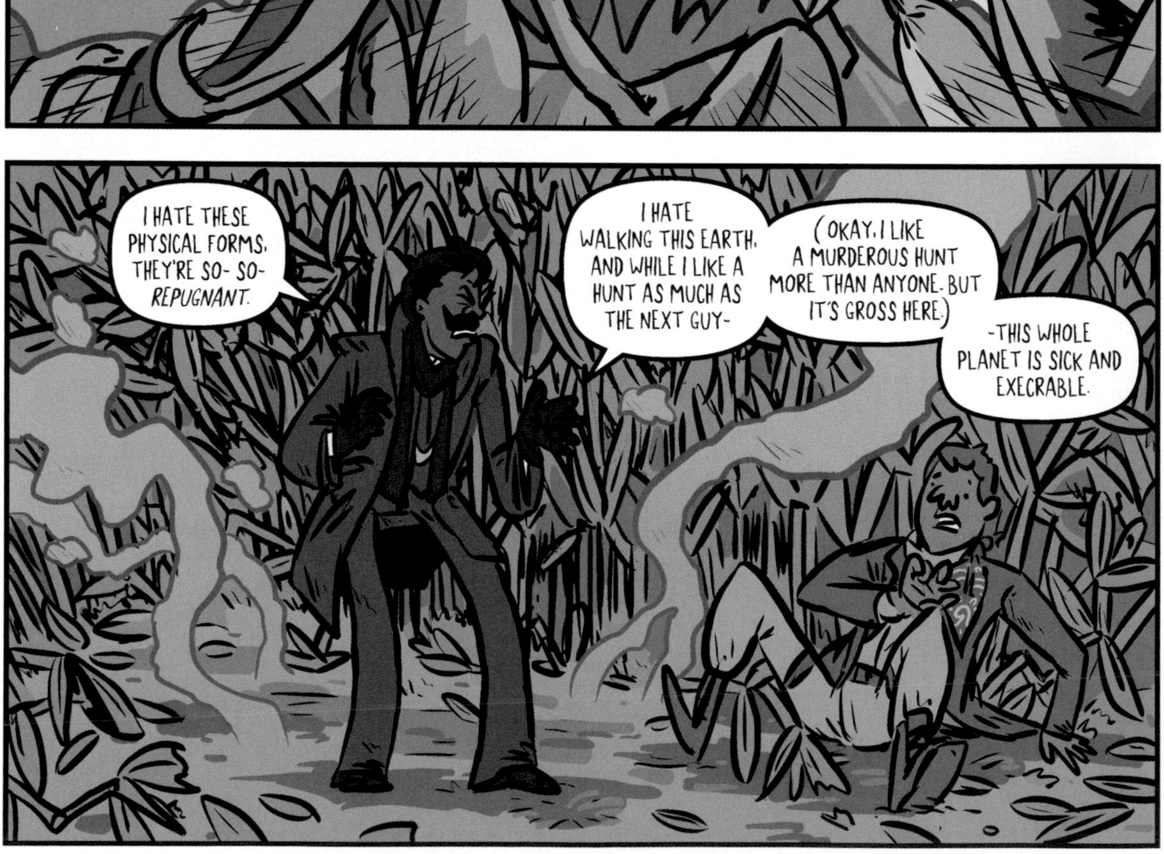
I HATE THESE PHYSICAL FORMS. THEY'RE SO- SO- REPUGNANT.
I HATE WALKING THIS EARTH, AND WHILE I LIKE A HUNT AS MUCH AS THE NEXT GUY-
(OKAY, I LIKE A MURDEROUS HUNT MORE THAN ANYONE. BUT IT'S GROSS HERE.)
-THIS WHOLE PLANET IS SICK AND EXECRABLE.

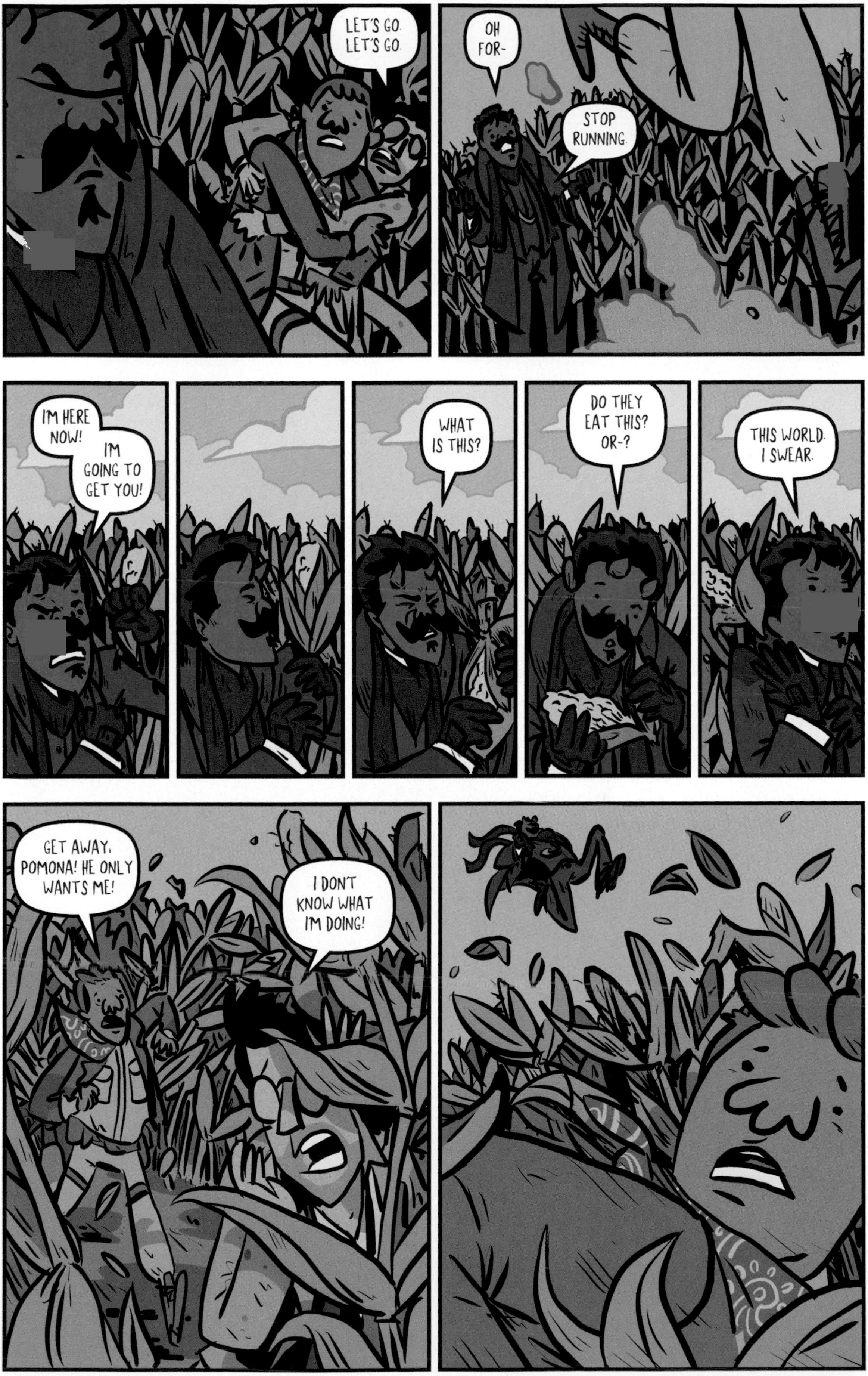
LET'S GO. LET'S GO.
OH FOR-
STOP RUNNING.
I'M HERE NOW!
I'M GOING TO GET YOU!
WHAT IS THIS?
DO THEY EAT THIS? OR-?
THIS WORLD. I SWEAR.
GET AWAY, POMONA! HE ONLY WANTS ME!
I DON'T KNOW WHAT I'M DOING!

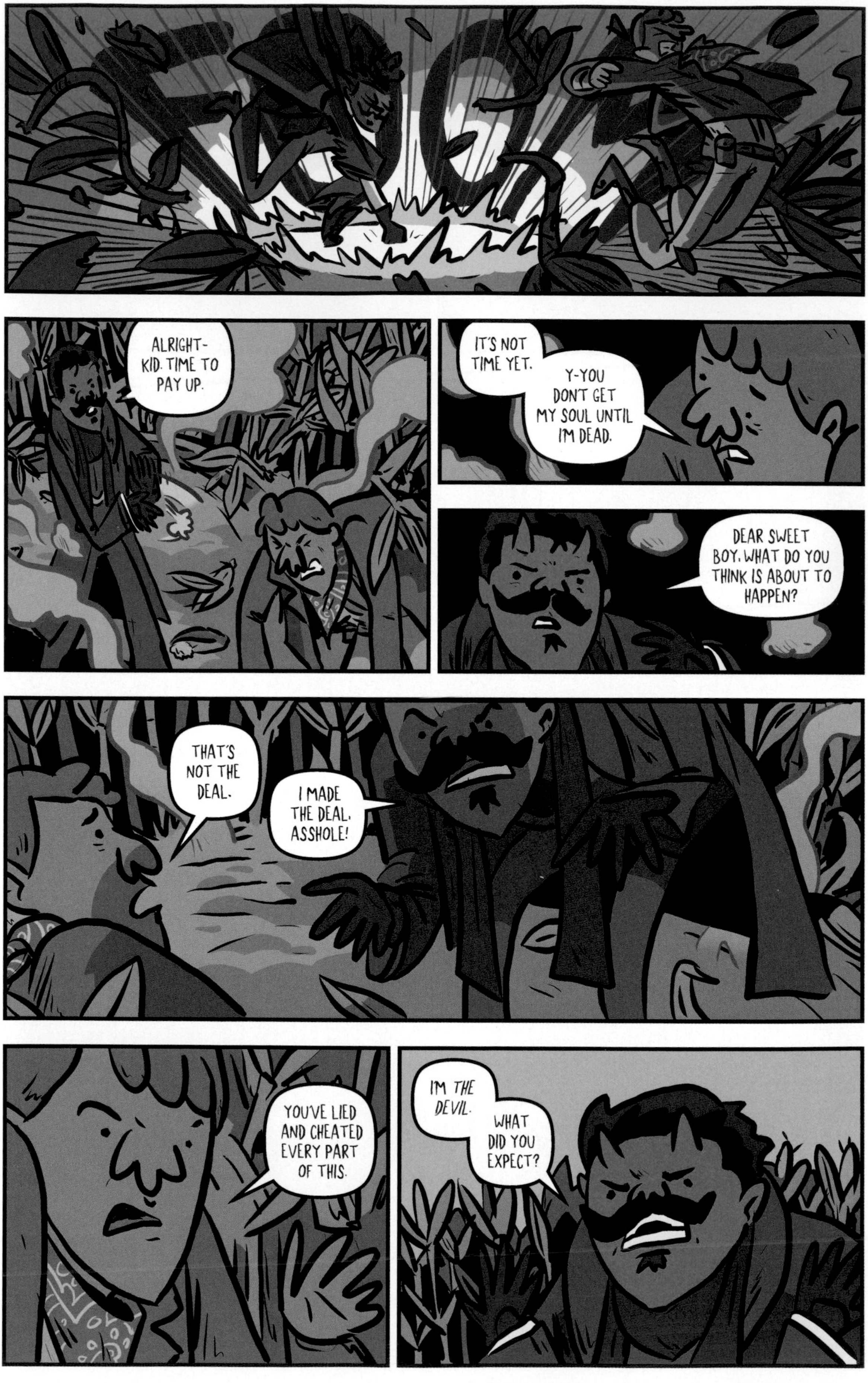
ALRIGHT-KID. TIME TO PAY UP.
IT'S NOT TIME YET.
Y-YOU DON'T GET MY SOUL UNTIL I'M DEAD.
DEAR SWEET BOY, WHAT DO YOU THINK IS ABOUT TO HAPPEN?
THAT'S NOT THE DEAL.
I MADE THE DEAL, ASSHOLE!
YOU'VE LIED AND CHEATED EVERY PART OF THIS.
I'M *THE DEVIL.*
WHAT DID YOU EXPECT?

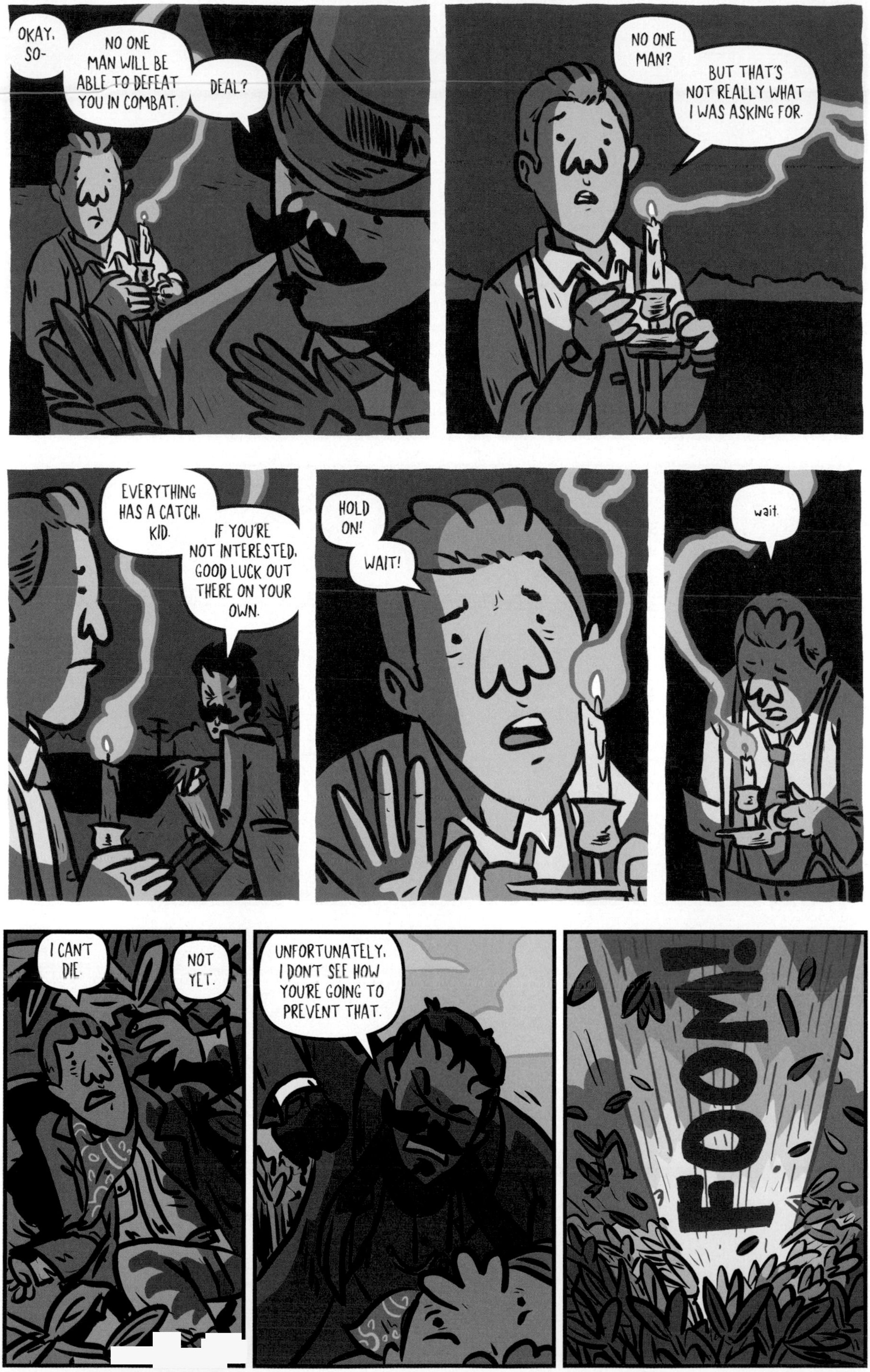
OKAY, SO-
NO ONE MAN WILL BE ABLE TO DEFEAT YOU IN COMBAT.
DEAL?
NO ONE MAN?
BUT THAT'S NOT REALLY WHAT I WAS ASKING FOR.
EVERYTHING HAS A CATCH, KID.
IF YOU'RE NOT INTERESTED, GOOD LUCK OUT THERE ON YOUR OWN.
HOLD ON!
WAIT!
wait.
I CAN'T DIE.
NOT YET.
UNFORTUNATELY, I DON'T SEE HOW YOU'RE GOING TO PREVENT THAT.
FOOM!

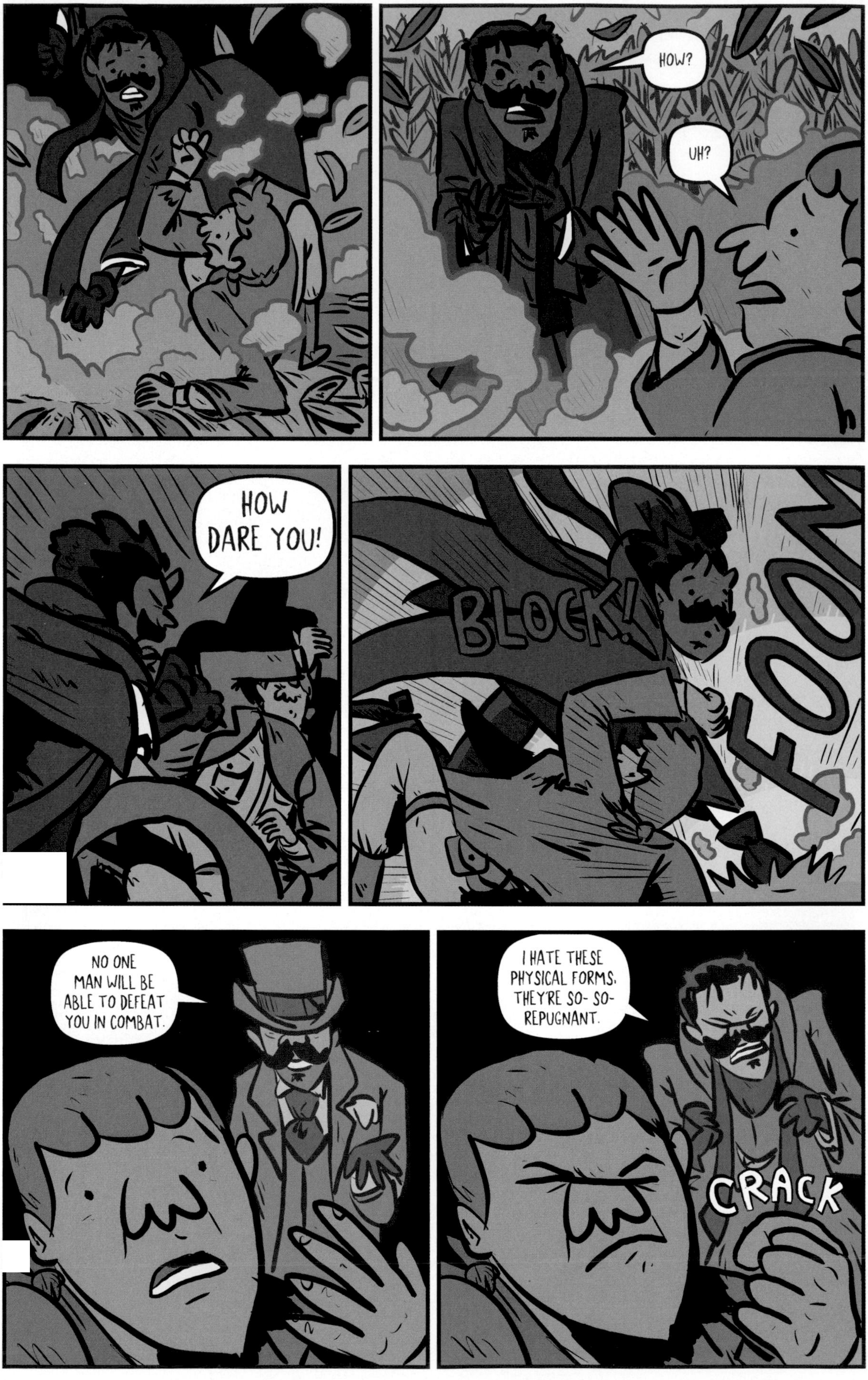
HOW?
UH?
HOW DARE YOU!
BLOCK!
FOOM
NO ONE MAN WILL BE ABLE TO DEFEAT YOU IN COMBAT.
I HATE THESE PHYSICAL FORMS. THEY'RE SO- SO- REPUGNANT.
CRACK

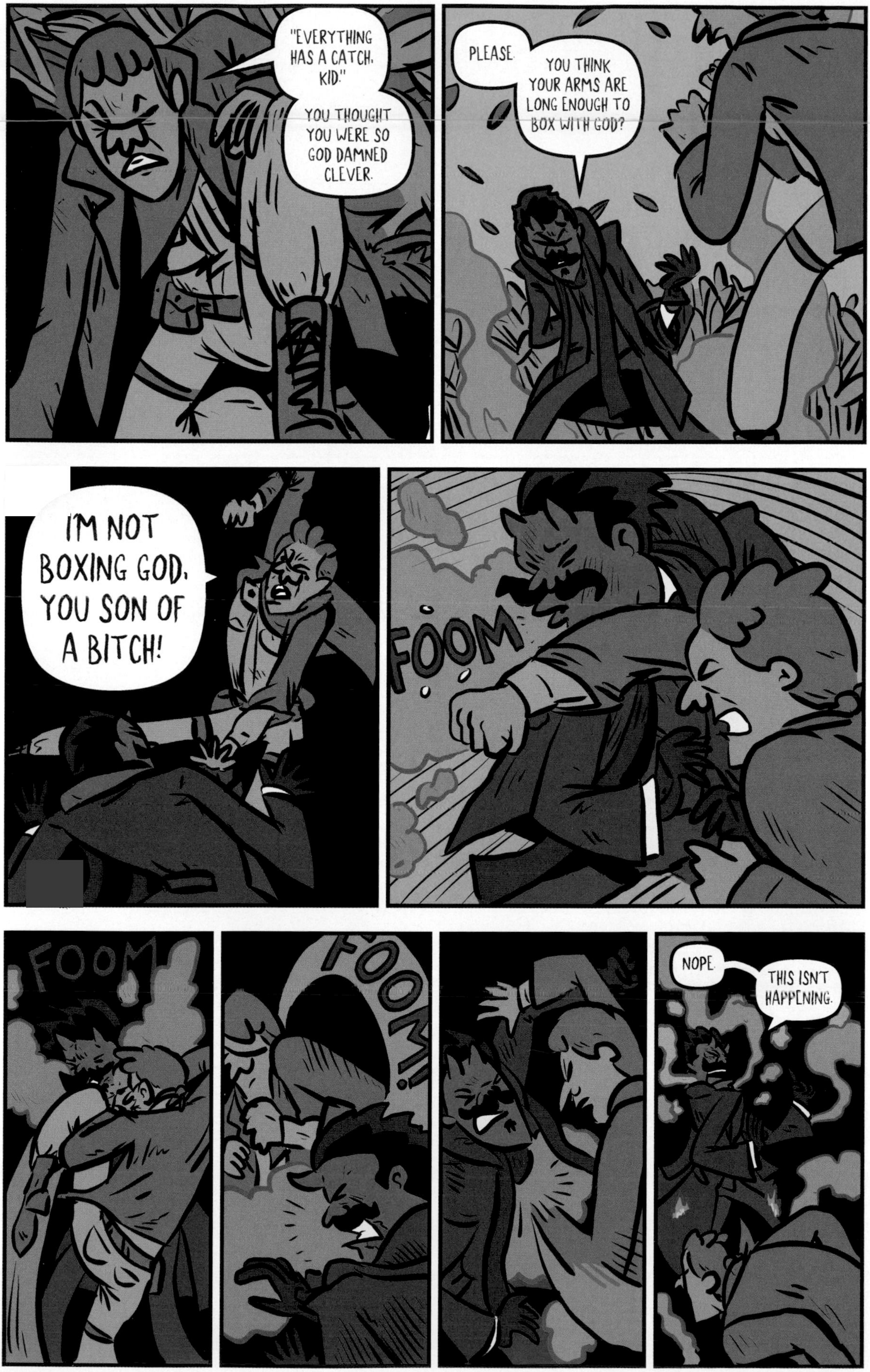
"EVERYTHING HAS A CATCH, KID."
YOU THOUGHT YOU WERE SO GOD DAMNED CLEVER.
PLEASE.
YOU THINK YOUR ARMS ARE LONG ENOUGH TO BOX WITH GOD?
I'M NOT BOXING GOD, YOU SON OF A BITCH!
FOOM
FOOM
FOOM!
NOPE.
THIS ISN'T HAPPENING.

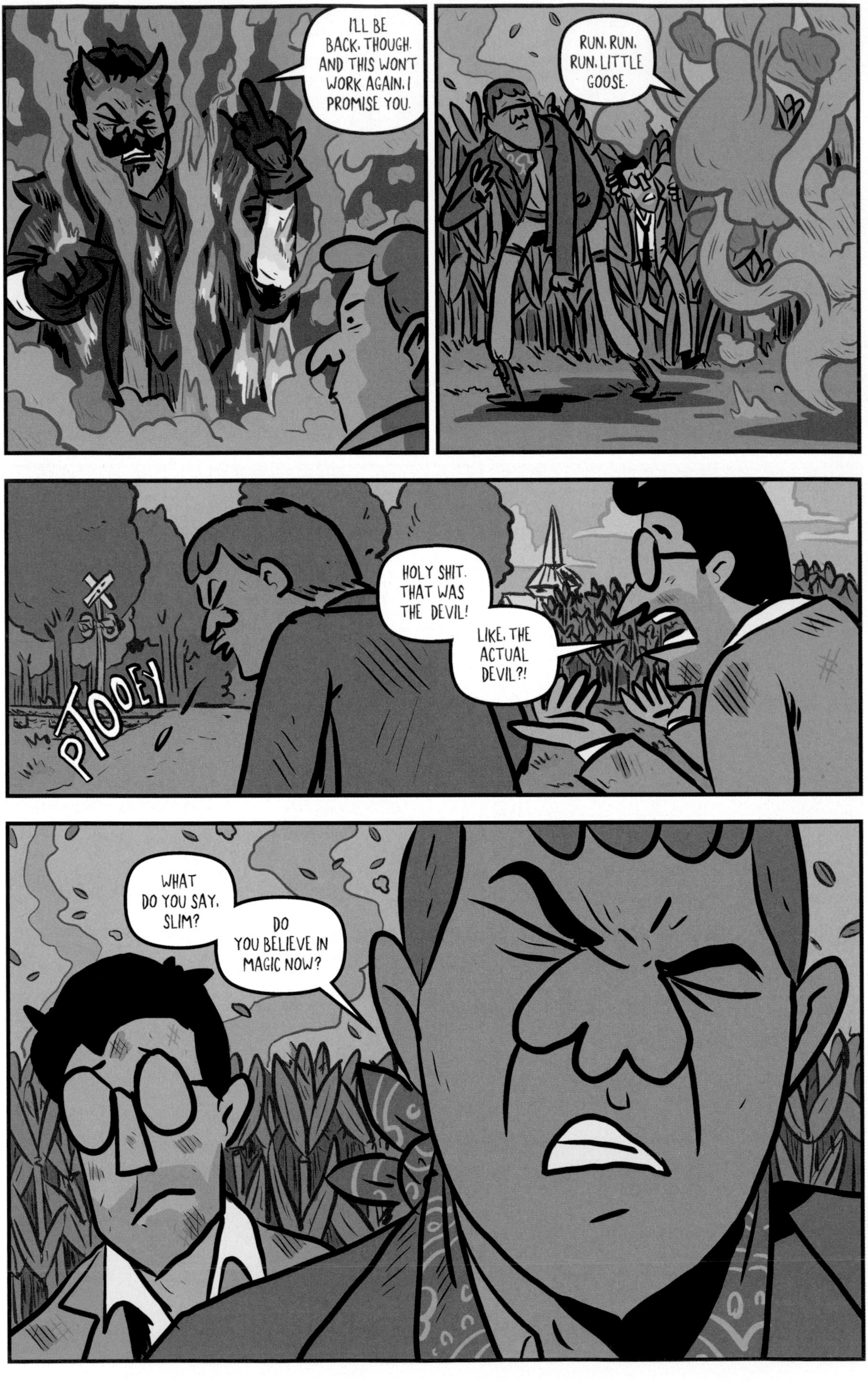
I'LL BE BACK, THOUGH. AND THIS WON'T WORK AGAIN, I PROMISE YOU.
RUN, RUN, RUN, LITTLE GOOSE.
PTOOEY
HOLY SHIT. THAT WAS THE DEVIL!
LIKE, THE ACTUAL DEVIL?!
WHAT DO YOU SAY, SLIM?
DO YOU BELIEVE IN MAGIC NOW?

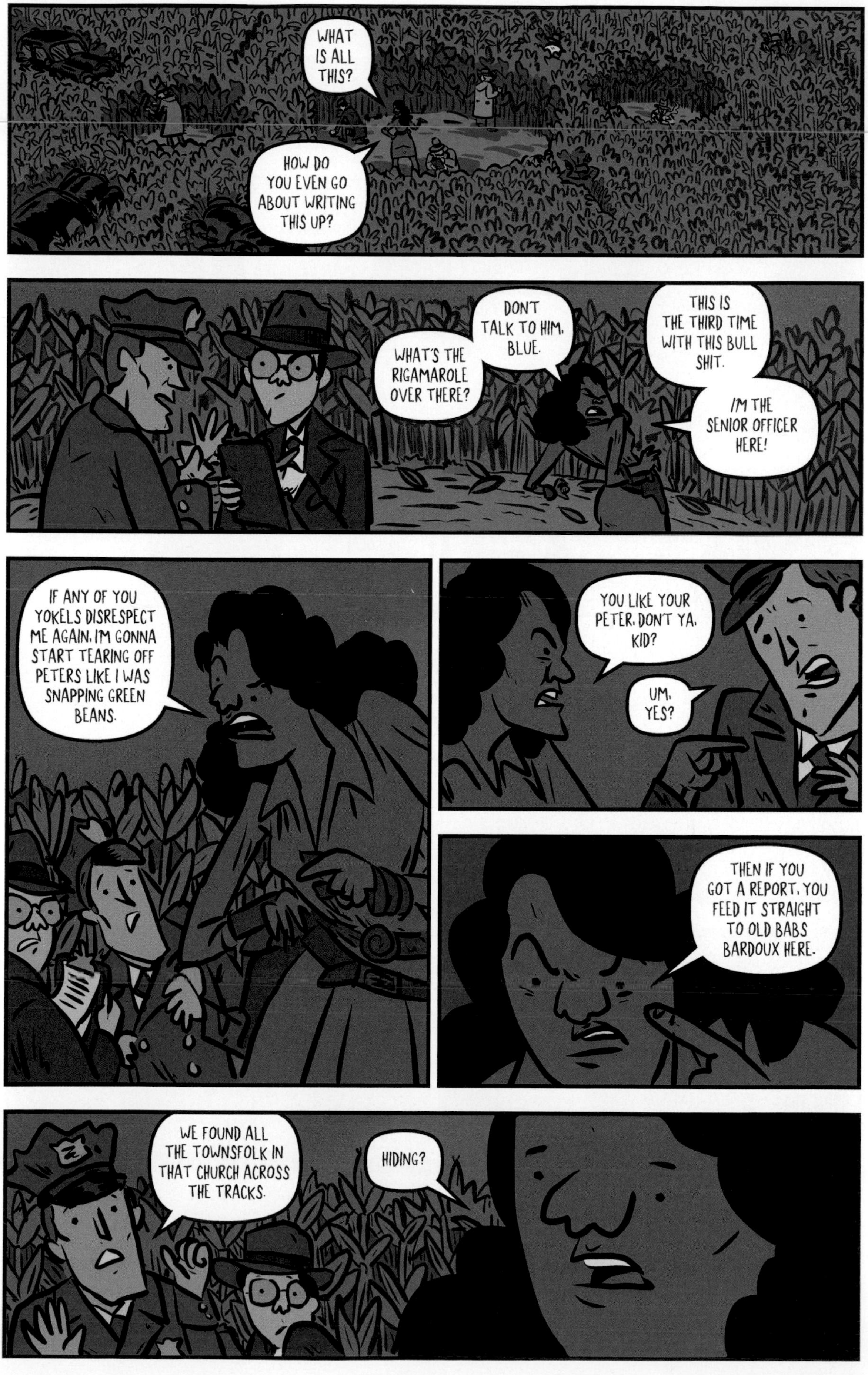
WHAT IS ALL THIS?
HOW DO YOU EVEN GO ABOUT WRITING THIS UP?
WHAT'S THE RIGAMAROLE OVER THERE?
DON'T TALK TO HIM, BLUE.
THIS IS THE THIRD TIME WITH THIS BULL SHIT.
I'M THE SENIOR OFFICER HERE!
IF ANY OF YOU YOKELS DISRESPECT ME AGAIN, I'M GONNA START TEARING OFF PETERS LIKE I WAS SNAPPING GREEN BEANS.
YOU LIKE YOUR PETER, DON'T YA, KID?
UM, YES?
THEN IF YOU GOT A REPORT, YOU FEED IT STRAIGHT TO OLD BABS BARDOUX HERE.
WE FOUND ALL THE TOWNSFOLK IN THAT CHURCH ACROSS THE TRACKS.
HIDING?

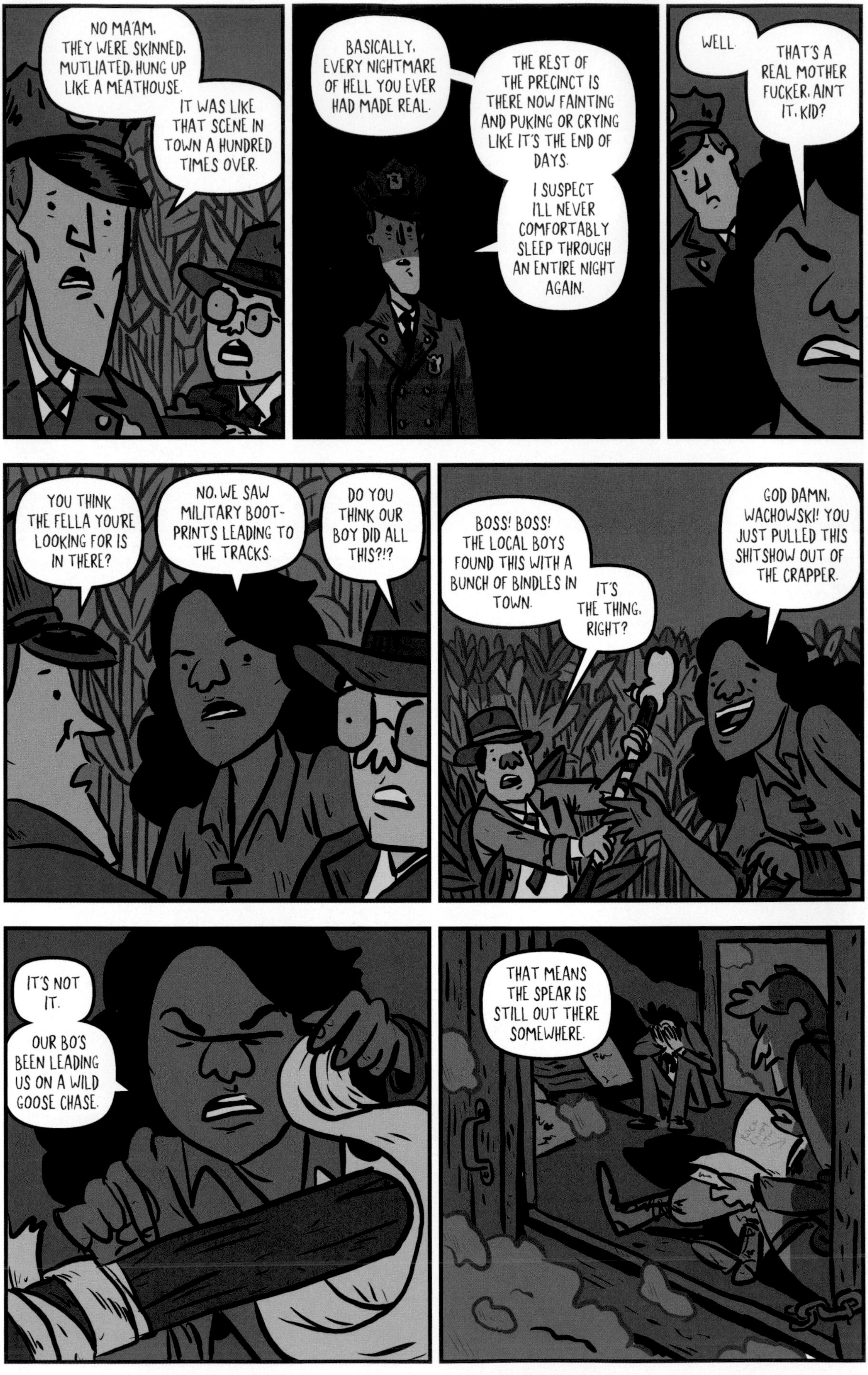
NO MA'AM. THEY WERE SKINNED. MUTLIATED. HUNG UP LIKE A MEATHOUSE.
IT WAS LIKE THAT SCENE IN TOWN A HUNDRED TIMES OVER.
BASICALLY, EVERY NIGHTMARE OF HELL YOU EVER HAD MADE REAL.
THE REST OF THE PRECINCT IS THERE NOW FAINTING AND PUKING OR CRYING LIKE IT'S THE END OF DAYS.
I SUSPECT I'LL NEVER COMFORTABLY SLEEP THROUGH AN ENTIRE NIGHT AGAIN.
WELL.
THAT'S A REAL MOTHER FUCKER, AIN'T IT, KID?
YOU THINK THE FELLA YOU'RE LOOKING FOR IS IN THERE?
NO, WE SAW MILITARY BOOT-PRINTS LEADING TO THE TRACKS.
DO YOU THINK OUR BOY DID ALL THIS?!?
BOSS! BOSS! THE LOCAL BOYS FOUND THIS WITH A BUNCH OF BINDLES IN TOWN.
IT'S THE THING, RIGHT?
GOD DAMN, WACHOWSKI! YOU JUST PULLED THIS SHITSHOW OUT OF THE CRAPPER.
IT'S NOT IT.
OUR BO'S BEEN LEADING US ON A WILD GOOSE CHASE.
THAT MEANS THE SPEAR IS STILL OUT THERE SOMEWHERE.

CHAPTER FOUR

"The jails are made of tin."

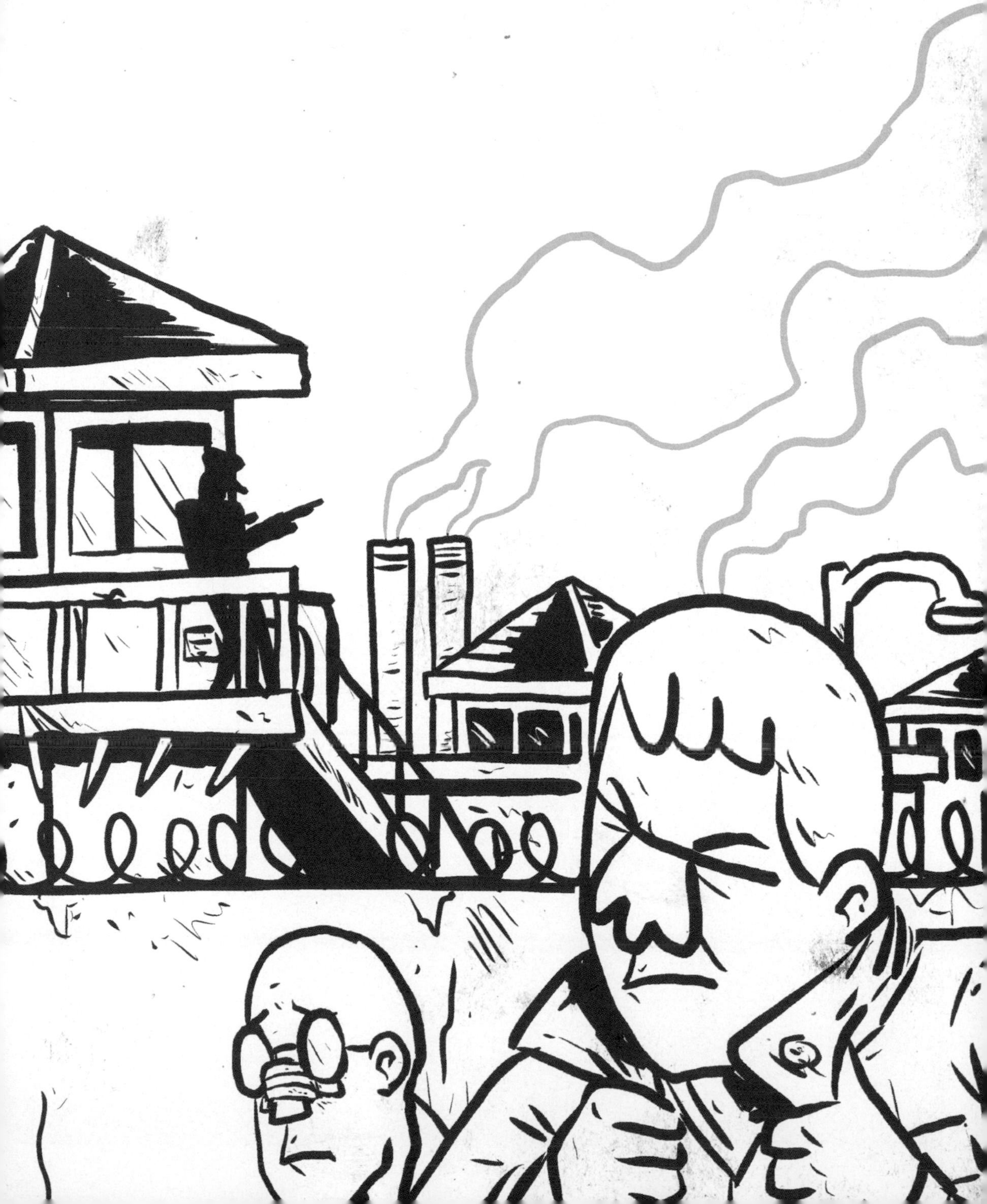

"hobos arrested
on sight."

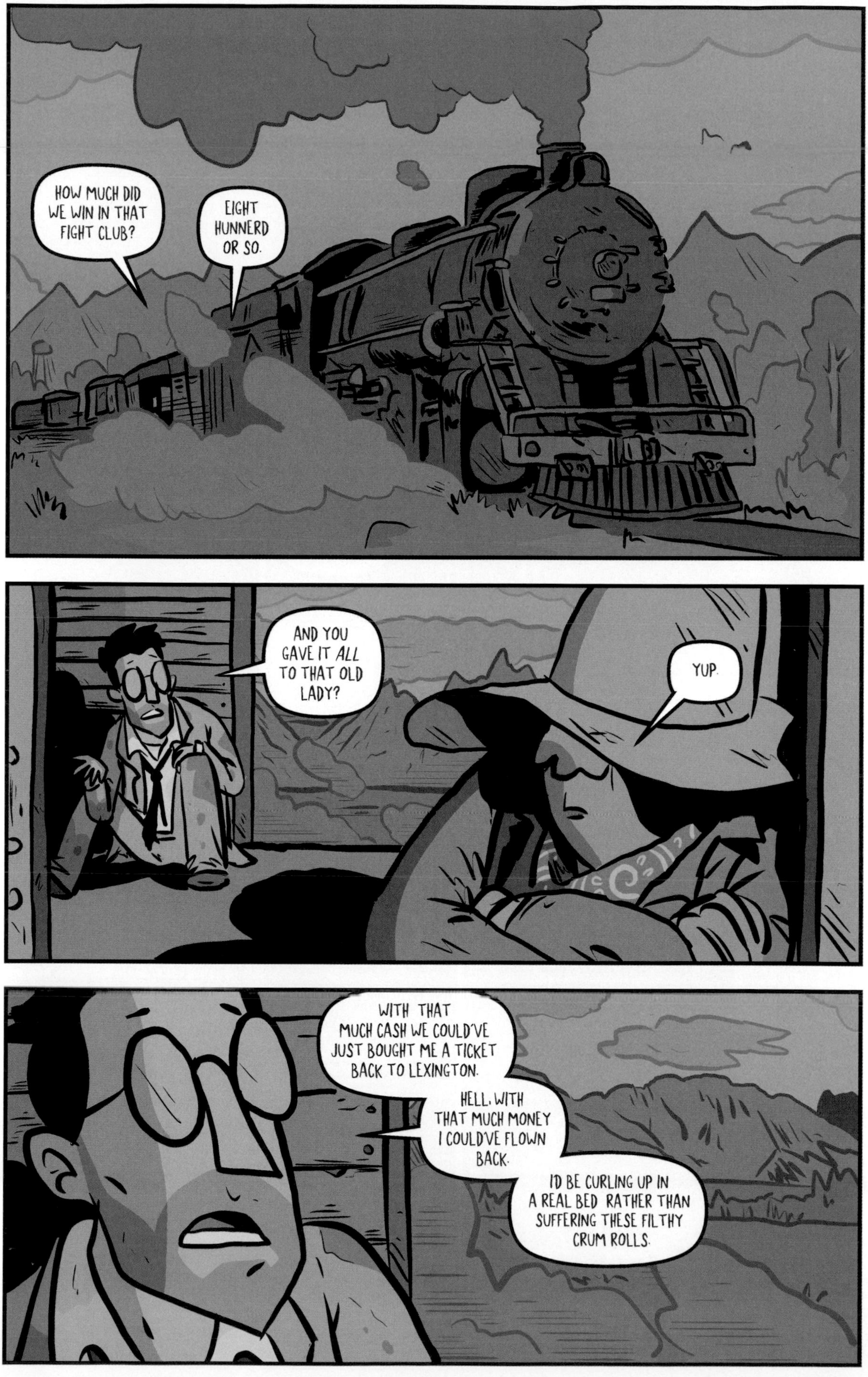
HOW MUCH DID WE WIN IN THAT FIGHT CLUB?
EIGHT HUNNERD OR SO.
AND YOU GAVE IT *ALL* TO THAT OLD LADY?
YUP.
WITH THAT MUCH CASH WE COULD'VE JUST BOUGHT ME A TICKET BACK TO LEXINGTON.
HELL, WITH THAT MUCH MONEY I COULD'VE FLOWN BACK.
I'D BE CURLING UP IN A REAL BED RATHER THAN SUFFERING THESE FILTHY CRUM ROLLS.

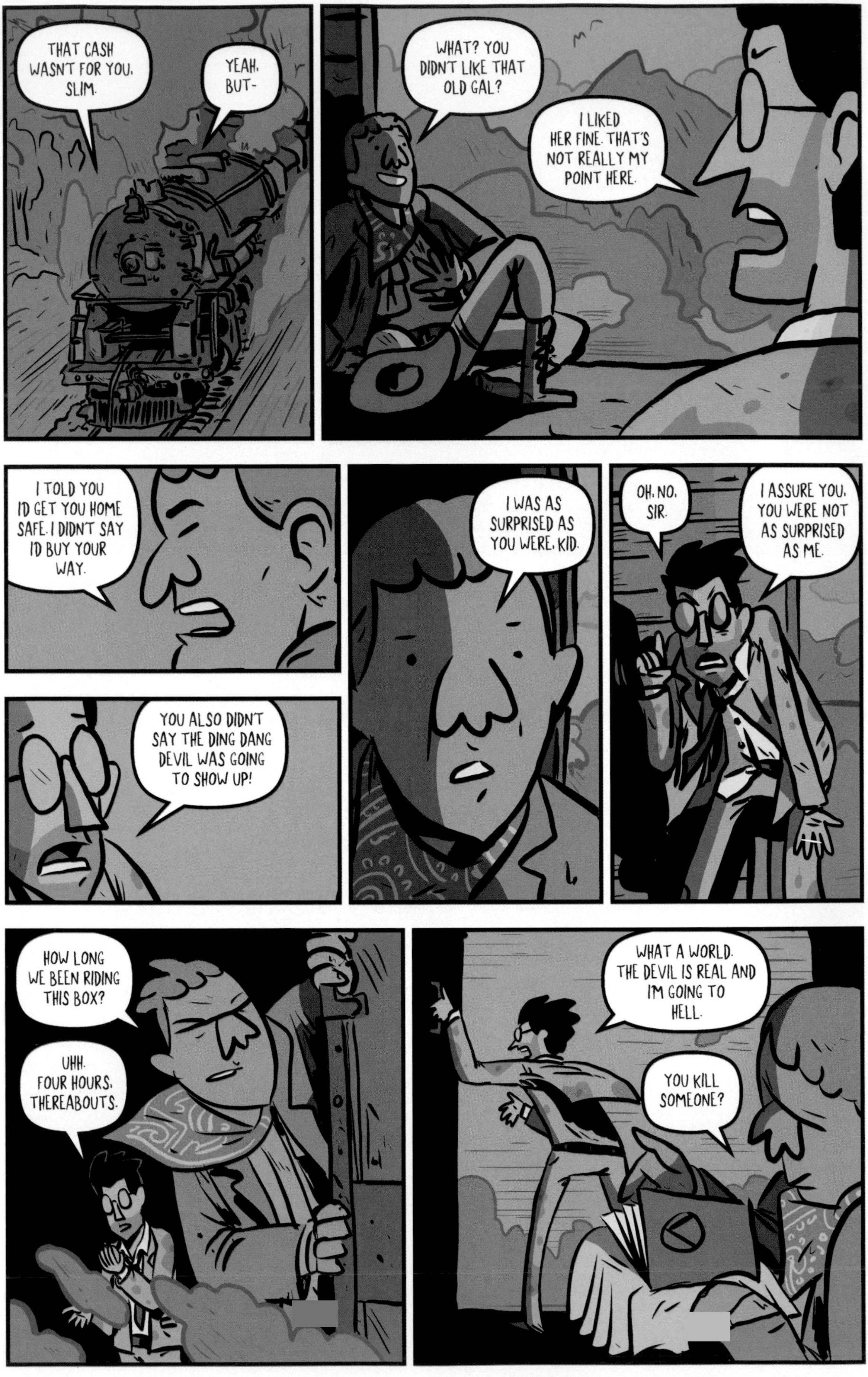
THAT CASH WASN'T FOR YOU, SLIM.
YEAH, BUT-
WHAT? YOU DIDN'T LIKE THAT OLD GAL?
I LIKED HER FINE. THAT'S NOT REALLY MY POINT HERE.
I TOLD YOU I'D GET YOU HOME SAFE. I DIDN'T SAY I'D BUY YOUR WAY.
YOU ALSO DIDN'T SAY THE DING DANG DEVIL WAS GOING TO SHOW UP!
I WAS AS SURPRISED AS YOU WERE, KID.
OH, NO, SIR.
I ASSURE YOU, YOU WERE NOT AS SURPRISED AS ME.
HOW LONG WE BEEN RIDING THIS BOX?
UHH. FOUR HOURS, THEREABOUTS.
WHAT A WORLD. THE DEVIL IS REAL AND I'M GOING TO HELL.
YOU KILL SOMEONE?

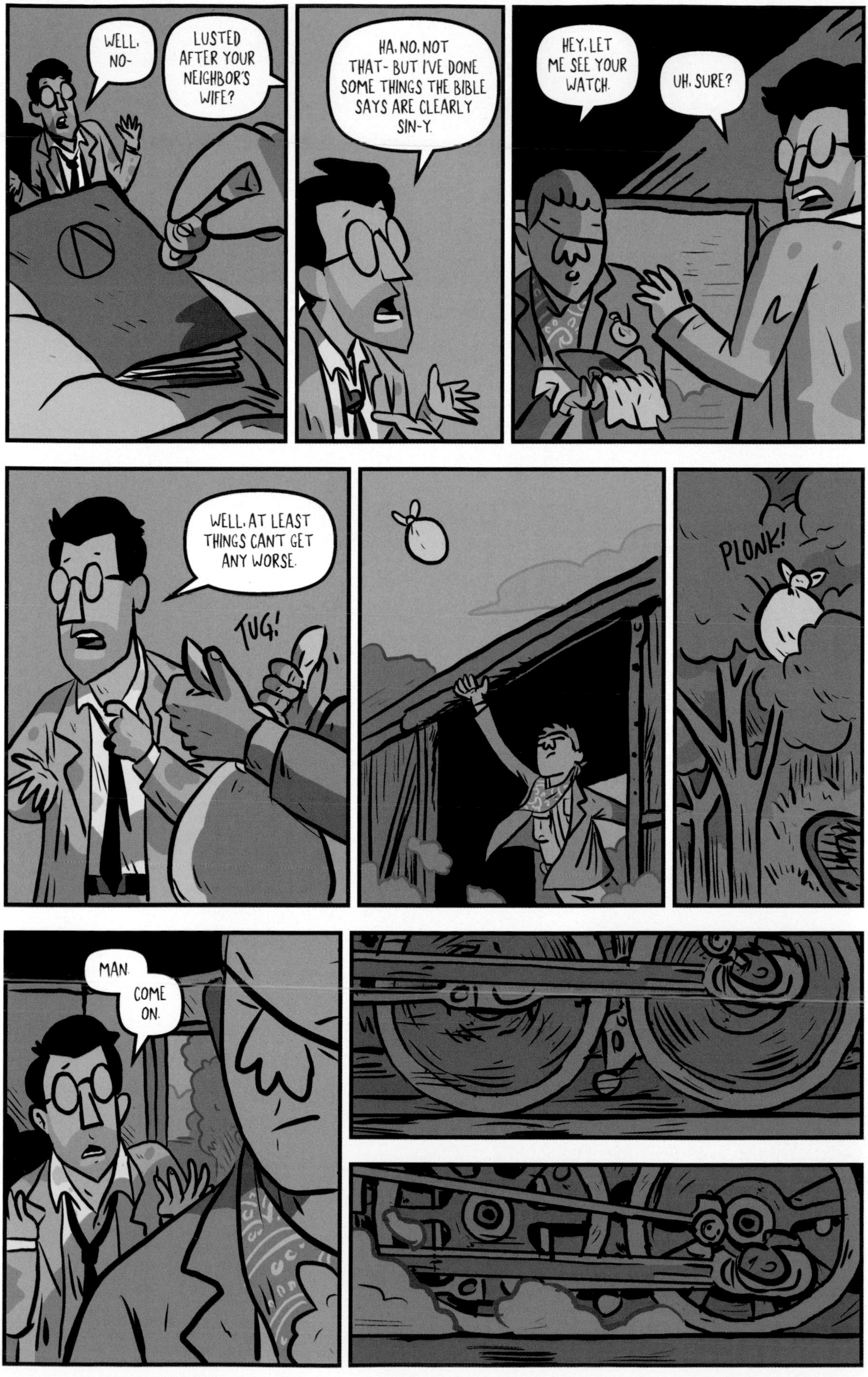
WELL. NO-
LUSTED AFTER YOUR NEIGHBOR'S WIFE?
HA. NO. NOT THAT- BUT I'VE DONE SOME THINGS THE BIBLE SAYS ARE CLEARLY SIN-Y.
HEY. LET ME SEE YOUR WATCH.
UH. SURE?
WELL. AT LEAST THINGS CAN'T GET ANY WORSE.
TUG!
PLONK!
MAN.
COME ON.

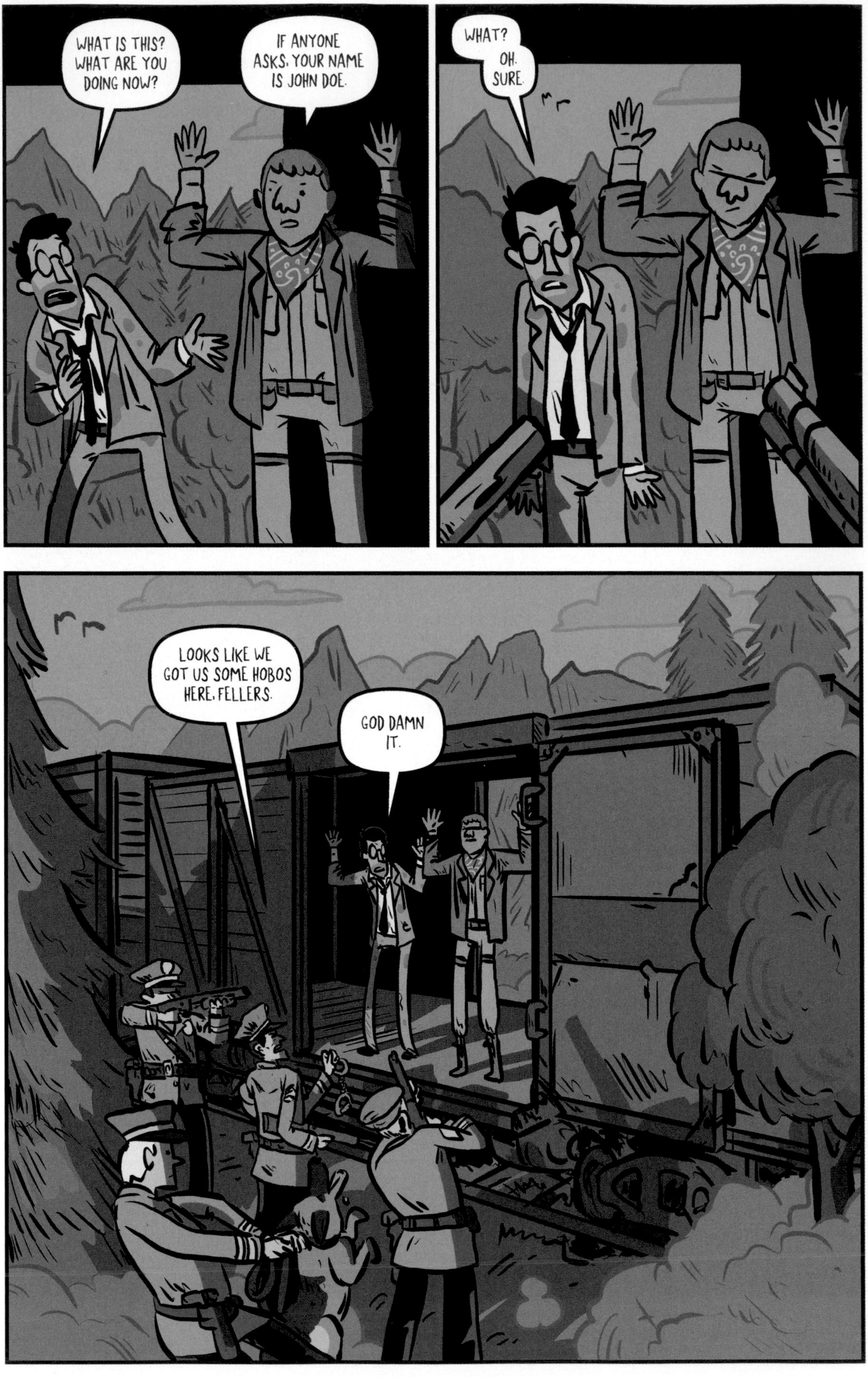
WHAT IS THIS? WHAT ARE YOU DOING NOW?
IF ANYONE ASKS, YOUR NAME IS JOHN DOE.
WHAT?
OH. SURE.
LOOKS LIKE WE GOT US SOME HOBOS HERE, FELLERS.
GOD DAMN IT.

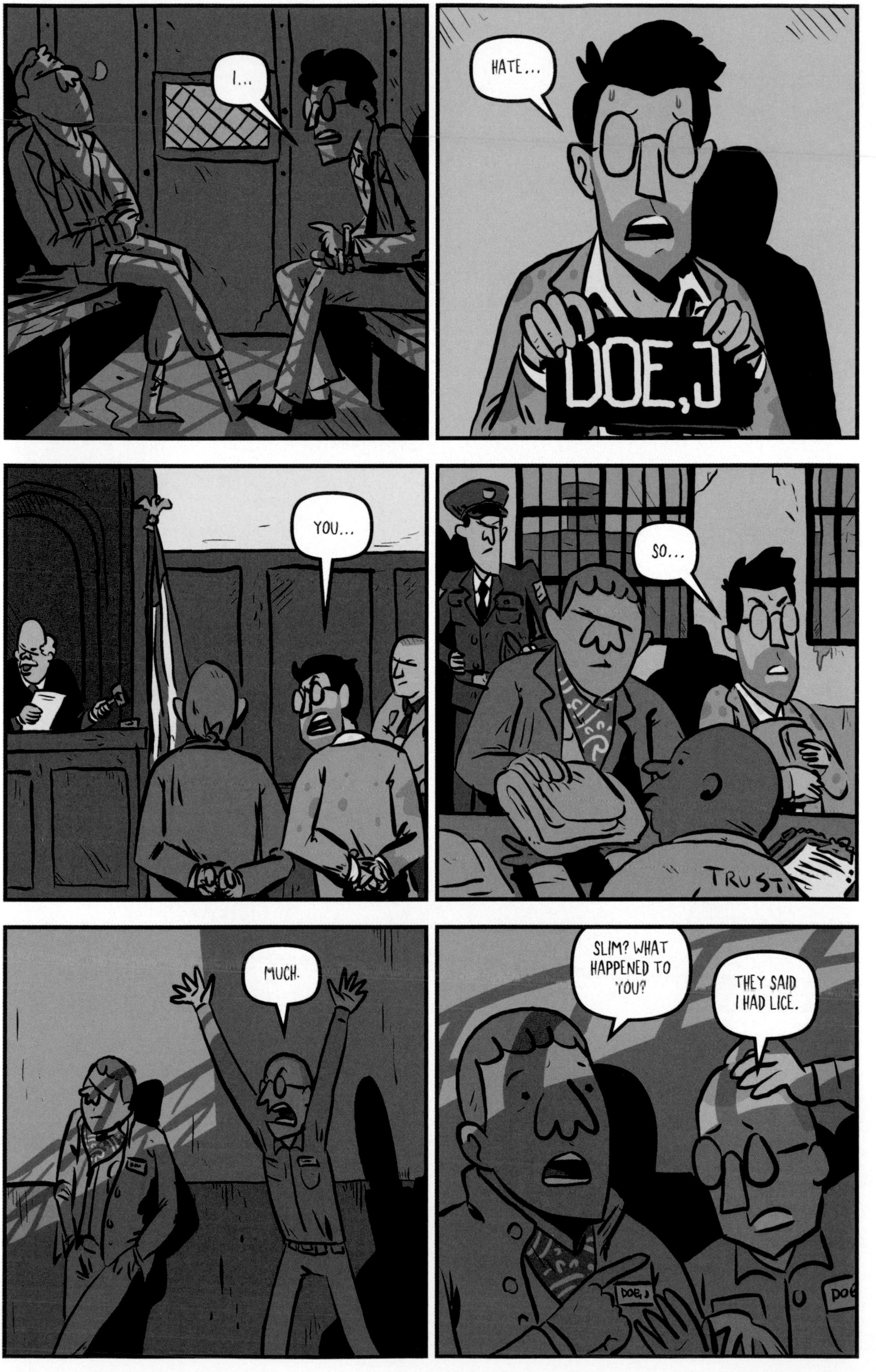
I...
HATE...
DOE, J
YOU...
SO...
TRUST
MUCH.
SLIM? WHAT HAPPENED TO YOU?
THEY SAID I HAD LICE.
DOE, J

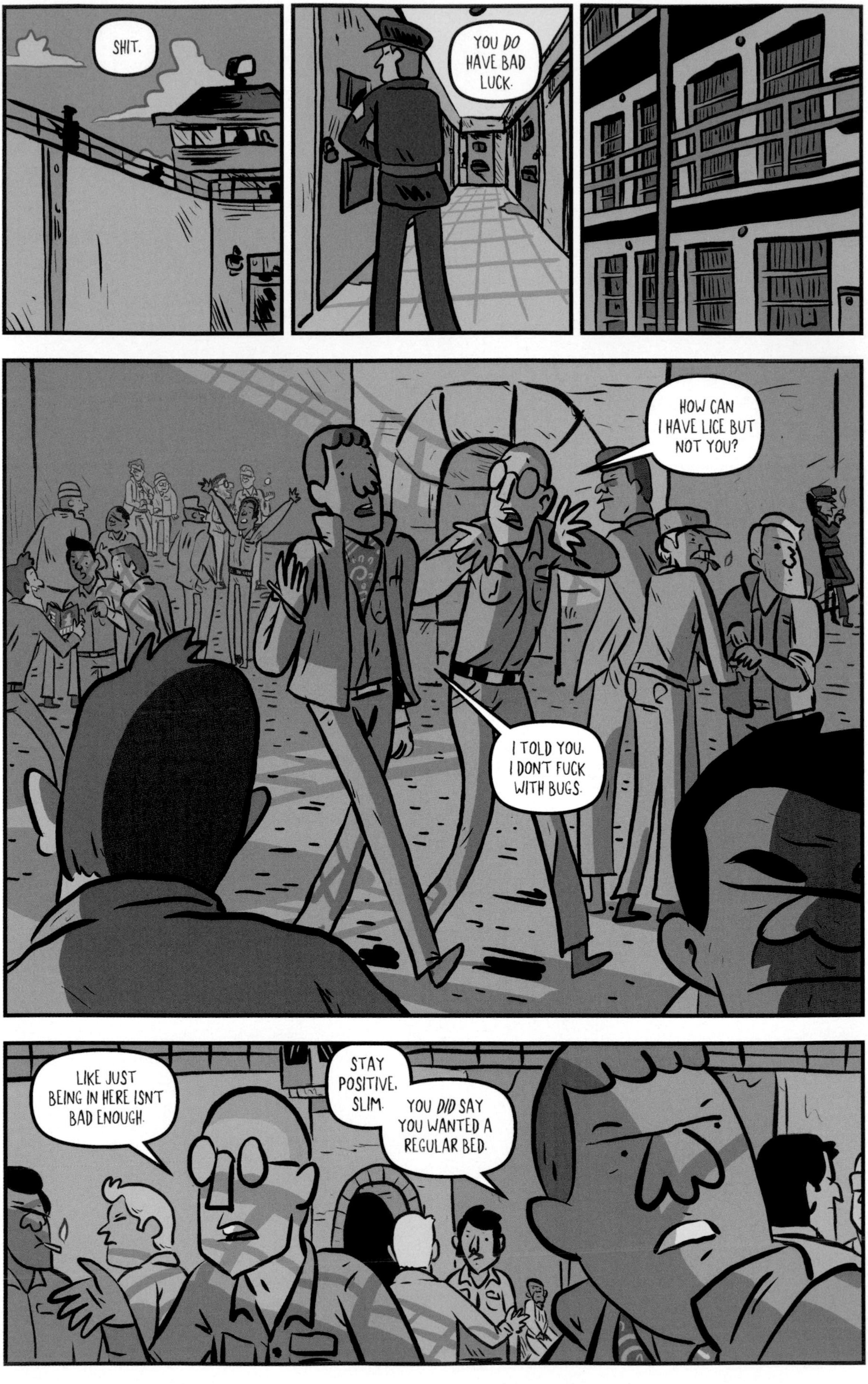
SHIT.
YOU DO HAVE BAD LUCK.
HOW CAN I HAVE LICE BUT NOT YOU?
I TOLD YOU, I DON'T FUCK WITH BUGS.
LIKE JUST BEING IN HERE ISN'T BAD ENOUGH.
STAY POSITIVE, SLIM.
YOU DID SAY YOU WANTED A REGULAR BED.

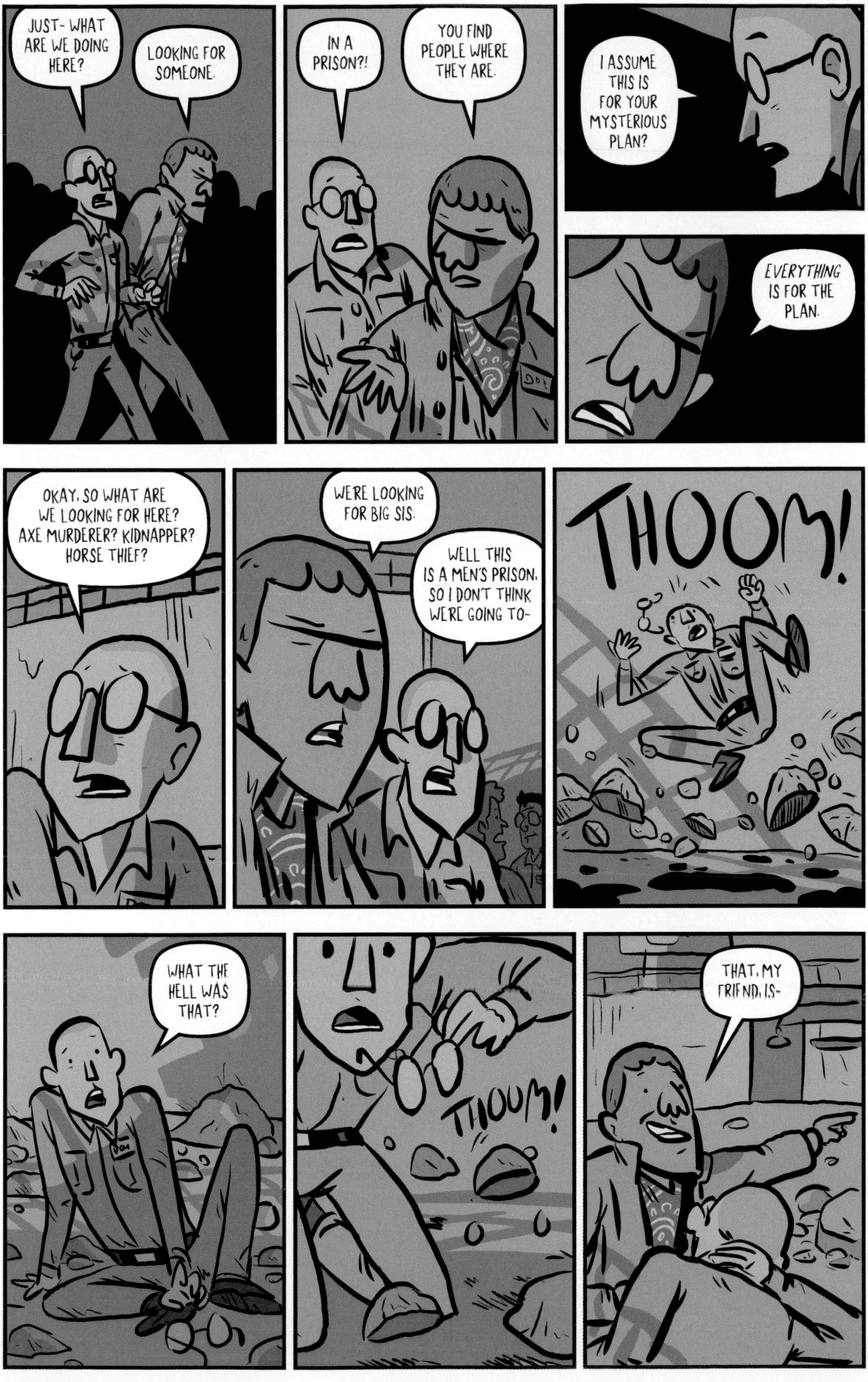
JUST- WHAT ARE WE DOING HERE?
LOOKING FOR SOMEONE.
IN A PRISON?!
YOU FIND PEOPLE WHERE THEY ARE.
I ASSUME THIS IS FOR YOUR MYSTERIOUS PLAN?
EVERYTHING IS FOR THE PLAN.
OKAY, SO WHAT ARE WE LOOKING FOR HERE? AXE MURDERER? KIDNAPPER? HORSE THIEF?
WE'RE LOOKING FOR BIG SIS.
WELL THIS IS A MEN'S PRISON, SO I DON'T THINK WE'RE GOING TO-
THOOM!
WHAT THE HELL WAS THAT?
THOOM!
THAT, MY FRIEND, IS-

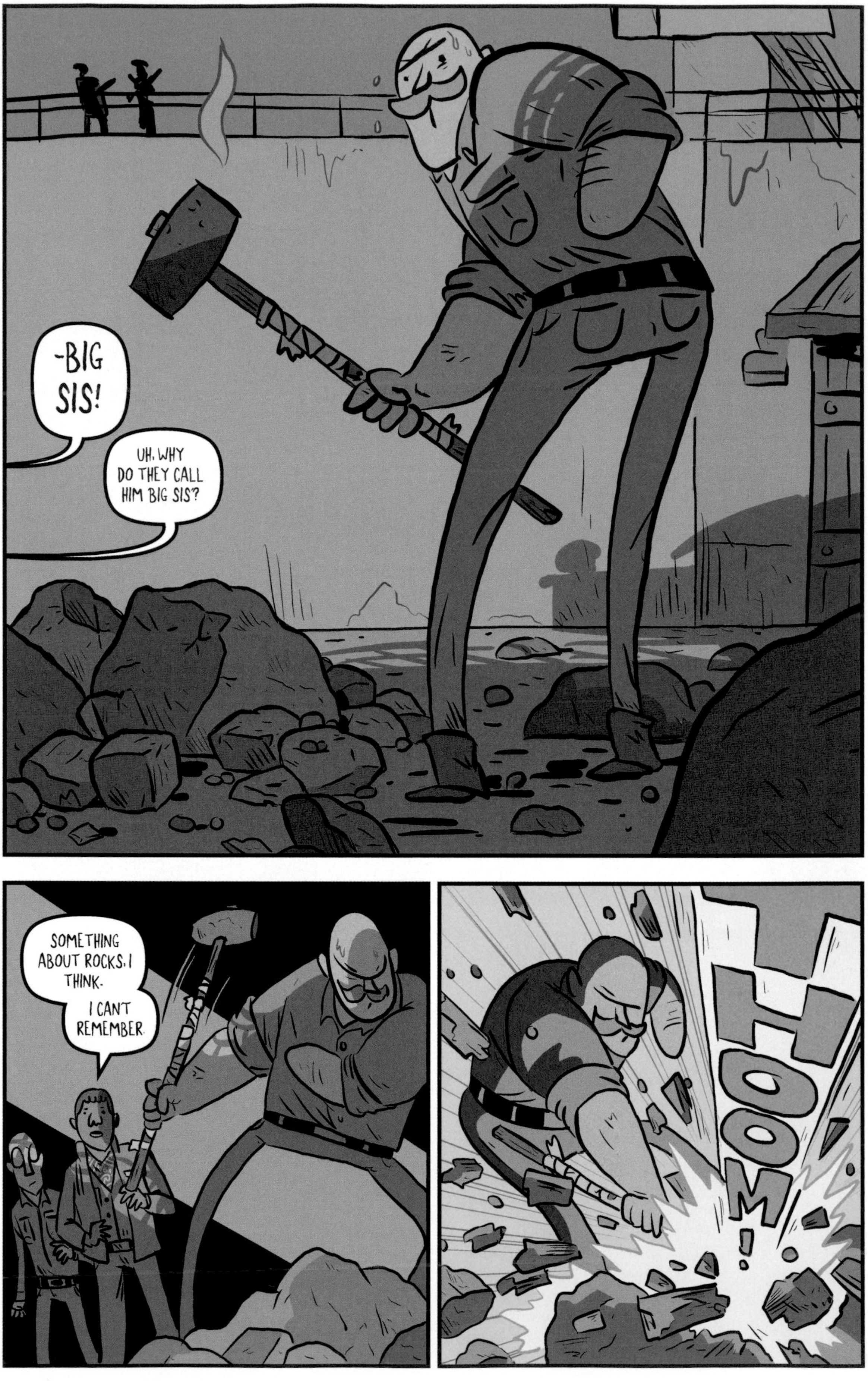

-BIG SIS!
UH, WHY DO THEY CALL HIM BIG SIS?
SOMETHING ABOUT ROCKS, I THINK.
I CAN'T REMEMBER.
HOOOM!

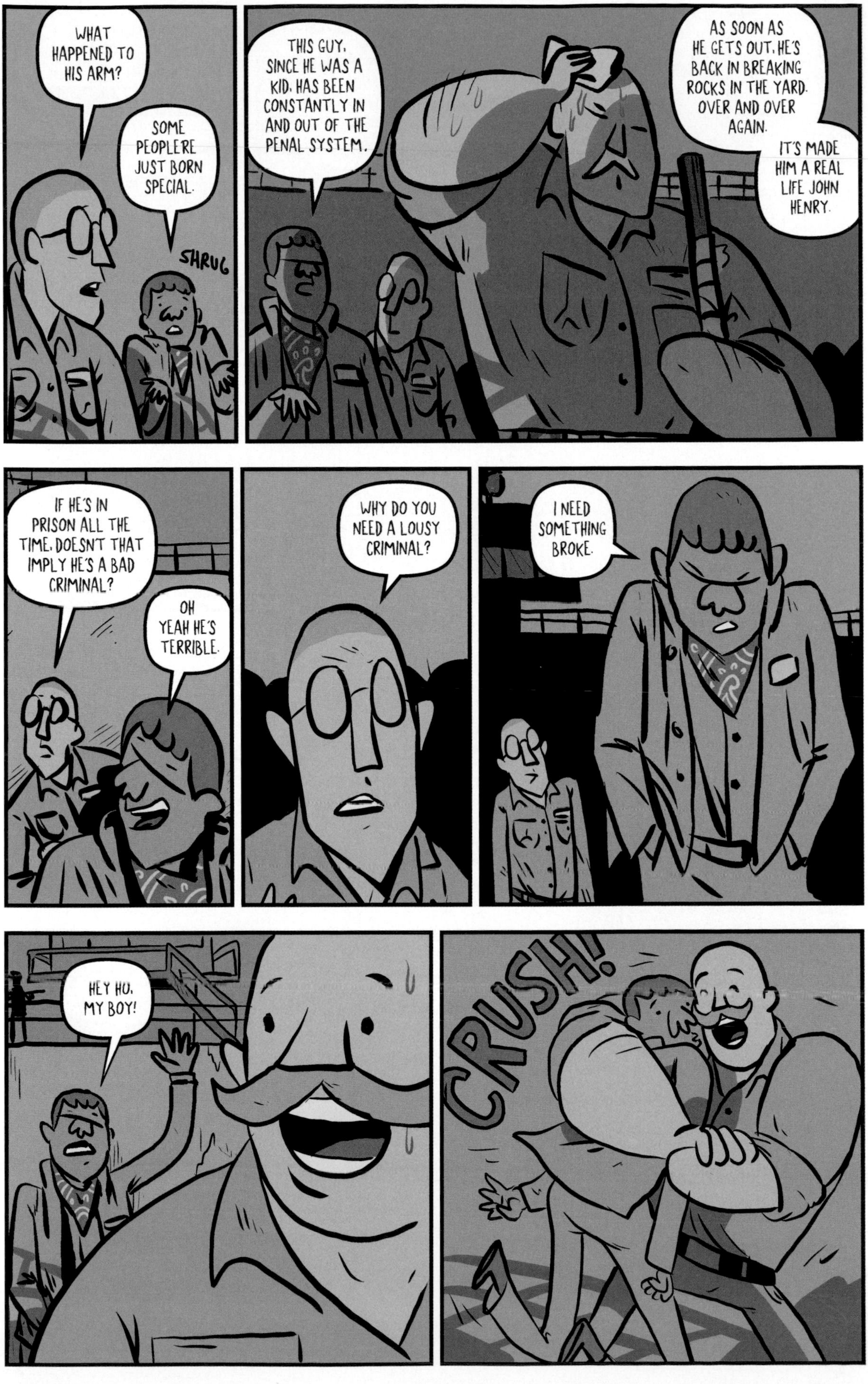
WHAT HAPPENED TO HIS ARM?
SOME PEOPLE'RE JUST BORN SPECIAL.
SHRUG
THIS GUY, SINCE HE WAS A KID, HAS BEEN CONSTANTLY IN AND OUT OF THE PENAL SYSTEM.
AS SOON AS HE GETS OUT, HE'S BACK IN BREAKING ROCKS IN THE YARD. OVER AND OVER AGAIN.
IT'S MADE HIM A REAL LIFE JOHN HENRY.
IF HE'S IN PRISON ALL THE TIME, DOESN'T THAT IMPLY HE'S A BAD CRIMINAL?
OH YEAH HE'S TERRIBLE.
WHY DO YOU NEED A LOUSY CRIMINAL?
I NEED SOMETHING BROKE.
HEY HO, MY BOY!
CRUSH!

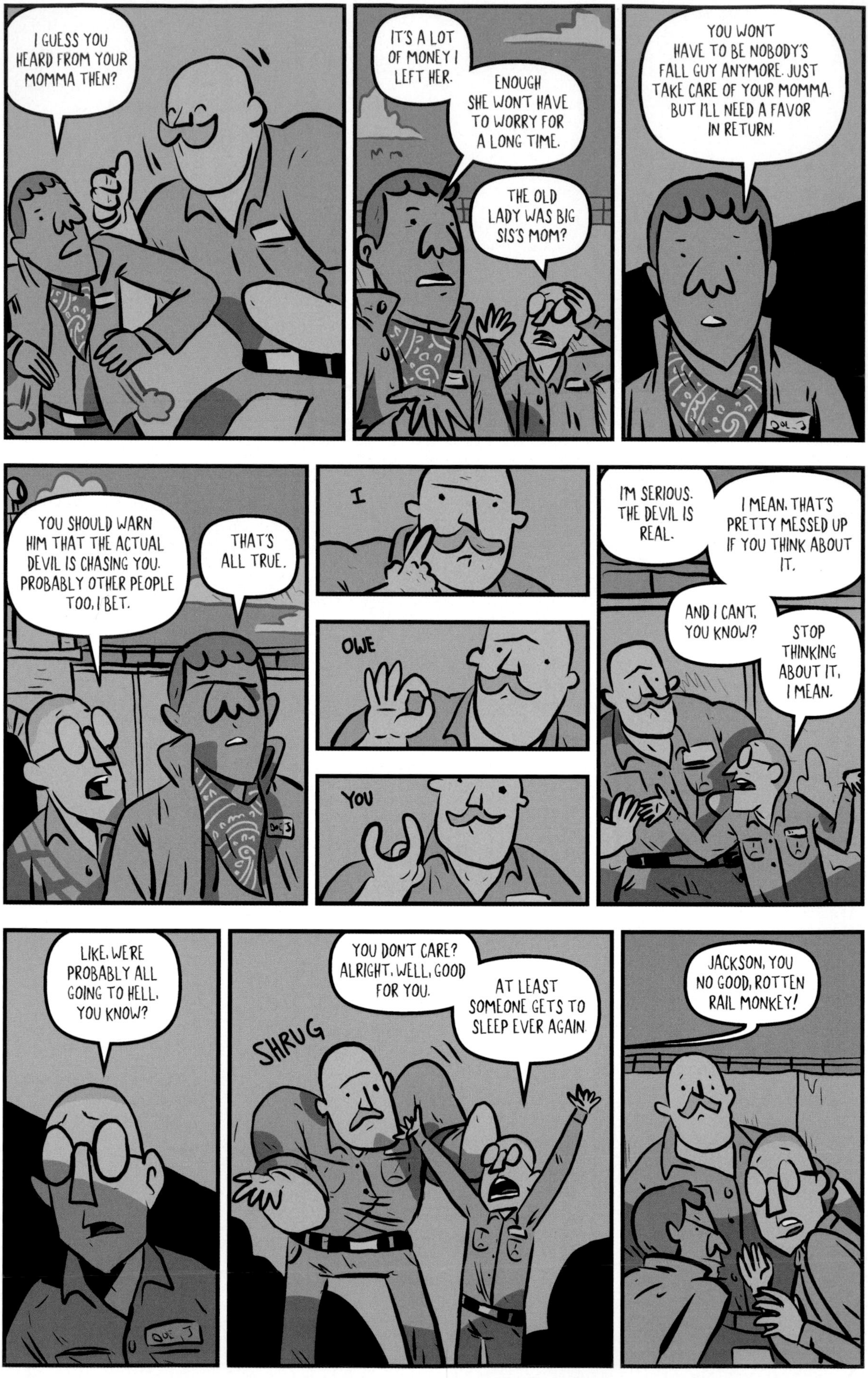
I GUESS YOU HEARD FROM YOUR MOMMA THEN?
IT'S A LOT OF MONEY I LEFT HER.
ENOUGH SHE WON'T HAVE TO WORRY FOR A LONG TIME.
THE OLD LADY WAS BIG SIS'S MOM?
YOU WON'T HAVE TO BE NOBODY'S FALL GUY ANYMORE. JUST TAKE CARE OF YOUR MOMMA. BUT I'LL NEED A FAVOR IN RETURN.
YOU SHOULD WARN HIM THAT THE ACTUAL DEVIL IS CHASING YOU. PROBABLY OTHER PEOPLE TOO, I BET.
THAT'S ALL TRUE.
I
OWE
YOU
I'M SERIOUS. THE DEVIL IS REAL.
I MEAN, THAT'S PRETTY MESSED UP IF YOU THINK ABOUT IT.
AND I CAN'T, YOU KNOW?
STOP THINKING ABOUT IT, I MEAN.
LIKE, WE'RE PROBABLY ALL GOING TO HELL, YOU KNOW?
SHRUG
YOU DON'T CARE? ALRIGHT. WELL, GOOD FOR YOU.
AT LEAST SOMEONE GETS TO SLEEP EVER AGAIN.
JACKSON, YOU NO GOOD, ROTTEN RAIL MONKEY!

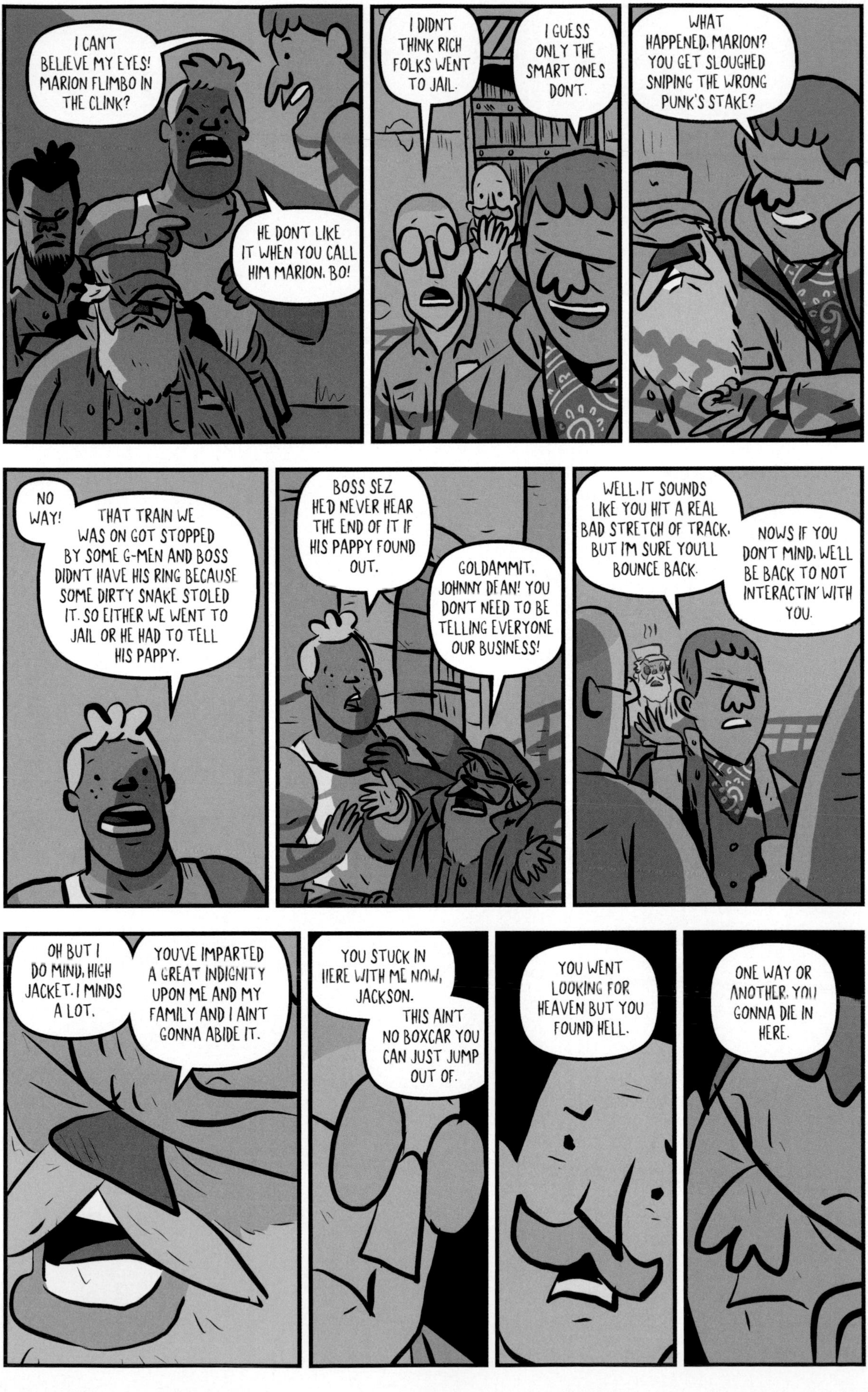
I CAN'T BELIEVE MY EYES! MARION FLIMBO IN THE CLINK?
HE DON'T LIKE IT WHEN YOU CALL HIM MARION, BO!
I DIDN'T THINK RICH FOLKS WENT TO JAIL.
I GUESS ONLY THE SMART ONES DON'T.
WHAT HAPPENED, MARION? YOU GET SLOUGHED SNIPING THE WRONG PUNK'S STAKE?
NO WAY!
THAT TRAIN WE WAS ON GOT STOPPED BY SOME G-MEN AND BOSS DIDN'T HAVE HIS RING BECAUSE SOME DIRTY SNAKE STOLED IT. SO EITHER WE WENT TO JAIL OR HE HAD TO TELL HIS PAPPY.
BOSS SEZ HE'D NEVER HEAR THE END OF IT IF HIS PAPPY FOUND OUT.
GOLDAMMIT, JOHNNY DEAN! YOU DON'T NEED TO BE TELLING EVERYONE OUR BUSINESS!
WELL, IT SOUNDS LIKE YOU HIT A REAL BAD STRETCH OF TRACK, BUT I'M SURE YOU'LL BOUNCE BACK.
NOWS IF YOU DON'T MIND, WE'LL BE BACK TO NOT INTERACTIN' WITH YOU.
OH BUT I DO MIND, HIGH JACKET. I MINDS A LOT.
YOU'VE IMPARTED A GREAT INDIGNITY UPON ME AND MY FAMILY AND I AIN'T GONNA ABIDE IT.
YOU STUCK IN HERE WITH ME NOW, JACKSON.
THIS AIN'T NO BOXCAR YOU CAN JUST JUMP OUT OF.
YOU WENT LOOKING FOR HEAVEN BUT YOU FOUND HELL.
ONE WAY OR ANOTHER, YOU GONNA DIE IN HERE.

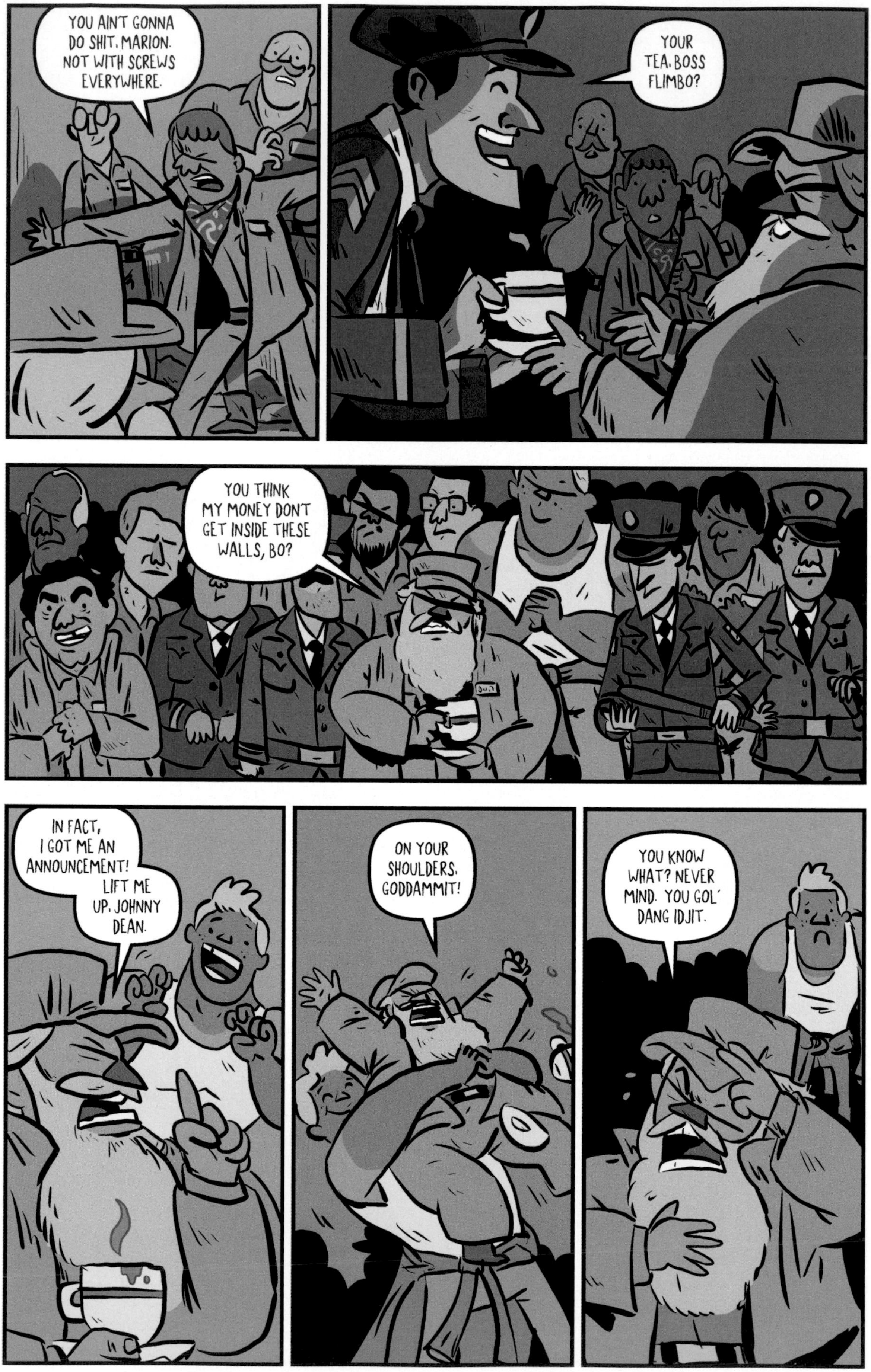
YOU AIN'T GONNA DO SHIT, MARION. NOT WITH SCREWS EVERYWHERE.
YOUR TEA, BOSS FLIMBO?
YOU THINK MY MONEY DON'T GET INSIDE THESE WALLS, BO?
IN FACT, I GOT ME AN ANNOUNCEMENT!
LIFT ME UP, JOHNNY DEAN.
ON YOUR SHOULDERS, GODDAMMIT!
YOU KNOW WHAT? NEVER MIND. YOU GOL' DANG IDJIT.

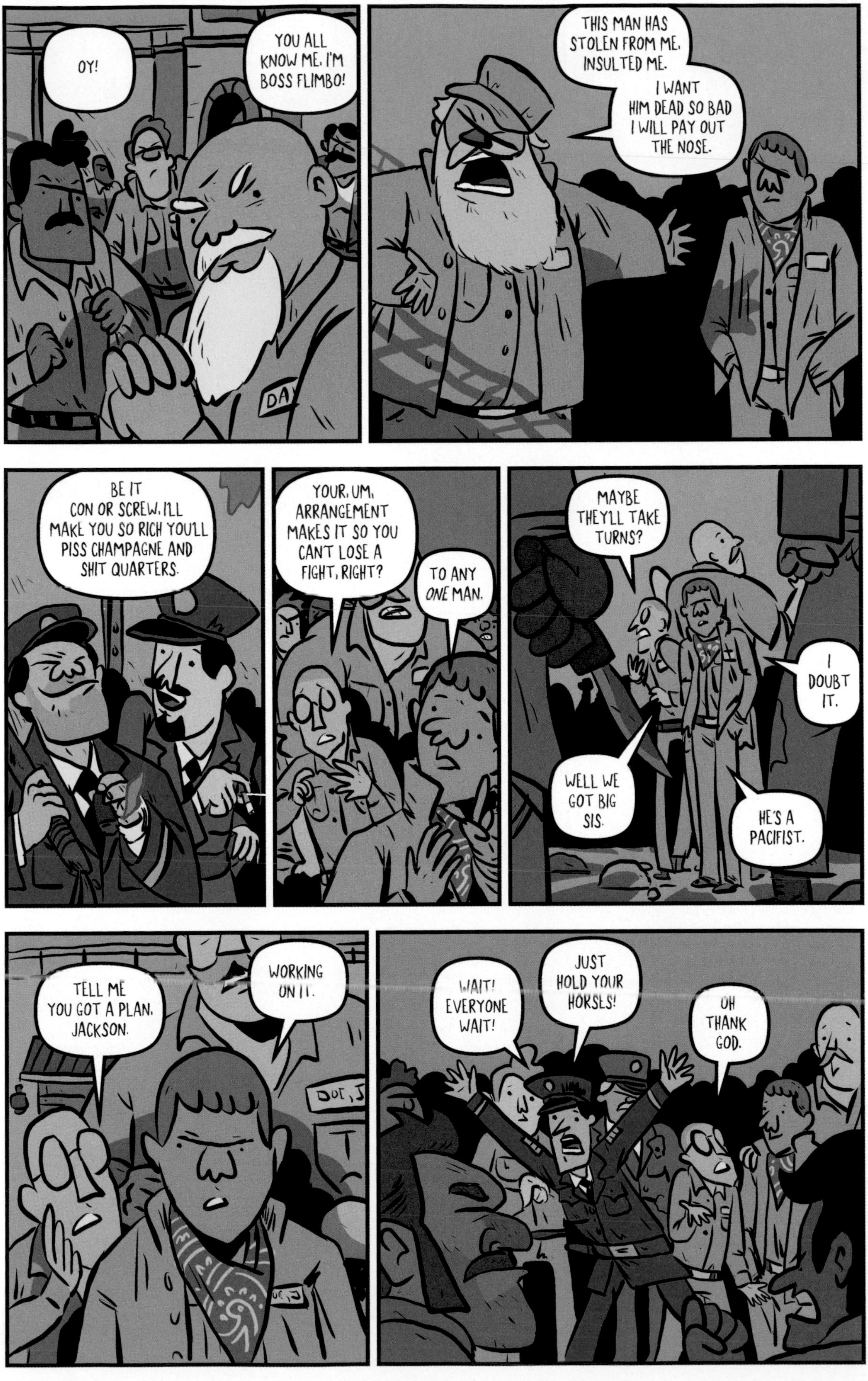
OY!
YOU ALL KNOW ME. I'M BOSS FLIMBO!
DAY
THIS MAN HAS STOLEN FROM ME, INSULTED ME.
I WANT HIM DEAD SO BAD I WILL PAY OUT THE NOSE.
BE IT CON OR SCREW, I'LL MAKE YOU SO RICH YOU'LL PISS CHAMPAGNE AND SHIT QUARTERS.
YOUR, UM, ARRANGEMENT MAKES IT SO YOU CAN'T LOSE A FIGHT, RIGHT?
TO ANY *ONE* MAN.
MAYBE THEY'LL TAKE TURNS?
I DOUBT IT.
WELL WE GOT BIG SIS.
HE'S A PACIFIST.
TELL ME YOU GOT A PLAN, JACKSON.
WORKING ON IT.
DOE, J
WAIT! EVERYONE WAIT!
JUST HOLD YOUR HORSES!
OH THANK GOD.

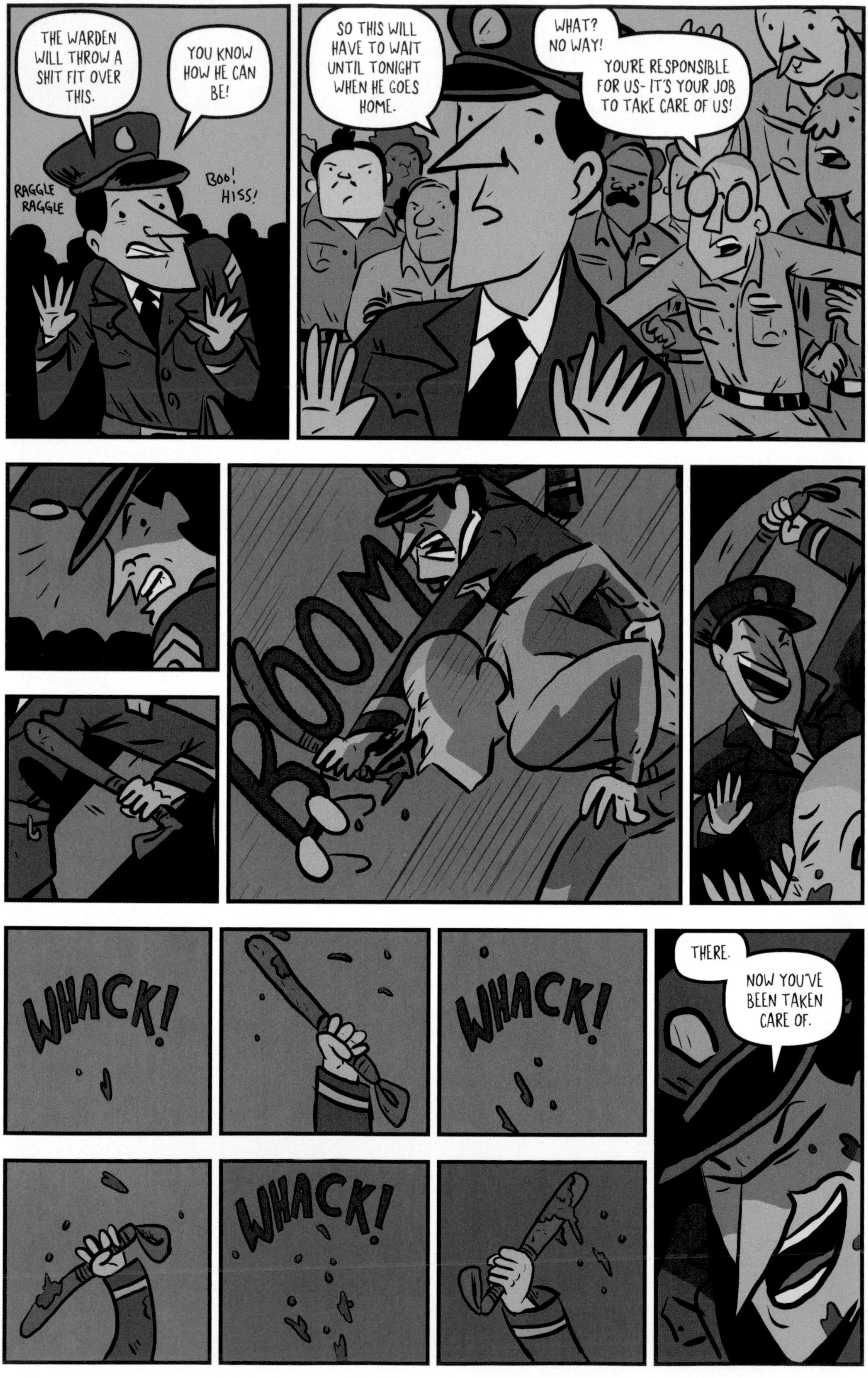
THE WARDEN WILL THROW A SHIT FIT OVER THIS.
YOU KNOW HOW HE CAN BE!
RAGGLE RAGGLE
BOO! HISS!
SO THIS WILL HAVE TO WAIT UNTIL TONIGHT WHEN HE GOES HOME.
WHAT? NO WAY!
YOU'RE RESPONSIBLE FOR US- IT'S YOUR JOB TO TAKE CARE OF US!
BOOM
WHACK!
WHACK!
WHACK!
THERE.
NOW YOU'VE BEEN TAKEN CARE OF.

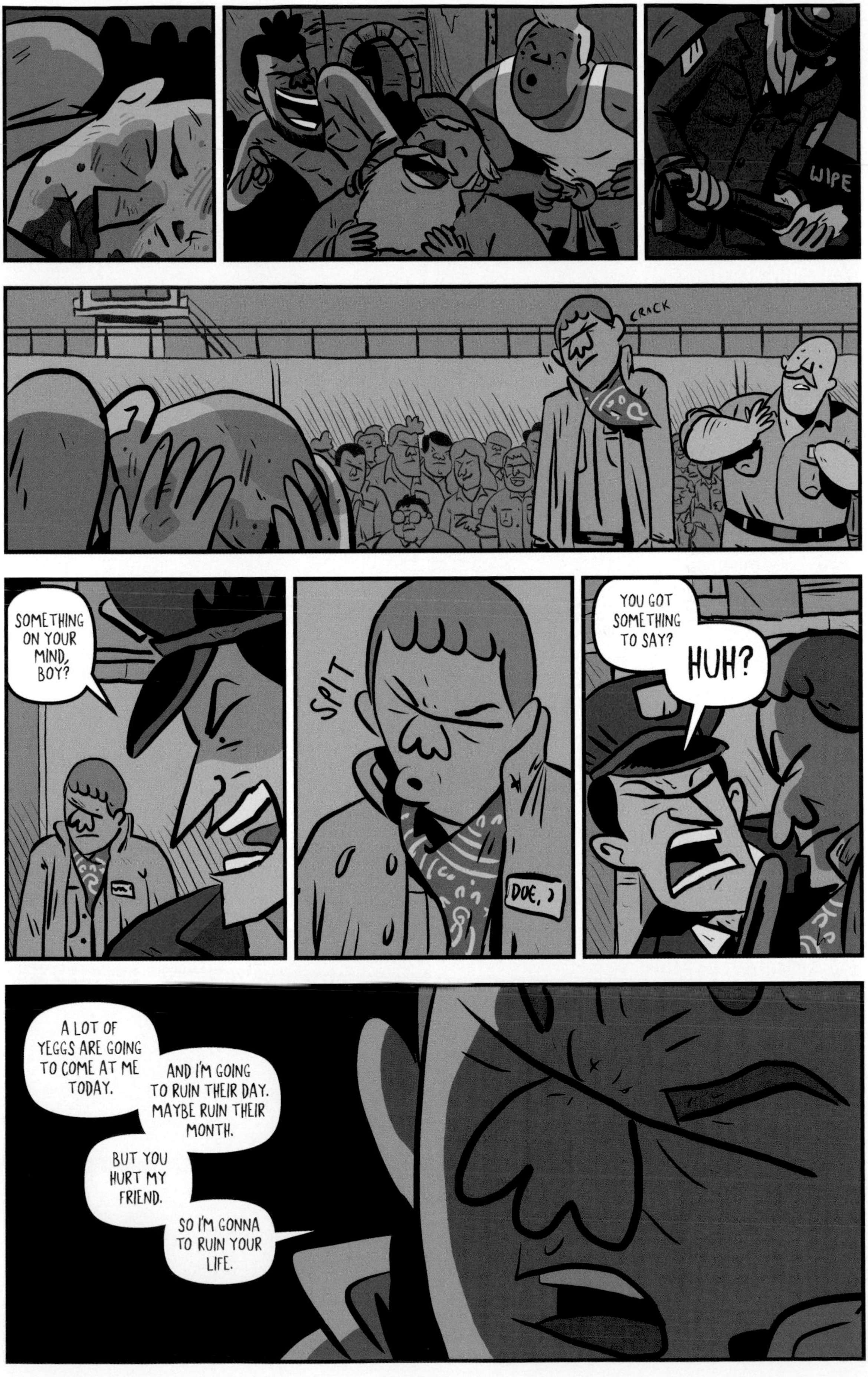
WIPE
CRACK
SOMETHING ON YOUR MIND, BOY?
SPIT
DOE, J
YOU GOT SOMETHING TO SAY?
HUH?
A LOT OF YEGGS ARE GOING TO COME AT ME TODAY.
AND I'M GOING TO RUIN THEIR DAY. MAYBE RUIN THEIR MONTH.
BUT YOU HURT MY FRIEND.
SO I'M GONNA TO RUIN YOUR LIFE.

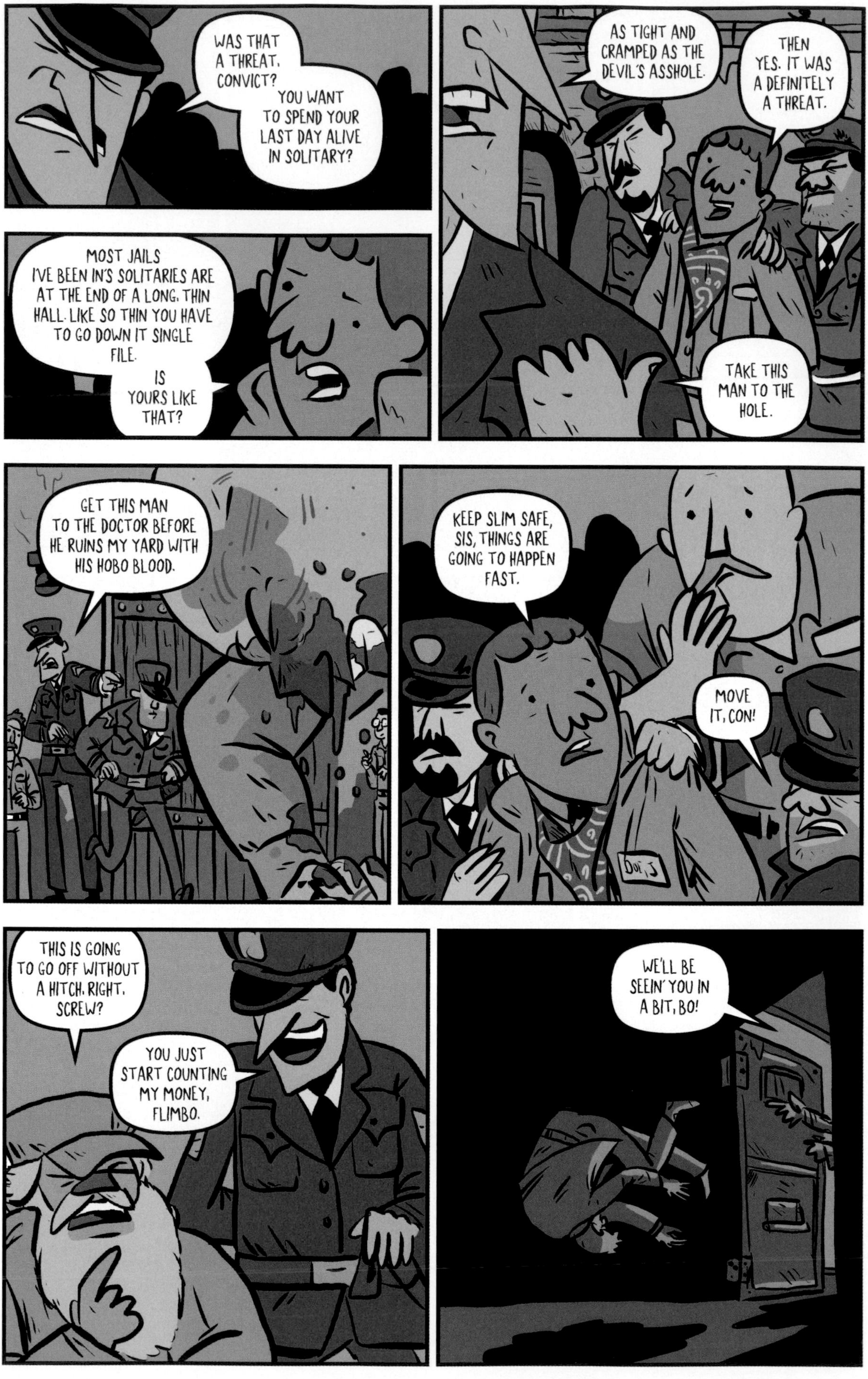
WAS THAT A THREAT, CONVICT?
YOU WANT TO SPEND YOUR LAST DAY ALIVE IN SOLITARY?
MOST JAILS I'VE BEEN IN'S SOLITARIES ARE AT THE END OF A LONG, THIN HALL. LIKE SO THIN YOU HAVE TO GO DOWN IT SINGLE FILE.
IS YOURS LIKE THAT?
AS TIGHT AND CRAMPED AS THE DEVIL'S ASSHOLE.
THEN YES. IT WAS A DEFINITELY A THREAT.
TAKE THIS MAN TO THE HOLE.
GET THIS MAN TO THE DOCTOR BEFORE HE RUINS MY YARD WITH HIS HOBO BLOOD.
KEEP SLIM SAFE, SIS, THINGS ARE GOING TO HAPPEN FAST.
MOVE IT, CON!
THIS IS GOING TO GO OFF WITHOUT A HITCH, RIGHT, SCREW?
YOU JUST START COUNTING MY MONEY, FLIMBO.
WE'LL BE SEEIN' YOU IN A BIT, BO!

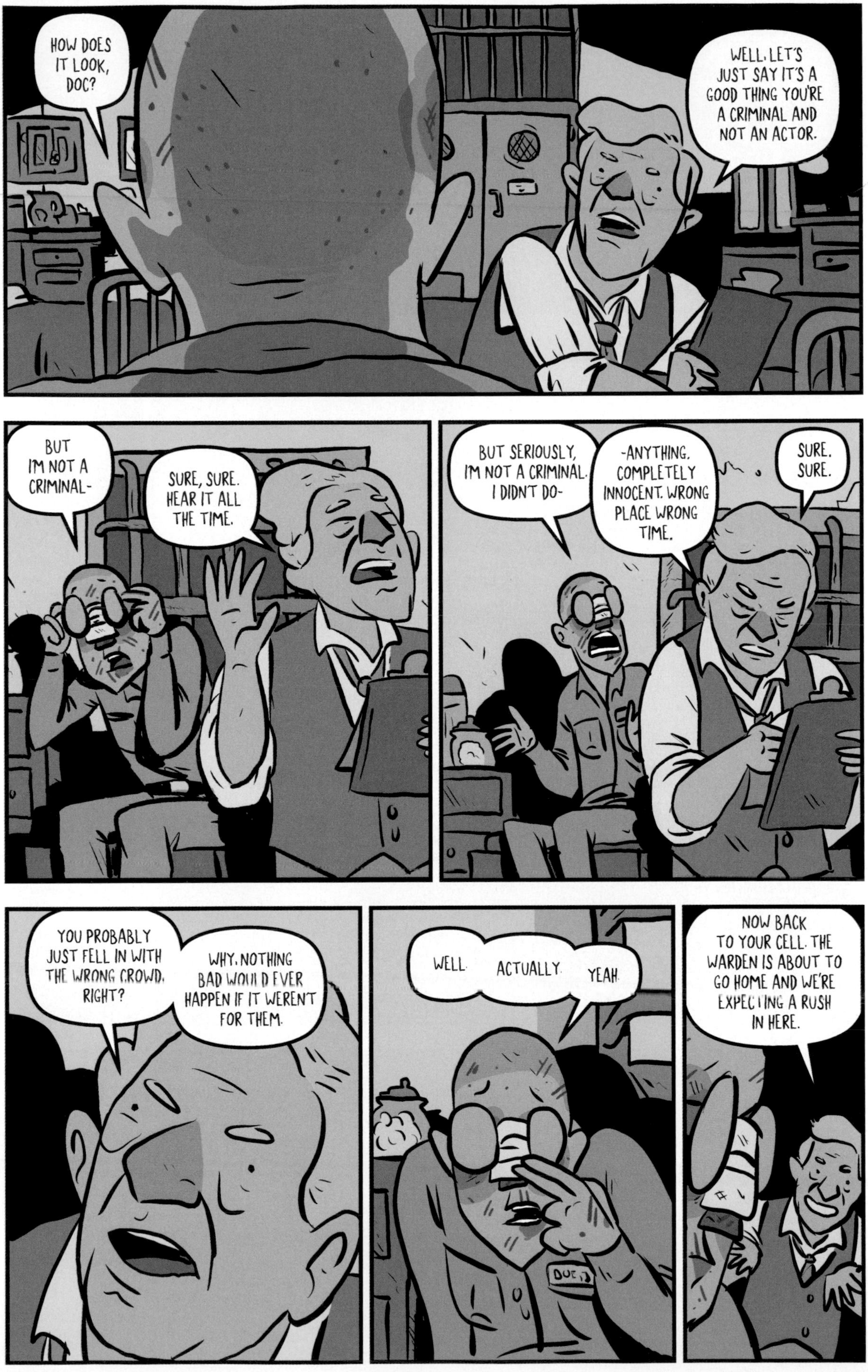
HOW DOES IT LOOK, DOC?
WELL, LET'S JUST SAY IT'S A GOOD THING YOU'RE A CRIMINAL AND NOT AN ACTOR.
BUT I'M NOT A CRIMINAL-
SURE, SURE. HEAR IT ALL THE TIME.
BUT SERIOUSLY, I'M NOT A CRIMINAL. I DIDN'T DO-
-ANYTHING. COMPLETELY INNOCENT. WRONG PLACE WRONG TIME.
SURE. SURE.
YOU PROBABLY JUST FELL IN WITH THE WRONG CROWD, RIGHT?
WHY, NOTHING BAD WOULD EVER HAPPEN IF IT WEREN'T FOR THEM.
WELL. ACTUALLY. YEAH.
NOW BACK TO YOUR CELL. THE WARDEN IS ABOUT TO GO HOME AND WE'RE EXPECTING A RUSH IN HERE.

BYE WARDEN, HAVE A NICE WEEKEND!

LET'S OPEN THOSE CELLS AND KILL US A HOBO!

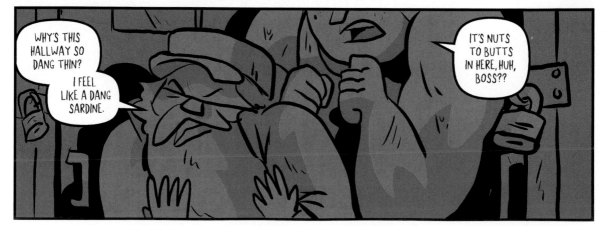

WHY'S THIS HALLWAY SO DANG THIN?

I FEEL LIKE A DANG SARDINE.

IT'S NUTS TO BUTTS IN HERE, HUH, BOSS??

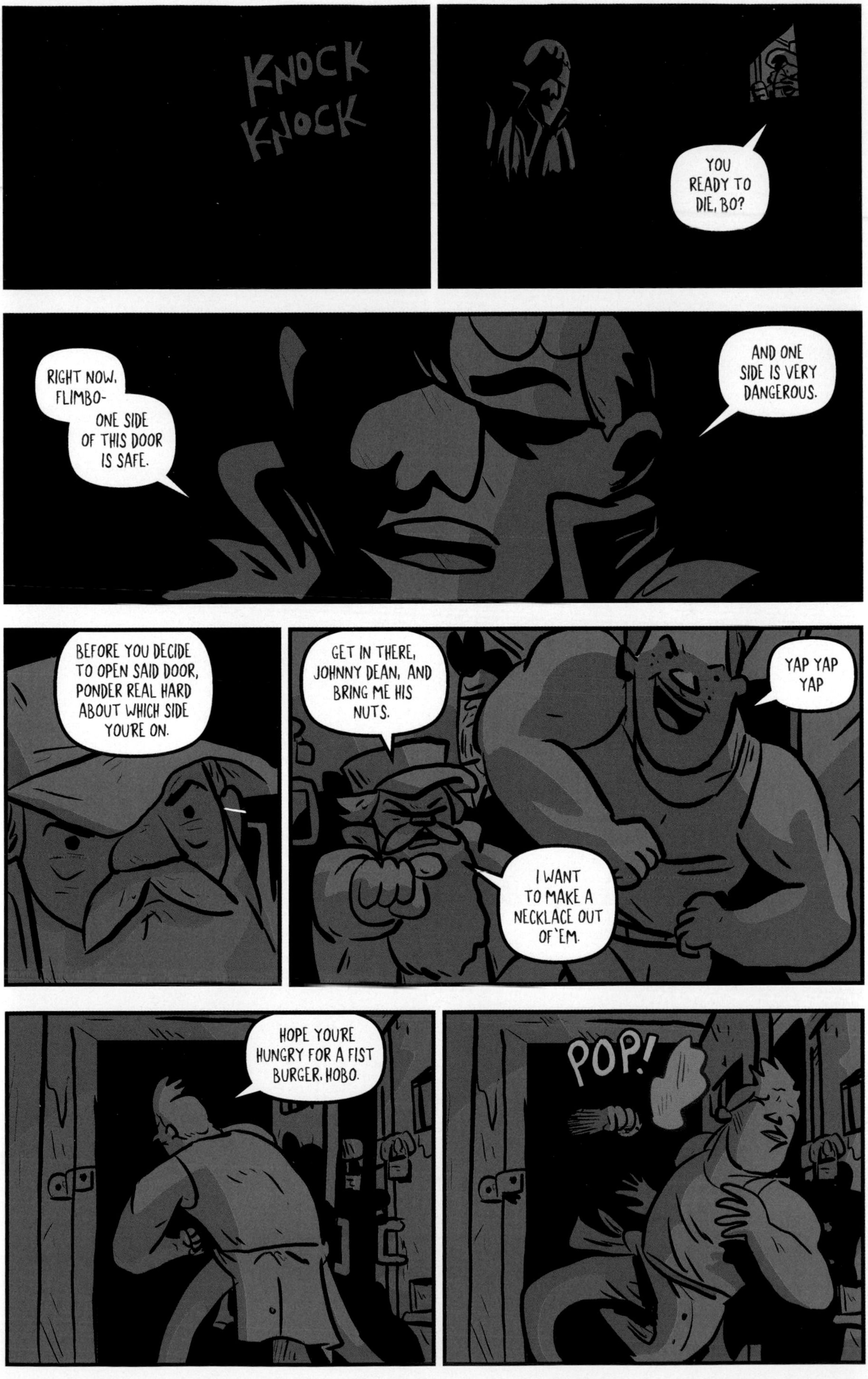
KNOCK KNOCK
YOU READY TO DIE, BO?
RIGHT NOW, FLIMBO-
ONE SIDE OF THIS DOOR IS SAFE.
AND ONE SIDE IS VERY DANGEROUS.
BEFORE YOU DECIDE TO OPEN SAID DOOR, PONDER REAL HARD ABOUT WHICH SIDE YOU'RE ON.
GET IN THERE, JOHNNY DEAN, AND BRING ME HIS NUTS.
YAP YAP YAP
I WANT TO MAKE A NECKLACE OUT OF 'EM.
HOPE YOU'RE HUNGRY FOR A FIST BURGER, HOBO.
POP!

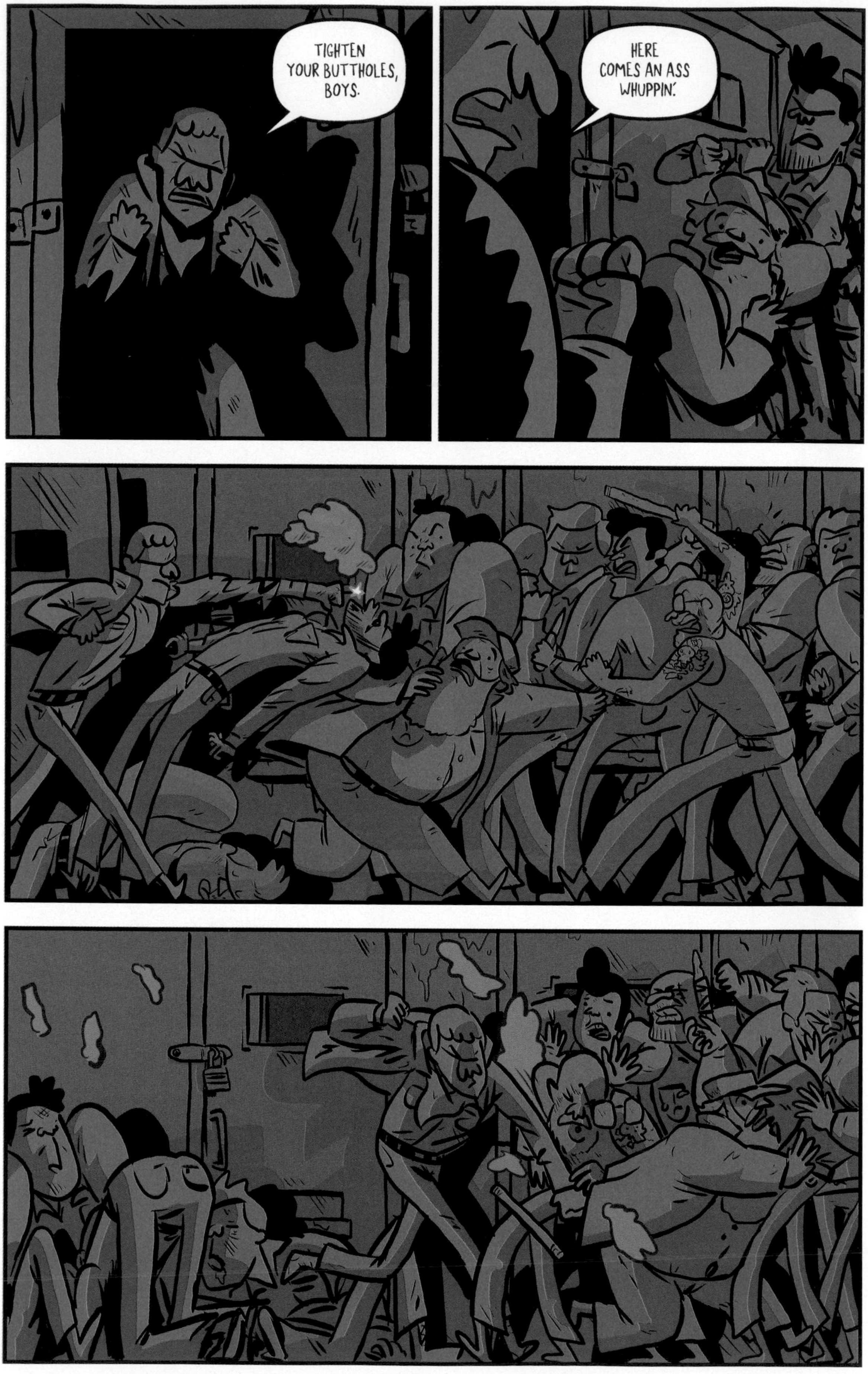
TIGHTEN YOUR BUTTHOLES, BOYS.
HERE COMES AN ASS WHUPPIN'.

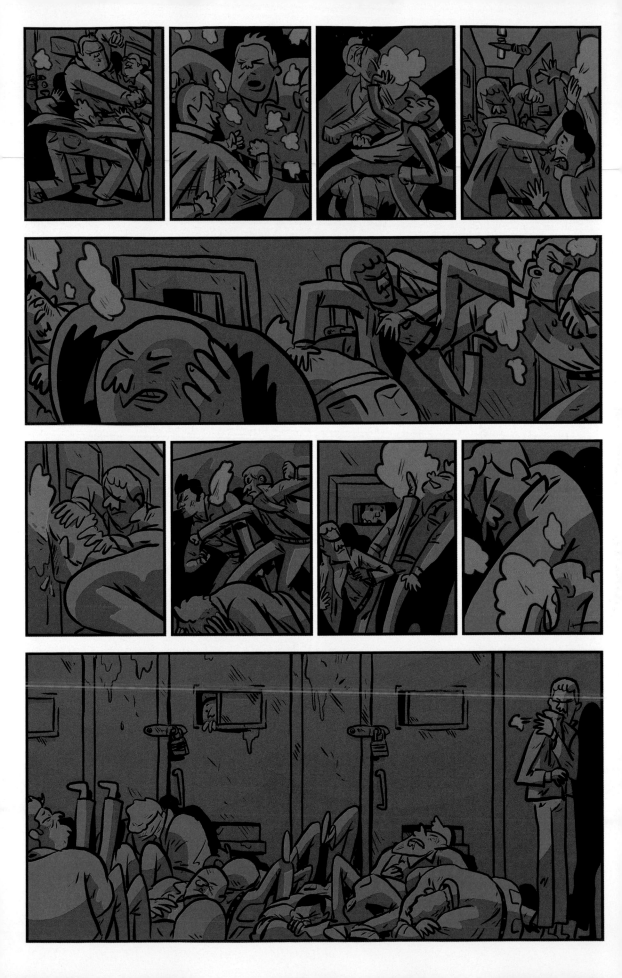

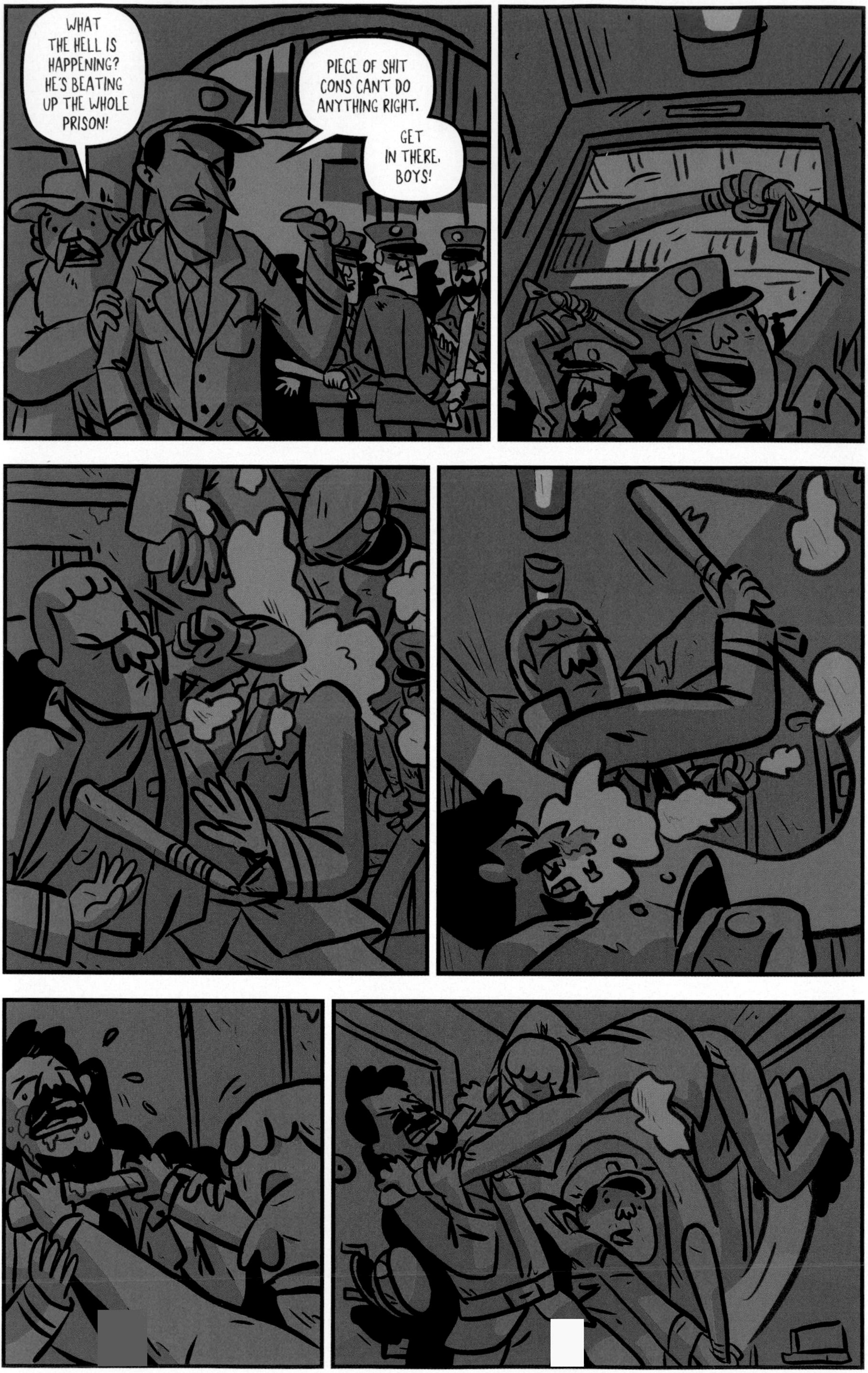
WHAT THE HELL IS HAPPENING? HE'S BEATING UP THE WHOLE PRISON!
PIECE OF SHIT CONS CAN'T DO ANYTHING RIGHT.
GET IN THERE, BOYS!

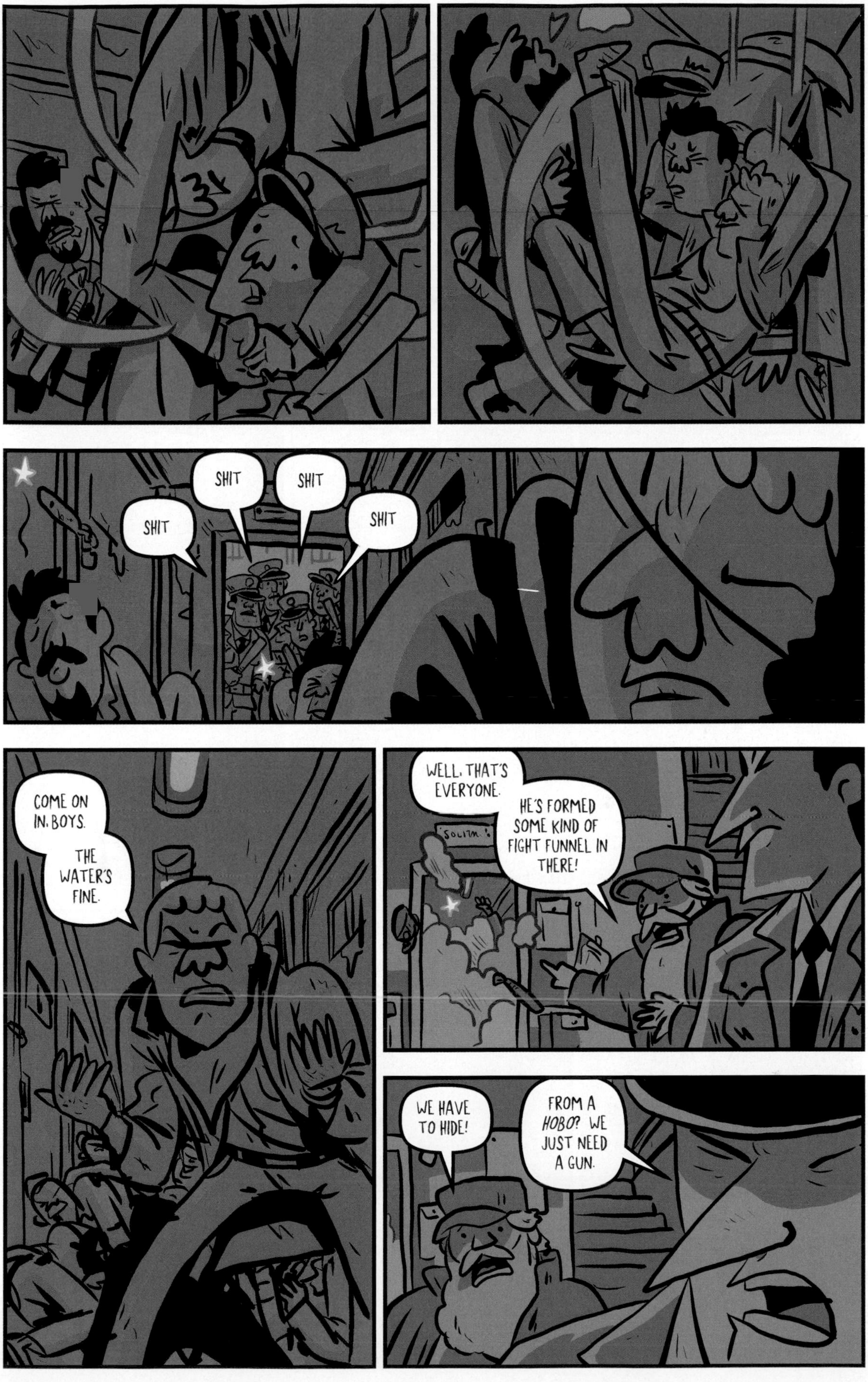
SHIT
SHIT
SHIT
SHIT
COME ON IN, BOYS.
THE WATER'S FINE.
WELL, THAT'S EVERYONE.
HE'S FORMED SOME KIND OF FIGHT FUNNEL IN THERE!
WE HAVE TO HIDE!
FROM A *HOBO*? WE JUST NEED A GUN.

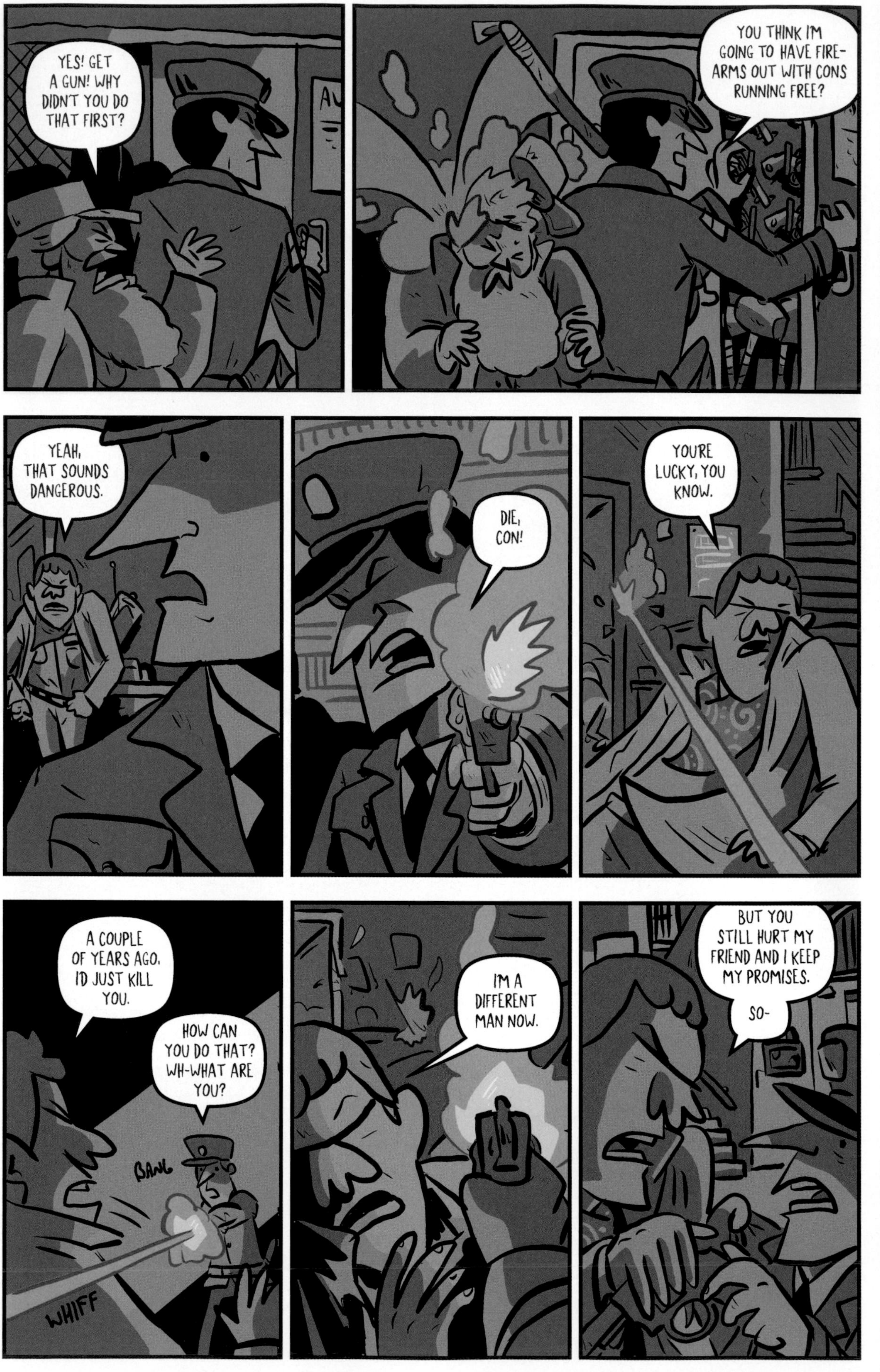
YES! GET A GUN! WHY DIDN'T YOU DO THAT FIRST?
YOU THINK I'M GOING TO HAVE FIRE-ARMS OUT WITH CONS RUNNING FREE?
YEAH, THAT SOUNDS DANGEROUS.
DIE, CON!
YOU'RE LUCKY, YOU KNOW.
A COUPLE OF YEARS AGO, I'D JUST KILL YOU.
HOW CAN YOU DO THAT? WH-WHAT ARE YOU?
BANG
WHIFF
I'M A DIFFERENT MAN NOW.
BUT YOU STILL HURT MY FRIEND AND I KEEP MY PROMISES.
SO-

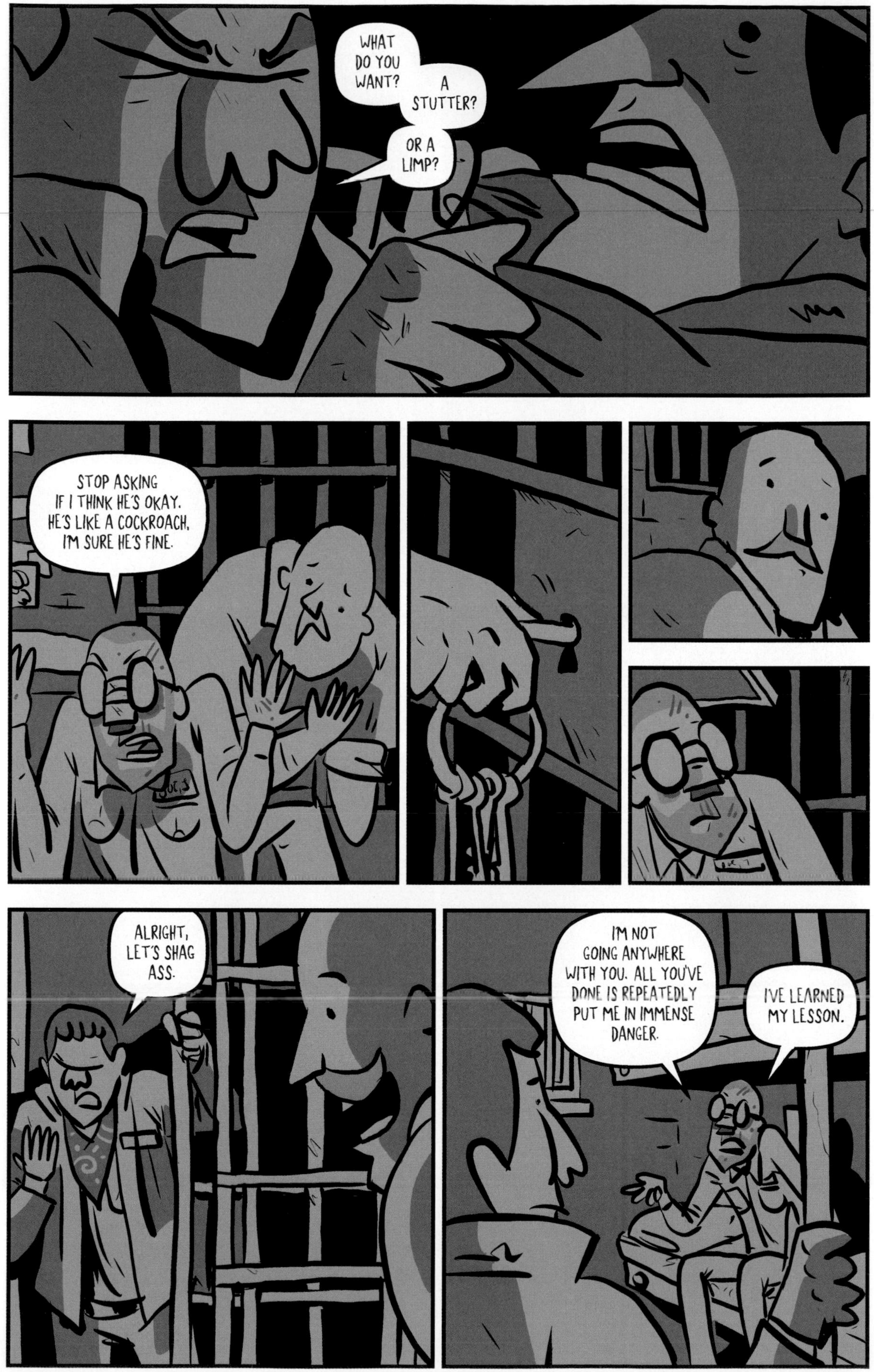
WHAT DO YOU WANT?
A STUTTER?
OR A LIMP?
STOP ASKING IF I THINK HE'S OKAY. HE'S LIKE A COCKROACH, I'M SURE HE'S FINE.
ALRIGHT, LET'S SHAG ASS.
I'M NOT GOING ANYWHERE WITH YOU. ALL YOU'VE DONE IS REPEATEDLY PUT ME IN IMMENSE DANGER.
I'VE LEARNED MY LESSON.

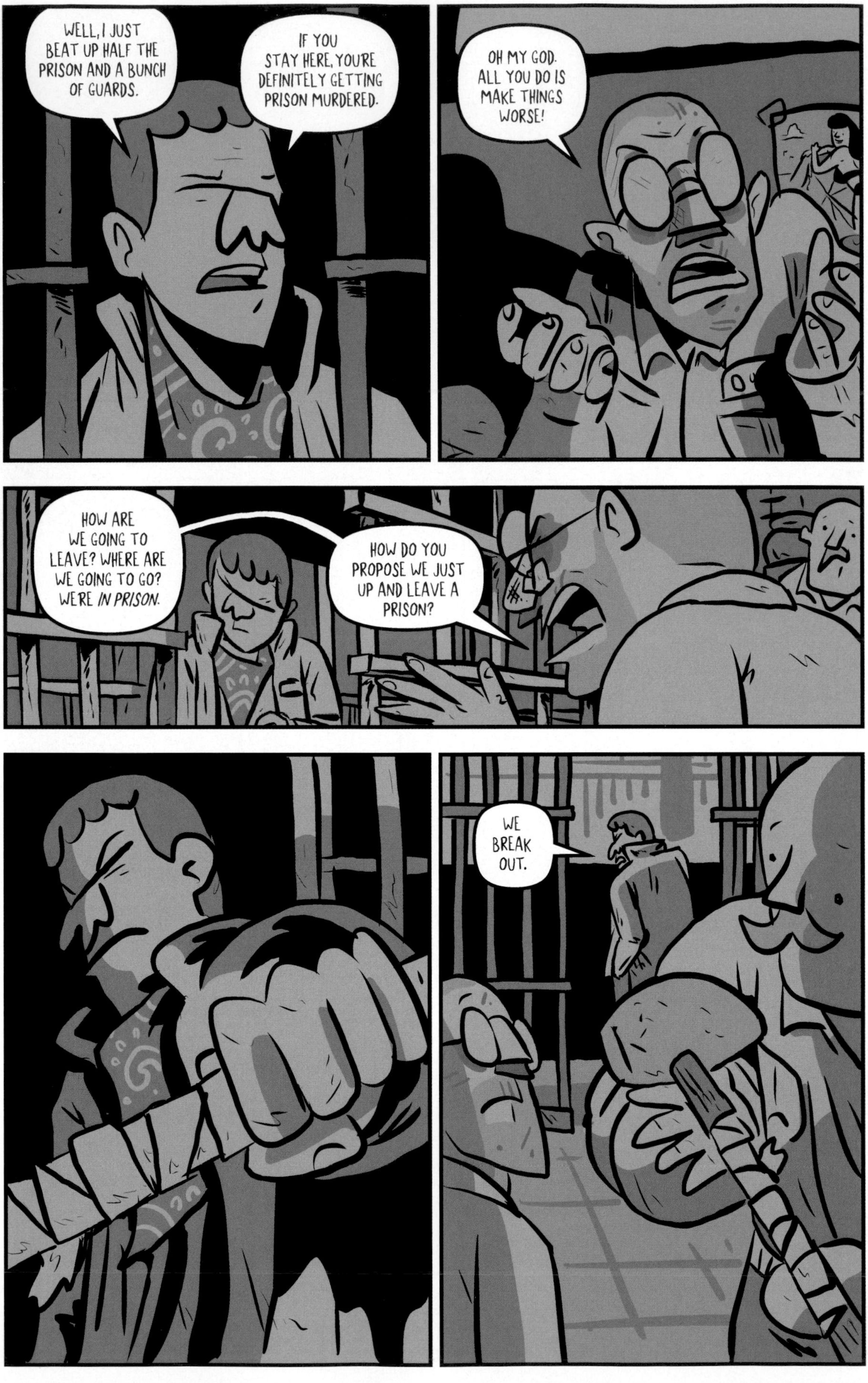

WELL, I JUST BEAT UP HALF THE PRISON AND A BUNCH OF GUARDS.
IF YOU STAY HERE, YOU'RE DEFINITELY GETTING PRISON MURDERED.
OH MY GOD. ALL YOU DO IS MAKE THINGS WORSE!
HOW ARE WE GOING TO LEAVE? WHERE ARE WE GOING TO GO? WE'RE *IN PRISON*.
HOW DO YOU PROPOSE WE JUST UP AND LEAVE A PRISON?
WE BREAK OUT.

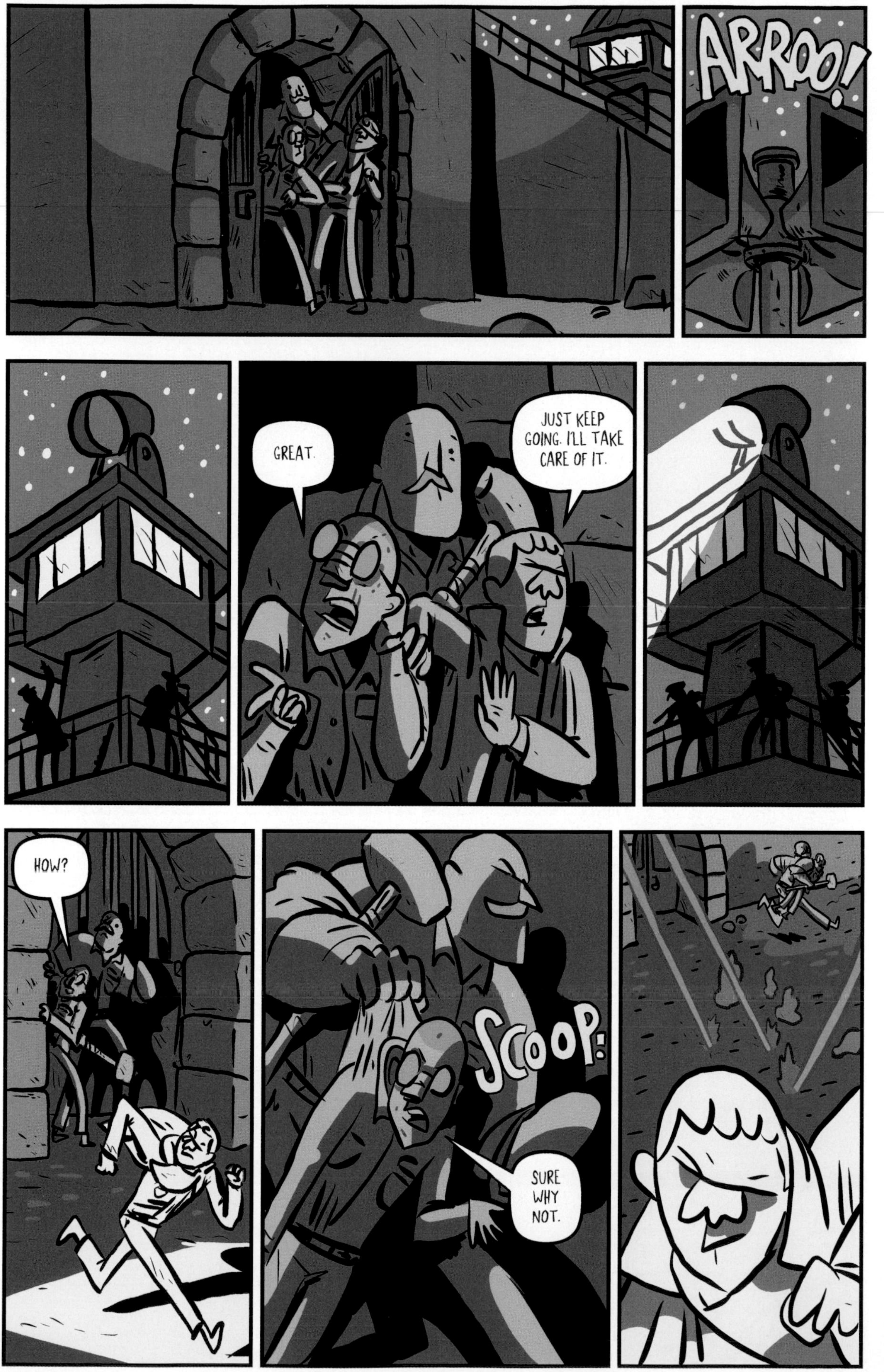
ARROO!
GREAT.
JUST KEEP GOING. I'LL TAKE CARE OF IT.
HOW?
SCOOP!
SURE WHY NOT.

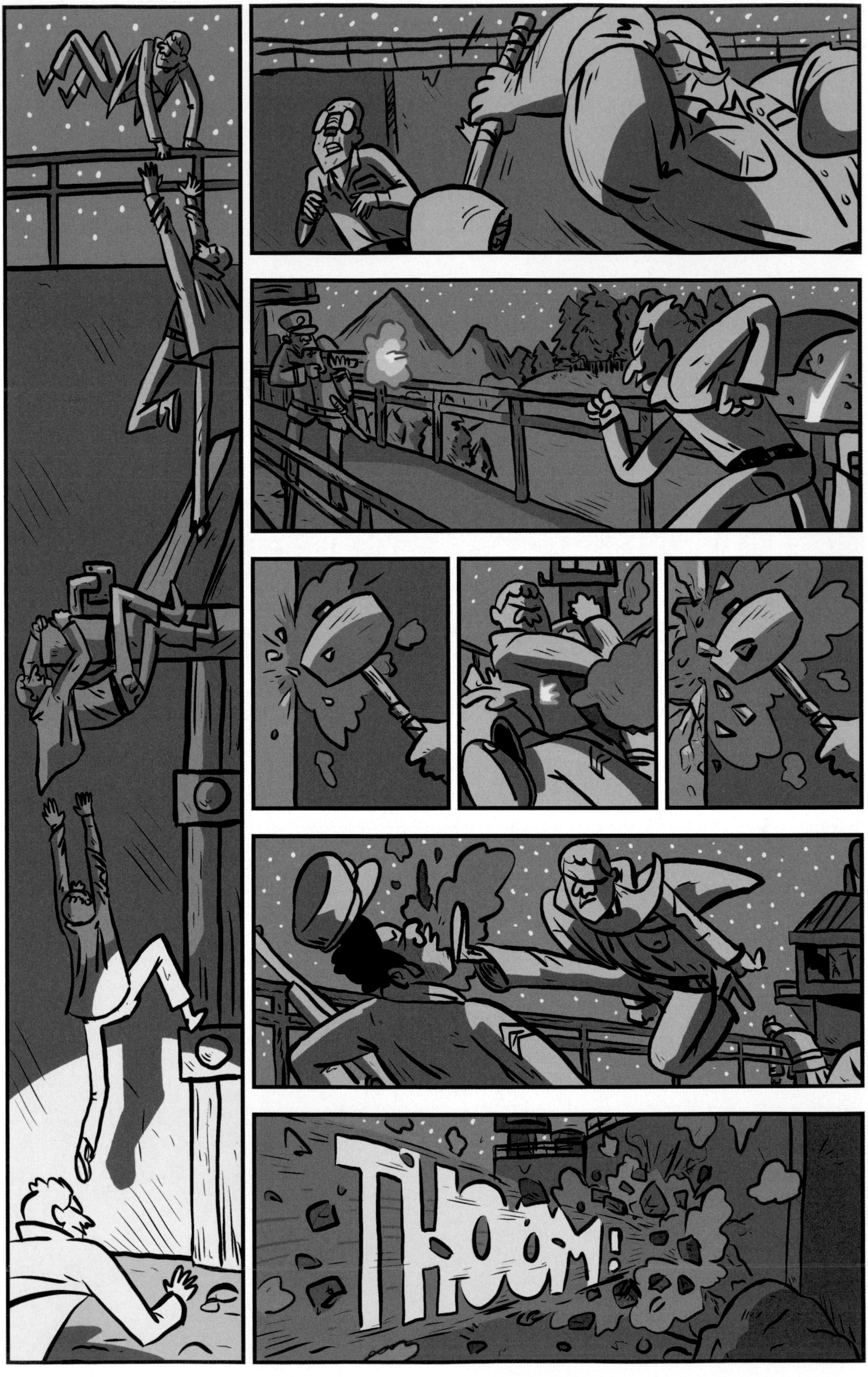
THOOM!

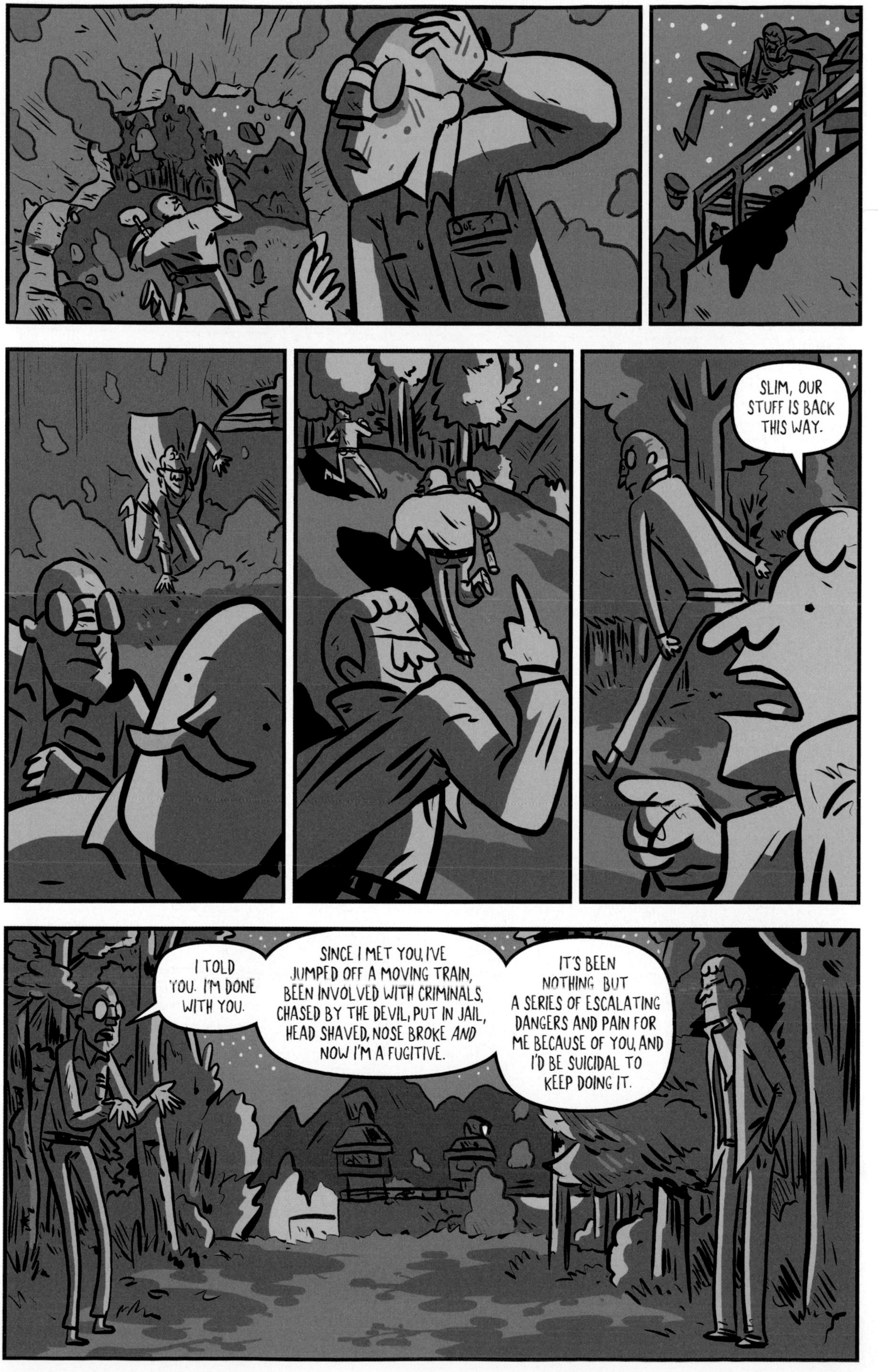
SLIM, OUR STUFF IS BACK THIS WAY.
I TOLD YOU. I'M DONE WITH YOU.
SINCE I MET YOU, I'VE JUMPED OFF A MOVING TRAIN, BEEN INVOLVED WITH CRIMINALS, CHASED BY THE DEVIL, PUT IN JAIL, HEAD SHAVED, NOSE BROKE *AND* NOW I'M A FUGITIVE.
IT'S BEEN NOTHING BUT A SERIES OF ESCALATING DANGERS AND PAIN FOR ME BECAUSE OF YOU, AND I'D BE SUICIDAL TO KEEP DOING IT.

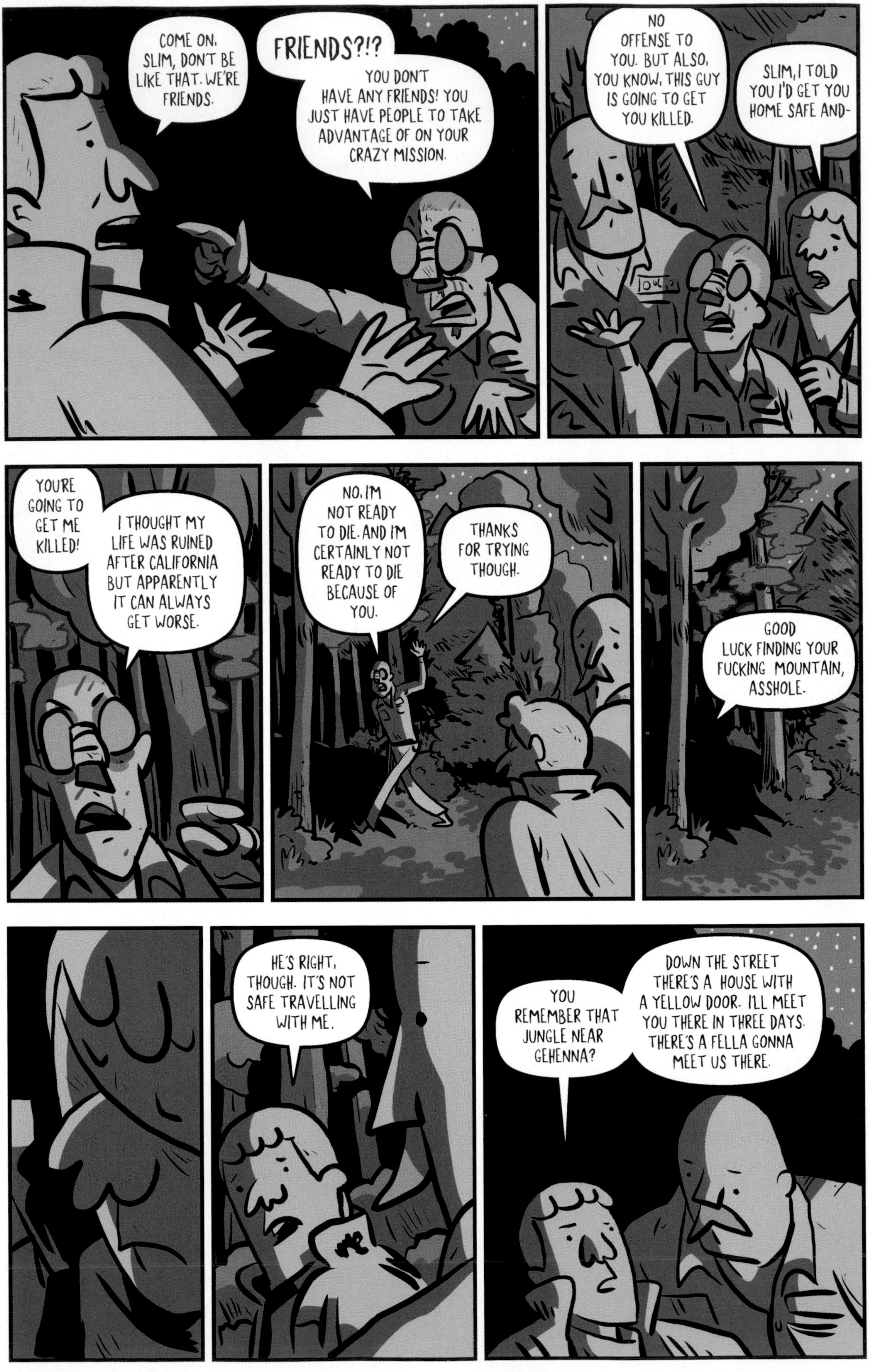
COME ON, SLIM, DON'T BE LIKE THAT. WE'RE FRIENDS.
FRIENDS?!?
YOU DON'T HAVE ANY FRIENDS! YOU JUST HAVE PEOPLE TO TAKE ADVANTAGE OF ON YOUR CRAZY MISSION.
NO OFFENSE TO YOU. BUT ALSO, YOU KNOW, THIS GUY IS GOING TO GET YOU KILLED.
SLIM, I TOLD YOU I'D GET YOU HOME SAFE AND-
YOU'RE GOING TO GET ME KILLED!
I THOUGHT MY LIFE WAS RUINED AFTER CALIFORNIA BUT APPARENTLY IT CAN ALWAYS GET WORSE.
NO, I'M NOT READY TO DIE. AND I'M CERTAINLY NOT READY TO DIE BECAUSE OF YOU.
THANKS FOR TRYING THOUGH.
GOOD LUCK FINDING YOUR FUCKING MOUNTAIN, ASSHOLE.
HE'S RIGHT, THOUGH. IT'S NOT SAFE TRAVELLING WITH ME.
YOU REMEMBER THAT JUNGLE NEAR GEHENNA?
DOWN THE STREET THERE'S A HOUSE WITH A YELLOW DOOR. I'LL MEET YOU THERE IN THREE DAYS. THERE'S A FELLA GONNA MEET US THERE.

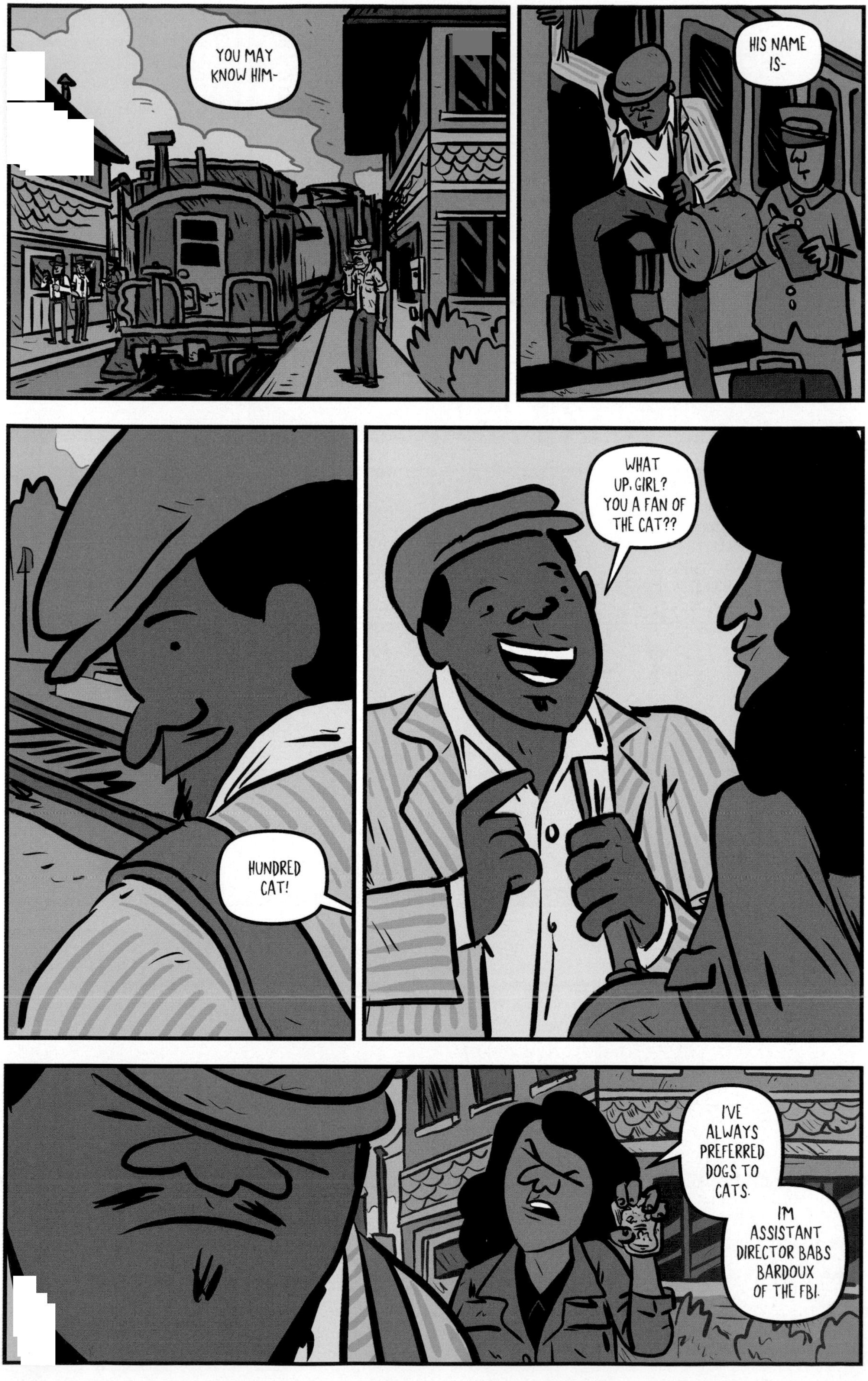
YOU MAY KNOW HIM-
HIS NAME IS-
HUNDRED CAT!
WHAT UP, GIRL? YOU A FAN OF THE CAT??
I'VE ALWAYS PREFERRED DOGS TO CATS.
I'M ASSISTANT DIRECTOR BABS BARDOUX OF THE FBI.

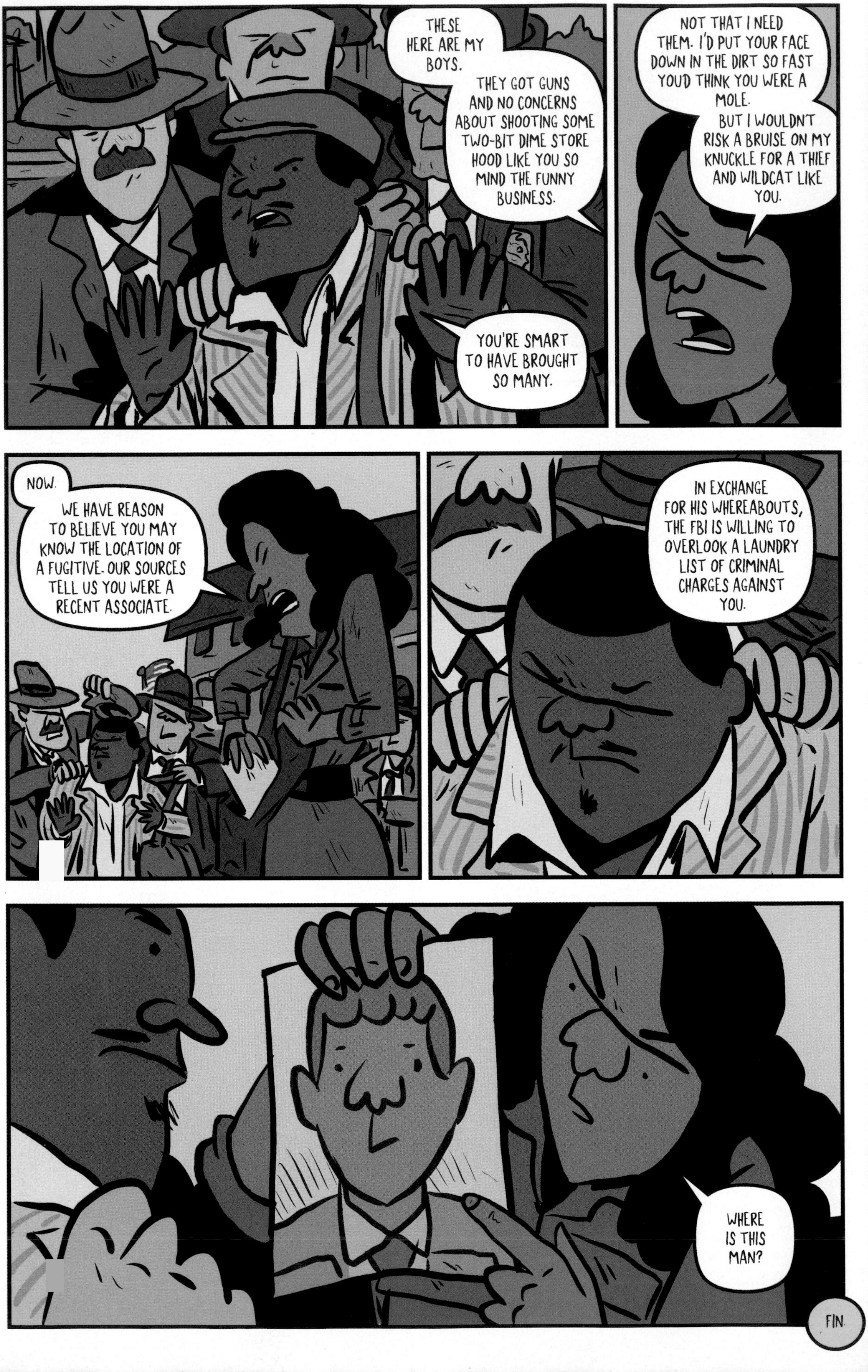

THESE HERE ARE MY BOYS.
THEY GOT GUNS AND NO CONCERNS ABOUT SHOOTING SOME TWO-BIT DIME STORE HOOD LIKE YOU SO MIND THE FUNNY BUSINESS.
YOU'RE SMART TO HAVE BROUGHT SO MANY.
NOT THAT I NEED THEM. I'D PUT YOUR FACE DOWN IN THE DIRT SO FAST YOU'D THINK YOU WERE A MOLE.
BUT I WOULDN'T RISK A BRUISE ON MY KNUCKLE FOR A THIEF AND WILDCAT LIKE YOU.
NOW.
WE HAVE REASON TO BELIEVE YOU MAY KNOW THE LOCATION OF A FUGITIVE. OUR SOURCES TELL US YOU WERE A RECENT ASSOCIATE.
IN EXCHANGE FOR HIS WHEREABOUTS, THE FBI IS WILLING TO OVERLOOK A LAUNDRY LIST OF CRIMINAL CHARGES AGAINST YOU.
WHERE IS THIS MAN?
FIN.

TO BE CONCLUDED IN

VOLUME TWO

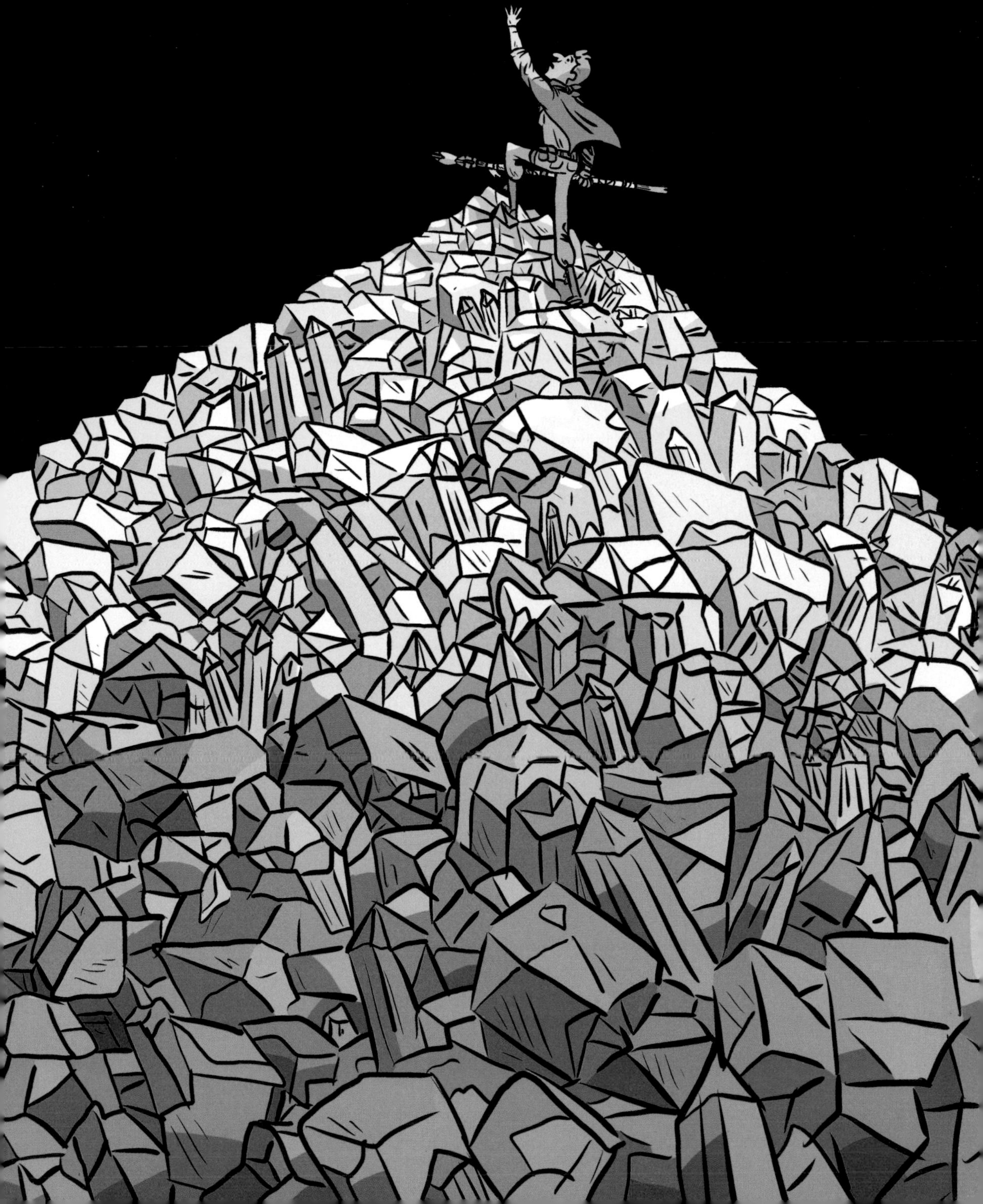

KYLE STARKS

Kyle Starks is an Eisner-nominated
cartoonist from Southern Indiana.

His hobo nickname would be "That City Slicker Isn't
A Hobo At All" and they would be right.

This book is dedicated to my wife and children who inspire
me daily and to the thousands of brave men and
women who rode our countries' rails.

Please do not try to hop on any trains.
Trains are nothing to fuck with.

If you are interested in reading more about hobos,
check out Roger Bruns' *The Knights of the Road*,
or Jack London's *The Road*.

CHRIS SCHWEIZER

Chris Schweizer is an Eisner-nominated cartoonist
who's written and drawn *The Creeps, The Crogan Adventures*,
and some nonfiction books about car maintenance and historical
mysteries for First Second Books. He's from Western
Kentucky, only a fifty-mile boxcar ride from Kyle.

His hobo nickname would be "Uncle Inky,"
because that's what his niece calls him and
he's often avuncular and ink-stained.

This is the first time he's colored someone besides himself
because he loved *Rock Candy Mountain* so much.

DYLAN TODD

Dylan Todd is a writer, art director and graphic designer.

When he's not reading comics, making comics, writing
about comics or designing stuff for comics, he can
probably be found thinking about comics.

He likes Star Wars, mummies, D-Man, kaiju and
1966 Batman. He's the editor of the 2299 sci-fi comics
anthology and, alongside Mathew Digges, is the co-creator of
The Creep Crew, a comic about undead teen detectives.

You can find his pop culture andw comics
design portfolio at bigredrobot.net.

He ain't never hopped a train, but he has eaten
himself a lukewarm can of beans a time or two.